Miss Peachy and the Floating World

GORDON JOHN THOMSON

ISBN:
ISBN-13:9781519021663

DEDICATION

For my sister, Hazel Thomson

.

Miss Peachy and the Floating World

This is the second instalment in the adventures of young American detective, Joseph Appeldoorn, and Miss Amelia Peachy, Edwardian actress and athlete, British secret agent, and mistress of disguise and intrigue. In this second episode, set in the mysterious and exotic world of Meiji Japan, the pair encounter even more danger than in Switzerland two years before...

January 1904. Joe Appeldoorn believes Amelia to be dead, and is now married to Eleanor and has left his work as a detective with the Pinkerton Agency behind to manage his father's old electrical company. Life should be perfect for him yet he has problems; he still can't quite free himself of the tantalising memory of Amelia Peachy.

Aiming to get a commercial foothold for his electrical business in Asia and to outflank his business rivals Westinghouse and Tesla, he sets out on a business trip for Japan...

Unknown to Joe, Amelia Peachy has survived her fall over the *Rheinfall* in Switzerland and is now in Tokyo too, working for the spymaster at the British Embassy, Clive Randall, trying to discover who is leaking British diplomatic and military secrets to the Russians. Japan and Russia are edging close to war in the Pacific, and Britain is secretly supporting the Japanese in their plans...

Amelia also learns, though, that her old arch-enemy, the assassin Herr Johan Plesch, is believed to be in Tokyo, planning the murder of a major political figure...

As the story unfolds further, Joe and Amelia must survive bombings and assassinations, a fight to the death on the roof of an express train, earthquakes and explosions, culminating in a flight in a primitive flying machine and a confrontation with a sword-wielding madman.

At the end of the story, Amelia must decide where her future lies, while Joe Appeldoorn has an even harder decision to make when his wife Eleanor arrives unexpectedly in Tokyo...

.

CONTENTS

PROLOGUE

Saturday, December 19th 1903

As the swirl of elegant couples waltzed with geometric precision around the dance floor, Joseph Appeldoorn watched them enjoyably from the side lines, studying the spectacular figures of the prettier girls with particular pleasure, and being more than a little diverted by their flirtatious smiles and the sultry rustle of their silk and satin gowns.

It did occur to Joe that he had probably never been happier in his life than at this precise moment. And surely that was the measure of true contentment, wasn't it? - to not only be perfectly happy, but to *realise* that you were happy...

This whole ballroom did present such a spectacular conjunction of colour and movement and sound that he consciously tried to freeze the moment in his memory so that he would be able to recall every detail for later enjoyment.

Yet, for Joe, even in this exquisite ballroom full of handsome women, there really was only one girl in sight that truly mattered: one girl in the corner of the room that his eyes kept returning to...

He moved around the dance floor and crept up behind her, as she swayed slightly in time to the orchestra and the lilting music of Johan Strauss. Unable to resist the enticing movement of that enchanting body any more, he slipped a discreet arm around her waist. She jumped slightly but otherwise made no response to this intimate assault. Emboldened, he let his fingers stray gradually higher, feeling the line of stiff whalebone corset under her bodice.

She still didn't turn her head but as his hand moved higher still, he felt her heart racing a little. 'I believe, sir, that you are touching my breast,' she

3

finally whispered breathlessly.

'That's quite correct, Miss Winthrop,' he breathed in her ear.

'Really, sir, this is most improper! I am a married woman now, and you should stop addressing me in that familiar fashion. And please remove your hand.'

'Nevertheless, Miss Winthrop, you appear to be rather enjoying the sensation of my hand on your breast...'

'You are not a gentleman, Mr Appeldoorn! People will see!'

'Then let's slip away from this throng and into the library behind us.'

A slight hesitation. 'All right, sir. If I must.' She repressed a delicious giggle. 'But only if you promise to be even more forward in private.'

'I swear.'

'And I've been a very naughty girl, ignoring you all evening...'

'Well, you have been very busy organising everything for your Uncle Arthur tonight...'

'...nevertheless, I do perhaps owe you some intimate reward for my inattention to you this evening...'

'Yes, I believe you do...' Joe glanced up and inadvertently caught the eye of her stern-faced grandfather, James Winthrop, standing on the far side of the dance floor. He just hoped that her grandfather couldn't lip read any of their private conversation; knowing that old buzzard, though, he was probably a past master at the art. Although he'd been a friend of sorts of Joe's late father, James Winthrop had nevertheless been less than overwhelmed when Eleanor had returned from Europe the summer before last, expressing a wish to marry the penniless detective he'd sent to find her. And even after eighteen months or so to get used to the idea, Winthrop still treated Joe with a certain coolness, as if he was some sort of outrageous fortune-seeker who'd seduced Eleanor deliberately and betrayed him personally.

But a relieved Joe could see that James was presently too busy for lip reading other people's talk, deep in a conversation of his own with the host of tonight's Christmas ball, his own brother, Arthur – a younger, and even more irascible, version of himself, if that were possible. The wealthy brothers had also included another distinguished local resident of Hartford, Connecticut in their conversation, this gentleman an elderly man with a thick mane of silver-white hair and silver moustache to match, and a roguish twinkle in his eye as he eyed up the pulchritudinous ladies in the room and their silky white bosoms. Joe wondered what the two Winthrop magnates might possibly have to say that could be of interest to Mr Samuel Langhorne Clemens, otherwise known as Mark Twain; but it did seem as if the creator of Huckleberry Finn and Tom Sawyer was finding their comments moderately amusing. It occurred to Joe – a wry thought that pleased him - that tonight the elderly writer was literally a Connecticut

Yankee in the court of King Arthur...

Eleanor's great uncle Arthur did truly live in a kingly style that put even his steel magnate brother James to shame; this new and sumptuous white-framed and porticoed Colonial Revival mansion, which he'd just had built on a wooded hillside above a bend in the Connecticut River north of Hartford, had clearly been designed to do just that.

While no one was looking in their direction, Joe quickly steered Eleanor away from the gaiety and babble of the ballroom. In the darkness of the library, with the sound of the *Blue Danube* muted behind heavy oak doors to a distant lilt, he kissed her long and passionately on the mouth. He remembered the first time he had ever kissed her, on that perfect blue and gold spring day on the shores of Lake Constance in Bavaria. How could he ever forget *that* day - the first time he'd ever felt the sensation of those wonderful breasts pressed against his body, the touch of those rose-petal lips? Except, as he now guiltily recalled, he had in fact slept with another woman that very same night...

Joe put that unfortunate thought to the back of his mind as he nuzzled Eleanor's bare shoulder and took in her exquisite shape and scent. She smelled wonderful, particularly compared to the musty book smells of these ancient tomes with which Uncle Arthur had filled his library. Books for a show of learning only, Joe suspected: these sad books were probably destined never to be opened again, never mind read. 'I can't wait to get you home and ravish you even more, Miss Winthrop,' he whispered in her ear.

She snuggled up to him and ran her hand down the line of his jaw. 'Neither can I. Actually, I have a surprise for you, Mr Appeldoorn. A new nightgown awaits in our marital bedchamber at home.'

'Will it fit me, though?' he asked doubtfully.

She giggled. 'It's for me, silly.'

'Ah! Is it lace? I hope it's lace.'

'It is, sir, and very fine too - all the way from Paris to remind you of old times - and so soft to the touch that it feels just like gossamer. And it's your favourite colour...*black!* Midnight black. It is quite the most outrageous thing I have ever worn for you. Why am I so kind to you, sir? Can you possibly explain it?'

'Because you love me - truly, deeply, madly?'

'Ah, such damnable male arrogance,' she sighed. 'And yet so depressingly true.' She kissed him on the brow, standing on tiptoe to reach, then moved her lips down to an eyelid, then back to his mouth again.

They held each other in companionable silence, gazing out through the darkened window at the wintry landscape outside, the vault of stars above, the line of snow and blue-white shadows below, falling away to the frozen banks of the Connecticut River. The waltz music had stopped by now and

5

the orchestra began to play something quieter - the initial chords of "Silent Night" – *Stille Nacht.*

Eleanor grew wistful at the sound of that haunting German carol. 'You still remember Switzerland, and everything we did together there?'

'Of course.'

She hesitated. 'Do you still ever think about *her*? Don't lie to me,' she added warningly.

'No, I no longer think of her at all.' It was a lie, but perhaps not much of one any more. He *did* still let his mind wander occasionally to thoughts of Miss Amelia Peachy, if the truth be known, but certainly much less often these days than before. Hard to admit it, but even the memory of such a woman as that was becoming fainter now; after all, Amelia's bleached bones had lain mouldering in the mud at the bottom of the Rhine for the best part of two years, and surely it was time for him to forget her absolutely...

Eleanor seemed relieved by the answer, as if she still thought of her rival as a living person who could threaten her happiness. 'What shall I do with myself while you are away?' she asked obliquely.

He kissed her again. 'Then come with me,' he suggested hopefully.

'I can't, you know that. Grandfather's health is still too fragile; he has just come through that awful operation on his stomach. Why do you have to go now without even waiting for the New Year?'

'It's the business opportunity of a lifetime, Eleanor. If I leave it, someone else will get there first. My rivals and competitors here are blocking every order I try to get for my new steam turbine generators, but in Japan we will have virtually no competition in the short term. Mr Maeda has promised me a huge order if I can demonstrate the technical superiority of our generators to him...'

'Why did this Mr Maeda write to *you*? How did he happen to hear of Appeldoorn Industries? You're hardly a challenger yet to Mr Edison or Westinghouse, are you?'

'I don't know how he got my name. But I'm certainly not going to look a gift horse in the mouth.'

'Is Japan not still a dangerous country for foreigners?'

'I'm no longer a detective, Eleanor, just a businessman and inventor trying to sell my company's engineering wares. There's no danger in that, is there?'

Eleanor still seemed unconvinced. 'There is more than one kind of danger,' she commented tartly. 'They say Japanese women are very beautiful and very tempting to Western men. Like porcelain dolls.'

'So I've heard too,' he agreed cautiously. 'But they could hardly have whiter or more perfect skin than yours, could they?' For such a sweet girl, Eleanor had a fearsome temper when roused so Joe had soon learned, early on in their life together, not to say anything even mildly complimentary about another woman.

Eleanor was often suspicious of his personal compliments to her too, though, suspecting ulterior motives – one unenviable trait she had picked up from her hard-nosed, bull-headed grandfather. 'Perhaps, for revenge, I shall take a lover while you're away,' she threatened seductively.

He suddenly realised how hard it would be for him to leave her for so long. Caught up in the excitement of the forthcoming business trip, he'd put any personal thoughts completely to the back of his mind. But now the reality struck home for the first time of just how much he was going to miss her. 'Perhaps you should,' he said lightly.

She put her hand to his cheek and lightly smacked it. 'Beast! As if I could.'

'I'll only be away for a few weeks,' he said apologetically.

Eleanor was not appeased. 'It will be *three months* at least! It will take you more than three weeks just to *get* there.'

Joe tried once again to convince her of the importance of his journey. 'It will be a great step forward for us if the Japanese buy my new generating equipment in quantity. Japan is a country in the throes of an Industrial Revolution, exploding with opportunities. They are hungry for new technology, desperate for fresh ideas. It will make our name, give us a huge advantage over our smaller domestic competitors...and perhaps even make Tom Edison and George Westinghouse sit up and take some notice of us, for once...'

Eleanor suddenly shivered, even though the library was warm with the heat of a crackling log fire. 'Please don't go to Japan, Joseph! I know you'll think this is just a silly woman talking but I really do have a premonition that something terrible might happen if you go there.' She sighed as she gazed out through the French windows at the wintry New England landscape outside. 'I'm frightened that I'm so happy. No one deserves to be as blessed as this so I'm sure that one day I'll have to pay an awful price for it - there must be something terrible lying in store for me in my future to redress the balance. If I lost you, I couldn't bear it...'

He put his finger to her lips, then gave her bottom a playful but hard smack with his other hand. 'Don't talk like that, my girl, even in jest. Don't you want me to succeed and make us lots of money?'

She wrinkled her nose and pouted; Joe was always enchanted by that particular expression. 'We're already rich,' she pointed out archly.

'You mean, *you and Grandpa* are already rich,' he corrected her.

Her eyes glittered momentarily with annoyance. 'What's mine is yours.'

He smiled uneasily, wondering why he didn't just accept his exceedingly fortunate situation in life; most other men certainly would. But the truth was that Joe Appeldoorn still needed to prove himself as an engineer and a man of business, and he was simply not content to rely on the largesse of a wealthy wife for a comfortable lot in life. 'Sounds so simple.'

'It *is* simple. It's only you that wants to complicate things so.' She frowned. 'If you really love me, how can you possibly want to leave me for three months or more?'

Joe sighed. 'There's no other way.'

'And yet you call yourself an engineer and scientist! If you are such a clever man as you claim, then why can't you invent a machine that would fly across the ocean to Japan like a bird, and be back to me in a few days?' she demanded unreasonably.

Joe smiled. 'According to reports, two brothers in North Carolina have done just that - flown a heavier-than-air flying machine that took off under its own power.'

'I can't believe that!' Eleanor shook her pretty head in bewilderment at the wonders of this strange new century. 'How can that be possible?' she asked. 'Can you explain such witchcraft to me?'

'There's nothing magical about it. The science of Aerodynamics, that's all. Actually, a man called Sir George Cayley flew a heavier-than-air machine fifty years ago in England. A little impractical and heavy, and it couldn't take off under its own power, but it worked after a fashion, I believe.'

She pouted again, pressing her breasts against him and falling back on her usually unassailable methods of persuasion. 'Please don't go, Joseph...'

Joe decided it was time to divert her from worrying needlessly about his trip, and began gently nibbling the lobe of her ear. As she sighed with satisfaction, he whispered, 'Miss Winthrop, tell me more about this French lace negligee of yours. That sounds much more like witchcraft to me than a mere flying machine. How soft to the touch is it, did you say?'

She leaned her gorgeous head of titian hair against his chest. 'Almost nothing to feel at all,' she whispered. 'One touch and it might just melt away in your fingers like morning mist. And I will be left entirely naked and unprotected, and quite unable to stop you doing anything disgraceful to me that you wish...'

CHAPTER 1

At that same precise moment that a Christmas ball was taking place in Hartford, Connecticut, ten thousand miles away, on the far side of the Pacific, a wintry dawn was stealing over a quite different world from that of Joe Appeldoorn's familiar New England: this other world a vast dark array of low-roofed houses, gables, graceful towers and mysterious gates, Shinto shrines and Buddhist temples, groves of bamboo and cypress - the endless sea of wooden rooftops of the Japanese capital...

Until recently this had been *Edo*, the home city of the Tokugawa Shoguns, the effective rulers of a feudal, Samurai-controlled society, a place of ancient history and time-honoured ways. The city had long been divided between the *Yamanote*, the High City built on the green hills to the west, with its temples and shrines and the grand houses of the elite; and the *Shitamachi*, the Low City, Edo's earthy plebeian heart, with its hugger-mugger of houses, workshops, timber and brick yards, flowing along the banks of the Sumida like a brown tide, that lapped right up to the castle moat of the Tokugawa fortress.

But now it was called Tokyo, and it *was* very much a new city for the twentieth century, a city of brick and steel rising from the ancient soil of Japan, dwarfing the historic buildings and washing away the old ways, much to the regret of many Japanese, and even to some of the foreign barbarians...

Clive Randall didn't quite see it that way, of course. An Englishman to the core, still young and idealistic in some ways, still a believer at heart in the inherent supremacy of his own race, the lure of Japan had left him mostly unmoved in the six years he had been with the British Embassy here. Old British hands talked endlessly to him of the feudal Edo of thirty years ago with nostalgic regret, but he couldn't see it. They remembered lanes bright with teahouses, neat houses with rice-paper windows, flickering small shrines, incomparable gardens, sacred carp swimming in unruffled pools. The Sumida in those days had been a wide clean river reflecting a glitter of light and the moonlit hump of distant hills, not the turgid polluted river flowing between grey factories and dirty quay walls that it was now...

Randall, on the other hand, could see only progress and enlightenment in the new belching chimneys and brick buildings of modern Tokyo, which had swept away the backwardness and inertia of the old feudal ways.

Watching the cold white dawn mist rising from the swollen murky surface of the Sumida River, he had to acknowledge however that he could clearly smell the acrid industrial smoke from the distant city, even this early in the day. Here, on this area of low marshy ground on the very northern edge of the city, thick with tussocky yellow grass and sedges, there was little to inspire anyone with the romance of the East. Here were only straight ditches and broad shallow tidal canals filled with dirt, unpainted wooden structures that looked derelict and forgotten, and rampant weedy growth that threatened to swallow everything.

He surreptitiously checked that he had his Remington Colt revolver in its concealed holster, then stepped down from his carriage and asked the driver curtly to wait under the branches of a nearby cypress grove. '*Unténshu-san, asoko ni matte kudasai!*' Then he walked up the slight rise from the water's edge, through the dank grey mist, a miasma of denser fog swirling in from the river, the only sounds the scuttle of rats by the canal, and the creak of an ancient boat. Randall shivered and pulled his cloak tighter about his upper body as he approached the Main Gate of the *Yoshiwara*, a high arched entrance to the old Pleasure Quarter of ancient Edo. This was the Nightless City, literally the "Place of Reeds", built within an enclosure of high wooden fences on a marsh at the edge of the Asakusa district of the city, where in spring croaking frogs added their own mocking commentary to the gaudy chorus of its pleasures. On one side of the main entrance stood a neat police box - empty at this hour, though, Randall saw – while on the other was a famous aged willow tree: the so-called "Willow of Welcome".

Randall had heard the old Oriental hands in the Embassy and elsewhere bemoan especially the degeneration of this place in the last few decades. Once, they said it had been a genuinely uplifting cultural experience to visit the *Yoshiwara* – the Streets of Flower and Willow – the "flower" being the courtesan, the "willow" the *geisha*; yet now, they complained, the art and subtlety were all gone, along with most of the delicate *ochaya* tea-houses and the *ryotei* restaurants, where assignments between client and courtesan had formerly been conducted with propriety and grace. Now the teahouses and *ryotei* were reduced in most cases to mere brothels and rooms for rent.

Randall had never seen the *Yoshiwara* in its heyday but its streets were now certainly an uninviting place at this time of the morning: indeterminate bundles of rags, which could have been old men or old women, begging for scraps; the whine of a homeless yellow mongrel, the suspicious glance from a brawny brown goblin of a man, working wood at a lathe and watching the yellow-haired barbarian visitor with a face both immobile and enigmatic. A blind shaven-headed mendicant monk in a grey robe wandered behind Randall, tip-tapping with his cane on the damp stone cobbles.

Yet even at this hour of a winter morning, Randall could also glance sideways into a seductive alleyway and happen to catch a sight that entranced even him: the glimpse of a butterfly kimono, a white stocking and cloven boot, and the delicate eyes of a local beauty, shyly gazing out at the world through a paper screen.

As the sun came out through the mist, Randall continued on his way in a better mood now, following the wide main street with its central beds of winter camellia flowers, and lined on either side by a series of stone and brick buildings with bell-towers, balustraded verandas and pillared doorways. Inside these buildings, Randall knew from personal experience, there dwelled gilded fragile women - sometimes even displayed in bamboo cages - with highly charged and erotic names: Jewel River, Miss Moonlit Foam, The Honourable Brilliance and Young Bamboo. Despite his public protestations to the contrary, Clive had found the spectacle of beautiful women in cages a titillating one, especially when it was the highest class of courtesan – the *oiran* - who could stir even a foreigner's stone heart with the melancholy sweetness of their singing, whose dances were sinuous poems of motion, who wore the most ravishing brocades, and who presented to their admirers the most expressionless pearl-white faces. At times like that, even Clive Randall could feel a stirring of the Old Japan hand's pleasures in this strange world.

He reached a teahouse with a little shrine painted with the image of a *tanuki,* a magical racoon-like animal that the Japanese regarded for some reason with mystical awe, then turned first left, following a meandering lane between older *ochaya* teahouses with still graceful timbered facades. An alley appeared on the right just as he remembered, then a mysterious doorway with a curtained entrance. He brushed aside the silk curtain and mounted the steps inside, the timber creaking under his weight. He took out his revolver and cocked it ready for action, just in case.

She was waiting for him in the bare room, sitting perched on her knees on a *tatami* mat, as expressionless as any *oiran.* 'You won't need that weapon, Mr Randall,' she said complacently.

Clive slowly replaced his revolver in its concealed holster. He had heard rumours that Miss Peachy had gone native recently, brazenly living among the prostitutes of the *Yoshiwara* as if she was one of them, and immersing herself completely in this so-called local culture. It did not endear her to him; it was one thing for a Japanese girl to behave this way, but she was an Englishwoman for God's sake! Sir Charles Gorman had warned him during his last visit to London of Miss Peachy's propensity for eccentric and sometimes outrageous behaviour, but he wondered if she knew that this affectation for Oriental ways might be putting her permanently beyond the pale with her own countrymen. *Or, knowing her, would she even care, perhaps?*

He concealed his annoyance; he was after all Britain's spymaster in the Far East at the age of only thirty-five, and able to equivocate and intrigue with the best of them. And, he reminded himself, *she* worked for *him*, not the other way around...

Yet - by God! - she was looking very fetching in that brocade winter kimono of peach and gold, he had to admit. She did have a slight Oriental caste to her features that seemed to fit well with the costume. *In fact, was it his imagination, or did she seem to be metamorphosing into a Japanese woman of pleasure entirely?* The morning sunlight was filtered by the shade on the window, and the muted rays were perfect lighting for her extraordinary face. He noticed for the first time that she'd allowed her dark hair to grow unchecked in the past months; now it was long and silky and dressed in the local style with gilded combs, her lips painted in vermilion. Was she truly turning into one of these enchanted women of the *Yoshiwara* herself, he wondered...and why was that thought arousing him so much?

She certainly didn't look much like an English government agent any more – yet this was a woman who, according to Sir Charles Gorman, had personally saved the life of her monarch twice in the matter of a few months back in '02. Her other exploits were equally legendary: former actress on the London stage, a renowned circus acrobat and high wire performer, and an entirely mysterious enigma to all her colleagues...

'Can I get you some tea, Mr Randall?'

'Yes, please.' He bowed awkwardly. *I can play this tiresome Oriental game of mutual politeness just as well as you, Miss Peachy...*

'Please sit down, although I'm afraid there are no chairs. I can bring you a cushion if you wish, though.'

'Thank you; I shall stand,' he said stiffly.

Miss Peachy frowned. 'Why did you send a message insisting on coming here today, Mr Randall? I asked you to stay away, except in emergencies. Your visit here could betray my real identity...'

'You haven't reported to me at all for several weeks. I was worried about you,' he lied.

Her scarlet-painted lips twitched. *Was that amusement on her part, or cynicism,* he asked himself? 'I am doing my best to make progress in the task that was originally given to me,' she claimed, slightly peevishly. 'I was brought here to Japan to collect secret information from our rival powers, which I am doing...'

Randall interrupted her brusquely. 'But I've since given you a more specific and important mission – to discover how details of our arms deals with Japan, and our other embassy secrets, are apparently reaching the ears of the Russians in Tokyo, as our own agents in Moscow have been recently telling us.'

Miss Peachy remained impassive. 'I know that, Mr Randall, but you did agree that I could do this in my own way. All the Russian agents and their informers in Tokyo are visitors to the *Yoshiwara*, as are the Germans, the French and the Americans. Here, with my own network of informers among the *geisha* and courtesans, I can discover almost everything that is going on in this city.'

'Then why can't you tell me yet who is betraying us?' Randall demanded impatiently.

Miss Peachy sighed visibly. 'Because it will take time and finesse. I've only had a few weeks so far. You must learn a little Oriental patience, Mr Randall. This person or persons - whoever they are - are being extremely careful about being drawn out into the open. I will have to bait my trap very carefully.'

'We can't let this go on too long,' Randall warned. 'War is looming between Japan and Russia, and we must be sure our own house is in order before that happens. Otherwise who knows what the consequences might be to our own interests if we have an unknown traitor in our midst?' Britain was Japan's natural ally among the Western powers because of their mutual distrust of the territorial ambitions of Russia, France and Germany in the Far East. The English tended to think of the Japanese almost as an Oriental, if obviously inferior, analogue of themselves – a cultured island race surrounded by ambitious Continental neighbours always trying to foment trouble in their own backyard. And the deepest suspicions of both the British and the Japanese these days concerned those inveterate troublemakers, the Russians. Yet Clive Randall had no doubt that if the Japs did try and take on the might of Russia, they would get a bloody nose for their pains – and he personally thought that perhaps that wouldn't be such a bad thing if Britain's uppity yellow friends were taken down a peg or two...

A wooden-framed paper screen door slid open and a girl brought tea on a black lacquer tray from another room. Clive was finally forced, reluctantly, to squat on the floor, something which he always found slightly troubling to his natural dignity. The girl prostrated her head very low and served him the cup of piping hot green liquid. '*Dozo.*'

'This is *sencha,*' Miss Peachy observed. 'I hope that it's to your taste.'

'Perfectly.' The attendant girl, one of Miss Peachy's network of courtesan informers, no doubt, was *certainly* to Clive's taste - far more than the insipid green tea anyway: a perfect porcelain face and willowy figure straight from a *Ukiyoe* print. She lowered her eyes as she backed away on her knees and got gracefully to her feet.

'*Domo arigato*, Sumiko-san.' Miss Peachy smiled and nodded to the girl as she retreated silently through the screen door again.

'I have news for you from Sir Charles in London,' Clive suddenly interjected, trying to surprise her.

'Yes...?' Miss Peachy raised an inquisitive eyebrow.

'Your friend, Herr Johan Plesch...'

Clive was pleased to note the stiffening of her face, the sudden tenseness in her voice. 'Yes, what of him?'

'According to a reliable informant of Sir Charles, he's here...*in Japan*...'

Clive was glad to see that he had for once taken the wind completely out of Miss Peachy's sails with that remark.

'We don't know what his mission is yet, though,' Clive continued smoothly.

Miss Peachy grimaced. 'If he is in Japan, Plesch will be here to kill someone. The business of delivering death for a price is all he knows. I wonder who his unfortunate target is...'

'That's another task for you to find out...and stop him if possible.' It occurred to Randall suddenly that Miss Peachy herself might be the target – Plesch had more than enough reasons for wanting her dead. Yet Plesch was known to be motivated only by money, not ideology or personal revenge. Perhaps in this case, though, because of all the trouble she had caused Plesch in the past, he might be prepared to make an exception...

'Does this duty take higher priority than unmasking the informer at the embassy?' Miss Peachy asked curiously. Clive wondered from her concerned expression whether she too might be considering the possibility that Plesch had perhaps pursued her to Japan to exact his revenge for past hurts...

'Absolutely not. Your priority remains staunching this steady drip of British secrets to the Russians. But I certainly won't object if you finally deal with Herr Plesch too, assuming it is in our interests to do so anyway...'

CHAPTER 2

Joe Appeldoorn was still having extreme trouble adjusting to the manners and style of this strange new Oriental world that he had entered, a world of such startling contrasts with any that he had known before, that it did make him feel occasionally as if he had fallen down the rabbit hole in *Alice in Wonderland*. And his difficulties in this strange new country were exacerbated by his feelings of loneliness: he was missing Eleanor even more than he'd ever thought possible. This was the first time since they'd got married a year ago that he'd been away from her for more than a couple of days, and he was finding her extended absence from his life particularly unsettling and painful when he was also faced with the business challenges of this bewildering new country.

The Japanese were certainly proving to be an enigma to deal with, and none more so than the particular gentleman who had invited Joseph Appeldoorn to Japan. Yet it seemed that Joe was an equal enigma to this Mr Maeda in return. On first meeting Joe in the lobby of the Imperial Hotel yesterday evening, Mr Maeda had seemed clearly taken aback at just how youthful his American visitor had turned out to be. Joe was still only twenty-five, of course, and looked perhaps even younger than that if anything, he had to admit, so he had begun to worry about the unfavourable impression that his relatively youthful appearance might make on his important potential Japanese client. This contract was far from in the bag yet, so Joe was desperate to make a good personal impression, as a necessary precursor to the difficult task of selling his new and relatively untried technology to a no doubt technically demanding company. Faced with these puzzled looks from Mr Maeda, Joe began to regret that he hadn't grown a moustache before the trip, as he'd wanted to, to add a few years to his appearance. But Eleanor, using her usual bedtime method of persuasion, had talked him out of that drastic step, preferring the clean-shaven smoothness of his face the way it was.

After shaking Joe's hand extremely vigorously at their first meeting (in what he obviously believed to be a typically American manner) Mr Maeda then kept looking around the lobby of the Imperial in slight perplexity as if waiting for a much older man to appear and take over the conversation from this young imposter. (*Had Mr Maeda perhaps been expecting his late father rather than him?* Joe wondered uneasily – *was this perhaps a case of mistaken identity?* But no - that didn't seem at all likely since it was Maeda himself who had made the first business contact with him by letter, and written expressly to him by name as "Mr Joseph Appeldoorn esq".)

But despite Maeda's initial discomfort at his American visitor's unexpected youth, he had this morning nevertheless treated Joe like a VIP bearing gifts, rather than as a businessman trying to drum up business for his own company. A car – an imposing and gleaming bottle-green English Lanchester with a uniformed chauffeur – had been dispatched by Maeda to pick Joe up at 9 a.m. at the Imperial Hotel and take him first on a scenic drive of the city, through streets lined with bare-branched cherry trees and covered in a fine dusting of snow. The car journey took Joe in regal splendour around the peripheries of the Imperial Palace and past the famous Nijubashi bridge, the stone arches of which were faithfully reflected in the skin of blue-grey ice on the moat, then back, via Hibiya Park, through the Ginza district of Kyobashi to *Tsukiji*, the former Foreign Settlement on the shores of Tokyo Bay.

A boat was waiting at the quayside to take Joe on a further scenic trip up the Sumida River, a brightly painted steam yacht with engine already throbbing and deck plates vibrating in readiness to depart. Before he could go on board, though, Joe had to put up with the ordeal of being treated like royalty, as Mr Maeda and several of his closest business associates were lined up on the jetty to greet him in formal bowing fashion, all of them dressed up uncomfortably in Western top hats and ill-fitting frock coats, pebble glasses and gleaming smiles.

However, to Joe's relief, these formalities didn't last too long, mainly because only Mr Maeda himself, and his delicately beautiful daughter, Motoko, could speak enough English to engage him in any significant conversation.

Joe was also relieved to learn that, apart from the crew, the party travelling on the boat for the planned sightseeing trip up the Sumida River was to be limited to himself and the Maedas, plus another youngish American businessman called Toby Pryor.

Mr Maeda himself acted as Joe's personal tour guide for the first part of the trip up river, sitting companionably in the stern with Joe, while his daughter did a similar job on Mr Pryor in the bows. Kenzoburo Maeda was in his mid-fifties, Joe judged, a neat and dapper man, with the untroubled brow of a much younger man, and a head of hair still suspiciously jet-black, and so thick and gleaming that even the cold blustery wind on the river couldn't manage to ruffle a single hair of it. Although Joe didn't yet understand much about the structure and ownership of Japanese companies in general, or this one in particular, it seemed that Mr Maeda was both the chairman and unchallenged top dog of *Nippon Electriku Kaisha*, and therefore the main man to impress in order to sell them his new steam turbine generating equipment.

'How is it that you speak such good English, Maeda-san?' Joe had already learned a few simple words of address in Japanese, which his host seemed to appreciate.

Maeda shrugged modestly. 'Oh, that is easily explained. I was lucky enough to travel abroad in my youth, Mr Appeldoorn. I was particularly fortunate because the generation before mine had been expressly forbidden to travel abroad, on punishment of death, if they disobeyed and then returned.'

'That would certainly discourage a bit of casual tourism, that's for sure,' Joe interjected wryly.

Mr Maeda smiled politely but his eyes didn't look amused. 'After you Americans arrived here in Tokyo Bay fifty years ago, we in Japan had to learn about the modern world quickly. When I was only twenty-two – that was the year the Emperor was restored to real power in Japan – eighteen sixty-eight in the Western Calendar - I was sent to Europe with a group of other young men to learn the ways of the West. As a member of a visiting delegation from Japan, I was fortunate to meet some of the great European figures of the time: politicians like Bismarck and Mr Gladstone, scientists like Lord Kelvin and Professor von Helmholz. But it was the great poets and writers of Europe who attracted me most: I was honoured to meet Mr Charles Dickens at his home in Gad's Hill, Kent not long before he died, and Lord Tennyson too. Ah, *The Lady of Shalott* is still one of my favourite poems...*"As often through the purple night, below the starry clusters bright, some bearded meteor, trailing light, moves over still Shalott..."*'

Maeda was clearly in nostalgic mood for that well-remembered visit to Europe in his youth. 'It was eye-opening for a young man like me to see magnificent cities like London and Paris and Berlin, yet also galling to realise how far my country was behind those European powers in their mighty technology and industry.' He interrupted his thoughts to point out some more of the sights of his home city. 'See, Mr Appeldoorn, over here on the left is the district of Nihombashi with the grounds of the Palace behind, while over there on the right bank is Fukagawa. This whole area of the city around the Sumida is called the *Shitamachi* – the Low City, where the common people – the *Eddoko* – live.' He glanced up as the boat steered between the piers of a large bridge. 'And this is the Shinobashi Bridge we're just passing under. If you look in the distance, you can just see the snow-covered tip of Mount Fuji on the Southwest horizon.'

Joe nodded. 'Ah, the symbol of Japan - the famous extinct volcano.'

'The symbol of Japan indeed, Mr Appeldoorn, but far from extinct,' Maeda corrected him. 'It last erupted in the reign of the Emperor Higashiyama, almost two centuries ago. But that is nothing compared to the age of the Earth; *Fuji-san* will stir again in time, no doubt.'

Joe wondered what would happen to Tokyo if and when it did – there couldn't be many such vast cities built this close to a live volcano.

Maeda seemed to understand his unspoken question. 'Our island nation was born out of the violence of these volcanic peaks as they rose out of the ocean. So the earth still trembles here, and as a result we always feel close to the Earth Goddess. It has made us strong as a nation, though, this feeling of intimacy we have with the shaking Earth. But we also have to accept the power of the Earth, and the pain it causes, when it comes to test our fortitude from time to time.'

Joe transferred his attention back to the exotic river scene. The west bank - on the port side of the steam yacht - was hillier and greener compared to the flat brown sea of rooftops on the east side of the river. A penny steamer was making its way down river, piled high with people in colourful kimonos; Joe could hear their euphonious chatter, which carried across the water like fevered bird song. Ferries criss-crossed the water in crazy and risky fashion ahead of their little steam yacht, yet somehow all this confused pell-mell of river traffic managed to avoid each other.

Maeda pointed ahead. 'This is the Ryogoku bridge coming up, and the Ekoin Temple over there on the right on the approaches to it. I was born very near there in the Honjo district, the son of a carpenter. I had no privileged upbringing, you see, Mr Appeldoorn, so I was blessed by fortune to have the opportunities I have enjoyed...'

'Why were *you* chosen to go to Europe as a young man, then, Mr Maeda, when you were just the poor son of a carpenter?' Joe's curiosity got the better of his manners for a moment.

Maeda smiled faintly, not apparently too put out at being interrupted. 'Many people here wonder at that too, but the truth is rather prosaic – I was one of the few people in Japan then who could speak any English at all, even if very poor compared to the way I speak now. It happened that an English sailor was shipwrecked here in Tokyo Bay when I was a small boy, and he was allowed to stay and marry a local woman in Honjo: it was he who taught me English as a child. I still remember him well; his name was Lieutenant William Wells from a place called Sandwich in Kent - we local children called him "Willy-san" and thought him as strange as a dragon or unicorn. But now we are more used to foreigners these days, like yourself,

Mr Appeldoorn.' He shook his head doubtfully. 'Many people see me now as a Westernised businessman only, a man who has lost his Japanese soul, and with no feeling left for the past. But they're quite wrong; I mourn the loss of old Edo as much as anyone. It's just that we Japanese cannot afford to stand still any more and watch the rest of the world go past us again.'

Maeda grew even more thoughtful. 'The Sumida has many moods, Mr Appeldoorn. I think Mr Charles Dickens would certainly have enjoyed coming here – this river has a history and an atmosphere as rich as his beloved Thames. Over there on the left is the conservative *geisha* quarter – the *Yanagibashi* in Kanda. My mother was an accomplished high-class *geisha* there but she gave it all up to marry a poor carpenter. In my youth, my family and I still used to spend much of our time on the river – it was our main thoroughfare then, rather than just an obstacle to be crossed, as it is today. I remember boats going up or down all day between here and Asakusa in summer, their awnings always spread against the hot sun, banners aloft; sometimes a sad chant would sound over the water for the repose of the souls of those who had died by drowning...'

A businessman with a poetic soul...? Joe wondered about this man as he listened to Maeda's interesting life story. Maeda seemed an unusual person even here in Japan, but in America such people didn't exist at all, did they? Joe couldn't imagine having a similar conversation with an American businessman on a boat trip up the Hudson – nothing was sacred in New York except the need to make a quick buck.

Maeda sighed nostalgically. 'Every summer evening, when I was a child, a boat would come to the stone embankment near my home and give us a shadow play. When it came up river to the sound of drum and gong and *shamisen*, my mother would look so happy, remembering the Floating World and her time as a *geisha*...'

*

After Mr Maeda had gone back to the bows to talk with his daughter, the other American businessman on board, Toby Pryor, came to the stern of the steam yacht and introduced himself properly, as he eased himself onto the gunwale next to Joe's canvas seat. Joe reciprocated and offered him his hand in return.

'How're you doin', Joseph? You enjoyin' this boat trip – personally I'm friggin' bored out of my skull. Still, you don't upset your host in this friggin' country if you can help it.' Toby Pryor was clearly not a man to stand on ceremonies, but Joe didn't mind that. 'You don't mind if I call you "Joseph", do yer?' The New York accent was thick and heavy, and sounded more Lower East side or The Bronx than Brooklyn or Queens.

Pryor was older than him but still probably under thirty-five, Joe guessed. Mr Maeda had to be suspecting by now that all American businessmen must be young greenhorns, Joe thought uneasily, although, to be fair, Toby didn't actually look particularly young, with his swarthy Jewish skin, blue jowls, close-cropped wiry hair already going a little grey at the temples, and incipient double chin. He looked instead like a man who enjoyed the good things in life, and who was already happy to surrender to the pleasures and vices of middle age. His crumpled baggy suit and the beer stains on his necktie were hardly a positive endorsement, though, for a man apparently trying to sell Western clothes to an increasingly discerning and fashion-conscious Japanese market...

'You're from Philadelphia, Joseph, so Mr Maeda tells me?'

Joe blinked in surprise. 'Then he's very well informed because I didn't tell him that.'

Pryor tapped his large nose knowingly. 'Oh, these guys do their research, believe me. Don't imagine, despite the impression they try to give, that we can really teach these Japs anythin' about business.'

'You're probably right about that,' Joe said, nodding in agreement. 'You sound like you're from New York, Toby…?'

Pryor smiled. 'Where else? Do you know New York well, Joseph?'

'Yes, I do…I was living and working in Manhattan – East Sixty-Forth Street - until I got married last year and moved out to Connecticut.' Joe explained. Then he told Pryor a little more about his background, growing up in Philadelphia, and then, later, studying in Europe.

'Yeah, I was born and brought up on the Lower East side,' Pryor confirmed when it was his turn to speak again. 'Couldn't live anywhere else in America, although I love to travel out here at least once a year. My papa arrived in New York Harbour from Lithuania forty years ago with nothin' but the rags he stood up in; he was one of the first immigrants from that part of the world, I think. The first thing he did was change his friggin' family name from Prylinski – thought he would get on better in the New Country that way. And all the people who came after him seem to have done the same thing. These days our local synagogue doesn't have a single Jewish name – all friggin' anglicised Goulds and Smiths and Johnsons. I don't know why; it didn't make a damned bit of difference! My old man was still a Jew, whatever he called himself, and everybody on the East Side knew it! But he worked in a sweatshop for sixteen hours a day until he had enough capital to start on his own. Now he's got no hair left and a stomach ulcer the size of Brooklyn Bridge but he owns a dozen factories all over New York and Joisey.'

'And you're here selling his range of Western clothes?'

'Yeah, been visitin' Japan for five years now and selling more every year. Women's underwear is the big growth market out here in the Far East, you see. That part of our company is called "Orpheus Underwear." Get it?'

Joe was puzzled by the mythological reference to the man who had followed his dead wife, Eurydice, to Hades to try and bring her back from the grave.

'*Orpheus in the Undieworld*,' Toby explained with a leer. 'Thought the name up myself,' he added proudly. 'These Japanese dames can't get enough of our corsets, chemises, bloomers and bodices. You have to understand –' Toby sniggered – '...they weren't used to wearin' underwear at all under those kimonos of theirs, so now they're making up for lost time in the silk undie business. This year we've got a nifty new line in little silk drawers for women, and the little Jap girls just love 'em. Just been tellin' Motoko-san all about them, and givin' her some samples from the new range as a present. I tell you, she disappeared straightaway below deck with them – probably couldn't wait to try them on, I bet.' Toby looked rueful. 'Wouldn't have minded helpin' that little doll on with them, if I could – she's been making eyes at me ever since I came on board - but maybe it'd be a little tricky gettin' to know her better with her old man watchin'.' He glanced at the front of the boat. 'But that is one provocative little girl...'

Joe glanced at the demure little figure, sitting in the bows with her father, with slight unease. 'You think it's a wise move to try flirting with Maeda's own daughter?' Joe asked him doubtfully. 'In a conservative society like this, you're asking for trouble, aren't you?'

Toby nodded moodily. 'I suppose so. From a business point of view, I'd probably be cuttin' my own throat if I even tried. But, my God! Just look at that girl, Joseph – she's like something out of a friggin' dream...'

'More likely a nightmare. If you want to chase Japanese skirt, Toby, you'd be better looking elsewhere, that's my advice.' Joe quickly changed the subject. 'How much do you know about her father, and his business deals, anyway?'

Toby tapped his nose again. 'Oh, I've done my research too. From what I've learnt, he came from a pretty ordinary background, but someone in the ruling Choshu clan clearly took a shine to him as a young man, and he never looked back. Got a lot of important friends in very high places now, if you know what I mean. You have to realise the big industrial changes only really began here fifteen years ago or so, and the Japs have still got a lot of catchin' up to do. Initially it was the government who started up all the main businesses here, and they taxed the peasants and the rice farmers heavily to pay for industrial development since they didn't want to have to use foreign capital. Didn't want to get into hock to no foreigners, and I can't blame 'em for that. Then the government passed over these industries they'd founded to their closest pals, the *Zaibatsu* – people like Mitsubishi, Mitsui, Sumitomo and Yasuda, who are all government insiders and part of the clan. Maeda was initially given the *Nippon Yusen Kaisha* – that's the Japan Mail Line that challenged the foreign domination of the Japan-China steamship trade - even though he's not one of the rulin' clan by birth. But he does probably have the best business brain of the lot, and since then he's branched out into electric power and department stores, and all sorts of other things. He's the man behind the new Mitsukoshi Department Store at the west approach to the Nihombashi Bridge. His big competitor is the Shirokiya store on the other side of the bridge, and Maeda wants to make sure *they* don't get any of my ladies' silk panties in their display cases. Yeah, he's a very important man here...'

*

Eleanor's prediction to Joe about the length of his journey to Japan had proved very accurate. It had in fact taken him more than three weeks to travel across the world from New England to the Port of Yokohama in Tokyo Bay.

He'd travelled first to San Francisco from New York by way of the Central Pacific Railroad across the still wild lands of the American West. On the way he heard the news of the devastating New Year fire at the Iroquois Theatre in Chicago that had killed nearly six hundred people, which gave him severe pause for thought. But he had his own problems to worry about too: there were still no proper stations between Omaha in Nebraska and Ogden in Utah so Joe had been forced to take along a four-day stock of provisions cooked by Eleanor's own fair hand to see him through that long hungry leg.

The train did halt occasionally at various desolate watering places in the middle of nowhere – Joe had never fully understood the vast scale and emptiness of his own country until now, but this long journey through this near untouched wilderness brought it home to him. He also saw real Indians for the first time in his life outside a Wild West show, even if only a poor downtrodden drunken crew of old men and fat squaws begging for nickels at the window of his coach. These were no fleet-footed, bronzed warriors, that much was certain, but a race degraded and demoralised, it seemed to Joe.

The coach attendant, a grizzled old Yankee veteran of the Sioux Wars himself, had been surprisingly sympathetic to the Indian visitors. 'It's a damned shame to see 'em reduced to this. See that guy there...' - he pointed out a hawk-nosed old man in filthy buckskins, with bloodshot eyes and trembling hands - '...that's Spotted Tail, son of the Brulé Sioux chief of the same name who fought with Sitting Bull thirty years ago. Look at him now! *We* Americans did this to them. I hope we're proud of ourselves; we should'a just left these people and their way of life alone, in my humble opinion, instead of turnin' them into this human wreckage. I hope we don't go doin' this to any other poor bastards in the rest of the world...'

Joe knew America hadn't yet learned the lesson to stop interfering in other people's lives, though; American diplomats and traders hadn't stopped when they got to California but had gone right on across the Pacific and started telling the Polynesians, Japanese, Chinese and Filipinos how to live their lives too. American missionaries in particular seemed to be spreading everywhere in Asia and the Pacific, determined to save the souls of the benighted foreigners and force them to change their backward lives. A bit like a poisonous plague, Joe thought cynically...

And what America had done to the Japanese had been particularly insensitive in Joe's opinion – Joe wondered how Americans would have reacted if some technologically superior foreigners had turned up in New York Harbour, like visitors from another planet, and started telling New Yorkers what they could and couldn't do in their own country. Yet that was precisely what the Japanese had had to put up with...

The train had eventually moved on, the empty arid spaces and wild mountain scenery of the West slipping endlessly past the carriage windows, together with fleeting glimpses of antelope, prairie dogs, bears and the odd remaining buffalo that Bill Cody had somehow missed slaughtering.

The monotony of the land journey was soon obliterated in Joe's mind by the even greater monotony of sea travel by steamer - an eighteen-day passage from San Francisco to Yokohama. The only excitement for Joe during the voyage had been the problem of how to avoid the man-hungry thirty-year-old widow of a US marine whose husband had been killed at San Juan Hill in Cuba, serving with Teddy Roosevelt's Roughriders. Eventually a bored Mrs L'Estrange had transferred her attentions to the man in the next cabin to his own – a missionary returning to the Far East – and Joe had been reduced for the rest of the voyage to listening unwillingly through the paper-thin bulkhead to Mrs L'Estrange leading her missionary astray into all sorts of strange and unheard-of positions...

*

Toby Pryor was still prattling on about the perils and pitfalls of doing business in Japan as they passed under the Umaya Bridge.

Toby's earthy view of women (he was unmarried, Joe had established by now) reminded Joe a little of his old Parisian friend, René Sardou. René was now living with his Creole temptress, Corazon, in Paris, and Joe could imagine their life together was probably a tempestuous one at best.

'This country has gone through some friggin' upheavals in the last fifty years,' Toby was saying. 'The Japs are still a little bit crazy and, if you know their history, you soon understand why. The Samurai class and the peasants suffered a lot when the Japanese government decided forty years ago that they had to westernise the country to survive. They forced the Samurai class to give up their shaven heads and top-knot haircuts, and made the wearing of swords punishable by death. That was hard for the warrior class to take because they'd always been top dogs until then, and now suddenly peasants no longer had to run around kow-towing to them, while merchants and shopkeepers and tradesmen actually became more important than them. The Samurais made one last stand about thirty years ago led by a man called

23

Takamori Saigo – the Great Saigo, they still call him here. Saigo wanted to try and protect the old feudal way of life of the Samurai class, and his final battle with government forces made our Civil War battles look like a picnic party. Thirty thousand were killed on each side in just one friggin' day, including Saigo himself. There is still a fringe of die-hard nationalist fanatics about, even these days, who would like to turn the clock back to a feudal Japan, as well as a few crazy anarchists and socialists who would like to transform this country into a worker's paradise. A few years ago the Foreign Minister Okuma even lost a leg after a nationalist extremist threw a bomb at him. But generally, things have settled down here in Japan domestically, if not in their relations with their neighbours, particularly Russia...'

'So what's the problem between Japan and the Russians?' Joe interrupted.

Toby shrugged and glanced up at the front of the boat where Maeda and his daughter were still deep in conversation. 'The Japs started to have international ambitions of their own, I suppose. Ten years ago they went to war with China and, as easy winners at the end – China is a friggin' mess after all - claimed the whole of Korea, the island of Formosa, and Port Arthur and the Liao-tung Peninsula in Manchuria, from the Chinks. But Russia, Germany and France later forced Japan to surrender their claim to Manchuria, after which these friggin' European powers themselves all seized possessions in China too, and the Russkis then had the nerve to rub it in even further by grabbing Port Arthur and the Liao-tung Peninsula for themselves. So the Japs were really, *really* pissed off after that. That's why many people think war between Japan and Russia is inevitable in the end – certainly the Russkis ain't anyone's favourite foreigners at the moment around here.'

Toby ran a hand through his wiry black hair. 'There may be a Japanese Parliament of sorts but there's still no real democracy here, of course. There are no "liberal" political parties in the European or American sense, and that's probably not a bad thing for us doin' business here, but it may spell trouble in the long run. For the moment, though, the government is still run from behind the scenes by this handful of rich men of the Choshu and Satsuma clans with unbelievable power. They call 'em the *Genro,* the 'Elder statesman", and Maeda is still very close to them so watch what you say to him...'

*

After a while Toby went off to talk to Maeda again, and Motoko Maeda approached Joe diffidently in return in the stern of the boat, carrying a tray. As she bowed and sat down beside him, Joe could see begrudgingly what Toby had meant – this was a *very* attractive girl, her skin glowing with a fine peach-like bloom that seemed entirely natural, and her eyes a perfect almond shape under graceful arched brows. In the few days since his arrival in the East, Joe had already become highly susceptible to the eyes of beautiful Oriental women; and he found there was something particularly exotic and tantalising about the expression in Motoko Maeda's almond eyes that seemed to combine a tranquil femininity with a suggestion of something deeper and erotic stirring just beneath the surface. Perhaps Motoko took after her *geisha* grandmother in that ability to combine demureness and wanton sexuality, all in the same placid expression.

She pointed out a tall brick tower in the Asakusa district of the city on the left bank. 'That is Asakusa Twelve Storeys, Mr App-re-doon. Tallest building in Tokyo,' she said with a note of pride in her voice. 'Best place for view over city – nearly seventy metre high. Also the first elevator in city – specially delivered from America.'

'I haven't been to Asakusa district yet. Is it nice?' Joe asked neutrally.

'Oh yes. "Sixth District" is home of music hall and theatre and other entertainments. Just opened is "Electricity Hall" – first movie theatre in land.' She shyly offered him some Japanese eating delicacies from the tray she had brought with her: *natto, umeboshi* pickled plums, *soba* and *udon* noodles, *miso soup*. Joe tried a little of everything and did his best to look as if he was enjoying it. 'What is this stuff? *Kore-wa nan desu-ka?*'

She clapped her hands in delight at his attempt at speaking Japanese. 'You are very clever, Mr App-re-doon. That is *natto,* fermented soya bean. So sorry if not to your liking. It difficult taste for foreigner to appreciate.' Her English was heavily accented, but surprisingly good since she'd told him she had never travelled outside Japan.

Natto did taste pretty much as expected from the description but Joe said, 'Delicious,' anyway, hoping against hope she wouldn't offer him any more.

Even if he didn't like the food on offer, Joe still couldn't help continuing to admire the clear-skinned beauty of the girl offering it, despite his own advice to Toby about the inadvisability of being over-friendly with Maeda's daughter - and also, for that matter, remembering that unequivocal warning he'd had from Eleanor on the subject of Japanese women. Motoko was wearing western clothes - high buttoned-up shoes, a dark blue full-length silk dress and grey Kashmir woollen coat - that suited her very well. Her slender figure looked natural rather than being heavily constrained by tight whalebone stays at the waist – a torture which most western women seemed more than willing to bear in their preoccupation with achieving an hourglass figure.

With a sudden guilty thought about Eleanor, Joe struggled to raise his mind from thoughts of Motoko's trim little body to rather less questionable things. They had passed the Asakusa district and the decorative ironwork of the Azuma Bridge by now and were leaving the city behind them, the river flowing between low marshy ground on each side. On the left bank Joe saw a distant gate and an area of buildings enclosed within a high wooden stockade, like a fort. 'What is that place over there, Motoko-san?'

She fluttered her eyelashes again in his direction. They really were something for a man to wax lyrical about, Joe thought, like miniature Chinese fans, especially when she lowered them so enticingly. 'That is *Yoshiwara*, Mr App-re-doon.'

'What happens there?' Joe asked naively.

She seemed perplexed as to how to answer the question, but Toby suddenly reappeared, to rescue them both from their slight mutual embarrassment. 'If you like, Joseph, *I'll* show you what happens there. It's one of the more interesting areas of this city...*if you know what I mean, boy,*' he added with a private wink.

CHAPTER 3

Monday 25th January 1904

Joe Appeldoorn wasn't yet sure how well his first full day with his Japanese hosts had gone but he hoped at least that he had not made any enormous cultural gaffes during the course of this interesting first day. Certainly Kenzoburo Maeda had turned out to be an interesting and cultivated man, and far more approachable and westernised in his outlook than Joe had any right to expect.

Yet Joe thought Maeda's diffident smile and polite manners might be deceptive – being unused to the manners of Orientals, Joe found that Maeda was still a difficult man to read, as were all Japanese. Joe had recognised the unusual qualities of these people almost immediately on his arrival in Japan; and the city of Tokyo, for all its distasteful smells and smoke and noise, had begun to exert a notable attraction on him. Yet many things about this vigorous city and its people were still inexplicable to his western eyes; despite the veneer of the twentieth century, this remained at heart an unmistakeably Oriental city, looking out suspiciously at the rest of the world from its own slant-eyed heavy-lidded perspective.

Joe had learned enough about business in the last year (thanks mainly to Eleanor's guidance) to know that the essence of being a successful businessman was only partly to do with the quality of what was for sale, and far more to do with forming the right personal relations with your potential clients. And although Joe was supremely confident of the technical superiority and the competitive cost of his new steam turbines and high voltage generating equipment, he was also uncomfortably aware that, if he upset Maeda in any way, his domestic competitors would soon be sailing out in convoys from San Francisco to offer Maeda their wares in his place.

To try and cement his newfound relationship with his powerful potential client, therefore, Joe had invited Maeda and his daughter to dine with him tonight at his hotel, the Imperial Hotel, and had included Toby Pryor in the invitation too. Joe wasn't quite sure whether that latter move was a wise idea or not, yet Pryor was turning out to be a surprisingly useful and valuable source of information about Japan. And being in the clothing business and apparently already well connected to Maeda, it seemed Pryor was no direct competitor of his anyway and would hardly therefore be a threat to Joe's chances of closing his own deal with Maeda...

*

After getting back from the trip up river, Joe had an hour to spare in the afternoon, and spent it wandering around the streets in the vicinity of his hotel, absorbing the atmosphere of this strange and exotic city. Marunouchi district was the pleasant area immediately to the east side of the Palace where most of the Japanese government buildings, including the new Diet Building, were concentrated, along with foreign embassies and Western hotels. This area was the administrative and political hub of the new Japan, and the nearest thing Tokyo had to a Capitol Hill or a Whitehall.

Marunouchi's "London Town" was a surprise, though. As he walked through these streets of English-looking terraced brick houses, Joe could see that the foreign influence had already been particularly strong in this area; the English architects who had perpetrated this particular architectural monstrosity certainly had a lot to answer for. Marunouchi "London Town" did indeed look like a bit of Piccadilly dropped unceremoniously into the middle of Tokyo, but hardly seemed to suit the mood of this city, or the people in kimonos and peasant wear walking its streets.

Turning south, Joe came to two bazaars by the Shimbashi Bridge and went into the more interesting-looking one. He wandered through some of the stores; from the back windows of the shops, he could see the premises of the nearby Shimbashi *geisha* district preparing themselves for a night of sensual and intoxicating business. The lines of small shops in this bazaar were selling everything imaginable: food, of course, in startling variety – giant blue tuna, squid and octopus; one of the shops even had a live python in its window, although Joe was unsure whether this was intended for the cooking pot, or was just a visual distraction. There was also woodcraft for sale, bamboo and lacquerware, painted screens, miniature trees, *geta* clogs, *yukata* summer kimonos, and even some ladies' silk underwear that looked suspiciously to Joe like Toby Pryor's supposedly innovative range. Joe was deep in thought about the sights and sounds of this strange city as he left the bazaar, and in that heavily preoccupied state was nearly knocked down for his pains by a speeding horse–drawn tram.

He came to Shimbashi Station, the main terminus for trains to Yokohama and the South. He could hear the hiss of steam escaping from the locomotives waiting at the platforms, and feel that unmistakable sense of anticipation and excitement that railway stations always aroused in him, the feeling one has when setting out on a great journey.

With a flash of déjà vu, probably induced by the very European architecture of this brick-faced railway station, he was reminded of a significant overnight train journey that he'd made two years ago, from the Gare de Lyon in Paris to Bern in Switzerland: *that* had been the night he had first encountered the extraordinary Miss Amelia Peachy.

The memory of that journey and his first meeting with Miss Peachy made Joe reflect a little and turned his mood gradually from relaxed to melancholic. But for some reason it also brought on a heightened sense of tension that made him feel as if someone was watching his every move...

He spun around to challenge whoever it was, but found only a ragamuffin boy of six or seven staring at him with saucer-shaped eyes, as if seeing a ghostly apparition. Joe chided himself for his ridiculous paranoia, gave the startled child a rueful smile and then a single yen (quite a lot of money for a beggar child), before moving on.

The streets of Shimbashi were full of young people, who obviously loved to go strolling here, even on a cold winter's afternoon in January. As it grew dark and a thin drizzle began to fall, the few remaining rickshaws plying for trade, with their hoods raised to keep off the rain, looked like colourful corpulent beetles with sheathed wings. Joe saw one Japanese lady emerge delicately from her rickshaw, like a butterfly from its chrysalis, a girl who seemed almost as beautiful as the fragrant Motoko-san. Joe decided that tonight he had better take his own advice and perhaps be a little more distant with Maeda's tempting beauty of a daughter than he had been on the river excursion this afternoon; any improper social intimacy with his client's daughter, even if unintended, was one complication better left out of this business negotiation...

Joe finally completed his loop through the busy streets of Marunouchi, Kyobashi and Shimbashi, and returned to his temporary home located on the outer moat of the palace. The Imperial Hotel was three storeys of portentous wooden architecture in a vaguely Italianate style, with the castle moat in front still full of carp and water lilies, despite the skin of ice on the surface. Nearby, facing Hibiya Park, was the famous government guest house, the *Rokumeikan* – the so-called "Pavilion of the Weeping Stag" – built in a very similar architectural style to the Imperial, where the Japanese had once demonstrated their willingness to accept western culture and ideas by giving displays of Western dancing and music and poetry recitation. Built during the time of the "unequal treaties" with foreign powers, when the Japanese had to grin and bear the humiliation of foreigners dictating events in their country, and now partly disused after being damaged by an earthquake, the *Rokumeikan* already seemed to Joe an anachronism in this newly confident, modern and increasingly militaristic Japan of the twentieth Century...

*

At seven, after changing for dinner, Joe sat together with Toby Pryor in the lobby of the Imperial waiting for Maeda to arrive.

Joe nodded coolly at a gentleman in passing, someone he'd met briefly in the hotel bar the previous evening, a middle-aged Swiss businessman from Zurich, one Herr Ernst Ludwig Maienfeld. Joe hadn't found Herr Maienfeld particularly good company - for a man supposedly from Zurich, he preferred strangely to speak in stilted English rather than in German (even though Joe spoke perfect Swiss-German) and, even odder, seemed to know very little about his own hometown (which Joe *did* know well, having been a student there...)

Joe now returned his attention fully to his companion again, and began to regret his impulsive decision to include Toby Pryor in the dinner invitation tonight. Toby didn't look any more sartorial in his evening suit than he had on the boat this afternoon, neck bulging over his white tie, his shirt buttons in front looking ready to pop. Toby didn't seem to notice Joe's look of unease, though, and surveyed the scene with wry good humour. 'You know, Joe, this lobby is supposedly the haunt of every friggin' spy in Tokyo. The British watch the French, the French watch the Germans, the Germans watch the Japanese, everybody watches the damned Russkis. That guy you just said hello to, he *has* to be a spy, for damned sure...'

Joe was shocked. 'Really?'

Toby gave Joe a knowing look at that naïve response. 'You don't do a little spying yourself for Uncle Sam on the side, do you, Joe? Is that why you're staying here in this hotel?'

Joe squinted at him in surprise. 'What would make you think that?'

Toby clicked his tongue. 'Well, you look the part, Joe, especially dressed in that penguin suit, just like friggin' Raffles. And bein' a businessman is a perfect cover for a spy...' Toby glanced up at a small party of westerners, in tail-suited and silk-gowned finery, who were just entering the hotel, and being ushered through the main glass door by the obsequious doorman. 'Talkin' of friggin' Raffles, here come the British. There's some sort of reception going on in one of the function rooms tonight. Some British diplomat going back to Blighty, poor bastard.'

'*They* don't look like spies,' Joe commented idly.

'No, not all of them. That's the British Ambassador, Sir Stephen Hawtry-Gough...' Toby pointed out a typical stiff-lipped Englishman in tail coat and top hat, tall, lean, balding, and with a back so ramrod straight, it looked to Joe as if he still had a coat hanger stuck up there. '...And that's his wife, Lady Rosemary Hawtry-Gough,' Toby continued. 'I've met 'em both – his wife has a discernin' taste for our range of Orpheus silk underwear: in fact Lady Rosemary's one of my best customers here.' Joe saw that the

Ambassador's wife was a faded blonde beauty with an apparently permanently sad expression, as if morbidly reflecting on the passage of time and the slow unravelling of her life. 'A little past her best but still a fine looking woman for her age,' Toby commented with an earthy leer. 'I certainly wouldn't say no to her, if she wanted a good bulling – the poor bitch looks like she could use one, that's for friggin' sure.'

Joe saw Lady Hawtry-Gough's eyes linger on him for a moment before she moved on. 'Who are the younger guys with them?'

'The foppish-lookin' one with the red hair is a trade delegate called The Honourable Peregrine Cavendish...No, I couldn't friggin' well believe that name either...'

Joe laughed as much at the disbelieving expression on Toby's face as anything else.

'But if you want to sell anything to the English in Japan,' Toby continued loudly, 'you have to try and get on with that stuck-up piece of shit...'

Joe coughed to shut him up. 'And the blond guy talking to Cavendish – he looks a bit more formidable.'

Toby scratched his nose. 'Oh, he's a spy all right. Officially head of their Japanese language section, but in reality top of their intelligence team at the Embassy. Name's Clive Randall. But everybody knows about him - he might as well walk around Tokyo with a sign hangin' around his neck saying "SPY". And another one saying "COMPLETE FRIGGIN' BASTARD", for that matter. They're *not* the most subtle people in the world, the English.'

'You know a great deal about this place, Toby, don't you?' Joe was getting a little suspicious that a man who was supposedly in Tokyo only to sell his company's fashion wear should know quite so much about the ins and outs of this country.

Toby caught the meaning of his look and grew defensive. 'Hey, you gotta know what's goin' on in this friggin' town if you want to do business here. And I understand what makes people tick – it's the same things the world over: money, sex, power. I might not make a bad spy at that,' he mused. 'But Uncle Sam would hardly hire a dumb, loudmouth sonofabitch like me, would he...?'

'You probably have a point there,' Joe observed with a smile. He glanced around the lobby again and, for no particular reason, picked out one particular woman for his attention, sitting at an alcove table by herself, in a rattan cane armchair beneath the browning fronds of a pair of tired-looking Phoenix palms. 'So, if you understand people so well, what about that woman sitting over there on her own? Looks like she's waiting for someone? You know her?' The object of Joe's mild attention was a middle-aged European lady, a little on the plump side, and also, judged from the other side of the lobby, apparently more than a little plain. Her greying hair was partly concealed under a green silk hat and veil but she was well dressed in an expensive-looking day coat of dark lamb's wool with fur collar. Now that he thought about it, Joe recalled that the Ambassador's wife, Lady Rosemary, had acknowledged the woman with a slight nod of recognition as she'd passed her on the way in.

Toby inspected the woman carefully, but didn't seem absolutely sure of himself for once. 'Don't think I know her but there's something familiar about her. Definitely English, though. And I bet *she* doesn't wear my range of Orpheus silk panties – long stiff cotton drawers would be more her style -' he frowned - '...although I don't know, though. She could be wearing something special tonight under all those petticoats. If you're asking me, she looks like the lonely expat wife of some friggin' missionary or engineer from out in the sticks up country somewhere, come to the fleshpots of Tokyo looking for a liaison with anyone desperate enough. But even I ain't desperate enough for you, lady!' he whispered under his breath. 'I should'a told you, Joe - this friggin' hotel is also famous for romantic assignations and makin' whoopie. Practically an English knockin' shop. Oh-oh, she's got her eye on you, Joe.'

The woman *had* turned her head and looked back just as Joe's eye had fallen on her again, and her reaction was extraordinary. She went white for a second, then fumbled her coffee cup which smashed on the floor, spreading a stain of coffee across the teak floor. Fortunately it missed the fine Persian carpet set beneath the round table at which she was sitting. The hotel's handsome French desk clerk, Jacques – known intimately to everyone staying at the Imperial, particularly the lady guests - rushed over to help her, his brilliantined hair gleaming like satin. From the familiar way Jacques addressed the woman, she was obviously a regular guest at the Imperial.

'Please don't concern yourself, Madame Smythe. *Ca ne fait rien!*' Jacques snapped a peremptory finger and a tiny uniformed maid with mop and bucket appeared almost instantly, as if by magic.

The Englishwoman had apparently recovered her composure by now, but, as she nodded her thanks absently to Jacques and the maid, she still seemed more preoccupied with Joe than anything else, staring at him from the other side of the lobby as if she'd just seen him materialise through a solid wall.

Toby had lost interest in Mrs Smythe by now, though, and was busy trying to persuade Joe to visit the infamous *Yoshiwara* with him the following night, after a planned reception at the American Embassy to which they'd both been invited. 'There's this one place I know called the *Gankiro* Tea-house, also known as Number Nine, where they have lots of sweet little Japanese lasses who'll serve you tea, sweetmeats, *saké*. They'll even play *chonkina* with you – that's a game of forfeits - in which every time a girl loses a round, she has to take off another piece of her clothes. If you've never seen a Jap girl takin' her clothes off, you've missed a real treat. They got the cutest little asses in the world...'

Joe thought about his promise to Eleanor. 'I'd better not, Toby. And you'll go to Hell, if you're not careful,' he added lightly.

'Oh, come on, Joseph!' Toby insisted. 'They got women there who are straight from friggin' heaven, so it's worth the minor risk of goin' to Hell...And I ain't no Catholic anyway...'

Toby's voice tailed away in embarrassment as Motoko Maeda, dressed in full formal Japanese evening wear, a brightly coloured *furisode* kimono, suddenly appeared from nowhere at his side.

'So sorry, gentleman...I afraid bad news. My father detained by business, so, tonight, will you make do with me?'

Toby grinned disingenuously. 'You bet.'

Motoko smiled again innocently. 'Tell me, Mr Pryor, what is this place I heard you mention – *friggin' heaven*? Where is that exactly?...is it near New York?

*

Joe had learned enough in his short time in Japan to know that for Mr Maeda to send his daughter alone to what was effectively a business dinner was highly unusual behaviour. (In fact, despite the suffragette movement in the States, Joe had to admit that it would still be a highly unusual thing in Hartford, Connecticut or even New York too.) It suggested that Maeda had a great deal of confidence in his young daughter - and this from a man who was one of the leading *Zaibatsu* in the country. This could only mean – assuming that Maeda wasn't simply indulging in a bit of nepotistic self-delusion, which Joe suspected was *not* the case – that Motoko was far from being the subservient little porcelain doll he had first imagined...

She and Joe sat alone together at the end of the meal, Toby having disappeared for a few minutes – for a private snort of bourbon in the bar next door, Joe guessed. Toby had looked a little unsteady on his feet as he left the dining room and Joe wondered whether he'd been drinking even before meeting him tonight.

But he certainly didn't mind Toby leaving him alone for a few minutes with this young woman who was proving a constant surprise and pleasure to be with. The snowy white table linen was a perfect foil for her colourful kimono and obi, the candlelight gleamed on her raven hair and perfect complexion, while in the corner of the room behind her, almost hidden by palms, a quartet of Japanese musicians played their slightly laboured way through a succession of Western tunes: *Goodbye Dolly Gray, Just a-wearyin' for you, Bill Bailey won't you please come home, In the good old summertime, Ida, Sweet Adeline...*

Joe was beginning to suspect from what more he'd learned of her life during the meal that Motoko Maeda might be a little older than he'd originally thought. He had taken her for no more than twenty on first meeting her on the boat today, but it seemed Japanese girls retained their youthful looks a long time apparently, and it could be she was nearer twenty-five – in fact the same age as himself, if that really were the case.

She apologised yet again – it must have been the tenth time tonight – for coming on her own this evening. 'So sorry that it is only me tonight, Mr App-re-doon. My father means no disrespect by not accepting kind invitation.'

'None taken,' Joe assured her quickly before his curiosity about the Maeda family's affairs overcame his reluctance to pry. 'Your mother has been dead many years, you told me, Miss Maeda. Have you any brothers or sisters, though?'

'I had two older brother, but regrettably both dead.' Motoko looked solemn for a moment. 'One – Onii-san – Elder brother - died of fever last year, and my other younger brother, Shin-chan – killed fighting in *Manchuko* – Manchuria – ten year ago.'

Joe grimaced. 'I'm sorry to hear that. And have you any sisters?'

'Two young sister.'

Joe nodded in understanding. 'So your father must rely on you a great deal.'

Motoko acknowledged that with a slight bow. 'Of course.'

The Japanese maitre d' came over at this point in the conversation and ostentatiously offered Motoko more red wine from the open bottle on the table, but she surprisingly refused that and ordered Scotch whisky instead. One of the less predictable things Joe had discovered about the Japanese was that in the last few decades they had formed a deep appreciation of Western booze in all its myriad varieties. 'Did you enjoy the Western food I ordered tonight, Miss Maeda? Personally I found the Kobe beef delicious, but you didn't eat much...' Joe happened to glance up at that moment through the open door of the dining room and saw Toby Pryor in the lobby, exchanging earnest and surreptitious words with someone just out of sight. Although Joe couldn't see whom he was talking to, Toby looked surprisingly sober – in fact a lot more sober than he'd appeared when he'd staggered out of the dining room a few minutes earlier. Then the man Toby was talking to leaned his head forward slightly and Joe got a glimpse of blond hair. A moment later the man stepped back completely out of sight again, although Joe was certain by now that the man Toby was speaking to with such apparent earnestness was the British spymaster, Randall. Yet, only a few minutes ago, Toby had been dismissing the man as a "complete friggin' bastard". *So how to explain this thaw in Anglo-American relations...?*

'We Japanese not used to eat red meat,' Motoko was saying. 'Fish only.

When American came here fifty years ago and try persuade us to eat wild venison, they had to call it "Mountain Whale" otherwise no one eat it.' She laughed delightedly at the thought behind her hand. 'You are married, Mr App-re-doon, I believe. What is wife like? Very beautiful?'

Joe smiled. 'I think so, of course. Her name is Eleanor. She has very white skin and red hair – the shade we call "Titian" because the Renaissance artist of that name painted so many beautiful Italian woman with that particular hair colour.'

Motoko blinked innocently. 'Does *Ereanor-san* have large breast and hip?'

Joe was surprised by the intimate nature of the question, and wondered how he could phrase a polite answer. 'I think you would say so...by Japanese standards anyway.' *And* by American standards too, Joe thought complacently, his mind dwelling with satisfaction for a moment on the delights of his wife's extravagant figure.

Motoko sighed. 'I envy foreign women such good body form and long leg.'

Joe shook his head wryly. 'I don't think you have anything to complain to the Almighty about in that department, Miss Maeda.'

She was puzzled. 'Please?'

Joe decided wisely not to elaborate further, though, aware that the discussion was taking him into dangerously uncharted waters.

Motoko asked him how he'd first met Eleanor, and Joe gave her a short and simplified version of the story of how he had been sent to Europe to find her after she'd gone missing.

'You were detective?' she said admiringly. 'And you rescue *Ereanor-san* from bad men?'

Joe was uncomfortable at giving her the impression that he'd been some sort of hero. 'Sort of,' he said self-effacingly, '...from minor criminals anyway.' Although Johan Plesch had hardly been a minor criminal, Joe reminded himself, but an evil assassin and criminal mastermind who had supposedly been responsible for the murders of both a US President and several European heads of state. Joe's search for Eleanor had ultimately led him into a confrontation with this man and *real* danger, before Plesch had met his fate at the hands of the British government agent, Miss Amelia Peachy. Still, tonight was hardly an appropriate time to talk about such unpleasant things...

'It's a romantic story.' Motoko smiled charmingly.

Joe quickly changed the subject, and listening to the quartet striking up a slow waltz, asked, 'Would you like to dance, Miss Maeda?'

She flushed and for one moment he thought he'd made an enormous faux pas. *Perhaps asking a woman to dance in Japan was as good as inviting them into your bed?*

But the pink flush to her cheeks was apparently just a sign of pleasure.

'Oh, I love Western dance, Mr App-re-doon. Thank you so much for asking. I hope you find me good dancer. I learn to dance at *Rokumeikan...*'

'Yes, I've heard of the *Rokumeikan*. It's just a short walk from here, isn't it?'

Toby Pryor chose this inopportune moment to return, though, and - strangely to Joe - seemed highly drunk again. Joe wondered if Toby was playing some sort of stupid game. He hoped that Toby wasn't really silly enough, though, to have any romantic designs on Motoko, although from what he'd said on the boat this afternoon, he might have. Joe decided that, whatever else happened tonight, he wasn't going to leave Motoko on her own with Toby, not for a single moment...

The maitre d' appeared yet again and whispered something in Japanese in Motoko's ear. She spoke up hesitantly. 'It seems I have telephone call – probably my father. He is only person who know where I am this evening. Will you excuse, please?' She stood up and bowed before returning to the lobby, shuffling on her *zori* sandals in the characteristic walk of Japanese ladies dressed in kimonos.

Joe watched her make her entrancing exit through the door of the dining room into the lobby. As she disappeared from sight, Joe saw the Englishwoman he'd noticed earlier, Mrs Smythe, finally get up and leave her lonely table in the lobby alcove. If she had been waiting for someone in particular, that person had clearly let her down. She went off in the direction of the birdcage elevator, presumably to go upstairs to her room. But as she passed the dining room door, she glanced long and hard again at Joe...

Joe was puzzled by the woman's odd look, which could have meant almost anything, as he sat in reflective mood with Toby in the dining room waiting for Motoko to return. Out of the corner of his eye, he noticed a Japanese man and woman in western dress finish dinner at a neighbouring table and get up to leave. Other diners turned their heads curiously to look at them as they left – not surprisingly perhaps since they were a strikingly handsome couple, the man considerably older than his female companion but equally photogenic.

'Who are they?' Joe asked Toby curiously. 'Do you know?'

Toby blinked through red-rimmed eyes. 'Sure...that's Shintaro Isogai. Politician. Some sort of liberal, so they say. Runs a political party called *Jiyuto* or something - the Liberty Party. Arch-enemy of the government, and the present Prime Minister, General Taro Kat...Kat...sura. Although I never know how they keep track of their friggin' Prime Ministers in this friggin' country – change 'em more often than I change my underpants.'

'I thought you told me there were no political parties in Japan,' Joe complained mildly. 'You're letting me down here, Toby.'

'S'not quite true. Isogai is one to watch. If he lives long enough...'

'Who was that with him? His mistress?' Joe asked.

Toby downed another glass of saké. 'I agree she's juicy enough for that. But that's his daughter, Fumiyo. Socialist "intellectual" like her old man. Studied math at Göttingen in Germany with a Professor called Hilbert. A little cold, they say – you'd freeze your dick off if you ever ventured into those drawers, Joseph, my boy - but beautiful enough. I guess she'd suit one of those long-haired poets that like to admire women from afar. Personally I like to get up close with a woman and feel her hot little breath on my private parts.'

Joe looked at Toby oddly after this long speech, wondering if he was really as drunk as he was making himself out to be. He was still puzzled by Toby's short but earnest conversation with the British agent Clive Randall in the lobby, and was tempted to press him about it now. But he let the moment pass, although it did also occur to him to wonder why a New York clothing manufacturer like Toby Pryor should have heard of the University of Göttingen, or indeed of a mathematician like David Hilbert. Those were hardly the sort of facts you would expect a man like Toby to be familiar with. Toby Pryor might just be turning out to be the strangest anomaly Joe had yet encountered in this odd country...

*

Toby finally retired for the night, without even waiting for Motoko to return. His eyes were glazed and cloudy as he said, 'So long, pal. I gotta go – feel as sick as a dog. Say good night to "Cutie Pants" for me.' He weaved an erratic path out through the dining room door and across the lobby to the birdcage elevator.

Motoko had still not reappeared and it was now over ten minutes that she'd been away, so it had to be one hell of a telephone call, Joe thought. A little concerned, he signed for his bill and went out into the lobby to look for her, just as the people from the British Embassy party in the function room next door also spilled out into the lobby and began to make ready to leave the hotel.

As Joe stood adjusting his vision to the brighter electric light of the lobby, Motoko herself finally appeared from the hotel office behind the desk where the telephone handset was housed – telephones were still a comparative rarity in Tokyo. Sir Stephen Hawtry-Gough, the British Ambassador, and his wife saw Motoko and greeted her politely, even deferentially – clearly they knew her as the daughter of a powerful business figure in the city – and exchanged a few further words with her before being helped on with their coats by hotel staff in preparation to step outside into the chill January air. The Honourable Peregrine Cavendish was also there, hovering not far behind them, as was the man Toby had said was the top British spy here, Clive Randall.

Randall, drawing at a cigarette in a long holder, stared rudely in Joe's direction as he waited, weighing him up like a rival, before he too began to put his overcoat on.

The Isogais, father and daughter, were also chatting to acquaintances in the middle of the lobby as they too made preparations to leave the hotel.

Motoko joined Joe and bowed apologetically. She looked puzzled. 'I thought must be father on telephone. But when I took call, it was disconnected, or whoever it was rang off without speaking. I wait for second call, just in case. But it seems silly hoax only.'

'No matter. Are you ready to leave, Miss Maeda?'

'Yes, I have carriage coming at ten, another five minutes. I go back to town house in Marunouchi, quite near here.'

'Then I'll wait here in the lobby with you until it comes,' Joe suggested.

Motoko raised her almond eyes to look up at him; in her kimono and *zori* sandals she seemed tiny and fragile next to his six feet three frame. 'Perhaps you not know, but we also have old house in Kamakura, Mr App-re-doon. You must come and see it. Kamakura is beautiful town, more tranquil place than Tokyo now. My father and I appreciate greatly if you visit there later this week...'

Suddenly there came a sound of glass shattering and Motoko spun around in alarm. Someone had smashed the large plate window next to the main entrance door with an axe, and something heavy had apparently been thrown into the lobby through the broken window from outside.

Joe saw the object roll across the floor, a round black metallic thing, and with a feeling of panic recognised that it was a loudly whirring contraption with some kind of visible internal mechanism...

The British Embassy party seemed more curious at the incident than truly alarmed, but perhaps they hadn't noticed exactly what Joe had seen rolling across the teak floor towards them. The Isogais – father and daughter - stood rooted to the spot as the device rolled past the British party and right to their feet, where it finally stopped. The desk clerk, Jacques, standing behind them, went white and dived for cover. Motoko screamed a frantic warning to the Isogais, and this galvanised Joe into unexpected action.

He couldn't explain to himself why he did what he did, but instead of diving for cover as everyone else seemed to, he ran to pick up the object. Before he hardly knew what he was doing, he found himself running in a panic for the main entrance with what he was sure was a ticking bomb in his hand...

Time seemed to slow to a crawl as he charged through the open entrance; he felt unable to run properly, as if he was wading through three feet of water rather than normal air. His body too felt massive and leaden, his limbs refusing to work to order, a sick bile of fear welling up inside his throat. The whirring of the mechanism sounded as loud as a shunting train to his fevered imagination, and Joe braced himself unconsciously for the moment of explosion that would tear his body into bloody shreds.

Outside, people scattered as he screamed for them to get out of the way. But one man, a blind monk, didn't move, apparently stricken by paralysis and staring at this strange barbarian as he approached. Joe shouted at him, 'Get down!' as he threw the bomb like a football high into the air, aiming at the moat in front of the hotel.

The evil black object seemed to arc through the air forever in slow motion as Joe flattened himself to the paving slabs of the forecourt and put his hands over his ears. He even had time for an absurd thought to occur to him: *what would Eleanor say if she heard that he'd been blown up by an anarchist bomb?* She would be so angry at his stupidity that she would probably never speak to him again...

Just when Joe was beginning to think the bomb had been a fake, it exploded with a mighty blast just beneath the surface of the water, lifting a huge pall of water in the air, and drenching him in a thick soup of dead carp and shredded water lily leaves that seemed to fall to earth forever...

CHAPTER 4

Tuesday 26th January 1904

The American Embassy, the grandest of the newer foreign embassies in Tokyo after the British, had recently been built on one of the prime remaining plots of empty land in Marunouchi, with a scenic setting overlooking the tranquil outer moat of the Imperial Palace. At dusk, with the winter light fading fast, Joe Appeldoorn stood on the rear terrace of this palatial building, enjoying the distant view of the high white stone walls and curving green tiled roof of the imposing palace, and also the elegance of the embassy's own Japanese stroll garden, which was lit by flaming torches for the evening to show off its maples and pines, and its still lake of dark green water, to perfection. But finally he decided reluctantly that he had better go back inside to the reception. He, after all, was the centre of attention tonight – if an unwilling one.

An even more distinguished and immaculately attired company had gathered by now for drinks in the grand ballroom, ahead of the formal dinner. The wine and saké were flowing along with the conversation, complemented by a string quartet of beautiful kimono-clad Japanese maidens playing a succession of pianissimo Bach concertos with consummate skill.

Joe was finding this the most embarrassing night of his life by far (with the possible exception of a disastrous fancy dress ball at the Old State House in Hartford seven years before - the first time he had ever escorted a girl to a ball, in fact - when he had slipped on a marble floor in front of a sixteen-year-old Eleanor and ended up upsetting a bowl of fruit punch all over himself.)

This dinner tonight hadn't been originally intended as a deliberate *homage* to a young American hero – Joe had merely been invited along to a routine embassy function as a visiting businessman doing his bit to increase

Japanese-American trade. But, to his acute discomfort, tonight's dinner was turning out instead to be a personal tribute to his supposed heroism. The events of last night at the Imperial had catapulted the name of Joseph Appeldoorn from complete obscurity into sudden local prominence, and he was therefore being forced to put up tonight with being feted by the American community in Tokyo (insincerely in most cases, he thought) for his heroism last night. Joe had found to his dismay that this evening's function had been turned into a rampant and unashamed piece of politicking and self-promotion by the American Embassy, and he certainly felt uncomfortable about being lionised and made use of in this way when he truly believed that all he had really done last night was to try and save his own damned neck.

His name had already appeared prominently in several inaccurate and highly coloured accounts in the local newspapers today. Joe knew the accounts in the Japanese *Shimbun Zashi* and *Asahi Shimbun* were inaccurate because Motoko Maeda had appeared at the hotel this morning and helpfully translated their contents for him. But he'd needed no such help with the English language *Japan Mail,* whose reporter, a forceful young woman from Minneapolis called Ada Blanchett, had interviewed him last night and had then gone to town in her account of the last evening's events, both in her various factual inaccuracies and in her uncompromising superlatives describing Joe's heroism. Joe had almost curled up in embarrassment when he had read her piece.

Joe just hoped that Miss Blanchett's piece wouldn't be picked up by any of the major International news agencies or by the American press where Eleanor would almost certainly eventually see them. '*No danger in Japan!*' he had assured her. If she read the *Japan Mail* account now, she would be on the next boat across the Pacific, even if her grandfather were back at death's door again...

'Ah, Joseph, there you are! The hero returns. Did you enjoy your walk in the garden? Superb, isn't it?' The American ambassador, who rejoiced in the name of Theobald Ignatius Reinhold, was a man built on a massive scale, like a piece of gargantuan marble statuary. He had to be six feet six, or possibly six-seven, Joe thought, and it made him feel almost a dwarf by comparison because the ambassador was also paunchy and of vast girth – a Rabelaisian figure come to life. He was a Bostonian but he'd spent most of his adult life in the Far East and he carried that patina of the Orient that so many of these old Japan hands seemed to. His most distinguishing physical feature, apart from his considerable size, was a vast dome of a baldpate, as hairless as an egg, and nearly as smooth. The Japanese, whom he loved apparently, and who seemed very fond of him in return, had a special affectionate nickname for him – *Hageyama* – literally "No-tree Mountain".

Hageyama's Japanese was absolutely perfect after several decades of practice – yet it was still peculiar for Joe to hear this quintessentially Japanese voice coming from such an unexpected source. The ambassador used his perfect Japanese to introduce Joe to a couple of winsome young Japanese ladies lingering nearby – daughters of senior government officials - who smiled and simpered at him before the ambassador excused himself and led Joe off into a quiet corner. 'Your exploits last night have done us a world of good with the locals, Joseph, my boy. Not only did you prevent any loss of life last night, you even saved the Imperial from any damage...'

'Apart from a lot of dead goldfish in the Emperor's moat,' Joe pointed out.

The ambassador smiled broadly. 'Well, I believe we can live with that.' He clapped Joe on the shoulder. 'The Japanese are still suspicious of foreigners, you know, particularly the Russkis, but they appreciate bravery and personal courage above everything else.'

Joe accepted the praise as casually as he could; Hageyama's good opinion was one of the few honest-sounding compliments he had heard tonight, and one that he really appreciated.

The ambassador now surprised Joe. 'I'm really glad now that it was your name I recommended to Mr Maeda, when he came to me a few months back, asking for the name of a suitable American electrical engineering company that he could tie up with.'

That did explain something to Joe that he'd not understood previously – why Maeda had approached him ahead of many more prominent American companies - but, still slightly puzzled, he was tempted to ask the ambassador how *he* had come to hear of Appeldoorn Industries in the first place.

'I've been here in Japan for over thirty years, Joseph, off and on,' the ambassador went on. 'In fact I was here almost right at the beginning of the Meiji era, as a young undersecretary to the US consul in Yokohama – that would have been the autumn of 'sixty eight, I think – and I was here when the Imperial court moved from Kyoto to Edo. I even saw the young emperor, Mutsuhito, arrive in state here at the Tokugawa palace, and was that a sight to see! – straight out of feudal Japan. In those days he still wore the full formal Japanese regalia: he had on these loose satin robes of crimson and white, and large lacquer sabots, and his head was bound by a fillet of fluted gold with a tall gold plume, like something out of *The Mikado*. I knew at the time, even though I was only a greenhorn of twenty-two, that I was watching the end of an era, the last act of the old Japan. I visited him at court only today to pay my respects – he and I are familiar acquaintances now - but these days he always wears Western clothes, a boring black coat lined with purple silk, and a military style suit with a high collar. With that cocked hat and dress sword he wears, I've heard people say he looks like a goddammed Limey admiral. But, today, he asked about *you* by name – so even the Emperor of Japan knows who you are now, Joseph! That's what I call real fame.'

'You must have seen a lot of changes here,' Joe observed, deftly trying to divert the subject away from himself again, and the events of last night, for about the twentieth time tonight.

Hageyama nodded. 'Too damned many, for my liking. The Japanese had to move on and join the modern world, I suppose, but it would be good if they didn't lose their souls and their culture completely in the process.'

Joe nodded sympathetically. 'Yes, it does seem a pity for them to have lost so much of the old ways.'

The ambassador patted Joe on the arm with a massive hairy paw – Joe felt almost like a child again next to this man's immense bulk. 'Your father – *Henry* - would have been exceptionally proud of what you did last night.'

Joe looked up in surprise at the particular emphasis in the ambassador's voice. 'I guess he would. Did you know my father, then, Mr Ambassador?'

'Sure I did; Henry and I were at Harvard together, back in the Dark Ages - class of 'sixty four. He was studying physics, which none of us law students could fathom at all. Cleverest guy I think I ever met. He was always telling me about things he'd invented, new theories, new bits of electrical hardware. I always knew he would do well...'

Joe interrupted eagerly, 'Yes, I've been working through his scientific notebooks this last year, and there are a phenomenal number of ideas in there to follow up. Especially an idea he had for a way for radio waves to carry sounds *directly* by varying the amplitude of the carrier waves a little. I've been working on the technical details of that concept to see if it might be possible to transmit decipherable speech or even music directly over the air. There are still a lot of practical difficulties to overcome before I'll know whether it's really possible or not, although in theory I can't see why it shouldn't work.'

The ambassador shook his head in wonder. 'Imagine that! Sound without wires!' He fell silent for a moment. 'Tragic what happened to your father, though! I always regretted that we lost touch later in life. And it was a real pity he couldn't have lived long enough to see what a fine young man he'd produced.'

Joe felt like sinking through the floor with embarrassment at the subject coming round yet again, with a certain inevitability, to his supposed heroism last night. He'd been scared witless, that was the truth, and had been acting purely on instinct. But what else could he have done with that damned bomb? If it had gone off inside the lobby, it would have killed him anyway...

So how many more times could he reiterate that he was no hero, just someone trying to save himself?

If Eleanor had been here, though, then she at least would no doubt have enjoyed seeing her husband being feted like this, and even more, seeing him so embarrassed...

*

Dinner was served for the thirty invited guests in the Neo-classical dining room, on a satinwood dining table of immense length. Oil paintings of dead Presidents and former ambassadors lined the walls; candlelight gleamed from a row of Federal-style silver candlesticks. Sitting opposite Joe, the stiff-necked English Ambassador, Sir Stephen Hawtry-Gough, was a refreshing change at least from all the embarrassing adulation Joe had received from everyone else tonight. Sir Stephen regarded Joe with a look that seemed to suggest he thought Joe must be some sort of village idiot for picking up a ticking bomb, as he asked in a condescending voice, 'Was that really the best thing you could think of doing in the circumstances, Mr Appeldoorn? It might have blown up in your hands. Or did you not realise that it was such a dangerous device?'

Joe shrugged deprecatingly. 'Yes, I really was that dumb that I couldn't think of anything better to do with it than throw it back outside.'

Lady Hawtry-Gough disagreed at once. 'You're just being modest, sir,' she said with a smile. Her beauty - faded or not - was more in evidence to Joe in the soft candlelight of this dining room setting than it had been in the harsh electric light of the Imperial Hotel lobby last night. She was sitting next to Joe, and in her low cut gown, seemed determined to reward Joe for his bravery last night by showing him a generous amount of her enticing white cleavage. 'And you're talking nonsense, Stephen, if you really believe Mr Appeldoorn didn't fully comprehend the extreme danger of what he was doing.' She turned to him and gave him another close-up view of her partially décolleté breasts. 'Is that not so, sir?' She glanced at her husband again. 'He saved all our lives, while you and the other gentlemen there did nothing helpful that I can recall.'

Red spots of anger flared briefly in Sir Stephen's gaunt cheeks; he certainly didn't like being upbraided by his wife in the company of others. But wisely he said nothing more for the moment, although looking balefully through narrowed eyes at her, as if promising her silently that he was going to give her a damned good thrashing when he got her home.

The Italian ambassador sitting on the other side of Lady Rosemary, a dapper little man with hair as shining as patent leather, defused the tension at the table by saying, 'As I was just telling Lady Rosemary earlier, Sir Stephen, I was in Milan six weeks ago, and I saw Signor Puccini conduct the rehearsals for his new opera, *Madame Butterfly*. It's based on that play by Signor David Bellasco about the romance of an American naval lieutenant with a Japanese woman. Knowing I live in Japan, Maestro Puccini wanted to consult me about the authenticity of some details of the country and its people.'

'I suppose it will be the usual sentimental nonsense about a devoted and tragic Oriental woman faithfully waiting with cherry blossoms and lanterns for her heartless Western lover to return?' Sir Stephen observed tartly. 'Let me tell you, sir, the average port girl of Nagasaki or Yokohama is strictly a mercenary businesswoman, and has a heart of stone. But I suppose that this more truthful and less sentimental view of Oriental women would be a difficult subject for a romantic opera...'

'I had no idea you were such an expert on the port girls of Nagasaki and Yokohama, Stephen,' his wife rejoined, a withering response that made the British ambassador lapse into another uncomfortable silence.

In the awkward hiatus in the conversation that followed, Joe nearly jumped as he felt a hand reach out and surreptitiously stroke his thigh under the table. He just hoped that it wasn't Sir Stephen, stretching improbably from the other side of the table. A few seconds later the hand returned to caress his thigh again and this time Joe quickly put his own hand over it, reassured at least to find that it was a soft and feminine hand. Lady Rosemary didn't even blink as Joe – in a sudden mood of devilment - stroked the back of her hand in return.

Why on Earth was he doing this? Perhaps just for the satisfaction of pleasuring this woman while her husband's penetrating eyes were peering down his haughty nose at him from the other side of the table.

'You seem happy tonight, Rosemary,' her husband observed, a little perplexed by the smile on her face.

'Yes, I am very content, Stephen.' Lady Rosemary turned her head to Joe and smiled warmly. Joe rather liked that smile, and kept his hand where it was, clasped with hers.

Sir Stephen accepted his wife's cryptic comment with only a mild show of surprise, before turning his attention to Joe again. 'Have you had no physical reaction yet to your heroics last night, Mr Appeldoorn? No nervous tension? No signs of delayed stress?'

Lady Rosemary had now moved her hand a little higher up Joe's thigh. 'Actually, now that you mention it, I do feel a little stiffness coming on,' Joe said...

*

Joe escaped to the ballroom as soon as dinner was over; although he had to admit that he'd rather enjoyed his secret under-the-table flirtation with Lady Rosemary, he decided it was probably better to nip that relationship in the bud. Sir Stephen Hawtry-Gough might be a pretentious bore, but he was also an important man in this town and one Joe couldn't afford to make an enemy of.

Other guests who hadn't been able to get here in time for dinner, Toby Pryor among them, were arriving for after-dinner drinks in the music room. As Joe accepted a brandy from a passing waiter, he saw Mr Maeda enter the room with Motoko, and went over immediately to greet them, still conscious that, regardless of the excitements of the night before, his prime reason for being in Tokyo remained selling his high voltage generating equipment to this man. Going home without getting that contract signed was simply unthinkable – the jobs and futures of the workers in his Philadelphia and Long Island factories depended on it.

Despite the fact that he was trying to concentrate his attention on Maeda, though, Joe still couldn't avoid having some of that attention wrested away by the physical impact of his daughter. Tonight she was dressed in an arresting western gown of saffron silk that almost took his male breath away, particularly the way the glossy fabric clung enticingly to her body and caught the candlelight, the colour contrasting so perfectly with her peach-like complexion. She herself seemed perfectly relaxed, displaying no after effects of last night's drama that Joe could see, her elaborate hair shining raven-black, her face calm and composed, if perhaps a little flushed.

When Motoko excused herself in order to say hello to some close acquaintances, Maeda discreetly drew Joe aside into a quiet corner. His eyes were moist and his voice became quite hoarse with emotion as he spoke. He bowed nearly to the floor. 'Mr Appeldoorn, *Domo arigato gozaimashita*! I owe you a debt I can never, ever repay. My dear dead wife thanks you from beyond the grave for the life of our daughter. Both my sons are dead, you see, and Motoko-chan is the main remaining hope of my life. I hope she will make a good marriage in time and perpetuate my bloodline, if not my name. If you hadn't saved her last night, that hope of mine would have been lost forever.'

Joe was highly embarrassed again by this encomium, justified or not, but also elated too because this debt of honour surely meant that Maeda would now almost certainly sign the agreement to buy his company's equipment. Although, knowing the Japanese by now, Joe realised that he would still have to haggle long and hard over price – sentiment would never be allowed to get in the way of making a profitable business deal.

'Have you a particular husband already in mind for her?' Joe asked curiously, wondering who the lucky man might be. He knew that marriages were still arranged here, of course, and that women from wealthy families like Motoko had very limited freedom over their choice of potential husbands. Glancing across the room to where Toby Pryor was now talking animatedly to Motoko, he wondered how Maeda would react if he knew that both of his barbarian business associates harboured disgracefully lustful thoughts towards his jewel-like daughter.

Maeda looked at Motoko talking and smiling on the other side of the room with slight unease written on his face. 'She was engaged to a man from a family of very ancient lineage, but regrettably the man turned out to be unsuitable. *Watashi wa, kenami no yosa yori, jinbutsu no hō o taisetsu ni kangaeru...*' Maeda looked rueful. 'Oh, I'm sorry – you don't understand, do you? For me, a person's character is much more important than their breeding, don't you agree?'

Motoko rejoined her father and she again bowed low to Joe, before giving him a secret enigmatic smile; he in turn hoped she hadn't overheard any of his recent conversation with her father about her private life.

Maeda apologised to Joe. 'Unfortunately I cannot stay long this evening; I have another important meeting later tonight. But I had to come along and thank you personally for my daughter's life. And to introduce you to someone who is here tonight – a fellow countryman of yours, and a gifted scientist and inventor in his own right.'

Maeda waved to the other side of the ballroom, and a man joined them, a man in his early forties with wild red hair, freckled complexion, a goofy smile, and a bone thin body, who looked like an archetypal crazy inventor. In his wrinkled evening suit, he made tough competition for Toby Pryor as the worst dressed man in the room. The thin man held out a skeletal hand to Joe; the sleeves of his coat were at least three inches too short, Joe noticed. 'Larry Longrigg,' the newcomer said, introducing himself with a jaw-wrenching smile.

Joe shook his bony hand and told him his name in return. 'Where are you from, Mr Longrigg?'

The man smiled again in that jaw wrenching fashion. 'Call me Larry! Originally I'm from Lansing, Michigan. But now a resident of the world.'

Maeda interrupted diffidently. 'Mr Longrigg is the technical engineering advisor to my electrical supply company. I have asked him to look at the design of your high voltage generators and transformers for me, and at the quality of the sample equipment you have shipped here from America. Your equipment is presently being stored in a bonded warehouse in the port of Yokohama, and Mr Longrigg lives nearby at Hakone, so perhaps I can let you arrange together the details of how and when you meet to discuss the technical aspects of your system. He will vet it for me and report back.' Maeda offered Joe his hand and shook it warmly. 'But I don't expect any problems and, once that technical evaluation is done, we can hopefully sit down together to agree price and to sign the contract between our companies.'

Maeda finally excused himself. 'Motoko will stay and talk with you, Mr Appeldoorn, for the rest of the evening. If you have any business questions, let her know. She will be your contact for the next few days as unfortunately I have to travel to Kyoto early tomorrow.'

Motoko went with her father into the adjacent Neo-classical entrance hall, where Joe saw Maeda pay his farewell compliments to Ambassador Reinhold; he and Hageyama were clearly old friends, Joe judged, from the affectionate smiles exchanged between them as Maeda put on his overcoat to leave.

Joe turned to Larry Longrigg. 'So, Mr Maeda says you're an inventor yourself. What kind of things do you invent, Larry?'

Longrigg smiled broadly, his Adam's apple bobbing up and down in his long thin neck like a snake trying to escape from under the flesh. 'Oh, lots of things, Joseph. Improved radio equipment, a new colour printing process, even a flying machine.'

Joe smiled. 'I think those bicycle makers, the Wright Brothers, have just beaten you to that last one, haven't they?'

Longrigg didn't seem put out by that comment. 'Maybe. We'll see anyway. Joseph, can we meet on Thursday in my house out at Hakone? It's up in the mountains near Fuji – be a nice day out for you, a chance to get away from the smoke of Tokyo. You can travel in luxury by train as far as Atami as Mr Maeda's honoured guest, and I can send a driver with a carriage to pick you up at Atami Station. I have a new automobile – a Daimler Benz – but it is a little temperamental, so I think you'd better make do with the old horse-drawn transport. It's slow but reliable...'

*

When Larry Longrigg too had left to talk to other American expatriates he knew, Motoko finally returned to Joe's side and gave him yet another deep bow of obeisance. 'I have not thank you properly for last night. You save us all!'

'You're trying to embarrass me too!' he said resignedly. 'It was nothing.'

'My life not nothing,' she scolded him lightly. 'I shall think of special way to thank you. You deserve...*special* reward...I believe...'

'Well, you never did give me that dance you promised me last night, did you?'

Her smooth olive brow wrinkled slightly. 'True. But I think you deserve something more...*interesting*...as a reward...'

*

Toby Pryor pigeonholed Joe as soon as Motoko had gone back to talk to her Japanese friends.

'I heard that! *Special* reward? You lucky sonofabitch! Weren't you the one yesterday advising me to lay off her...?'

'She just meant a dance, that's all. She hasn't promised to have my children. Anyway, I am already married, Toby, as Motoko-san is fully aware.'

'I saw the way she was lookin' at you, my friend. And if you really believe that she was just talkin' about havin' a dance with you, then you don't know much about women, do yer, Joe?' Toby mocked him scathingly. 'I wish *I'd* stayed downstairs last night to save that cute little ass from a bomb.'

'In your condition, you wouldn't have noticed that bomb even if it went off right next to you.' Joe suddenly remembered that Toby had been behaving very strangely last night: there'd been that secret conversation he'd had with the unpleasant English spy, Randall for one thing; then the way he had appeared to be acting much drunker than he really was; and then finally the fact that he'd ducked so quickly out of the dining room at the end of the evening claiming to be feeling ill. And that had only been a few minutes before someone had tossed a bomb into the lobby, Joe reminded himself. It was almost as if Toby had had some presentiment of what was going to happen last night...

'Tonight, though, I'm goin' to show you my own appreciation for what you did last night, Joseph. I promised you I was going to take you to the *Yoshiwara* after this party, and that's where I'm friggin' well goin' to take you, pal! After last night you deserve it. I know a real high-class place to visit - a famous bathhouse in the *Yoshiwara* called the House of the Red-Crowned Crane? It's *really* a special experience.'

He seemed insistent about it, and Joe, despite his slight misgivings about what he'd promised to Eleanor, and his continuing suspicions about Toby, did finally allow himself to be persuaded. Tonight he did feel like a taste for the exotic world of the *Yoshiwara* and a chance to meet a real life Madame Butterfly...

It was a truism, of course, but there was nothing like being delivered from a violent premature death to make you realise that perhaps you had better take your pleasures in life while you could...

*

Joe hadn't seen any sign of civilian police after the explosion last night.

Instead, within a few minutes of the explosion, with sirens wailing over the rooftops of Marunouchi district, half the Japanese army seemed to descend on the hotel instead. Joe had sat on the raised stone edge of the moat and tried to get his racing heart and ragged breathing under some sort of control again, while uniformed troops milled about in what looked like total confusion.

Eventually he went inside and found a still-shocked Motoko, and waited with her until her carriage arrived to take her to her nearby home.

The officer in charge at the scene, an army major called Sawada, had been reluctant at first to let any of the witnesses go, but in the end - after he'd discovered Motoko's identity – had meekly allowed her to board her carriage and leave without complaint.

He led Joe back into the hotel after Joe had seen Motoko off in her carriage, and, seeing Joe's hands were still trembling slightly, sat him down in a cane chair in the lobby where he fetched him a double whisky with his own hands.

'It seems everyone here in the hotel owes you a great debt of thanks, Mr

Appeldoorn.' Major Sawada was only about thirty and spoke exceptionally good English with an American accent. Joe was sure that he must have spent some time in the States to be able to speak the language so proficiently. Despite his comparative youth, though, Joe could tell from the way his minions rushed to do his bidding that this man was someone very important in military counter-intelligence. He continued to treat Joe with nothing but bland courtesy, though, as he questioned him about tonight's events, apologizing for what had happened with apparent sincerity. He never raised his voice once, not even to his own men, but his juniors were clearly terrified of every soft-spoken order, that much was certain.

'Did anyone see who threw the bomb?' Joe asked as he glanced around the lobby. The lobby was mostly deserted now; there'd been no structural damage to the hotel apart from a few blown-out windows and the dead fish in the moat. The hundred or so guests had all retired to their rooms by now, reassured of their safety by the presence of a phalanx of armed soldiers guarding each entrance to the hotel, who were checking everything and everyone going in an out.

'We have two witnesses who claim to have seen the man responsible for this outrage,' Sawada announced. 'A man wearing a Western suit and homburg hat pulled low over his eyes, but definitely Japanese and probably young.'

'So he got away?'

Sawada narrowed his eyes. 'For the moment. But the people responsible for this cowardly and despicable deed will be caught and punished in time, Mr Appeldoorn. You have my word on it.' Sawada was an extremely handsome man, with an almost boyish face, a clean jaw with neat sculpted features, and hair as smooth and precise as a mannequin's. With looks like that, it might have been difficult to take the threats or actions of such a man seriously. But Joe, remembering the way his officers nervously dashed around to do his bidding, didn't doubt his ruthlessness for one moment.

'Who do you think it was?' Joe asked curiously.

Sawada shrugged. 'Although there is nothing left of the bomb itself, from your description I believe I recognise the type, which has been used several times before: it probably used cakes of Atlas dynamite manufactured by the Repauno Chemical Works near Philadelphia –'

'My home town,' Joe couldn't help interjecting.

Sawada's eyes narrowed again. '...Unfortunately dynamite is a readily available explosive in this country, where so much is needed to blast new railway tunnels through our mountainous interior. And this device almost certainly used the usual detonators - a mixture of potassium chlorate and fulminate of mercury – and probably also had some sort of simple revolving winder alarum to set off the detonators, which would have been started manually with a switch before the bomb was thrown. So, from that evidence, I believe this attack has all the hallmarks of one of the ultra-nationalist groups: perhaps the *Kokuryukai* - the "Black Dragon Society" – who are members of former Samurai clans who dislike the westernisation of our country and think the clock can be turned back to another age.' He laughed sourly. 'Or perhaps even the *"Society of the River Amur"* – a group of ex-military officers disgruntled with the recent diplomatic policy of appeasement with our Chinese and Russian neighbours. But no matter who they were – they will wish they had never been born when I catch them...'

*

At the embassy function, Joe found he had even further personal gratitude to withstand, as Shintaro Isogai and his daughter came forward to speak to him, apparently also intent on personally thanking him for his actions last night. Unlike last night, though, both were dressed in formal kimonos, and Fumiyo Isogai had her hair dressed in a severe Japanese style that made her look quite different from the rather Western-looking woman Joe had seen in the Imperial last night.

It seemed the handsome and patrician-looking Mr Isogai wanted to say something himself but, as his daughter explained, had only limited English so she would have to translate for him. Joe hadn't seen them at the dinner table earlier so presumed they must also have been one of the later arrivals at the function. He began to wonder why a socialist politician who led a fledgling political party should even have been given an invitation to a prestigious American Embassy business function like this one, but perhaps Hageyama saw the need to cultivate the friendship of a man who might possibly be a major political figure of the future.

Joe could instantly detect a certain degree of arrogance about this man, though – for one thing he seemed to take it for granted that *he'd* been the real target for the assassin with the bomb last night, rather than any of the other VIPs in the lobby at the time, including the British ambassador and his wife.

His gratitude was also far less effusive than Maeda's; in fact Joe had trouble detecting any real gratitude at all in the man's haughty manner for what he'd done. 'My father believes he would perhaps have been able to deal with the bomb himself in similar fashion, if you hadn't intervened, Mr Appeldoorn,' Fumiyo said, translating smoothly, without a falter.

Joe didn't know whether Isogai might have managed to deal with the bomb himself or not, but in the circumstances it still seemed a less than gracious way to express his thanks...

Isogai continued speaking, and his speech was followed by Fumiyo's instant translation, '...Nevertheless you have his sincerest thanks for what you did. He admires a display of bravery even when...' His daughter looked embarrassed and clearly omitted to translate the end of her father's Japanese sentence.

51

Joe guessed the rest of the unfinished phrase might have been, '...*even when it's displayed by a foreigner...*'

A typical damned politician! - that was Joe's opinion of this man by now. Politicians were always calculating the potential advantages or disadvantages of every situation, but perhaps the impact of last night's events on an up and coming political career was difficult for Mr Isogai to assess. Being saved by a *gaijin* was perhaps not the best image for a Japanese politician, though – even a socialist politician - in a country beginning to burst with resurgent national self-confidence again after so many years of being humiliated and disparaged by foreigners. But then again, Joe had heard that the incident had brought Isogai some, no doubt, welcome attention in today's local newspaper headlines, since many liberal Japanese editors seemed to agree that last night's events must have been an attempt on the life of an important left-wing politician by ultra-nationalist elements who disliked the idea of Japan one day becoming a Western-style democracy.

With a formal bow, Isogai thanked Joe again, then excused himself to go and speak to Ambassador Reinhold.

Fumiyo stayed behind and had the honesty to look a little apologetic. 'I'm sorry, Mr Appeldoorn. That probably sounded an ungracious way to express his gratitude; but believe me, my father really is very appreciative for what you did. Otherwise he would hardly have come along especially tonight to thank you in person.' She relaxed her own stiff and formal expression slightly. 'But he has so much on his mind at the moment, so many things competing for his time and attention. Our nation is at a turning point in its history, and he feels that only he can stop us turning into an Eastern copy of the militaristic German Empire, or perhaps even worse, a country like...like...'

'Like America, you mean?' Joe suggested dryly.

'Perhaps.' She smiled, disarming the sting in her words. 'Believe me, I have nothing against America, or Americans per se, Mr Appeldoorn, yet you Americans should stop believing that Capitalism is the universal panacea for every problem, or that your particular form of government is so superior to all others, or even that it is appropriate to all other nations.'

Joe decided wisely not to be drawn into a political argument with this woman; for one thing he mostly agreed with her and, for another, she looked far too smart for him anyway. She was very tall for a Japanese woman – five seven at least – and as willowy and elegant as an actress, but with her beauty almost deliberately subverted by a permanently severe expression. Behind that smooth high forehead resided a really formidable intellect, Joe guessed. 'Someone - the ambassador - told me that you studied physics at the ETH in Zurich, Mr Appeldoorn. That is a school with a prodigious reputation.'

Joe shrugged wryly. 'I did have to struggle to keep up.'

She almost smiled in response. 'I believe you're being modest.'

'And you, Miss Isogai? You studied in Germany, I believe? Did you not study mathematics at Göttingen with Professor Hilbert? If so, you must be one of the first women to do so, and certainly the first *Asian* woman.'

Fumiyo thawed a little more in her manner. 'I'm impressed, Mr Appeldoorn. You're well informed. Perhaps you are a spy too, like so many other people in this room.'

Who on earth did she mean? Joe wondered, glancing around uneasily. 'No, I'm much too dumb to be a spy.'

'Oh, I think not.' She studied his face curiously. 'I know you are a businessman and an engineer rather than a mathematician, but have you ever heard of Professor Hilbert's Programme, I wonder?'

Joe nodded curiously. 'You're right that I'm not a mathematician, but as an engineer I do maintain an interest in the subject. I presume you mean the list of twenty-three major unsolved theoretical problems in mathematics that Professor Hilbert set out at the Congress of Mathematicians in Paris four years ago?'

Fumiyo's eyes lingered even longer on his this time. 'I'm impressed even more. And have you perhaps heard of the details of some of these particular unsolved problems - Cantor's continuum Hypothesis, for example?'

Joe wondered what she was trying to prove with these testing questions but answered honestly anyway. 'I have,' he admitted, 'but I don't understand most of them, since they fall well outside the field of engineering mathematics that I am familiar with.'

Fumiyo seemed to assess him quietly. 'Well, let's see. Do you happen to know, for example, whether any polyhedron can always be dissected into a finite number of pieces, and reassembled to form a cube of the same volume?'

Joe felt as if he was playing a game of intellectual tennis with this woman, as he returned her difficult shot and sent it deftly back across the net. 'No, it can't. I do happen to know that that's the *only* one of Hilbert's problems that's already been solved - by a man called Max Dehn, I believe.'

Fumiyo nodded triumphantly, her point proven. 'Then you are certainly no fool, Mr Appeldoorn. But probably no spy either...'

*

The man strode into the US Embassy ballroom like some visitation from an older and more exotic Japan. He was dressed in full formal Japanese wear: the *montsuki*, the formal black silk kimono, over which he wore striped *hakama* ankle-length loose trousers, and a *haori*, the outer coat. He had *setta* sandals on his feet and a pair of braided cords at his waist. All that was missing, Joe thought, as he wondered who this man was, were the Samurai swords and the topknot haircut...

Motoko had returned to Joe's side a few minutes before, and she whispered in his ear. 'I astonished! This is Yukio Kiratani; we call him "Conscience of Japan". He *never* accept invitation to party of this kind.' Motoko's eyes were wide with surprise. 'He rarely leave his home in Kyoto these days. He was one of leader of Samurai revolt twenty-five years ago, you know, and fought with the great Saigo - Takamori Saigo – in final battle in Kyushu in tenth year of Emperor.' Her voice began to flutter with excitement. 'Look, he coming over to speak. This great honour for you, Mr App-re-doon.'

Kiratani introduced himself with a deep formal bow. Joe tried his best to bow a bit deeper in return, as he knew the rule by now that polite custom dictated. Motoko bowed almost to the floor, which made Joe realise the true esteem this man must be held in by the Japanese.

He was an old man, over seventy, small of stature, and bent by age, with arthritic hands. Yet there was nothing remotely pathetic about him – on the contrary there was something magnificent about this grey-haired man and his quiet dignity.

He made a long speech, which Motoko translated. '*Anata ni yuube tasukete moratta koto o, watashi wa issho on ni kimasu...*' 'Mr Kiratani thanks you for saving people last night; he owes you a personal debt for what you did, Mr App-re-doon.' Motoko's eyes were shining with emotion while Joe was cringing with even deeper embarrassment, even though a little puzzled as to why Kiratani should feel any personal gratitude for what he'd done. Joe got the distinct impression throughout the long speech, and Motoko's sometime stumbling translation – a slight gesture of acquiescence between them, or a nod of mutual understanding - that she knew Kiratani rather well, though he couldn't be absolutely sure.

Kiratani finally excused himself, bowed and departed. There was a hush in the room afterwards as if the Emperor himself had just quit the room.

Motoko clapped her hands with delight at this honour bestowed on her barbarian friend, Mr Appeldoorn.

Joe had a question for her. 'If Kiratani fought with the Great Saigo at this last battle, how come he survived? I thought to give your life in battle was everything to a samurai. They weren't allowed to just surrender, were they?'

Motoko looked at Joe as if he had just said something unmentionable in polite society. 'It true he lost everything. And he did indeed try kill himself, but was prevented. Afterwards his wife, on deathbed, made him swear to stay alive, look after only son.' Motoko sighed. 'It not fair but sometime we have to bear the unbearable. Perhaps your own country has to do same, sometime.' Motoko watched Kiratani leave with regret. 'He very sad man.'

'You seem to know him quite well,' Joe suggested shrewdly.

'I know him, and respect him highly.' Motoko's expression became even more melancholy. 'Was engaged to his only son.'

CHAPTER 5

Only a few hours after leaving the Embassy party, Joe Appeldoorn found himself transported back from the frantic pace of the twentieth century to a different time and a different world. A world that felt almost like heaven...

Here in the House of the Red-Crowned Crane, both a bathhouse and a *ryotei* restaurant, located in the heart of the *Yoshiwara* pleasure district, he and Toby Pryor reclined in a vast sunken bath of fragrant steaming water, served by a trio of beautiful white-skinned kimono-clad girls who ministered to their every need. They brought fresh pails of piping hot water when called for, scrubbed the difficult places to reach on their backs, and served them up late-night delicacies on sky-blue dishes: prawns, quails' eggs, lily bulbs, eels and red seaweed. *And* all the drink they wanted: *genmaicha* tea, beer, o-saké, barley *shochu*, whisky, Fuji Beer....

Toby stretched luxuriantly in the hot water. 'Is this place not everythin' I said it would be? A place to friggin' die for.'

Joe mentally agreed with that judgement – it certainly would be a place to die for if *Eleanor* ever found out about his late-night visit to the *Yoshiwara*... But he'd nevertheless made a mental promise to his faraway wife that his pleasures tonight were going to be limited to bathing and drinking only, and definitely not sampling any of the more decadent pleasures on offer in this place. Still, it was odd how little embarrassed he felt about being naked among these pretty nubile young women. Perhaps because they didn't see anything offensive in his nudity at all – to them it was perfectly natural.

Joe glanced across at Toby as his companion took yet another long and admiring look at one of the kimono-clad beauties. 'Remember what the ambassador told us about how to behave here, Toby. This is a bathhouse and a *ryotei* restaurant, *not* a brothel. So, I don't know how you behaved before here, but tonight let's try a bit of propriety and decorum, even if you are looking for a girl for the night, later on.' He caught the unmistakable gleam of lust in Toby's eyes. 'Toby, these girls are serving girls only *so don't you dare proposition them*, otherwise you'll get us thrown out.'

Toby smiled up at Sumiko, a wondrously pretty girl, as she poured another pail of water over his wiry head. 'It might just be worth it,' he said slyly. 'I am only friggin' flesh and blood after all, Joseph...'

*

After they had left the embassy at ten, a boat hired by Toby had brought them up the Sumida from *Tsukiji* to the *Yoshiwara*. The boat was an old type of galley with a short bank of oars on each side, but it had no proper wheelhouse or cabin for its passengers to shelter from the intense cold; instead only a makeshift awning of some nondescript cloth over the middle section of the boat. Despite the cold wind on the river, though, Joe had preferred to sit outside in the unprotected stern to clear his head. Through the paper doors of the makeshift cabin, transparent in the light of the lantern behind, he could see two shadows moving inside, those of Toby and the elderly skipper, apparently engaged in deep conversation throughout the trip. Despite having little Japanese - or so he'd claimed anyway - Toby seemed to have an awful lot to say to the captain of this little boat, as the man's four muscular sons tirelessly worked the oars on each side in stolid silence.

The contradictions in Toby's behaviour seemed even more pronounced as Joe got to know him better. Joe sensed the man was acting a part sometimes, or at least exaggerating his natural cruder characteristics. Toby was clearly not the moron he sometimes pretended to be, and Joe did wonder if it was wise to allow himself to be taken God knows where tonight by this unpredictable individual...

Joe enjoyed the journey, nevertheless. At night on the river, it was still possible to imagine the Sumida as it had once been, the boat slipping by under darkened bridges, the lap of water against the wooden hull, the river wide and serene in the moonlight, reflecting a silvering of light and revealing the distinctive rounded profiles of distant hills...

*

Once they'd arrived in the *Yoshiwara,* Joe found that the House of the Red-Crowned Crane also seemed to belong to a vanished era. With its finely proportioned wooden façade, its dainty paper screens and inviting curtained entrance, it was the gateway to a different world and a different time. Inside the entrance there were soft slippers to change into, and a passageway lit by globular red lanterns, that in turn led to a mysterious doorway and the bathhouse beyond, overlooking a tiny dry landscape garden with arcane swirls of white gravel and distinctive-looking rocks...

Ambassador Reinhold - Hageyama, the old Japan hand - had overheard

Joe and Toby talking at the Embassy about their prospective trip to the *Yoshiwara* later that night, and had given Joe a few words of advice before leaving. With a roguish smile he enlightened him in particular about the distinctions between *geisha* and *oiran*...

'"*Geisha*" literally means "talented performer", Joseph,' he explained. 'These ladies are principally performers designed to entertain men with songs and music, with elaborate dances, with jokes and conversation, and with their grace and womanly perfection. Being designed to bring contentment to men, there is always an unavoidable element of the sexual in their behaviour too, of course, but primarily theirs is the kind of female beauty meant to be admired from afar, not sullied with the physical touch of a man. Whatever you do, Joseph, *never* proposition a *geisha* – it will just cause severe embarrassment all round. The *oiran* on the other hand are not true *geisha* but courtesans, skilled in the physical arts of making love, yet still a long way above the status of common prostitutes. Although - these days - the boundaries have become blurred and common prostitutes often pretend to be *oiran,* while courtesans pretend to be *geisha*. Actually there are very few real *geisha* left in the *Yoshiwara,* so I've been told.'

Joe was curious about the origins of the *Yoshiwara*.

'Ah,' the ambassador said meaningfully. 'It would take a long time to tell you the whole story of the *Yoshiwara*. The place has been there for over two hundred years, and its ways are esoteric, harsh and subtle - not surprisingly, since they were perfected by the same race of men who for centuries cultivated the beautiful distortions and rigid postures of the miniature *bonsai* tree.'

The ambassador added a few other words of advice for Joe as he personally escorted Joe and Toby from the embassy. 'Make sure that you know what sort of woman you're dealing with tonight: *geisha, oiran,* ordinary courtesan or just serving girl. Whatever you do, don't confuse their identities or roles, otherwise it could cause trouble, or get very expensive for you. And something else about bathhouse etiquette...make sure you put on different slippers if you go from the bath to the toilet. That's the classic barbarian *faux pas,* to walk back into the bath area still wearing toilet slippers.' He grinned like a boy. 'It took me years to live that mistake down, the only time I did it...'

*

Toby was busy distributing free pairs of pink silk underwear to the three girls in the bathhouse, which generosity was met with much giggling on their part. The sauciest girl, Setsuko-san, pretending ignorance of the garment's true purpose, tried placing a pair jauntily on her head to see what they would look like there.

'Are you *sure* these girls are not hookers, Joseph?' Toby asked hopefully, his eyes lingering on the enchanting face of Setsuko as she danced pertly around the room with a pair of pink panties on her head, while the other two girls collapsed into hysterical giggles.

'*You're* asking *me*? You're the one who's supposed to know the ropes here,' Joe said acidly, before adding, 'But yes, I'm sure about these girls, Toby, although if they like you well enough, perhaps you might still get lucky...' Joe didn't finish his sentence, though, as another young Japanese woman entered the room with a further pail of steaming water to replenish the bath. This one was dressed quite differently from the three other serving girls, though, in an exquisite kimono, and with a white fragrant Jasmine flower in her hair.

'Who are you, beautiful?' Toby asked.

The girl bowed. '*Dozo Yoroshiku. Atashi-wa Aiko desu.*'

Ah,' Toby said, with heavy emphasis, '*you* are Aiko-san. *Hajimemashite.* I've heard *a lot* about you...'

*

The new arrival, Aiko, could not be a *geisha*, Joe decided, if he had understood the ambassador correctly, because – to put it simply - a *geisha* would not be working in a bathhouse or teahouse like this one. Yet, to Joe's inexpert view, she seemed to look almost the part, with her mound of jet-black glossy hair, her face heavily made-up with pale cheeks and scarlet rosebud lips, her *furisode* kimono gaudy with silks and sashes.

Whether she was a real *geisha* or not, though, Joe was still stunned by this immaculate vision of an older Japan. He felt an undeniable male stirring as he watched her pouring more beer for Toby, imagining deeply erotic thoughts about the lure of Japanese women, the stirring of slender white bodies in the dark of night, the whisper of ancient ecstasies...

'Do you know who she is?' Joe asked Toby in a whisper.

Toby seemed quietly amused. 'Oh, I think you'd be very surprised if you really discovered who she is, ' he said mysteriously, before adding hurriedly, 'I believe she's no ordinary working girl, you see, but the owner of this fine establishment. Although, I have to say, she doesn't look much like my Aunt Mabel, who owns a couple of fleapit hotels and Turkish baths of her own in Atlantic City,' he went on. 'You *do* own this place, don't you, Miss Peach Blossom?' he asked, turning his head to look directly at Aiko.

Aiko obviously understood some English because she nodded slightly in response to Toby's question. "*Ee. Soo desu.*'

Toby laughed, and whispered in Joe's ear. 'You're beginning to friggin' drool, Joseph. Bad form to give yourself away so easily.'

Aiko suddenly spoke up in sing-song English, but which was also surprisingly fluent, it seemed to Joe. '*Okyaku-sama*, would you like any other service?'

Toby nudged Joe. 'Do you want a girl, Joe? I think we're being offered the chance to make a deal with a nearby house of pleasure.'

59

Joe was tempted - sorely tempted - despite his earlier mental vow of faithfulness to Eleanor. But, to be honest, looking at the elegant face and figure of Aiko, he decided that he preferred to stay here anyway, where he could perhaps drink and talk with this startling porcelain vision.

'Well, I'm goin' to damn well indulge myself, Joseph,' Toby declared without further deliberation. It was soon arranged that the saucy Setsuko would act as his guide for the rest of the evening, and in a few minutes Toby was dressed and ready to follow his pert consort to an assignation at a nearby house of pleasure. Toby grinned in anticipation as he left. 'I'll be back in an hour or so, then we can go back together to town by boat. Don't go without me, though!' he added warningly.

Joe watched him go with a slight sense of envy – it seemed things in the *Yoshiwara* hadn't changed quite as much as Ambassador Reinhold might have imagined.

Joe got out of the bath and dried himself, before Sumiko, one of the remaining girls, bowed and passed him a *yukata* to put on. She said something in rapid staccato Japanese to Aiko as she did. Joe picked up only the word *"Saru"* – which he knew meant "monkey".

Aiko sat on her knees by a squat short-legged table and invited him to sit with her. Sumiko and the other girl withdrew with a shy giggle into their hands, leaving Joe and Aiko alone. She asked his name then and he told her.

Joe felt a little uncomfortable now at being alone with this woman, who was clearly a very different proposition from the other younger serving girls in this establishment. It was difficult, though, to read the thoughts behind that expressionless mask of pearl-white.

'What did Sumiko say just now?' he asked suspiciously. 'Does she think I look like a monkey?'

Her eyes barely stirred in the immobility of her painted face. 'She said you have a good strong body for Western man, App-re-doon-san. Almost hairless, just like Japanese man. She doesn't like hairy Western men – too much like monkey, she said.'

Joe accepted the probable accuracy of the translation. 'You speak very good English, Aiko-san.'

'A little. Not good. English teacher here taught me.'

'Did you train as a *geisha*?' Joe wanted to know. 'You seem like a *geisha* to me.'

She giggled into her hands. 'Of course not, App-re-doon-san. Geisha very high class woman. I ordinary woman.'

"Ordinary" was not a word Joe would have ever used to describe her. 'Are you from Tokyo?'

'No, App-re-doon-san, I come from Nagano prefecture, in the Northern Japan mountains.'

'What's it like there?'

She let her eyes wander for a moment. 'Small villages, forests, waterfalls, *yuki* - heavy snow - in winter. In my village of Iiyama, sometimes two or three metres of snow can fall, enough to bury houses up to roofs.'

'Sounds more like an alpine village in Switzerland,' Joe suggested.

For a moment the fixity of her expression faltered slightly. 'I never been to Switzerland.'

Joe finally smiled across the table at her. 'Then Switzerland has really missed something...'

*

Joe was fully dressed and waiting in the entrance of the teahouse when Toby returned. Joe glanced at his pocket watch – it was already after 2 a.m. - and yawned heavily. 'Are you finally ready to go?' he asked Toby.

Toby nodded. 'Did Miss Peach Blossom have anything interesting to say while I was away?'

'No, not much,' Joe lied. 'And what did you get up to? Not much talk either, I bet.'

Toby winked. 'No, not much at all. Instead I had my wicked way with a young lady called Miss White Chrysanthemum – buttocks as firm as baseballs and thighs that could crack a walnut. And I think I may even have learned an entirely new position tonight, Joseph. You see, I've always been one for extending my cultural horizons - whenever I get the friggin' opportunity, that is.' He slapped Joe on the arm. 'C'mon. Let's go.'

They walked together through the near deserted streets of the *Yoshiwara*. Toby surprised Joe by saying, 'Sometimes I think I really would like to stay here, you know. Surprisin' for a New York boy like me, but there's something about this place that gets into the blood after a while. The women here are really like nowhere else on earth.' Toby seemed in an oddly reflective mood to Joe, surprising in itself after he'd just been enjoying himself with a woman.

'Yeah, I'd like to stay here and start a local clothing business. I could live out here like a *daimyo* with my own harem.' Toby stopped suddenly and eyed Joe warily. 'So tell me. What's your wife like, Joseph? Beautiful, I suppose?'

Joe shrugged. 'She is certainly that. And red-haired. And awfully cute.'

'It still didn't stop you eyeing up Miss Peach Blossom back there, did it? Were you really tempted by her?' Toby asked.

Joe mused on that question honestly. Yes, he had been tempted by the woman's exotic beauty; that was the unfortunate truth. Yet, at the same time, there had been something alien and intimidating too about Aiko's manner that had dampened his ardour a little and kept his feelings in check. He had found it quite impossible to read the mind behind that white-painted mask of a face, which made him reluctant to be intimate with her when he had so little comprehension of her feelings towards him in return.

Whatever the reason, he had in the end not given into temptation, and had done nothing but talk with her pleasantly about inconsequential things. Thinking of Eleanor and his marriage, perhaps that was for the best...

They walked on and passed a man in the street heading the other way – from his size clearly a European. The man turned his face quickly away but Joe had already recognised him by the light of a red lantern: this was the supposed Swiss businessman that he'd met in the bar of the Imperial Hotel. What was his name again? *Herr Maienfeld*... That was it. The man who said he was from Zurich yet apparently preferred speaking English to German, and who knew almost nothing about his own hometown. Yet, the coincidence of running into that man here gave Joe a sudden chill presentiment – a premonition that something awful was about to happen...

'What's wrong, Joseph?' Toby asked. 'You look like you've seen a friggin' ghost! Who was that man? I didn't see his face.'

Joe turned his head and saw that Maienfeld had already disappeared from sight.

'No one you know,' he said distractedly, although he remembered now that Toby himself had suggested the man must be a spy of some sort last night in the Imperial Hotel. Joe forced himself to shake off this sudden unaccountable feeling of foreboding. He was a rationalist after all, he reminded himself, not someone given to illogical superstition and nonsense. 'It's nothing,' he told Toby brusquely, moving on rapidly. 'Let's just get out of here. This place is making me uneasy.'

A minute later they were approaching the entrance gate of the *Yoshiwara* when suddenly, without warning, three men in dusty black coolie clothes jumped out at them from the side alleys on each side of the main street, barring their way forward and flashing evil-looking knives in their faces...

*

They all looked mean individuals to Joe, small but muscular, with brutal, scarred and pockmarked faces straight out of an Oriental nightmare. Their weapons looked disturbingly more like short stabbing swords rather than knives, and all three appeared to know how to use them to good effect.

'*Okane!*' one of them screamed in Toby's face. His companions then took up the same manic chant.

'I think they want our money,' Joe said, backing away slightly.

Toby squared up to them. 'Like hell I'm goin' to give 'em my friggin' money!' He reached for his inside pocket and pulled out instead a little silver-handled revolver, which he pointed at the leading robber.

But the lead robber had lightning fast hands and before Toby could stop him, the Jap had knocked the revolver out of Toby's hand with one deft sweep of the handle of his long knife. The revolver flew through the air and clattered somewhere on the stone cobbles. The robber then launched a blow at Joe with the knife, which Joe parried skilfully before kicking the man viciously behind the knee, sending him into a heap on the cobbles.

Joe kicked the prone man again, this time in the face, then jerked Toby back by the shoulder – 'Are you crazy? Run!' he ordered.

They turned and retreated at a gallop into the warren of lanes and alleyways behind them, slipping and sliding on the dry dusty cobbles, as they weaved their way between unlit teahouses and brothels. The twisting streets became narrower and darker, but they kept on going, hearing the steady footsteps and restrained breathing of their implacable pursuers close behind them. *Could there be even more than three of them?* Joe wondered worriedly. It sounded from the noise like an army of scurrying rats closing on them relentlessly...

Cats and clucking hens scattered before them; once a dog howled and barked at them in a frenzy as they ran through a cobbled yard with a kennel at one side. Despite the fact that they were slowing down themselves with fatigue and leaden muscles, they seemed to be pulling ahead of their attackers as the sounds of pursuit gradually faded into the distance. Eventually, with lungs heaving, Joe and Toby came to a tentative halt and listened for the sound of any continuing pursuit. Joe was reassured that they did seem to have lost their pursuers somehow, although he was a little surprised at how easily they had achieved that feat when the robbers presumably knew the byways of the *Yoshiwara* intimately.

Joe noticed that Toby was breathing no more heavily than him after this testing run, so was obviously fitter than he looked. And he had been armed too, Joe had seen with surprise, although it was perhaps not unusual for a European or American man to carry firearms for self-protection in this city. In fact Joe had brought his own revolver to Japan just in case, but hadn't seen the need to carry it with him so far.

He saw that the place they had stopped in was a quiet back lane, with a small carpenter's workshop on one side and a dark doorway on the other. The moon had set by now but enough starlight filtered down from above to reveal the basic geometry of the buildings. From a window above the doorway, Joe heard the plaintive notes of a *shamisen* – perhaps a *geisha* still plying her sensuous trade in an upstairs room at three in the morning. On a bench in front of the carpenter's shop, Joe found a piece of carpenter's timber shaped like a baseball bat, and gratefully took hold of it as a makeshift weapon, in case the robbers found them again.

'Shit, that was close!' Toby stood with his back to the doorway and almost laughed. Then he coughed violently and his head jerked back convulsively as a long sword-like blade suddenly erupted through his chest from behind and impaled him savagely through the breastbone.

Joe looked on in horror as the blade was withdrawn with savage brutality, like hacking a joint of beef in two, and blood spurted high and wide from Toby's chest. Toby sunk to his knees, gasping, as his hidden attacker, concealed artfully in the doorway behind him, jumped out into full view and thrust viciously at Joe with the same bloodied blade.

Somehow Joe managed to sidestep and avoid the first lethal thrust. The man was overbalanced for a moment by his misplaced blow and tumbled to the ground for a second, giving Joe a slight chance. His fingers took a tight grip on his makeshift baseball bat, and he swung it in one sinuous movement at the man's head as he tried to rise from the floor, almost decapitating him with the power of the blow. The man grunted like a pig as he collapsed.

Joe sized up the situation rapidly: this attacker seemed to be here on his own, although he was clearly one of the three men who had attacked them earlier. Perhaps he had just tracked them better, or else knew another way into this warren of alleyways, and guessed where they would end up. Joe wondered bleakly how long he had before the other two men found this alleyway too.

Joe went over to the slumped body of Toby, lying in the deep shadows on the straw-covered ground, and bent down to cradle his head with his arm, trying to see how bad the injuries were. Yet Joe had seen that blade go right through his chest, so knew that it was futile to hope. Even if the blade had missed Toby's heart by a miracle, it must still have cut through many other vital blood vessels, muscles and nerves. As if to confirm that, Joe saw that the front of Toby's evening jacket was already drenched with his own blood, so it was only a surprise that he was still breathing at all.

Because of the noise in the alleyway, someone had lit an oil lamp in an upper room above the carpenter's shop and Joe could see a little better now in the extra light it provided. Toby's eyes were glazing over fast, he saw, but in his last lucid moments he seemed desperate to say something to Joe before his lungs filled with blood and his brain died.

Joe struggled to hear what Toby was trying to say.

He heard a name on Toby's quivering lips, but refused to believe he had understood him properly.

'Say again, Toby. What is it?' Joe demanded in a whisper.

Toby made one last brave effort to speak. Joe heard the name so clearly this time that he could no longer deny to himself what Toby was trying to say. This was a name that filled Joe with dread - the last name he ever wanted to hear from the lips of a dying man, or from anyone else for that matter...

CHAPTER 6

Wednesday 27th January 1904

In the early hours of the morning "Aiko" sat in front of a mirror, as Sumiko helped her remove her heavy face make-up before taking her bath. The pieces of prosthetic thin latex rubber she used to disguise the shape of her eyelids were glued on, and always difficult to remove. Yet, complemented by her own naturally small features and oval face, they gave such an authentic Oriental look to her face that it was worth the extreme discomfort of wearing them. She could perhaps have managed without such a refinement but then, as an actress, she'd always been a perfectionist and wanted to get the look of her face as authentic as the speech and the mannerisms. The use of prosthetics to change the appearance of her face – false noses and chins and cheeks - was a trick she'd learned in her time in the theatre, particularly during a run of David Bellasco's play in Drury Lane; when playing the Japanese heroine Madame Butterfly, she'd used a Japanese stage name and had managed to convince even the dour and cynical London drama critics that she really had to be an unknown visiting Japanese actress.

She watched now as the English face of Miss Amelia Peachy emerged from beneath the expressionless oriental visage. The real thing that gave her away was her eyes, of course – distinctly blue, even if very dark blue. Yet in the dim light of the *ryotei* she could get away with it as they drew no particular attention...

In a way "Aiko" felt far more real to her than her "Madame Butterfly" stage role in London had ever felt. When Amelia put on the costume and the make-up of Aiko, she did feel inhabited – taken over almost - by a real flesh-and-blood individual. Aiko was in a sense as real as she was – perhaps more real in her essence, if anything. Deep inside, Amelia could feel exactly what this Japanese woman was feeling – it seemed to her more a spiritual bonding of two genuine souls than a mere act of pretence...

She relaxed the stiff muscles of her shoulders, enjoying the sensuous touch of Sumiko's skilful hands on her face and neck, as caressing as the soft wings of a dove. Amelia had to admit that she felt a stirring of excitement at the touch of another woman's hands on her body – perhaps at the thought of an illicit and forbidden kind of love? To be frank, she had sometimes wondered what it would feel like to make love to another woman, yet whatever little remained of her conventional English middle-class psyche had so far refused to ever let her take that adventurous step.

Sumiko regarded her with something bordering devotion, she knew, and had done so almost from the first moment they had met. Amelia still recalled that first meeting with a quiet glow of satisfaction. She had been touring the *Yoshiwara* looking for a suitable nest for her spying activities, dressed as it happened in the guise of a young bearded Frenchman. Male impersonation had been her forte during her brief career in the London music halls, and she could hardly walk around the *Yoshiwara* dressed as a Western woman, after all. And so it was in this oddly dressed situation that she had seen Sumiko for the first time, cleaning in the street in front of the House of the Red-Crowned Crane, bedraggled and abused, and half-starved by the vicious old woman who owned and ran the place.

Even in that state, Amelia had seen that, beneath the grime, Sumiko was a truly delicate porcelain-skinned beauty. Certainly few Victorian English ladies had ever possessed such impossibly white and perfect skin as this, and Amelia had naturally wondered at the profligacy of an establishment in the *Yoshiwara* that could afford to treat such a natural beauty in this way, or keep her working as a drudge only. She was the sort of girl any sensible man would have paid a fortune just to look at. The girl had soon become aware that she was under close scrutiny by this strange if handsome *gaijin*, and Amelia had quickly walked on.

But the more she learned about the House of the Red-Crowned Crane the more perfect it seemed for her purposes. In particular because it was a well-known haunt and meeting place of foreigners, and particularly *Russian* foreigners...

Still in the guise of the Frenchman, Amelia had soon entered into negotiations with the elderly owner to buy this bathhouse and restaurant with her own money. The old woman had charged what was for her an exorbitant price, believing that she was selling to a strange foreign man, but the amount of money seemed well worth the expense to Amelia, particularly as she acquired the workforce too as part of the sale.

Sumiko was the true pearl in this establishment, though. The seventh of a family of eight children from Akita prefecture, the daughter of a poor rice farmer, she'd been sold by her father to this house in the *Yoshiwara* at the age of eight in order to keep the rest of his family alive. Amelia could imagine that it must have broken the farmer's heart to have to sell such a beautiful child as Sumiko. But the owner of the House of the Red-Crowned Crane had taken a strange dislike to her as she grew up and treated her as the lowest kind of menial, even though it would have brought her far more profit using Sumiko as a serving girl or *oiran* inside.

After Amelia was installed as the new owner of the bathhouse, Sumiko had soon become her dedicated acolyte – or, that is, once she realised that her new employer was not a French*man*, but rather an English*woman*. (It had been a tricky matter revealing this deception to Sumiko – Amelia did make a very convincing if diminutive Frenchman, even if she said so herself - and she had been forced finally to remove her false moustaches and to partially bare her bosom to convince Sumiko that she was indeed a woman.)

All of the ten girls who worked in the bathhouse and the *ryotei* restaurant were in on the deception now of course, and had become dedicated acquirers of sensitive information for their generous employer. But Sumiko had become Amelia's special intimate accomplice in her spying activities on her Russian, French and German clientele.

Amelia, now installed in the House of the Red-Crowned Crane, soon found she needed a Japanese *alter ego* in order to move freely in this strange little world of the *Yoshiwara* (foreigners attracted far too much attention) and it was Sumiko who had taught her enough of the language to pass for Japanese with foreigners. (Because of her remaining lack of fluency in the language, Japanese visitors to the House of the Red-Crowned Crane however usually took "Aiko-san" for a Korean woman, despite her Japanese name.)

Sumiko had shown her how to apply the *geisha* and *oiran* make-up when needed, the pearl-white face, the rosebud lips, and also how to walk and talk like a Japanese. Amelia's great talent for language and mimicry had helped too of course, plus a natural affinity she'd instantly felt for this country and its people. In a way she felt strangely as if she'd finally come home...

Using this *ryotei* restaurant and adjacent bathhouse as her base, Amelia had found the perfect arrangement for her covert spying operations. She could spend half of her time here, living on the fringes of society in the city's decadent underbelly, and spying on the conversations of foreign male visitors to the *Yoshiwara* - embassy staff and government agents; while the other half of her life she spent residing in comfort in the Imperial Hotel or other hotels in the central districts of town in a variety of European guises, spying mainly on the wives and mistresses of diplomats. Even *British* diplomats, it had to be said...

After six months of this frantic activity, there wasn't much Amelia didn't know about the intimate lives of Tokyo's diplomats, or the secrets of the Intelligence world in Tokyo generally. The only problem being that she'd been so seduced by this lifestyle that eventually her existence as Aiko in the twilight world of the *Yoshiwara* began to seem much more real and important to her than her life away from it.

Every other week, Sumiko accompanied her down river to Nihombashi on a special houseboat, a hired steam launch equipped with a cabin and bed. On the boat journey she could transform herself at will into any one of several women. But the usual persona she adopted for her stays in town was that of the horse-faced Mrs Evadne Smythe, who was so plain and so lonely that all sorts of diplomatic wives felt the urge to confide in her. A saucer-eyed Sumiko had been amazed, even disturbed, at the transformation of Amelia into Mrs Smythe the first time she'd witnessed it. But with her in-bred Japanese love of drama - *Noh* theatre and *Kabuki* - Sumiko had soon taken a delight in this idea of being able to change identities and appearances at will. Amelia had based the character of Mrs Smythe on her own stern Aunt Georgina, and that was probably why she had a soft spot for Evadne...

Amelia had received word only recently from England that the real Georgina had died – her last blood relative – and she had been overcome with competing feelings of guilt and grief and bewilderment at the news. *How could Aunt Georgie be gone, without a last word to her, without a last kind thought?* But then, why should she have a kind remaining thought for her wayward niece? Their relationship had never been an easy one. Amelia had been a wilful child, while Georgina was a strict Victorian who simply did not know how to show affection, particularly to a difficult child. At the age of sixteen, Amelia had left her behind without a qualm and had hardly made more than token contact with her afterwards.

She, Amelia Peachy, this independent woman who needed no one close in her life, and who for the last few years had looked down on humanity mostly with contempt and bitter amusement, had finally realised the emptiness and sterility of her own existence. It was a shock to her to realise that what she needed in her life was some human warmth and friendship again. While she was always on the move from place to place, it seemed she had been able to put such melancholy musings to the back of her mind, but her relatively settled life during these months among the fragile and beautiful women of the *Yoshiwara* was teaching her profound and uncomfortable lessons about herself, and about life.

Apart from the guise of Mrs Smythe, Amelia still had the clothes and props for her other old *alter ego*, Miss Charlotte Cordingly, in her room at the Imperial. Amelia had a soft spot for Charlotte too, as with Mrs Smythe. Charlotte was the plain, sensible sister she'd never had, and sometimes Amelia felt the need to bring the spinsterish teacher Charlotte back to life in these new and exotic surroundings.

So Miss Charlotte Cordingly or Mrs Smythe would regularly re-emerge into the world of modern Tokyo, to take tea with their particular friends and acquaintances from the British Embassy – even Lady Hawtry-Gough herself, who was an even lonelier woman than herself in Amelia's opinion, and who often opened up her heart to "Mrs Smythe" about the state of her life. It almost pained Amelia to deceive Lady Rosemary, but she told herself she had a job to do and there was no room for sentiment – she was here to protect the Empire against a dangerous traitor and criminal, and she had to find the person responsible...

Once, Amelia had come back to the quayside from a week-long stay in town, inadvertently dressed as Miss Cordingly rather than as Mrs Smythe, and a scared Sumiko (who hadn't seen this particular guise before) frankly hadn't believed it was her. As a tribute to her acting skill it was probably the highest accolade that Amelia Peachy had ever received, but it was annoying nevertheless having to remove Charlotte's fake front teeth almost in full view of everyone on the quayside in order to be allowed back on board her own boat.

Sumiko had been so taken with the costume of Miss Cordingly that she had spent the entire trip back up the Sumida trying on the clothes herself, and even the fake front teeth, admiring herself in the mirror and turning herself into a very odd-looking and odd-sounding Charlotte...

*

Amelia stood up and stretched as she studied her own naked figure in the glass.

Sumiko had filled the bathtub for her by hand, and was watching her surreptitiously from the other side of the room. Amelia frankly enjoyed the sensation of Sumiko looking at her, almost as much as the touch of her strong fingers massaging her neck and shoulders. She stretched and arched her back, flexing the muscles of her buttocks, and teasing her friend with a sly smile in the glass. Sumiko, slender and supple as a willow, was envious of the length of Amelia's legs, her large rounded breasts and particularly her curvaceous Western bottom. 'Why is my *o-shiri* so flat, when yours is so curvy?' she complained ruefully, standing sideways to look at herself in the mirror.

'Don't complain, little one,' Amelia said in Japanese. 'All the men who come here look only at you, not me.'

Sumiko pulled a funny face. 'Not that handsome *Amerika-jin* who was here tonight. He never took his eyes off you once after you came into the room.'

Amelia smiled complacently. 'If only that were true, little dumpling,' she said...

Amelia was not really in such a complacent mood tonight as she suggested to Sumiko from her manner. It seemed that many figures from her past were all suddenly reappearing in her life, and she was finding these unexpected changes increasingly disconcerting. Just this evening, a little before midnight, Amelia had been up in this room adjusting her make-up and had spotted a silent figure, skulking in the street below. It was difficult to see the man with his face mostly obscured under a fedora hat, and the shape of his body disguised under a thick cloak. Clouds had drifted across the face of the moon, eclipsing the already dim light in the alley. But then the man chose to light a cigarette and, by the brief light of the flaring match, she saw his features clearly for just a second. *It was Shelepin...*

She'd always known deep down that it would be him the Russians would have sent. If the Russians were getting important secrets from a British traitor in Tokyo then it all had to be orchestrated by a man like Shelepin, of course. Who else but their best agent could organise such a coup of espionage?

Now that she had confirmation he was here, it was almost a relief to know who her main adversary on the Russian side was. But did Shelepin know *she* was here in Tokyo? It might just be chance that had brought him tonight to the House of the Red-Crowned Crane; many Russians patronised the place, after all. But there was a more ominous possibility why he was standing brazenly outside her own window - someone might have given her secret identity away...

Perhaps this explained her failure so far, if the Russians were so well informed about everything. For all the useful information she had uncovered and passed onto Randall since coming to Tokyo, Amelia had been frustrated by her lack of success in finding the specific thing she'd been asked to investigate in the last few weeks: the source of the recent leaks from the British Embassy to the Russians. Randall had sneered at her failure to discover the identity of the traitor and it was hard to take contempt from such an odious man. She didn't rule out the possibility that *he* was the person selling the secrets, of course. But she doubted it; Randall didn't have the imagination to be a traitor. Just an obnoxious human being who needed a good hard kick up the backside, she thought peevishly.

Nor had she detected yet any direct evidence that her archenemy, the assassin Johan Plesch, was here in Tokyo. The thought of Plesch being at large in Tokyo was an additional complication in her life that she certainly didn't need at this moment. The intelligence reports provided by Randall that claimed Plesch was operating here were only second-hand at best, so could easily be wrong. The usually cocksure Randall certainly wasn't absolutely convinced of his facts in this case, it seemed. Yet Amelia's instincts told her that Plesch probably was here – the looming threat of war between Russia and Japan, and the volatile nature of domestic politics here, was just the sort of atmosphere of crisis in which Plesch thrived. And, if Plesch were here, then that meant that some significant outrage was being planned...

And now Joseph Appeldoorn had turned up in Tokyo too... She hadn't foreseen that unexpected turn of events; she'd thought it was highly unlikely that she would ever see him again and had as a consequence managed to relegate him safely to a seldom-used part of her memory.

Shelepin and Joseph Appeldoorn…

The only two men she still really cared about, and both here in this city. It did seem like the working out of a strange predetermined fate, but Amelia Peachy did not believe in such brazen coincidences, so suspected there had to be more than the hand of fate in this unlikely coming together.

Was Joseph here as an official agent of the American Government? It had to be a possibility, at least, yet somehow she didn't think it likely. The newspapers accounts this morning of the attempted bombing in the Imperial Hotel had all referred to Joseph Appeldoorn as an "American businessman" and, as far as Amelia knew, that was the simple truth these days. At the time she had met him in Europe two years ago, he had, it was true, been working as a detective with the Pinkerton Agency, but he had apparently given up all that sort of work for a conventional business career, after his marriage to the wealthy heiress, Miss Eleanor Winthrop.

The other man who had been with Joseph tonight, Toby Pryor, certainly *was* an agent of the Secret Service in Washington, though, and a very effective and experienced one, she knew, particularly as his genuine role as the Far East representative of his family's clothing business gave him the perfect cover for his spying activities. Amelia had known about Pryor's activities here for some time, and his regular sniffing about in the *Yoshiwara* for information, thanks to her own web of spies and informants. Pryor had even had the temerity to try and recruit Sumiko to his cause the last time he'd been in the House of the Red-Crowned Crane a week ago, but hadn't succeeded, of course. Sumiko was absolutely loyal to Amelia, and had quickly reported her conversation with Pryor.

Pryor was more than just a collector of information, though, so he had to be here on a specific mission, Amelia realised. It could be anything; the Americans were certainly anxious to know what was going on in the Far East - they too were worried about Russian expansion in the Pacific - and to position themselves to take best advantage of the present situation. But Pryor was not a subtle spy sent to ferret out diplomatic deceits and secrets. He was more of a hunt-and-kill destroyer of America's enemies, from what she'd heard – in fact he seemed to perform a similar function to her own in the British secret service, and to take on similar missions.

When he had slipped out of the bathhouse tonight with Setsuko-san, it certainly hadn't been in order to have a sexual liaison with Miss White Chrysanthemum in the House of Pleasure next door, as he'd claimed. Or at least not *only* for that reason anyway: according to Setsuko-san, Miss White Chrysanthemum was a regular supplier of information to Mr Pryor. *But what information might she have?*

And then suddenly Amelia understood the reason why Pryor was here - *he had been sent to Japan to find and eliminate Plesch*. Of course, that had to be it...!

The Americans, after all, had even more reason to want to bring Plesch to justice than the British did – Plesch had not actually succeeded in his mission to kill the King two years ago, but he had certainly organised the murder of the American President McKinley back in '01, even if he hadn't actually fired the shots that killed him.

And that must be why Joseph was here too...

After returning to America two years ago, Joseph must have told his government about his encounter with Plesch. And now that Plesch had apparently turned up alive in Japan, it was natural that the Americans should bring Joseph over here to help track him down. He, after all, was one of the few people in the world who could identify Plesch.

But was Joe helping Pryor voluntarily or was he being pressurised to help? *Or could it be that he didn't even know he was here to help track down Plesch?* Knowing how the American Secret Service worked, that last one seemed the likeliest scenario to Amelia. Joseph had probably been brought here unwittingly as the live bait to draw Herr Plesch out into the open where Pryor could try and pick him off...

Last night, in the lobby of the Imperial Hotel, Amelia had been there, disguised as Mrs Smythe, secretly spying on her own compatriots from the Embassy. She'd had information from one of her sources that the Russians might make contact that very night with their traitor inside the British Embassy, and "Mrs Smythe" had been the perfect person to observe the goings-on in the lobby. Amelia had paid particular attention to the undersecretary, Mr Peregrine Cavendish, who had the right kind of access to secret information, and who was reputed to have built up enormous gambling debts since his arrival in Japan last year.

With amusement Amelia had also spotted Vladimir Obodovsky prowling the lobby – the man's disguise as a Swiss businessman was amateurish to the point of being farcical. Probably that was the reason why Shelepin had been brought from Russia to mastermind the operation instead – the Tsar's Intelligence Service simply couldn't trust this oaf of a colleague to carry out such a complex operation.

But who was she to talk about amateurs? Amelia thought ruefully. She too had behaved like a rank amateur last night, dropping her cup in her extreme surprise when she had first spotted Joseph sitting on the other side of the lobby. But at least he hadn't recognised her, she was sure of that – she'd walked past his view several times after that just to satisfy herself that he was paying her no particular attention.

Nor had Pryor seen through the guise of Mrs Smythe, she was also sure. The make-up and mannerisms of Mrs Smythe were quite impervious to suspicion, even if she said so herself. Thank God she hadn't been there last night dressed as Miss Cordingly, though – Joseph would certainly have recognised that *alter ego*.

It had been less of a surprise tonight to Amelia that Pryor and Joseph should turn up together here in the *Yoshiwara,* and at the House of the Red-Crowned Crane of all places. Pryor had been here several times previously and clearly knew that this particular bathhouse was the haunt of Russian and German agents, a place where secrets regularly exchanged hands. And it was probably inevitable that Pryor would have brought Joseph here eventually, if he was using Joseph as bait.

Tonight had still been a difficult experience for Amelia, though – she'd worried that something - some familiar gesture or look - would give her away. Yet Joseph had not recognised her tonight either, she was convinced of that - he wasn't a good enough actor to have pulled that deceit off. But Pryor? She wasn't so sure about Pryor any more.

Pryor had been looking at her in a very deliberate way tonight, as if trying to peer with X-ray vision to make out the real woman beneath the pale face paint. And he had deliberately called her "Miss *Peach* Blossom" several times tonight – which was far too much of a coincidence. Somehow he'd learned who she was…

And what's more, he wanted her to know for some reason that he had finally seen through her disguise…

Perhaps someone had betrayed her secret to Pryor, either deliberately or inadvertently – he had slept with so many girls in the *Yoshiwara;* one of them might easily have said something to make him suspect her.

But then a new thought came to her and she instantly knew the truth… *Randall* might have told Pryor of her secret identity here…

Yes, that had to be it! Now that she thought about it, she had even seen Randall exchange a word and a significant look with Pryor in the lobby of the Imperial last night. *But why would Randall have given her secret identity away to the Americans?* Perhaps the British Intelligence Service and the Americans were cooperating secretly to track down Plesch, and Pryor wanted her help in particular? But if that were the case, Randall hadn't told her of it. And if Randall *had* revealed to Pryor that Aiko-san and Miss Amelia Peachy were one and the same person, then - an even more worrying thought - who else might he have told?

If her secret identity here was compromised, then perhaps it was time to let Aiko-san disappear for good, and to remain in the guise of Mrs Smythe or Miss Cordingly for the present – even Randall didn't know about the true identity of those two ladies, and therefore couldn't give her confidence away this time.

She thought again about seeing Joseph tonight. Sitting so close to him again, reliving the memories of their time together in Switzerland in her mind, it had been difficult to keep her face under control. Her heart had been beating wildly under the costume and her face longing to relax under the thick make-up. There had been one moment when she'd almost finally given in and revealed herself to him - the moment when he'd mentioned Switzerland himself with that familiar half-smile of his, and she'd felt an almost irresistible urge to lean across the table and say, '*Joseph, it's me...!*'

She remembered that last desperate moment they'd shared together two years ago in Switzerland, though, and that had given her pause for thought – Joseph had just been shot by Plesch and was near death, lying in an expanding pool of his own blood on a cliff face above the Rhine Falls - the *Rheinfall...*

*

Afterwards, she had relived endlessly in her mind those last few seconds of that cliff-top encounter with Plesch and tortured herself with doubt. *If only she'd done this – if only that...*then the end might have been different...

The fact was she had completely misjudged the timing of her intervention, and Plesch had unexpectedly shot Joseph twice just as she was about to jump the assassin from the cover of the trees.

And yet, despite the lateness of her action, she had still nearly succeeded in driving Plesch over the cliff to his well-deserved fate; that was, until the man had locked a sinewy hand around her leg and started dragging her over the edge too. She remembered the look on Joseph's face as she had finally succumbed to Plesch's deathlike grip and slid over the cliff face to her apparent death...

She *had* nearly died in fact – she came as close to it that day as she ever had. Somehow she missed the jagged rocks on entry into the foaming water, but she was instantly sucked under by the savage current and swirling waves, which swept her over the Rheinfall, smashing her body against rocks, battering the life out of her.

She didn't know how she survived the massive hundred-foot fall or the pummelling on the boulders below, but she came to, a few minutes later, gasping for breath on a shingle beach half a mile downstream of the falls. To her astonishment, she found that she was even able to move, with no apparent serious injuries to her body, although naturally suffering considerable bruising and superficial injuries. She realised that something truly miraculous had just happened, since she should by rights be dead. She doubted that one person in a thousand would have survived such a fall, never mind doing so without any serious injuries, as she just had. Climbing wearily to her feet, she had quickly scanned her surroundings, looking for any signs that her arch enemy might also have survived the fall. But there'd been no sign of Plesch in the river or on the banks, and almost in exultation she'd really thought that she must have finally triumphed over him, and that the devil must be dead.

But her exultation was short-lived as she remembered that Joseph had been bleeding to death on that rock face above the waterfall.

Still dressed only in a bodice, corset and silk drawers, she had dragged her weary and bruised body up and retraced her steps upstream, through the matt of dense pine forest clinging to the slopes, to the top of the cliff where she had left Joseph. But when she got back to the narrow shelf of rock overlooking the falls, perhaps an hour after he'd been shot, she found that Joseph was already gone, together with the middle-aged tourist who'd been there with him, whoever he was. She'd touched the ugly slime of Joseph's blood on the rocks, and nearly wept with self-pity and grief.

But she soon recovered – Amelia Peachy was made of sterner stuff than this! She went and recovered the skirt and overcoat and boots she'd discarded earlier in the woods above the cliff, and, looking slightly more presentable now, walked back three miles in the cold rain to the hotel. It was at this point she realised that to all intents and purposes she was dead, and what a convenient state that was for a person in her line of work. Until she was absolutely sure of Plesch's fate, she definitely preferred to keep news of her miraculous survival secret, and started to tread warily.

She managed to enter and leave the Hotel *Rheinfels* without being seen by the staff, taking only her passport and other important things, notably the clothes and make-up of Miss Cordingly.

After finding herself a room in another hotel where she could transform herself into the guise of Miss Cordingly again, she then went to the local hospital in Schaffhausen and was overjoyed to learn that Joseph was still alive – even if his life was hanging by a slender thread. Amelia had been tempted then to try and see him, or perhaps Miss Eleanor Winthrop, who was maintaining a lonely vigil at the hospital too, as if she was already Joseph's grieving and distraught wife.

But the shadow of Plesch still loomed large in her thoughts and Amelia, nervous of discovery, elected to leave the hospital without making her presence known. She later made discreet enquiries with the local police, reporting an imaginary husband to be missing; but it seemed no bodies had been found in the Rhine in the last few hours. If *she* had survived the fall over the *Rheinfall*, it was beginning to seem equally plausible to Amelia that Plesch too had somehow managed to achieve that unlikely feat.

Amelia took the overnight train to Southern Germany and reported back to her Foreign Office boss, Sir Charles Gorman, still in Friedrichshafen, who, despite still expressing deep dissatisfaction with her recent performance of her duties, ordered her to try and pick up Plesch's trail again.

The King had returned to London from Germany by now, and Amelia had soon followed him there, after first hearing the wonderful news that Joseph was out of danger in Schaffhausen and expected to make a full recovery in time. Less wonderful was the news that he was now being nursed personally and full-time by Miss Eleanor Winthrop, the American heiress he'd been sent to Europe to find...

In London the King adamantly refused to bow to the government's pressure and change his playboy lifestyle or bohemian habits. Amelia was sure that Plesch would not have given up his mission, and might well make a third and even bolder attempt to assassinate the King – and in London, the heart of the British Empire, this time. Plesch had to be fully aware of what the impact of such a crime would be, but seemed to have lost all his previous professional restraint in his determination to see his thwarted mission through to its bitter end.

The King was normally well protected when in England by his detective guard, but not at a certain house of ill repute in Mayfair that Amelia knew he frequented at least once a week. She persuaded Sir Charles to let her be introduced into that favourite House of Pleasure to protect the King at these times. And so Miss Amelia Peachy was transformed yet again, this time into the blonde and curvaceous "Miss Trixie Delight" – a low and common role which she had taken on with a real relish, particularly because of the risqué wardrobe she had to adopt in order to be convincing. (This was also the name Amelia had adopted during her brief stab at a career on the music hall stage several years before, when she had made an ill-judged attempt at being a male impersonator in the style of Vesta Tilley - an experiment which she had soon wisely abandoned for the theatre proper.)

The King had been allowed in on the deception this time – Amelia didn't want to go through similar problems to those she'd encountered in a certain establishment in Zurich where similar shenanigans had taken place, and where "Bertie" had not been in the know. Yet Bertie had proved insufferable, though, once he knew the truth about "Miss Trixie Delight", treating her like one of his fancy women, rather than a government agent trying to protect his worthless neck. Amelia had soon grown used to his clumsy fumbling and his fascination with pinching her bottom. "Miss Trixie Delight" soon had the most black-and-blue buttocks in the entire establishment, which was saying something. Miss Peachy had soon begun to tire of playing a blonde tart and resolved *never* to do so again if she could possibly help it...and certainly not with the lecherous King of England anywhere in the vicinity.

Then one night in June - the 24th to be precise - Plesch had finally made his move. His disguise had been absolutely brilliant – even Amelia hadn't suspected the doddery Italian gentleman with the gleaming baldhead. They'd searched the clientele for weapons at the door, of course, but it transpired later that Plesch had somehow got hold of a kitchen knife once inside the building. And that was more than enough for his purpose after he'd found "Miss Trixie Delight" and the King together in one of the private salon rooms, and then done his best to skewer the most powerful monarch in the world.

Despite being taken completely by surprise, she'd managed somehow to parry his first knife thrust at the King. But she missed the second follow-up blow, and the King had taken it full in his abdomen and collapsed onto the thick carpet like a blood-filled sack. By this time others had come to the private room to help and Plesch was forced to flee, while Amelia, her own heart pounding with fear and thoughts of her probable disgrace, tried desperately to halt the flow of her sovereign's blue blood.

Though it had looked red enough to her, as it spilled out in vast quantities over the plush cream carpet.

As soon as a doctor came, she armed herself with her trusty Browning automatic pistol and went looking for Plesch, determined to finish him for good this time. She knew he couldn't have got out of the building: the doors had been guarded by Special Branch bobbies; and her trap was well set, even if the outcome, with the King being rushed to St Bart's Hospital for emergency surgery, hadn't been exactly what Amelia had been planning.

She organised the search of the building in the next hour, bringing in Special Branch detectives to investigate every nook and cranny of this four-storey Georgian house, and finally narrowing Plesch's location down to one place — *he had to be on the roof...*

She found him standing calmly on the flat roof, next to the parapet, gazing out at the rooftops of night-time Mayfair. It was after 9 p.m. by now but there was still enough dusky light to see by. Gaslights were being lit in Bond Street below, where she could hear the ribald laugh of a hansom cab driver waiting for a fare. To the south she could see the silhouettes of Big Ben and Westminster Abbey outlined against a pale lilac late evening sky. There was no way off this roof for Plesch that she could see - a full twenty-foot gap separated it from that of an adjacent building - but she nevertheless approached him cautiously, knowing this man, even if finally cornered, was probably the most dangerous man she'd ever encountered, and would kill her just for pleasure if he had half a chance.

He saluted her with a mocking bow. 'Miss Peachy, how nice you look! In all that excitement earlier, I did not have time to compliment you on your arousing appearance.'

'And I compliment you too, Herr Plesch! A pity you had to sacrifice your hair, though, in the interests of crime.'

'A temporary loss only, I assure you, Miss Peachy.'

She tut-tutted. 'Perhaps permanent. It may not have enough time to grow back before they hang you at Wormwood Scrubs.'

He smiled humourlessly. 'Then perhaps you would spare your country the expense and formality of a trial. And spare me a little boredom too before I depart this life...'

With that Plesch slowly mounted the three-foot high stone balustrade parapet, and tottered on one foot on the narrow sloping top.

'Get down, Herr Plesch,' Amelia commanded coldly. 'You can't escape from there.'

But then, with no more than a casual flexing of his legs, *he jumped*...

The gap to the neighbouring building looked too far for any mortal man to make from a standing jump and Amelia could only watch in amazement as he seemed to fly through the air as if ejected from a cannon. Despite herself, she was so enthralled in the performance of the jump that she didn't attempt to shoot him in mid-flight as she should have done. Before she could even react, he'd reached the other roof and rolled across the tarred felt, onto a fire escape and was gone...

In her ridiculous "Miss Trixie Delight" outfit, with high heels and short flounced skirt and pink tights, she'd had no chance of following him. Amelia had been a circus performer herself but didn't know of another man alive who could have made that jump successfully...

And so, the ignominy of it – *Plesch had escaped justice once again.*

Was the man human? Or was he a spectre, a devil? She had half begun to suspect so – this was the only man who had ever truly frightened her.

Afterwards, faced again with the savage censure of her chief Sir Charles Gorman over this debacle, she had considered leaving the strange underworld business of spying and returning to the stage. Fortunately the King did survive but his coronation in June had to be postponed; the government had been forced to put out a false story that he was suffering from Appendicitis.

Although she hadn't earned the government's secret five thousand-pound bounty for the head of Johan Plesch, Amelia still had more than enough money to satisfy her material needs, having earned a lot from her different careers, and investing the money wisely. She was now in fact a very wealthy woman, with more than twenty thousand pounds sterling nestling in her account with Coutts Bank, and much more in various Swiss bank accounts. She had also just bought herself a stylish Georgian house in Hampstead overlooking the Heath – and so she could afford to tell Sir Charles what to do with his job with impunity.

At the beginning of July '02, still undecided about her future life, she went back to the Continent to see Joseph who, she had been reliably informed, was now out of hospital and about to return home. It was going to be a difficult reunion of course because he obviously thought her dead these many months. Yet the frank truth was she wanted him to stay with her, and was even prepared to humble herself in the process to get the man she wanted. She missed him in Paris, though – he had already left the city – but she finally caught up with him in Cherbourg on the quayside as he was getting ready to board the *Kaiser Wilhelm der Grosse* of the North German

Lloyd Line, bound for New York and home.

But Miss Winthrop had been there with him, which Amelia had not been expecting (although perhaps she should have done, given her understanding of normal human behaviour.) From the cover of a large packing case, and with a sinking heart, she watched them together, arm-in-arm walking down the quayside. They looked so happy together, she thought, so ideal for each other in every way. In the end she'd simply waited for them to board the gangway, then turned and walked away. *What could she possibly say to him now...?* As far as he knew, she was dead and buried, and she told herself she could hardly blame him for finding another woman so quickly. Yet somehow she still couldn't help feeling, in some obscure and entirely unreasonable way, that he had betrayed her memory and let her down...

On the train back to Paris, she reconciled the situation in her own mind, and to her own satisfaction. If she was honest, she couldn't ever see herself as a sober married woman, living in Finchley or Harrow or even upstate New York, raising children, attending church fetes, planning dinners, supervising the downstairs maid with petty tyranny, watching her own hips gradually spreading and her husband's eyes straying elsewhere. She knew in her heart that this was not sort of life she was intended for. She felt inside that she was the type of person destined never to grow old, but to burn brightly for a short time and then to fall to earth again like a brilliant but short-lived comet.

She stayed only a few days in Paris, before contacting Sir Charles again at the Embassy, then taking the overnight train to Berlin where a new report of Plesch had just been received at the British Embassy in *Under den Linden*.

*

She finished her bath and stood up in front of the mirror again, feeling the slight ridging of the scar in her left abdomen. At the age of twenty-eight, there were still no signs of her hips spreading quite just yet, she was glad to see. That scar, though, she would carry with her for the rest of her life, a permanent memento of Joseph since *he* had left that scar there, although probably saving her life in the process.

Even in her preoccupation last night she'd been happy to see how little he'd changed in the past two years. Still so annoyingly handsome, but at least, unlike most good-looking men, he wasn't insufferable. (Unlike Randall, who made it so obvious to Amelia that he wanted her, yet at the same time clearly despised himself for his weakness in doing so.)

Amelia Peachy was usually completely immune to handsome men, and she had certainly not taken to Joseph Appeldoorn at first either. But Joseph did have a natural charm that most men of her acquaintance lacked...

She'd known that feeling for sure the first time he had looked at her that *special* way in a certain naughty room at *Le Royale,* that infamous brothel on the shore of Lake Zurich. An odd place to fall in love with a man...

Last night she'd been upstairs in her room at the Imperial, standing at the window, when she'd heard the sound of breaking glass below, then seen Joseph charging outside with that thing in his hand. She hadn't realised what it was until he threw it – a bare second before she stepped back from the glass and it exploded. He must have saved thirty or forty lives at least by his brave action – later she'd felt almost a proprietary pride on his behalf, as if he still belonged in some way to her...

Amelia put on her sleeping kimono and sat down again in front of the mirror, regarding her sombre image in the glass. Sumiko, now taking her own bath on the other side of the room, seemed to sense her melancholy mood and was equally quiet.

Amelia realised that, although she could never see herself as a bored suburban housewife, she was also growing tired of the spy game, tired of the deception and the deceit, tired of death, tired of being mostly friendless and alone. She thought of her Aunt Georgina slipping away, dying all-alone in that awful nursing home in Cobham, and was determined that she would not end up that same way. As Amelia drifted off to sleep in the chair, she was reminded for some reason of playing Miranda in a production of *The Tempest* at the Shaftsbury Theatre; the last lines of that play had always made the hairs stand up on the nape of her neck as she listened in the wings to them at the end of the performance...

'These our actors, as I foretold, were all spirits and are melted in air, into thin air'. That was what she was – a spirit, a dream, not a real person. *'We are such stuff as dreams are made on, and our little life is rounded with a sleep...'*

Then she woke up sharply as she heard the sounds of a sudden commotion of some sort outside. A distant scream, yells, a grunt, the sound of running footsteps. She frowned; sounds like that were unusual here. Even in the *Yoshiwara*, violent robbery was as rare as anywhere else in Tokyo, while murder was almost unheard of, although picking pockets and snatching money belts were becoming more commonplace crimes these days, with so many rich foreigners frequenting the alleyways of the "Place of Reeds".

Amelia listened with concern to the continuing sounds of commotion; then the running footsteps receded and the streets of the *Yoshiwara* fell silent again.

Amelia moved cautiously to the window. 'Did you hear that?'

'*Neko* – cat, probably,' Sumiko said facetiously from the bathtub, with a shrug. 'Boy cat looking for love, I think...'

'I hardly think so, little dumpling – it would take the biggest cat in the world to make that much noise.' Then Amelia heard in the distance something even more sinister, the sound of a blow striking flesh with huge force and then a scream of agony that made the goose pimples rise on her back. Then silence again – *absolute silence.*

What was going on? Could it be Joseph in trouble?

Then she heard a distant shot...

*

Joe had cradled Toby Pryor in his arms for what seemed an age, while he had watched him die. His own heart was sick and heavy with a sort of grief – he'd hardly known this man really but liked him nevertheless. And his mind was still reeling at the name he'd heard Toby say — the name of an evil and degenerate assassin whose bones, by all rights, should have been rotting by now in the mud at the bottom of the Rhine. What could it all mean...?

It was just as Toby breathed his last and the alleyway had grown completely quiet again that Joe realised his own danger was certainly not past. The man he'd hit with that makeshift weapon had vanished...

Now, as he heard several footsteps returning, he wished he'd hit the man even harder.

Regretfully he laid Toby's head with tender care on the cobblestones and turned to look for a means of escape. But it was already too late, he saw; there were figures approaching from *both* sides of the alleyway, knife blades at the ready.

Joe knew he was as good as dead, and for a moment Eleanor's words of warning flashed through his mind. And the thought that he would never see her sweet face again almost made him panic...

But he turned to fight anyway, determined to take at least one of these cowardly devils with him. He backed into a narrow little cul-de-sac against a brick wall so that they could only come at him one at a time.

He tripped the first man who rushed him, then kicked him viciously in the back of the head as he fell on the ground.

Yet another man had appeared, though, in the alleyway to augment the three original attackers. *Four* robbers to kill one man! The thought incensed Joe even more and he lunged out angrily at the next in line, forcing him back.

But the newly arrived figure had a surprise for the others, and instead of taking their side, pulled out a pistol and calmly shot the last robber in the back of the head without any ceremony at all.

The remaining robber still on his feet turned at the sound of the shot and promptly fled, leaving his hurt confederate behind, even though the man Joe had kicked to the ground was beginning to groan and might soon be fully conscious again.

'Are you hurt?' the newcomer asked curtly, stepping forward.

His English was good but he was certainly no Englishman, Joe decided instantly. German, or Russian, possibly. In the dim light of a nearby lantern, Joe could just make out a handsome mocking face and longish black curls.

He was nearly as tall as Joe.

Joe bent down to examine Toby's body again, at a loss to know what to do.

The foreign man shook his head wryly. 'You have no time for this sentimentality, I'm afraid. Your friend is dead, sir, as is this rogue I dispatched. And if you wait here, you will soon be too. This robber -' he indicated the groaning man on the ground – 'will shortly be fully awake and the other one who fled will also no doubt be back in a few minutes with reinforcements to avenge his dead companion. Personally I don't care to wait for them.' He looked at his pocket watch. 'It's nearly three and I was about to go back to town anyway. I have a boat on the river near here - do you want to go back to Nihombashi with me? It seems like a sensible course of action, in the circumstances.'

Joe looked up at the man. 'I can't just leave my friend here. Can't we take his body back with us too?'

The man seemed annoyed. 'I suppose so...if you have to,' he agreed peremptorily. 'But don't expect me to help you carry him. I've done my one good deed for the night...'

CHAPTER 7

Wednesday 27ᵗʰ January 1904

In his room in the Imperial Hotel, Joe Appeldoorn paced back and forward, still distraught and angry, despite the hours he'd had to get used to the idea that Toby Pryor was dead. His business trip to Japan was turning into a nightmare; yet he had no idea why this was happening or what he could possibly do about it. He was sorely tempted, though, just to go down to the booking desk of the Asia-Pacific Steamship Company in the lobby and get a berth on the first ship heading out from Yokohama to any American port. Or indeed anywhere else for that matter...

Bright winter sunlight suddenly flooded the room as the sun finally broke through the overcast sky for the first time today, but the late morning brightness brought no similar optimism to Joe's mood. He looked out of his second floor window and regarded the panorama over Nihombashi and Kyobashi districts with weary and disinterested eyes – this city was fast losing its appeal for him.

Major Sawada was being relatively patient with his questions today - Joe had to give him that much credit, at least. Sawada had not really pressed him at all about last night's events with any urgency yet, but instead seemed content to sit quietly in an armchair, and listen to what this American visitor to his shores might have to say for himself. Blue-grey smoke coiled upwards from the cigarette in his mouth, but the cigarette seemed more like an actor's prop than anything, a device for distracting attention from the point of his subtle probing questions.

Yet Joe was in no mood to be questioned by any interrogator at this moment; all he wanted was to quickly pack his bags and leave this damned country for good. He remembered again Toby's last gasping words. The man had known he was dying but he'd still struggled, with an almost superhuman effort of will, to try and make Joe understand something...*something about Johan Plesch.*

And that only made sense if Toby Pryor not only knew all about the assassin Plesch *but also knew of Joe's prior connection with the man.* So could Johan Plesch still be alive, and – an infinitely worse possibility - be here in Japan? That seemed to Joe the only possible reason why Toby Pryor should have struggled in the last few moments of his life to say the man's name. He was trying to warn *him* about Plesch...

*

The boat that Joe and his rescuer had returned in had been similar in size to the one that he and Toby had used to travel upstream only a few hours before, in search of a little harmless pleasure. But this later boat, for the far more sombre return journey, had neither cabin nor awning, just a single oarsman on each side and a tiller in the stern where a boatman, as wizened and shrunken as an ancient ape, had steered the vessel casually with one hand as he sucked at a Chinese opium pipe. An oil lantern, swinging from a pole amidships, provided a little smoky light for the melancholy journey.

With the first quarter moon already long set and no hint of dawn yet in the Eastern sky, nor scarcely a single gleam of light from the distant sleeping city, the Sumida had been as black as Joe Appeldoorn's mood. Unlike Mr Maeda, who clearly loved this river and would always see positive things in it that others didn't, Joe Appeldoorn could derive no similar feelings of poetic inspiration in his bleak surroundings tonight. He watched the ghostly wharves and jetties and darkened houses slip soundlessly by on both sides, only the regular splash of the oars and the muscular grunt of the rowers disturbing the pre-dawn calm. In the bows of the vessel, a small girl, as perfect and pretty as a little doll, lifted her head from the deck for a moment to look at Joe, yawned in disinterest, then went back to sleep beside a young woman lying next to her, presumably her mother.

The tall man who had saved Joe's life earlier that night (whose nationality, Joe had definitely concluded by now, had to be Russian) did not seem at all interested in the other living occupants of this boat, nor even in the inert and sad object bound up in a canvas bag and stored amidships.

The Russian sat on the gunwale of the boat near the lantern so that the swaying beam of light threw the planes and features of his handsome face into changing relief all the time. Despite the long black curls and the almost pretty features, Joe could see this man was no fop but a formidable individual.

The man had talked so far only in monosyllables but now Joe, studying him curiously from the other side of the boat, tried to draw him out a little. 'Thank you again for your help, Mr...?'

The man ignored the prompt for his name, but otherwise seemed philosophical about his current situation. 'I had to do it. I couldn't just let those Japs kill a fellow Westerner, could I?' he commented. Despite his earlier vow, he had in fact helped Joe carry the bloodied body of Toby on a borrowed cart across the marshy ground to the wooden jetty where his boat waited. Not surprisingly perhaps, the boatman and his family had been highly reluctant to take a dead body on board, and especially the body of a *gaijin*. The Russian had chosen not to intervene in the visual pantomime of negotiation that had then ensued between Joe and the elderly boatman, and at the conclusion Joe had been forced to hand over a small fortune in yen to the old man in return for transporting the body and himself back to *Tsukiji*. Because the boatman had both his daughter and granddaughter on board, there had been a further protracted delay in departing even after the fee had been agreed, while one of the boatman's sons had out of decency first sewn the body up in a canvas bag made up of bits of old sail.

You haven't told me your name yet, sir,' Joe pointed out to the Russian, deciding to be direct this time.

The man deliberated for a few seconds, before saying with a shrug, 'No, I haven't, have I? But call me Raskolnikov, if you will.'

Joe sniffed disbelievingly. 'Then you can call me Petrovitch in return.'

The Russian smiled knowingly. 'Ah, I could, but it's not your name, is it? Your name is actually Mr Joseph Appeldoorn and you come from the United States, I believe.'

Joe looked up sharply. 'Then, Mr "Raskolnikov", you're very well informed.'

The Russian shrugged. 'Your name and photograph were in the *Japan Mail* today. The hero who foiled the anarchist bombing of the Imperial Hotel yesterday evening. How does it feel to be a feted hero, Mr Appeldoorn?'

Joe almost smiled. 'Wearying, sir. But you did very well to recognise me from that picture in the newspaper, Mr "Raskolnikov". You see, it wasn't *my* picture that appeared in the *Japan Mail*. They printed another man's picture by mistake.' Joe wasn't sure whether that intense young reporter woman from Minneapolis, Miss Blanchett, had indeed made a genuine mistake, or whether — after he had declined to have his photo taken for the story - she had simply gone and used a passport picture of someone else she knew who bore a passing superficial resemblance to himself.

"Raskolnikov" didn't look chastened by that revelation and just shook his head wryly. 'Then I must have seen your picture in a different newspaper.'

Joe stuck out his jaw angrily. 'My real picture didn't appear in *any* newspaper today. Perhaps I'm getting a little sensitive, Mr "Raskolnikov", but so many people in this damned town are turning out to be not what they pretend to be.' He locked eyes deliberately with the Russian. 'So how did you really know who I was?'

The Russian squinted dangerously at him in return. 'Might I remind you, Mr Appeldoorn, that I saved your life back there? I'm not absolutely sure it was the right thing to do, so please don't press the point with me, otherwise I might change my mind and finish the job here myself.'

Joe wasn't sure how serious that threat was, but wisely decided to lapse into a resentful silence.

They had passed Nihombashi and were nearing *Tsukiji* by now, the old foreign settlement at the mouth of the Sumida where it emptied into Tokyo Bay. Thirty years ago, Joe knew this had been the only place in Tokyo where foreigners had been allowed to live under the terms of Japan's treaty with Western Powers, and the headquarters of many of the hongs - the foreign trading establishments - were still there, as were many godowns and warehouses, western shops and small hotels, bonded stores, custom houses, banks, shipping offices, and a jetty where the mail packet steamers still called twice a month.

For the moment this inner part of Tokyo Bay at the mouth of the Sumida still remained busy with shipping, although the forest of masts of the previous century was dwindling fast these days, as sail was finally driven off the high seas by the smoking funnels of the tramp steamers. In the pearly dawn half-light Joe could see a whole phalanx of steamships manoeuvring in the roadsteads further out in the bay, these new twentieth century steel and iron monsters quite immune to the vagaries of the trade winds, unlike their nineteenth century counterparts.

At six in the morning, Joe had found himself abandoned on the quayside in *Tsukiji*, with the canvas bag and its grim contents laid on the concrete jetty by his side. He could see no point in hurrying for help at this early hour so sat on a mooring bollard for a few minutes, watching the sun come up over the Pacific. Joe saw the roseate rays of light steal gradually across the rooftops of this vast metropolis, a city bursting with commerce and vigour, but also a city with disturbing and threatening undercurrents running just beneath its orderly surface...

*

Sawada studied the thin line of blue smoke rising from the end of his cigarette. 'So, who was this mysterious man who came to your aid, Mr Appeldoorn?'

'I told you: I have no idea who he was. But he called himself "Raskolnikov".' Joe described the man as best he could.

'A Russian?'

'Almost certainly.'

Sawada frowned. 'But you didn't think "Raskolnikov" was his real name?'

Joe shrugged wryly. 'Hardly. It's the name of the hero of Dostoyevsky's novel *Crime and Punishment*. So I introduced myself to him in return as

"Petrovitch".'

Sawada narrowed his eyes at that. 'Ah, the police detective in the same story, I believe. Was there something deliberate perhaps in your particular respective choices of literary identities, do you think?'

Joe shook his head tiredly. 'No, he'd already taken the murderer's name, hadn't he? So I had to take the policeman's.'

'And was the robber that this "Raskolnikov" shot really dead, do you think?'

Joe blinked for a moment at that disturbing suggestion. 'I'm not sure, to be honest. I certainly didn't hang around to check. The Russian said he was dead and I believed him...'

At seven o'clock this morning, the local harbourmaster had rushed down to the quayside in *Tsukiji*, soon after arriving for work, to investigate the report of a *gaijin* waiting on the quayside with a canvas article that seemed suspiciously to resemble a corpse in a sack. Joe had managed somehow by sign language to convince the harbourmaster that he should be allowed to make a telephone call from the harbour office handset to the American Embassy; he hadn't known whom else to call. He had spoken directly to Ambassador Reinhold, who had come down immediately to *Tsukiji* to deal with the situation. Hageyama had been grim-faced, and seemed to take the loss of Toby Pryor personally. 'I should never have allowed you to go to the *Yoshiwara*,' he kept repeating mournfully. 'It must be a more dangerous place these days than it ever was in my day...'

Joe told him the gist of what had happened, but the boat with the Russian had long since disappeared back up the Sumida, lost among a thousand other similar boats. The ambassador had made the arrangements for Toby's body to be taken to the morgue. Joe didn't ask the ambassador any searching questions about Toby Pryor, not even sure that he could trust Hageyama to tell him the truth. But he was now privately convinced from what had gone tonight that Pryor had been working in Japan as an agent for the US Government, in addition to his no-doubt real commercial role as a salesman for his father's company. That was the only plausible explanation for his strange behaviour and for all that inside information about Japan he seemed to possess. Joe remembered that Pryor had accused *him* of the very same thing, but now realised that had probably just been a clever diversion on Toby's part: to accuse someone else of doing exactly what *he* was really doing...

A preliminary examination had confirmed that Pryor had died from a stab wound to the chest that had ruptured one lung and caused massive internal bleeding...

Sawada had been told all this but still seemed suspicious of Joe's own part in last night's events. 'May I ask one thing? Are you by any chance an agent of the United States government, Mr Appeldoorn?'

Joe was taken by surprise by the question. 'You're the second person in two days to ask me that.'

Sawada looked interested by that. 'And who was the other?'

'Mr Pryor himself.'

Sawada exchanged a wry smile with one of his attendant officers, a look which Joe thought he understood. Sawada seemed to know already that Pryor had been an American agent, it seemed. 'You still didn't answer my question,' Sawada commented mildly.

'No, I am not. I'm just an ordinary American citizen, here trying to make a buck,' Joe declared wearily.

Sawada didn't seem convinced by the reply. 'Are you perhaps a patriot, though, who would do anything that your country asks you to do, Mr Appeldoorn?'

Joe shrugged. 'Not exactly...it would depend on what they wanted me to do.'

'Then, if you're not an agent, active or otherwise, of the American government, you seem to be having extremely bad luck. First an anarchist bomb, now this.' Sawada flexed his handsome jaw and ran a hand through his smooth hair.

'You could say that,' Joe agreed warily.

'What exactly were you doing in the *Yoshiwara*?' Sawada wanted to know. 'Or is that a stupid question?'

Joe gave him a withering look that said it was a very stupid question.

Sawada almost smiled at that response. 'Where did you go exactly?'

Joe sighed. 'To a bathhouse and *ryotei* called the House of the Red-Crowned Crane.'

Sawada looked at his aide again with another cynical smile, as if to say, *Is there no end to this man's evasive lies?*

Joe decided to take the initiative. 'Could the attack on Mr Pryor and myself last night have had anything to do with the bombing on Monday night? Could it have been organized by the same people?'

Sawada made a carefully considered reply. 'We have been continuing our investigations of that incident at the Imperial Hotel. We do believe it to be the work of one of the ultra-nationalist groups – most likely, the one I mentioned to you, the *Kokuryukai* - the "Black Dragon Society"...'

'So could they have a particular grudge against a couple of American businessmen?'

Sawada grimaced. 'They certainly have no love for America or its people. But an individual assault on a couple of ordinary American "businessmen" in the *Yoshiwara* is not really their style. So the chances are that there is no *direct* connection.'

Joe heard the subtle emphasis on the word "direct" and felt like pressing him about what "indirect" connections there might be, if any. 'So you think the attack on us last night was just a casual robbery gone wrong?' As he asked the question, Joe was already sure in his own mind that the real answer was No. He had tried his best to convince himself that he might have simply misheard or misunderstood Toby's dying words. But he knew he was only fooling himself. Toby had said that name, Johan Plesch, without a doubt. And his only reason for saying that name could have been as a warning. The way Toby had fought to stay alive for a moment longer to get that dreaded name past his lips – it was almost as if he thought that with his last breath he owed Joe that final warning...

If Toby had been an American agent, then it seemed likely that the American government thought the assassin was still alive somehow, and in Japan of all places. Perhaps Toby's mission had been to hunt him down...

Sawada smiled enigmatically. 'Yes. Perhaps it was just an opportunistic robbery after all. It's not impossible. But I can't say for certain yet.'

'Are you planning to go to the place where this happened and investigate in detail?' Joe asked doubtfully.

'Me personally? No, I don't think so. I doubt that I would have the time to investigate a straightforward street crime.' Sawada seemed highly amused by the idea that he would involve himself with such trivia. 'But I shall send a report to the local Asakusa police to visit the scene and make their own enquiries. However I'm sure that the body of the man that the Russian apparently killed will be long gone, as will the two surviving robbers...'

Joe looked Major Sawada straight in the eye. 'Do you think I'm in personal danger? Could somebody here in Japan want me dead?' He was tempted, just for a moment, to tell Sawada the name that Toby had whispered with his dying breath (a fact which he had deliberately omitted from his account so far.) But he knew that if he did, then he would also have to elaborate on his own personal history, and his direct involvement, with the supposedly dead assassin Johan Plesch. And Joe was not prepared to do that when he did not trust this man Sawada one iota, who seemed to be a rather sinister agent of Japanese state security rather than any normal trustworthy policeman. Joe could see no advantage in making this information known to such an individual until he had a much better idea of what was going on himself...

Sawada certainly didn't seem particularly interested in Joe's personal safety, that much was certain. 'It seems unlikely that you would be the target for any extremist groups, Mr Appeldoorn, *provided you are what you claim to be anyway...*'

Joe was getting annoyed now. 'I've told you already, Major Sawada. I am *not*, nor ever have been, an American agent!'

Sawada nodded soothingly. 'Then of course I take your word for it, and I can therefore think of no reason why your life should be under any particular threat in this country.' He paused thoughtfully. 'I would like to find this Russian saviour of yours, though.'

'Why? Not to reward him for his civic responsibility, I take it.'

Sawada grunted cynically. 'No, certainly not. From your description of the man, I believe he is an agent of the Tsar and, for the record, his real name is Gregor Nikolaivich Shelepin. If it was Shelepin who helped you, then he is here illegally and is almost certainly plotting some mischief against my country.'

Joe made a mental note of that name. 'I've told you everything I can remember about this Russian, and the boat crew who brought us downriver.'

'I'm sure you have. But if you remember anything else or, better still, if you see this man again -' Sawada passed over a *meishi* – a Japanese business card – of which Joe already had an impressive collection after scarcely three days here in Japan – 'please come to this building near the Imperial Palace and let me know. And also, should you wish to leave the city, please let me know where you are intending to go so I can contact you at short notice. Is that quite clear...?'

*

Motoko was waiting in the lobby for him as Joe came down the main staircase.

She bowed low and seemed genuinely upset. 'I hear sad news. Please accept humble condolence. I very sad to hear of Pryor-san's departure from world. My father still in Kyoto. What can I do to help?'

Joe shook his head and tried to smile. 'There's nothing more to be done, Miss Maeda. The ambassador has telegraphed Toby's father in New York to break the bad news.'

Motoko reflected on that. 'You look so tired, Mr App-re-doon.'

Joe ran a weary hand across his stubbly face. 'No, I'm all right. I just need some fresh air.'

'Then can we walk a little together, Mr App-re-doon?' she suggested eagerly.

It was clear to Joe there was something private she had to discuss with him. 'Of course. Just let me get my overcoat from my room. It still looks cold out.'

It was at this moment that the birdcage elevator descended from the second floor to the ground and Sawada and his entourage of uniformed aides and minions walked out into the lobby. Sawada bowed to both of them as he passed although Joe suspected the bow was aimed more at Motoko than himself.

Joe watched him leave the hotel with some unease. 'Do you know Major Sawada personally?' he asked her.

Motoko too was looking at the departing group with some discomfit written on her beautiful face. 'I acquainted with him. He has very high

90

connection in military. Better you stay away from Major Sawada, Mr App-re-doon.'

Joe smiled ruefully. 'I shall try, Miss Maeda. But it seems people in this city of yours keep trying to kill me, and every time they do, *he* turns up afterwards.'

*

Motoko and Joe walked eastwards into the Ginza district.

'It's a pity you see city only in winter,' Motoko observed. 'In springtime the city is adorable and the streets bloom with wild cherry, plum, willow. Frogs sing and fireflies dance in gardens.'

'And the summer? What's that like?' Joe wanted to know.

She fluttered her eyelashes again. 'Too hot and humid. And then the rains come, and the streets turn to mud and rushing streams.'

Joe hoped he wouldn't still be around in Tokyo by then to witness all this summer heat and rain, but nodded diplomatically.

They were walking down a narrow street of stalls near the rear of Shimbashi Station, where kite and balloon sellers in particular proliferated, their airy toys streaming behind them in the dry winter air. Even is his present dark mood, Joe was still interested in all the myriad mad things that were for sale in these market stalls. Sellers of poison offered a choice of potions to kill off the coming spring's fresh crop of rats – these particular salesmen had sharp rat-like features themselves as if imitating their intended prey. In the late morning sunshine, aged flute players with wastepaper basket-shaped hats over their heads made fey music, while toy peddlers paraded for sale flamboyant trays of painted butterflies, plaster kittens, gourds of emerald and violet, bunches of tiny bells, or puppet-sized priests that clapped their hands in prayer when a string was pulled.

Motoko played idly with the string on one of the more realistic puppets on a stall. 'Mr Pryor not marry, I believe.'

'No, I think not,' Joe confirmed, wondering why she seemed so visibly upset at Toby's murder, almost as if she thought she had some personal culpability for it.

Motoko's raven hair gleamed in the sunshine. 'No wife or children to grieve is better, but still very sad. Who do such terrible crime?'

Joe was still thinking of Toby's last words but he decided not to burden Motoko with such things. 'Probably it was only an ordinary robbery. I guess we must have flashed too much money about and attracted unwanted attention.'

Motoko put down the puppet and looked up at him, frowning into the bright sunlight. 'Where were you last night when this happened? In *Yoshiwara*?'

Joe nodded sheepishly.

She gave a knowing nod. 'I never been, although I curious to see it.

Man's place only.' She gave an enigmatic nod. 'Men are fortunate here in their freedom.'

They walked on a little further through the willow-lined streets of Ginza, then entered the rabbit warren of streets of Shintomiza. The way took them through more narrow back lanes with shops selling coloured sugar candies, and stalls protected by little wooden gods of longevity, their heads elongated with age. Child street-tumblers, wizened dirty little creatures apparently made of India-rubber, grinned and made wheels of themselves before the rich foreigner, trying to get some *rin* and *sen* coins, all shiningly imprinted with rising suns, chrysanthemums or coiled dragons, for their begging bowls.

'Do you like the way I dressed today, Mr App-re-doon?' Motoko asked in a brighter voice as they finally left the alleyway and came out into a broader avenue.

'Very pretty.' It was an understatement, to say the least; she looked adorable in a Western skirt of dark grey and a fur-trimmed satin coat of Royal blue. Her hat was blue too, perched on top of her mass of raven hair, and decorated with Hepatica flowers.

'I design myself,' she said proudly.

'Really?' Joe was no judge of women's wear but it looked professionally designed and made.

'*And* the yellow gown I wear at the embassy last night. I design also.'

'Then I'm impressed. You obviously have a talent for fashion design.'

'I still have much to learn about Western fashion. *Oto-san* – my father – allows me to order Western fashions for Mitsukoshi department store. Many Japanese woman like Western dress, and underwear. I want to study more so I can design good clothes suitable for Japanese figure. I want go to New York to study. Mr Pryor offer me help.'

I bet he did, thought Joe cynically.

'Mr Pryor say he speak to *Oto-san*. He suggest I go to New York college to study Western fashion; perhaps my father accept idea. Now Mr Pryor dead, I don't want to lose chance. Selfish, I know, after this terrible tragedy.' She turned those entrancing eyes on Joe again. 'Can *you* help, Mr App-re-doon? Per'aps you can talk to *Oto-san* about this, and to Pryor-san's father when you return America?'

Joe wasn't sure how to answer this so only nodded enigmatically. They took a shortcut through another side alley, where the light was dimmer, and the street was alive with sounds: the plaintive call of masseurs touting for business, the caterwauling of the medicine-men, the sly bird-catchers selling sparrows on a spit. Joe saw with disquiet, though, that they were entering a poorer area now where sleazier denizens of the back alleys predominated: rag pickers and beggars with mildewed straw sandals, who scuffed over the stones of these streets from dawn until midnight, their faces muffled with dirty cloth, their eyes bloodshot, sickened from probing refuse pails and cesspools.

Joe was glad when Motoko finally turned back towards the distant green tip of Atago Hill and the richer streets of Kojimachi.

'Your father says you may marry soon,' Joe said after a while, pointing out a potential difficulty in her plan to go to America.

'He want it. It is a shameful thing - at twenty-four not yet married. I old woman.'

Not from where I'm standing, Joe decided, looking at the radiance of her skin glowing in the winter sunlight.

'I will marry man *Oto-san* choose, but first I want go to New York. I want a career in fashion too. I modern woman. I want *Oto-san* to agree.'

'Then you must talk with him.' Joe suggested, not wanting to get involved in this delicate family matter.

'He already respect you, Mr Appeldoorn. If *you* suggest...'

'Err...I don't know. I'd have to think about it.' Joe could see himself being caught in a yawning trap here, trying to stay in the good books of both father and daughter.

Motoko smiled triumphantly, as if everything was agreed. 'If we friends, can I call you Joseph-san? Or Joe-san?'

'If you like.'

'Then it shall be Joe-san.' She laughed.

'Why are you laughing?'

'It so rude. Joe-san sounds like *Zo-san*, Japanese word for "elephant".'

Joe smiled. 'That's me. Mr Elephant Man.'

Motoko looked him up and down with unusual directness. 'You big enough for elephant, certainly...'

*

They were almost back at the Imperial Hotel now, but Motoko took a further diversion into Hibiya Park with its bare maples and gingko trees.

She hailed a noodle vendor, who was carrying two large wooden cabinets slung across his shoulders, and clanging a bell as he came. The man ran over, put down his cabinets, and placed a board across them to make an instant table. After Motoko had told him what she wanted, he scooped a dollop of noodles into a wire basket, dipped the lot into hot water, bounced and tossed them, slithered them into a bowl with a sliver of seaweed and a boiled onion top, and served her.

Motoko tucked into her noodles with enjoyment; obviously there was no social stigma attached here in Tokyo to a lady eating *al fresco* as there still was in America. 'I told you, I think,' she said demurely, 'that my father owns beautiful old house in Kamakura, Mr App-re-doon. My father and I appreciate greatly if you visit there tomorrow evening and stay the night...'

'Isn't your father still away?' Joe wondered aloud.

'Yes. But I want you to meet someone else. And I shall think of special way to thank you tomorrow.' Motoko smiled at Joe in a dangerous way that almost made him blush. 'You still deserve that....*special*...reward I promise...'

CHAPTER 8

Wednesday January 27th 1904

Randall was having trouble concentrating with Miss Peachy looking as provocative as this. She was wearing *trousers*, for God's sake – if you could call them that – actually they were more like tight cotton pyjamas - *and* she was smoking a black cheroot...

'Why are you dressed like that, may I ask?' he asked. 'In male attire?'

She shrugged enigmatically, obviously enjoying his acute embarrassment. 'I've just been exercising. This is Japanese peasant attire and very comfortable for gymnastic exercise. And this is my own home, Mr Randal. I wasn't expecting you, after all.'

They were in their usual rendezvous place – the small room above the bathhouse in the House of the Red-Crowned Crane. Randall had rushed out here unannounced after hearing the news of the murder of the American, Pryor. He was worried that his own unofficial actions might have caused this problem, and he was anxious therefore to cover his tracks as much as possible so that no possible blame for the man's death could accrue to him afterwards.

Randall saw that she did indeed seem to have been exercising violently - her clothes were damp with perspiration and her brow and cheeks were glowing pink with a shine like dew. 'Wouldn't you really like to change?' he asked her, giving her an opportunity to show some decorum for a change. 'I can wait.'

'No, it's not necessary.' She looked at him with brazen effrontery and blew a smoke ring with her lips. 'Say what you've come to say, Mr Randall.'

He decided to rise above her outrageous insolence. 'I came because I have important news, Miss Peachy. The American agent, Pryor – he of the vulgar speech and inadequate dental hygiene habits – was murdered last night. I don't know all the details but apparently he was stabbed to death by person or persons unknown.'

Randall could see Miss Peachy's expression falter for a moment and was pleased he'd managed to ruffle her normally implacable exterior, if only slightly.

She frowned, apparently deep in thought. 'Perhaps you didn't know, but Pryor was *here* last night.'

Randall blinked slowly. 'You mean in the *Yoshiwara*? I knew that much already.'

'No, not just that. I mean he was *here* - in the House of the Red-Crowned Crane. He took a bath here, ate some sweetmeats, drank saké.'

Randall detected some suspicion in her voice so decided to feign ignorance of what might have brought Pryor to this particular bathhouse. 'And then what?'

Miss Peachy was watching him carefully. 'I didn't see Pryor again afterwards. I believe he went to partake of the services of one of the courtesans in the House of Pleasure next door – Miss White Chrysanthemum, to my knowledge.'

Randall grunted contemptuously. 'Courtesan? That's a polite way of putting it. One of the painted whores, you mean.'

She stood up angrily, stubbing out the remains of her cheroot into an ashtray, and glared at him. 'I know for a fact that you personally enjoy the services of these "painted whores" yourself on occasion, Mr Randall, so please, in a spirit of lessening your general hypocrisy, do not dare disparage Mr Pryor's name for doing the same thing.'

Randall felt his cheeks burn bright red, and was about to make a tart rejoinder but was distracted by the sight of Miss Peachy as she paced angrily back and forward. In those tight cotton trousers – scarcely more than drawers really – she seemed practically naked.

This woman really was absolutely shameless...

But Randall now understood her motivation completely. She was clearly trying to seduce him – to ensnare him in her spider's web, as she had done with so many other men in the past, if all the reports were true. That was why she hadn't chosen to change her clothes after his arrival. She was deliberately exposing the shape of her breasts and those enticing little buttocks in order to entice him; there could be no other reason for this brazen show of flesh. Well, he would show her by maintaining the dignified reserve of an English gentleman...

Yet his resolve wasn't working perfectly. As she turned her back on him and he saw the curvaceous shape of her buttocks again, he suddenly realised with embarrassment that he was becoming physically aroused.

Feigning discomfort in his knees, he quickly shifted his sitting position on the *tatami* mat and tried to disguise his arousal as best he could.

'There was another American here last night with Pryor,' she observed, her back still turned angrily to him. 'What happened to him?'

'Ah, you mean Mr Joseph Appeldoorn, the supposed hero of the bomb incident at the Imperial Hotel on Monday night.'

Miss Peachy turned around to face him again. 'I do.'

Randall nodded. 'Yes, Appeldoorn could be an American agent too, although Pryor assured me that he isn't, merely a visiting businessman who could provide him with useful help in his mission. Appeldoorn was with Pryor when he was attacked last night, according to my information, but apparently escaped unhurt from the incident. From what I've been told, three robbers attacked them near the entrance to the *Yoshiwara.*'

Was that a slight look of relief on Miss Peachy's face? Randall wondered. *Intriguing...*

Was there a possible connection perhaps between Miss Peachy and this American Appeldoorn that he didn't know about? Randall decided to make some enquiries and discover what he could of any possible link between these two, unlikely though it seemed. But he could also test his theory straightaway perhaps by deliberately slandering the man...

'This Mr Appeldoorn certainly seems to lead a charmed existence, considering the events of last night, and the bomb thrown into the lobby of the Imperial on Monday night. Having met Appeldoorn that night, I found him to be a very obnoxious and arrogant individual – a typical Yank. Imagine this idiot! Picking up that bomb in such a panicked funk and charging outside with it like a complete oaf. I was there – he really had no idea what he was doing! He deserved to get his stupid neck blown off...'

Even Randall didn't believe this version of events entirely; he had certainly been frozen with fear himself when that sinister black object had careered across the floor of the Imperial lobby and threatened them all with sudden oblivion...

But Miss Peachy didn't rise to his carefully baited insults. Either she cared nothing for the man, or she was very good at hiding her feelings...

Instead she rounded on him with sudden viciousness. '*You* told Pryor about my secret identity here, didn't you? That's why he came here last night! He knew who I was, didn't he?' Her face had grown hard and accusing.

Randall was tempted to deny it but decided wisely to brazen it out instead. 'I had to tell him, in the interests of Anglo-American cooperation. He'd been sent to Japan specifically to find Plesch and eliminate him. Although he had only indirect evidence of it, he was convinced that Plesch is here in Japan and planning some major assassination. That's where my information about Plesch came from – the Americans. So I had to give them something in return.'

'You betrayed me in return for *prior* information, you mean?' Miss Peachy suggested dryly.

'Oh, very good, Miss Peachy. I enjoy a good pun as much as the next man, but that's not very funny in the circumstances.' Randall sniffed coldly. 'Pryor simply wanted your help to track Plesch down so I saw no harm in telling him of your rather theatrical guise here. I'm not sure *why* he wanted your help, though, since you have been singularly unsuccessful so far in your personal mission to find the traitor within our own camp.'

Miss Peachy was still pacing the room. 'Have you told anyone else that I'm here?' she demanded.

Randall hesitated. 'No, I don't believe so.'

Miss Peachy exploded with anger. 'You don't *believe* so! This is my life we're talking about, Mr Randall. Your careless release of privileged information about me might have got to anyone's ears, including Plesch, for all you know or apparently care. Who else has Pryor told, for example? Can you say?'

'He promised me your secret identity would stay with him alone,' Randall said stiffly

'But he's dead, Mr Randall,' Miss Peachy pointed out icily. 'So how on earth do I know whether my identity is secure any longer? You say Pryor was attacked by robbers? But that's quite unusual here in the *Yoshiwara...*'

'Unusual, perhaps. But certainly not impossible, if he was flashing money about rashly.'

Miss Peachy stopped in her tracks. 'Pryor was a clever man, Mr Randall. He did *nothing* rashly. That uncultured persona he adopted was deliberately designed to deter suspicion from his activities in my opinion. Whereas you seem to think he was really as crude and ill-mannered as he pretended.'

Randall was shocked, but tried not to show it. 'You think it could have been Plesch, or men employed by Plesch, who had Pryor killed then?'

Miss Peachy was sombre. 'Quite possibly...'

Randall shook his head doubtfully at that suggestion, preferring not to countenance the unpleasant possibility that Plesch might already be wise to the fact that he was being hunted here. 'Are you reaching any conclusions in your own mission?' he demanded with mock anger, trying to divert the discussion away from his own incompetence and double-dealing in the matter of the hunt for Plesch. 'Time is pressing. War between Russia and Japan may only be weeks away and we simply can't afford our embassy here to be compromised in any way. If any British diplomatic secrets were to reach the ears of the Russians which subsequently jeopardised our Japanese friends' plans, then, Miss Peachy, there would be all Hell to pay.' And it will be *your* neck rather than mine in the block, if that happens, he wanted to add...

Miss Peachy reflected for a long moment. 'I do have a possible candidate for our traitor.'

Randall blinked slowly. 'Who?'

'Cavendish, that's who...'

Randall was outraged by the suggestion. 'Young Cavendish! That's ridiculous. He's the son of an Earl.'

'He's also penniless and in debt. Yet he manages to gamble still. *And* he visits the "painted whores" of the *Yoshiwara* too...sometimes in your company, I believe.' Miss Peachy glared at him. 'Which is *your* favourite of these local young ladies, Mr Randall, may I be bold enough to inquire? Is it Sapphire Water, Miss Evening Moon, The White Chrysanthemum herself - or perhaps even Graceful Bamboo?'

Randall flushed again, but his anger had at least put paid to his physical arousal, which was fading fast in the face of the derision of this impossible woman. He got to his feet, ready to leave. 'Forget Cavendish,' he told her peremptorily. '*He* can't be our traitor. Find the real traitor before the balloon goes up, that's my advice...'

She nodded slowly, suddenly a model of docility again. As he reached the door, she said to him, 'Perhaps you should also be aware that the Russians have their best man here in Japan now.'

'Who? Not Shelepin?' Randall was aghast.

Miss Peachy gave him a wintry smile of farewell. 'Indeed so...'

*

Amelia watched from the window as Randall made his way down the dismal alley at the back of the House of the Red-Crowned Crane, and disappeared from sight.

How she hated that man! And how difficult it had been controlling her face when she heard the news that Pryor was dead by an assassin's hand. It had been such a relief to learn that Joseph had not suffered the same fate, yet she was still deeply worried for him, convinced now that he had been dragged unwittingly into the hunt for Plesch by his own duplicitous government. Even now, he might not realise the danger that he had been drawn into...

Could it really have been Plesch who sent those three robbers to murder Pryor? Or had they perhaps not been local robbers at all, but rather trained assassins or *ninja* merely pretending to be ordinary street ruffians? These ruthless mercenary killers still existed for hire in this city, if you knew the right people to contact. If Pryor had been getting uncomfortably close to Plesch, then Amelia knew her old adversary well enough to realise that he might have got wind of it and chosen to strike first. Plesch was never one to be taken by surprise – always thinking ahead, always making contingency plans. And especially so, if he had an imminent operation of his own to carry out and needed to lose the attentions of Western intelligence agents who were closing in on him...

Randall had clearly been worried to learn that Shelepin was now here in Tokyo masterminding the Russian Intelligence effort. And that was one

99

thing Amelia had to agree with Randall about. Apart from Plesch, Shelepin was the most formidable man Amelia had ever come across in her professional capacity.

She remembered the first time that she'd encountered him had been in an interrogation cell in the bowels of the Butyrka Prison in Moscow. The Butyrka was one of the favourite residences for dissidents and political prisoners opposed to the Tsar's regime, so naturally it was a heavily patronised establishment these days, with often a hundred or more inmates in a cell designed originally for no more than a dozen. It was a place where prisoners had to sleep sideways between their latrine buckets, and where interrogations almost always happened in the dead of night when the human spirit was at its lowest ebb...

*

The lead about Plesch had led Amelia eastwards from Berlin in the autumn of '02 to Cracow, then Kiev and finally Moscow.

The city of Moscow had been a revelation to Amelia – a different world – like stepping back fifty years into the past.

She arrived in Paveletsky Station on a wintry late November afternoon, the sky like beaten pewter and the River Moskva already full of twisted ice floes. Strangely for her, she was travelling under her own name for once - believing she was still unknown to the intelligence services here - and checked openly into a room at the Hotel Metropole. That had proved to be her first mistake...

At the border she had given her profession to the Russian guards as musician (which in fact was what her own passport showed – she had just enough skill with a violin and piano to convince a non-musician that this was her metier.) She'd flashed her eyes at the boyish guard who'd inspected her papers and assured him, in deliberately bad and girlish Russian, that she was *desperately* anxious to train at the Tchaikovsky Conservatory of Music. Despite the thinness of this cover story, her papers were quickly stamped and she was allowed to cross into Imperial Russia.

She spent her first full day in Moscow innocently, exploring this city of violent contrasts. The size of the place was the first thing that surprised Amelia. The original small settlement at the foot of Borovitsky Hill on the north bank of the Moskva River, where Ivan III had built the castle of the town, the Kremlin, had long since proliferated into a vast city of a million souls.

The other things that struck her were the unsettling contrasts within this city. Particularly striking was the deep contrast between the grandeur of the Renaissance, Classical and Russo-Byzantine architecture in the heart of the Russian capital, and the miserable suburbs ringing the centre - row upon row of small houses, grim apartments, untidy barracks, derelict hovels.

Amelia wandered the streets in the heart of the city, admiring the hulking Mausoleum in Red Square, the five-domed Cathedral of the Assumption, the monumental senate building, and Paskov Palace on its hill overlooking the Kremlin. All this sublime architecture gave her the impression of a city living on unrealisable dreams of grandeur, an island of wealth and privilege buried within an ocean of poverty and ignorance that was the real Mother Russia. The privileged areas of the city were easy to appreciate: the famous Mamontov's Art School, the prestigious music conservatories and ballet schools, the theatregoers in furs and silk stockings, and the rows of footmen in powdered wigs standing watchfully at the doors of vast mansions...

The Flower Market at the foot of the Kremlin was also a delight, yet only a few blocks away was the other Moscow, the Moscow of grimy streets, drab and grey with dim gaslights, peopled by Muscovites far removed from the rich industrialists and prettily dressed women Amelia had seen in the Hotel Metropole. Here, in the slums around the Khitrov Market, the populace – mostly ragged, hungry, and shivering - wore padded coats and felt boots, walked cracked pavements, and stepped over bulging unfilled holes in the muddy roads. These Russians did not enjoy the privileges of luncheon parties, racecourse meetings, or gala performances at theatres. Here in the real world were only wrinkled peasant women selling potatoes for a pittance, grey-bearded priests, beggars and pickpockets, old men barely alive playing gypsy songs for a few *kopeks*, uniformed doormen doffing caps.

Amelia returned that evening to the Metropole Hotel, deep in thought.

That night she waited as arranged in the main restaurant, a long high room with a maze of small tables and a blaze of light and colour. There were balconies at first floor level running on each side of the room with private rooms behind - "*Kabinets*" - where the dissolute youth of Moscow sang debauched gypsy songs and indulged themselves with loose women. The room was full of army officers in badly cut uniforms, Russian merchants with scented beards, German commercial travellers with sallow features, and painted blousy women.

Amelia felt exposed here by reason of her normality for once – as if she was the only one not in fancy dress at a masked ball. On a high balustraded dais at one end of the room, an orchestra in resplendent red coats played a selection of Viennese waltzes at frenzied speed. Amelia hoped she wouldn't have long to wait; already a dozen sets of predatory male eyes were sizing her up from various corners of the room. It was a relief when a man did finally approach her, clearly her contact from the British Embassy, and asked her if he could join her and buy her a drink. In Russian she said to him the agreed code, 'I prefer Scotch whisky to Russian vodka, if that's all the same.'

The man smiled unpleasantly at her and replied in heavily accented

English. 'I'm afraid you won't get much of either where you're going, Miss Peachy...'

*

The accommodation at the Butyrka was not what Amelia had been used to because she had never been caught and imprisoned like this before. Although she had often faced extreme danger over the last five years in her career as a government agent, her acting ability and her mastery of disguise had always allowed her to escape from danger and evade capture by her enemies.

But now she faced an entirely new experience. Now, for the first time, she was caught, trapped with forty other women in a cell barely ten metres by six. There were all classes of society represented here among the prisoners, from upper class ladies being punished for being married to dilettante gentlemen unwisely dabbling in politics, to murderesses and the dregs of womankind. Amelia was soon befriended by one middle-aged genteel-looking woman, Irina Reveskova, who had been in the Butyrka for six months already, held as a bargaining chip to persuade her liberal politician husband in Paris to lessen his activities against the Russian state.

Amelia had only been there twenty-four hours but she had already seen the way that prisoners were subjected to acute physical stress and near starvation. In particular she had noted the drastic changes in temperature in the cell during the day and night, something which had to be quite deliberate...

'They weaken our physique and our resolve that way,' Irina explained in Russian. 'First, they use the hot air system to fill the cell with ice cold air, then hot stinking air. Sometimes they block up all the ventilation until we nearly asphyxiate.' She looked at Amelia with huge solemn dirt-smudged eyes. 'It's much worse for the men, I've heard. Sometimes they turn up the heat so high in their cells that blood oozes between the pores of their skin. They cook them alive almost...' She turned to look at the single small barred window with a smear of wan grey light just penetrating the gloom of the cell. 'So what is an Englishwoman doing here? Are you a spy?'

Amelia shrugged, hiding her fear. 'No, of course not. It's just a mistake...'

*

On the third day she was finally interrogated – at three o'clock in the morning. She was dragged from her uncomfortable sleep on the straw next to Irina and frogmarched by guards to a room in a long stone corridor on the upper floor.

There were no windows in the room, but there was a table with hard wooden chairs that looked like the most comfortable things she'd ever seen in her life. Somehow she found the resolve to keep standing.

A uniformed man came into the room, wearing high leather boots and a pistol in his holster. She recognised him as the man who'd arrested her at the Metropole.

'My name is Captain Vladimir Obodovsky, Miss Peachy,' he announced in halting English. 'Of the Imperial Russian army – Intelligence Division.'

'How do you do,' Amelia said facetiously in English.

Obodovsky nudged a chair with his boot. 'Please take a seat. Can we talk in Russian? Irina informs me that you speak *very* good Russian, Miss Peachy, probably much better than my poor English.' He smiled knowingly. 'I can see you're disappointed with her but Irina has to do what she can to survive here. So please don't hold her human weakness against her. Can I get you a drink? Coffee? Tea?'

Amelia took the seat, but continued to speak in English. 'Coffee, please, and a cigarette too, if you have one. I trust from this meeting that you now realise you have made a grave mistake. That I'm just a visiting musician, no more.'

'I think not, Miss Peachy. On the contrary, you work for the British government, and you are here to spy on my country. Please don't deny it! You are a spy, Miss Peachy!'

'I am not here to spy on your country, Captain. You have no right to hold me here, Captain Obodovsky.'

'So what are doing here in Russia?' Obodovsky demanded.

Amelia smiled innocently. 'I came here to improve my technique with the violin. Russia has the greatest music teachers in the world, after all, and particularly at the Tchaikovsky Conservatory of Music...'

Obodovsky smacked his fist theatrically on the table. 'Liar! You will be shot as a spy, unless you tell me the truth!'

Amelia didn't even twitch but just looked at him pityingly. 'Then, are you saying that Russia does *not* have the greatest music teachers in the world...?'

Another man had entered the room, together with the guard bringing the coffee. This new arrival took a seat in the corner and sat watching with detached amusement as the guard placed the cup of coffee on the table and the rich tempting smell of delicious Russian coffee filled the room.

Amelia tried not to look at the man in the corner but it was as difficult to ignore his handsome face and dark curls as it was the tempting aroma of the coffee. This was a man far removed from the usual dour Russian male, Amelia could see. She wished that she looked and smelled a lot better than she did – it was mortifying to be paraded in front of a man like this in such a filthy and malodorous state.

The new arrival listened to Obodovsky's laboured and halting interrogation of her for five more minutes before finally curtly dismissing him from the room. Amelia had never been in any doubt who the real boss here was: this man carried the unmistakable stamp of genuine authority.

'My name is Major Gregor Nikolaivich Shelepin, Miss Peachy,' the man introduced himself in perfect English, taking the seat opposite her at the table after Obodovsky had reluctantly left the chamber. 'We already know a great deal about you. An impressive personal history, I must say. Circus performer with the legendary Luigi Belzoni in Italy. Music hall artiste and male impersonator. Accomplished actress on the London stage. Your family origins are a little vague, though. Your only living relative appears to be a lady called Georgina Pevensey of Cobham, Surrey – she is your aunt, I believe. And I see you have had several distinguished lovers, including the infamous British agent John Ballantyne.'

Amelia tried to remain impassive yet it was difficult to conceal her shock. How could this man know so much about her? It surely meant only one thing - there had to be a British agent working for the Russians...

Yet at least he hadn't mentioned the name Joseph Appeldoorn, so perhaps he wasn't aware of her most recent escapades...?

She took an ostentatious drink of the coffee. 'It seems you do know a great deal about me, Major Shelepin. If so, you should also know that I saved the life of your ruler, Tsar Nicholas earlier this year, and risked my own life to do it. Or do you not know that the Head of the House of Romanov almost died at Friedrichshafen in Germany last March in an elaborate assassination plot?'

Shelepin did seem interested in what she said, and clearly knew something of what had gone on there. 'Tell me exactly what happened in Friedrichshafen, then,' he said.

Amelia took another sip of coffee, the best thing she had ever tasted in her entire life. Finally she deigned to reply. 'The story begins in January this year. A man called Johan Plesch – a well-known professional assassin - was hired then to kill the King of England.'

Shelepin raised a curious eyebrow. 'By whom, may I ask?'

Amelia had nothing to lose now in telling the truth, so continued. 'By ex-President Paul Kruger of the Transvaal Republic, I believe. You see, I am being perfectly frank with you, Major.'

Shelepin grunted. 'You have no choice, Miss Peachy. But go on with your story anyway.'

'Plesch, for reasons that are unclear to me, decided to extend his brief to include Kaiser Wilhelm and the Tsar in his victims – perhaps only because they were meeting their English uncle at Friedrichshafen, and they all therefore made an opportune target. He may have also received an additional commission from one of the Tsar's political enemies, which seems more likely. Whatever the reason, Plesch and his confederates would have killed the Tsar along with everyone else there.'

Shelepin remained expressionless. 'And?'

'I prevented Plesch from succeeding in this insane plot,' Amelia said with quiet modesty. Although, if she was being fair, she could have added that she wouldn't have succeeded in foiling the plot but for the help of Joseph Appeldoorn that day.

Shelepin grunted cynically at her feisty response. 'I believe you, Miss Peachy, if that's any comfort to you. But I would advise you not to go around boasting of your actions in this country without knowing the loyalties of the people you are talking to. Some people here may not thank you for saving the Tsar's life,' he added dryly.

For a moment Amelia thought she might have made a huge mistake in boasting of saving the Tsar, until she saw a slight smile on Shelepin's face.

'So have you come here looking for a medal from the Russian empire, Miss Peachy? Is that it?' Shelepin asked in amusement.

'No, I came here to finish my job. Plesch escaped me in Germany in the end, but now I believe he is here in Russia. I have information that he is working for one of the dissident groups here, possibly with the aim of making another attempt on the Tsar's life.'

Shelepin pondered that. 'Will this man work for anyone then?' he asked contemptuously.

Amelia nodded. 'Oh yes. He is no great believer in ideology, or even in politics. He simply kills people for a price.'

Shelepin grimaced. 'Then, Miss Peachy, you had better tell me more...'

CHAPTER 9

Wednesday January 27th 1904

Amelia was just finishing her make-up as Aiko, preparing for the coming evening's entertainment in the House of the Red-Crowned Crane.

She disliked the very thick white face paint that she had used, but it seemed the extra level of disguise and anonymity it provided might be necessary tonight when there was a chance that Obodovsky or even Shelepin might turn up. She finished applying the red to her lips in a delicate bow.

'So, do I look the part, little dumpling?' she asked Sumiko, standing behind her.

Sumiko tidied up the back of her hair and pronounced herself satisfied with the result. 'Yes, a true Japanese, Ameria-san. Even I cannot believe your ability to transform yourself into a Japanese.'

Amelia studied her face in the mirror and saw Aiko-san brought back to life for one more evening. But it couldn't go on like this, she knew - in her heart she realised she wasn't safe here any longer now that Randall had given her secret away to God knows who. And while she herself could put up with an enhanced level of personal risk without worrying too much about it, there was a considerable chance she might also be bringing danger unwittingly to the girls of this establishment too. And *that* possibility she couldn't accept. In truth, after nearly six months living here, she did feel almost like a mother to these girls even though she was only seven or eight years their senior.

Amelia looked at Sumiko sadly. Their special time together was nearly over, she realised. She would soon have to leave this place for good and go back to the Western world that she sometimes loathed and often despised.

But she showed nothing of her emotions to Sumiko, as she stood up and put on her evening kimono.

She had already decided that she would give this place - lock, stock and barrel - to Sumiko when she left. Now the gift would have to be made a little sooner than she had expected, that was all. But it was still going to be hard to say goodbye to her perfect Akita *bijin*.

On reflection, it seemed to Amelia that she was always on the move for one reason or another. Sometimes the reasons were not convincing ones at all, and had more to do perhaps with her own irrational fear of staying in one place for too long. For once, though – in this completely alien place - she had felt tempted to stay for a little longer, but this time, ironically, circumstances were forcing her to move on before she was truly ready.

Yet did she really want to change that life of danger and constant challenge that she'd enjoyed over the last twelve years, for a more settled existence? The truth was Amelia Peachy thrived on change and tumult – it was what she needed to make her feel fully alive, and not simply breathing. A repetitive life in one place was simply not for her, and would, she knew, eventually drive her to distraction and make her melancholic and moody again.

A year ago in Russia, she had certainly come alive again during that mad dash across that vast unknowable country, as she had tried finally to catch and destroy her nemesis, Johan Plesch...

*

The train thundered through the Russian night, on its way eastwards. After three weeks working with Russian intelligence, the trail was taking Amelia and Shelepin a thousand miles east of Moscow to the Volga and a town called Kuibyshev.

The night was like a deathly shroud blanketing the earth, the cold intense. The rattle of the carriage on the tracks was a reassuring noise to Amelia when faced with the empty immensity beyond those darkened windows. The locomotive, snorting steam into the frozen night air, was a thin chain of yellow light in a wilderness of snow-covered hills and ghostly white birches.

Moscow had been a city of contrasts but out here, far from the capital, little of Imperial Russia remained. Only Peasant Russia - an unfathomable place in its size, its emptiness and its total brutish detachment from the rest of the world. From what Amelia had seen of it so far – the scattered villages of hovels, the frozen earth, the impoverished wretches trying to make a living from this unforgiving land - it could still have been the time of Peter the Great, so little appeared to have changed here.

This area of the country was a hotbed of revolution, though: a place where Marxists and anarchists - mostly outsiders according to Shelepin - were plotting the demise of Imperial Russia and trying to stir a reluctant bovine peasantry into action.

During the last three weeks Amelia had formed an uneasy relationship with Major Shelepin. He was charming, handsome and seemed entirely amoral; yet she was attracted to him, she couldn't deny.

Was it perhaps because they were so much alike in their essentials? Was that why she was so taken with this confident and worldly man?

He still didn't trust her entirely though, or perhaps not at all, and she certainly didn't have complete confidence in him in return. He hadn't allowed her, for example, to make contact with the British Embassy since she'd been apprehended and she realised worriedly that, as far as her government was concerned, she had simply disappeared somewhere within the vastnesses of the Russian state.

She remained a virtual prisoner in everything but name, not being allowed to go anywhere without an armed escort, but at least they had found her more pleasant accommodation than a cell in the Butyrka for the rest of her time in Moscow. Shelepin referred to her now as a "guest" of the state rather than a prisoner, but Amelia was by no means sure whether, after finding out everything she knew about Plesch and his possible contacts in Russia, he wouldn't simply toss her back into the Butyrka Prison on returning to Moscow.

Or perhaps he wouldn't even bother doing that. Amelia looked at the endless drift of birch and pine trees out there in the frozen darkness. In this country Shelepin had the power of life or death over her, and could simply rid himself of her annoying presence any time he wanted.

Yet she had begun to sense that her physical attraction towards him was now being returned, if only in the subtlest ways. In particular he had definitely become more solicitous of her physical comfort these last few days – or was she merely fooling herself?

The compartment was cold, despite the heating wheel being turned up to its maximum. Amelia lay shrouded in thick borrowed furs in one corner next to the window; Shelepin, dressed still in greatcoat and leather boots, sat in the opposite corner by the door to the corridor, where he was trying to read in the poor overhead light. Amelia recognised the book of course as Dostoyevsky's novel *Crime and Punishment*.

'Is that really appropriate reading for an Army Intelligence officer, Major?' she mocked him gently.

He looked back at her with an amused expression, but wasn't apparently in a mood to give an answer to her deliberately provocative remark.

'Are you married, Major?' she persisted, needing a diversion of some sort from the boredom of this endless journey.

He gave up his book with a sigh for the present, recognising that she wanted to talk and wouldn't give him any peace until he did. 'No, I have never found either the time or the urge to devote myself to a single woman as yet. And you – are you married?'

'I thought you knew everything about me,' she responded tartly.

'I doubt if it's philosophically possible for one human being to know *everything* about another. Not even for a man and wife.' Shelepin smiled. 'Certainly, the facts I've heard about your life mentioned no husband, but you may have slipped one in somewhere without people noticing.'

She was amused by that. '*Slipped* one in? No, I have never been married, Major. The closest I ever came to that blissful state was with Signor Belzoni, whom you do seem to know all about.'

Shelepin offered her a cigarette, but she declined with a rueful shake of her head, having tasted enough Russian tobacco by now. Shelepin put a cigarette to his own lips, though, and lit up using his exquisite gold lighter. 'I know Belzoni by reputation; he was certainly a wonderful trapeze artiste and a legendary high wire performer.'

Amelia felt a pricking of moisture in her eyes at this unexpected praise for her old lover Luigi. 'He was a wonderful performer. He taught me much, not only about performing, but about life itself.'

'I even saw him perform once, you know,' Shelepin announced unexpectedly. 'In Florence, I think, about fifteen years ago. Before you joined him, I presume.'

'Fifteen years ago...yes, I was only twelve at that time,' she pointed out dryly. Surviving in a dreadful girl's boarding school for most of the year, and then being forced to live through school vacations at her maiden aunt's home in Cobham. Perhaps those experiences explained so much of her character and the woman she had grown into...

Shelepin was still remembering the remarkable things he had seen Belzoni do in Florence. 'Yes, Belzoni walked across a single wire stretched between two of Florence's landmark buildings, sixty metres in the air. It was extraordinary to watch such presence, and such complete fearlessness.'

Amelia shook her head. 'He was *always* afraid, he told me, but he had simply mastered the art of rising above those fears.'

Shelepin nodded. 'I suppose that is what all brave men do. He did have amazing grace and skill, though, to complement that bravery. Later, before two hundred thousand spectators in a park in Florence, he performed the triple loop from one trapeze to another, the only man to achieve that feat so far, I believe.'

'The only *man* possibly. But I did master that trick too, eventually,' Amelia said with quiet assurance.

'Really?' She could see Shelepin was impressed by that. 'And were you there the night he died? In Vienna, wasn't it?'

Amelia was solemn. 'I was there with him, of course. But I had injured my wrist a few days before so I couldn't go up with him that night. I had to be content with watching from below.'

'He was trying to perform a *quadruple* loop that night, wasn't he? Something that no one has been able to achieve so far.'

'Yes, he was trying to perform a quadruple. For Luigi, life was all about a continual search for excellence, you see, and a need to push himself to his limit...'

Shelepin came over and sat opposite her. 'And are you the same, Miss Peachy? When you have reached your own personal limit, achieved all the goals you have set yourself in life, what then? Will you too choose to plunge from the high wire rather than face sad mediocrity and the inevitable disappointments of old age?'

She didn't answer that question, though, but instead turned her gaze back to the window, seeing her reflection against the endless melancholy forest and hearing the lonely howl of the wind in the trees...

*

They stayed in a remote if comfortable *dacha*, a rustic country villa, which Shelepin had somehow commandeered for the use of himself and his men. It reminded Amelia a little of a Swiss chalet, but with all the prettiness and comfort removed, and only the functionality remaining, a house of birch plank walls and moss-covered roof surrounded by a wilderness of birches and snowy hills.

Yet it was warm inside at least, with a log fire roaring in the main living room, and thick quilts on the hard wooden beds, and the windows boarded up against the shrieking wind.

The information that Amelia had acquired from informers in Cracow and Kiev now stood her in good stead as she was the only person in the party who had privy information of a planned rendezvous between Plesch and his new clients. Amelia had been wise enough to keep this information to herself as long as possible, but finally she had to reveal her secret hand to Shelepin and hope for the best

Armed with this information, Shelepin had soon set a trap around the village ten kilometres from Kuibyshev where Plesch was allegedly due to attend a clandestine meeting. Plesch was coming apparently to meet a group of local dissidents to agree the timing of his mission. The target had to be the Tsar, of course, Amelia thought, and possibly his wife and family too – Plesch did not do things by halves. After all, he had already killed a President and the King of Italy, and almost succeeded in shooting the King of England, so what did another Tsar and his family matter?

The only problem with Amelia's information was the timing – she didn't know precisely when the meeting was to be held, only its location. So patience was called for, while a team of Shelepin's men kept close watch on the village and the main meeting hall, the most likely venue.

Amelia thought she would look very stupid indeed if it turned out that the meeting had already taken place, and their first news of its outcome was hearing about the subsequent murder of the Tsar. If that happened, Shelepin might well prefer to drop her body into a frozen lake somewhere and pretend that he'd had no prior inkling of such a heinous plot. Amelia didn't know if Shelepin was ruthless enough for such a plan, but, knowing the amoral nature of the spying profession, she preferred not having to put the matter to the test.

January dragged into February, and the earth was gripped with such an intensity of cold that Amelia had never known or even imagined before - the mercury even froze solid in the barometer on the outside wall of the *dacha*. She became bored and bad-tempered in this little frozen kingdom in which she found herself trapped like an unlikely princess in a nightmare fairy tale. Shelepin behaved unfortunately like a perfect gentleman throughout this grim winter, as did his men, and a peevish Amelia became even more cross at being incarcerated with these dull and stolid individuals. In her lonely bed at night, she did begin to entertain some hopes that Shelepin at least would find the resolve to knock on her door one night and offer her some physical consolation of a sort, but he never did.

One late afternoon in February the call finally came through to break the deadening monotony of her existence. Furtive visitors had been spotted descending discreetly on the village, and a suspected clandestine meeting was apparently being convened soon in the village hall. It seemed that this night might finally be the moment when Amelia could finally deal with Johan Plesch...

Shelepin accompanied Amelia on the five-kilometre journey from the *dacha*. They travelled by *troika* – the only feasible way on the narrow rutted ice-covered tracks through the forest. The driver was one of Shelepin's own men and the horse was a fine black Arab stallion. Wrapped in rugs to try and stave off the numbing cold, it was a journey she would long remember because of the landscape on the way: the monstrous spectral trees festooned in ice, the drifting of snow, the stinging of a million pellicles of ices, the banshee wind howling, the stars mere frozen pinpricks of light in a sky like velvet. She was dressed in furs, trousers, boots and cap, yet still the cold seeped into her very bones. They crossed a frozen lake, an arctic nightmare of ice, the surface groaning and creaking against buried rocks.

Yet she felt outrageously happy to be finally doing something after all the weeks of inactivity. And she couldn't deny that part of the enjoyment was having this man Shelepin at her side in this wild venture. He too clearly came to life when there was a chase on, assertive and confident again now that he could sense imminent success.

They left the *troika* finally under a weeping spruce and joined Shelepin's men as they formed a cordon around the village. Amelia watched from a distance with Shelepin as what looked like a group of village and country elders trooped into the small assembly hall, fiery torches lighting the entrance.

From the shelter of branches weighted down with snow, they watched the village hall, waiting for someone to leave. Shelepin ordered his men to move in further and tighten the ring of steel around the village, while he and Amelia waited for the signal to act.

Amelia tested the weight of her trusty Browning pistol in her hand, which Shelepin had finally returned to her in a rare moment of generosity. She was just feeling the touch of the metal, cold even through her gloves, when out of the corner of her eye she saw a coal-black *troika* making a dash from the other end of the village.

She realised the truth at once, and pulled at his shoulder in alarm. 'I think the village hall meeting is a decoy, Gregor Nikolaivich; Plesch has been meeting somewhere else in the village all the time.'

Shelepin cursed viciously but didn't argue with her judgement. He leapt into the front seat of the *troika* and took the reins himself. Amelia had only enough time to scramble into the back seat before he whipped the Arab stallion into a frenzied gallop.

Plesch – if it was Plesch – had a considerable start on them, and seemed to know exactly where he was going. Amelia knew the general geography of the area a little better now and guessed that Plesch was making for the town of Kuibyshev. And the most obvious reason for that destination was that it was a major stop on the Trans-Siberian Railway. If he managed to get there and onto a train, they had no way of catching up with him.

It was a strange and silent pursuit across the wintry wasteland with its pale birches and frozen shapes ghostly in the starlight – only the creak of the leather harness, the hiss of the runners on the ice, and the panting of the horse as he strained to catch his quarry.

They *were* gaining, though, their Arab stallion a significant cut above the shaggy Cossack horse he was chasing. Amelia could see the driver of the *troika* ahead but the light was too dim for her to know if it was really Plesch at the reins or not. Yet her instincts told her that it was, and she felt a rush of blood to her frozen face at the thought she might finally be about to settle her score with this devil.

By now they had reached the same ice-bound lake that they'd crossed on their outward journey to the village. On the far side of the lake, the road ahead would soon diverge, the left branch to Kuibyshev, the right to their temporary *dacha* home.

Plesch was urging his horse across the ice, the steel skis flying over the surface. The gap had opened up a little as the local horse proved better on ice than the Arab thoroughbred. Amelia saw with dismay that Plesch had already made it across the three hundred metres of ice and was now back on the track again on the west bank.

Shelepin was urging his horse on yet again when there was a gigantic explosion ahead of them, and a huge gaping rift appeared in the ice. There wasn't time to stop the terrified horse, but Shelepin, with consummate skill, managed to slew the direction of the *troika* to the left of the hole. But it threw the *troika* over on its side and Amelia was flung out and across the frozen surface, plunging into the hole in the ice and the inky black water...

*

The shock of the ice-water almost stopped her heart dead. She could feel the water enshrouding her in its deathly embrace and knew she was as good as dead. She couldn't move her limbs even to struggle, and she was about to be dragged down permanently into the frigid depths by the weight of her leaden clothes when she felt herself being suddenly lifted up from the water by magically strong arms.

She was a stiff as a corpse already but still vaguely aware of what was going on as she was carried across the ice by that same pair of muscular arms. Somehow Shelepin managed also to right the *troika,* and before Amelia was hardly aware of it, he had dropped her into the back seat again and set off at a renewed furious gallop.

But not in pursuit of Plesch any more; instead in a race to get her back to the *dacha* before she froze to death.

Amelia could feel the life ebbing out of her body, her eyes growing dim, her hearing fading...

Suddenly she felt a roaring inside her head, though, as if her hair was on fire. A voice penetrated through the fog of her brain. She felt a blow across her face that brought a feeling of thousands of hot needles penetrating her flesh. She gasped with the frightening pain...

Then she realised she was lying in front of the roaring, smoking, wonderful fire in the dacha, and she saw Shelepin, as if through a red haze, pummelling her body and striking her face to restore her circulation.

Gradually she returned to life, a little at a time. Her muscles were aching, her eyes sore and streaming, her mind in a daze. Only after thirty minutes or so of this severe treatment did she realise that she was entirely naked on the rug in front of the fire.

It would have seemed ungracious to complain about this treatment, though, she thought...

When she had recovered some semblance of normal feeling in her limbs again, he wrapped her in homespun blankets and brought her a glass of whisky. He smiled grimly at her. 'I take it, Miss Peachy, that you still prefer Scotch whisky to Russian vodka...'

The spirit stung her throat but left a warm glow spreading through her innards to match that on the outside.

Her voice was hoarse. 'Why did you save me, Gregor Nikolaivich ? You could have left me and caught Plesch. If he has reached Kuibyshev and got on a train going east, then you'll never catch him now.'

Shelepin looked at her in the firelight, smiling faintly. 'I weighed up the alternatives and decided in favour of you, Miss Peachy.'

113

She was genuinely puzzled. 'Why?'

He smiled, more warmly this time. 'Perhaps because it would have been recklessly profligate of me to let a woman die who can do a triple loop on the trapeze. Such gifted people are rare and not to be squandered.'

'Thank you,' she said with mock solemnity. She tried to raise her head, but her eyes were drooping with reaction and fatigue. 'I think I feel well enough now to retire to bed, if it's all the same, Gregor Nikolaivich.'

He picked her up at once, even though she tried to protest weakly. 'I believe I am well enough to walk unaided now, Major Shelepin.'

'Nevertheless I insist...'

He carried her up to her room on the first floor, which was snug and warm with a log fire still blazing in the hearth despite the late hour. He laid her down on the bed, and pulled the thick quilt over her. 'Good night, Miss Peachy,' he said. 'I'm glad I could save you. And don't be too disappointed. We'll have another chance to settle with Herr Plesch in due course, no doubt.'

He turned to go but her hand snaked out from under the quilt with surprising speed, and held his arm in a strong grip. 'Don't go, Gregor Nikolaivich,' she whispered. 'I'm still cold...'

*

A week later, her lover saw her off at Kuibyshev Station. The rime-covered trees crowding the back of the platforms were sculpted with ribbons of ice, and the rails rang like iron on the frozen earth at the approach of a heavy locomotive. 'Will you not get into severe trouble with your superiors for letting a British agent just walk free?' she asked him uncertainly.

'Not with these local officials, I won't,' Shelepin assured her. 'They wouldn't dare cross me.'

She smiled at his bravado and wondered to herself why she was leaving him at all when she had so many compelling reasons to stay. Was it that old fear of standing still while the world moved on relentlessly past her? Was she afraid of finding herself putting down roots even here, in the impoverished soil of this Godforsaken country?

Shelepin had not made any attempt to persuade her to stay, as if knowing such a gesture would be a waste of time with such a free spirit as Amelia Peachy. But he did have a question. 'Why are you going east to Vladivostok, Amelia?' he asked her as they stood shivering together, watching the powerful locomotive finally approaching the platform out of the early morning mist.

Amelia wondered that herself. 'Because I'm sure that's where Plesch has gone. And I was supposed to report to the British Embassy in Japan when I finished here in Russia anyway.'

Shelepin ran his gloved finger delicately down the bridge of her nose. 'I hope, *dushinka*, that if we do ever meet again, then at least we won't be enemies.'

Despite the cold, Amelia leaned forward and kissed him firmly on the lips. 'I hope so too, Gregor Nikolaivich...'

*

Amelia's journey had led her from Kuibyshev to Vladivostock, but there, despite all her best efforts, she finally lost Plesch's trail. So then, reluctantly, she had no other choice but to take the branch line across Manchuria to the Liaotung Peninsula and the bleak harbour of Port Arthur, from where in March 1903 she finally took a sea passage across the Yellow Sea and around the southern tip of Korea to the Japanese port of Nagasaki...

CHAPTER 10

Joe Appeldoorn realised with dismay that it was already growing dark and so far he hadn't even been able to find his way back to the scene of Toby's murder.

Some detective he was now...

In the face of the complete lack of interest of the cynical Major Sawada, or apparently even of the local Asakusa police, in investigating Toby Pryor's murder seriously, Joe had decided to take some drastic measures of his own. After all, he told himself, he *had* been a detective with the Pinkerton Agency for the best part of three years and had learned a lot in that time, both about investigating crimes, and about how to defend himself.

So, as soon as Motoko had left him after their lunchtime walk together, he'd gone back to the Imperial in early afternoon and armed himself with his reliable Webley-Fosbery revolver. It was a weapon he'd learned to trust over several years, thirty-eight calibre, eight-shot – he had bought this particular gun to replace the similar one he'd lost above the Rhine Falls in Switzerland two years ago.

Sawada's apparent indifference to last night's events had disturbed Joe deeply and made him wonder what deep and murky waters he was getting himself into in this bewildering country; it seemed that Sawada was actually far more interested in apprehending his Russian rescuer than in catching the actual perpetrators of the crime. Logic told Joe that, since he clearly couldn't trust the police or the security forces here, he should be sensible and keep a low profile for the present – particularly if it were true that Johan Plesch was still alive, and possibly in Japan stalking him. Joe could still think of no other plausible reason why Toby, with his dying breath, should have tried so desperately to get that dreaded name past his lips. But at the same time, part of Joe's subconscious was still in denial over the possibility, refusing to believe it when he was sure that he had seen that evil assassin fall to his death two years ago at the Rhine Falls in Switzerland.

For any normal visitor to a foreign country, such a threat to their safety, no matter how implausible, would no doubt have sent them scurrying back to the permanent protection of their hotel. But Joe Appeldoorn was not built for giving in to fear and, regardless of the danger or the complete stupidity of what he was doing, had gone down to the quayside of *Tsukiji* in mid-afternoon and hired a boat to take him back up the Sumida to the *Yoshiwara*...

He'd convinced himself that he would achieve two things by stepping back into the lion's den. One was to disprove Sawada's complacent belief that nothing at all could be learned from the scene of the crime. Joe himself doubted that the body of the robber who'd been shot would still be there after more than twelve hours - even if the Russian had actually killed him - but that still didn't mean that valuable clues might not have been left behind.

And the second point of visiting the scene of the crime was his intention to be deliberately provocative. Still in two minds about the possibility that Plesch could really still be alive, and that he could have been behind last night's attack in the *Yoshiwara*, Joe wanted to try and provoke some response to test that possibility - almost hoping that, if Plesch really were here in Japan, then this blatantly reckless gesture might smoke him out into the open immediately. If that happened, then perhaps even Sawada would be forced to take some positive action.

But Joe had found that the hope of achieving either of his objectives was proving entirely farcical, since he had been unable so far to even find the right alleyway again in the maze of the *Yoshiwara*. And now it was growing dark – the boat journey here having taken much longer than he'd expected – so that even if he found the right place, the light would be too poor by now to make anything useful of the scene of the crime.

Joe had no better idea now than to make for the House of the Red-Crowned Crane instead, which at least was the one place in the *Yoshiwara* he was reasonably confident he could still find in the rapidly descending wintry dusk. It also struck him that Aiko-san, the enigmatic white-faced proprietor of that bathhouse, might be privy to any rumours among the residents of the Yoshiwara concerning the identity of the men who had carried out the attack on him and Toby.

Realising with frustration that he had taken yet another wrong turning, though, in trying to get to the House of the Red-Crowned Crane, Joe stopped suddenly in his tracks and retraced his steps back to the broader street he had just left. It was then, though, that he realised he was being watched as he saw a head suddenly pull back out of sight behind the corner of a darkened teahouse at the next alleyway.

Joe made no sign that he knew he was being observed but felt for the reassuring handgrip of the Webley in the holster under his tweed overcoat, ready to use it at a moment's notice. Then he sauntered casually towards the spot where the man was hiding. The man's head reappeared for a moment and Joe saw at once with a shrug of disbelief that it was not a local as he'd expected. Instead it was that damned man Maienfeld yet again...

Suddenly Joe remembered that he had last seen that man only a few minutes before he and Toby were attacked last night, which sent a flood of fresh suspicion through his mind. His suspicions about the man deepened even further when he remembered that Toby himself had declared the man to be a spy of some sort. At the time, Joe had thought Toby must be simply joking, but that joke seemed to be wearing thin now...

Suddenly furious, he ran forward to the side alley where Maienfeld was concealed, only to see that the man had already fled somewhere into the dark.

Joe could hear his footsteps ahead of him, though, and he followed him down the twisting side alleyway at a run, startling the doormen, beggars and courtesans who watched this strange barbarian careering past the inviting curtained entrances of their modest places of business, as if the devil himself was on his tail.

After five minutes of running Joe realised dismally that he had not only lost Maienfeld, but he was also completely lost again in the seediest area of the *Yoshiwara*.

With a sigh, Joe gave up with his futile pursuit and leaned tiredly against a large decorative plinth of granite, some four feet high, placed as a feature outside the dimly lit entrance of a *ryotei* restaurant. From inside the restaurant he could hear the chink of glasses, the babble of drunken Japanese conversation, and the peal of a woman's laughter as she probably indulged herself in some *geisha* party game. Joe felt badly in need of a drink and a childish game, himself, as he wondered what to do next. He heard something that distracted him, though, from his gloomy thoughts – the tip-tapping of a blind man's cane on the cobbles behind him. Joe turned his head to see a blind shaven-headed monk in a grey robe feeling his way along the dimly-lit lane toward him.

Joe watched the man's slightly irregular crab-like approach, as he felt with his stick for the projections of posts and porch entrances and *engawas*. But it was only when the man ducked slightly to avoid a red lantern that Joe noticed something familiar about the man...

Joe was sure he had seen this same monk before, yet struggled to think where, until the truth suddenly hit him...

It had been at the bombing at the Imperial Hotel two nights ago...

This was the same blind monk who he'd seen standing outside the hotel as he ran frantically through the entrance with the ticking bomb in his hands.

The man had *stared* at him...

Why on earth would a blind man *stare*? Joe wondered suddenly in alarm. And why, for that matter, would a blind man duck to avoid a red lantern...?

Joe had only a moment to fling himself behind the granite plinth before a fusillade of gun shots thudded into it, sending rock fragments and stone chips flying in all directions. Joe had his own revolver in his hand in a second, and looked cautiously from behind the shelter of the granite mound for the murderous monk. But like Maienfeld, the monk was gone, apparently melted into thin air.

Cautiously Joe eased himself to his feet and poked his head out from behind the granite plinth, wondering about the monk's strange disappearing act. Perhaps he'd simply fled after he'd used all his ammunition. Joe tried to remember how many shots the man had fired – at least five or six times. Joe finally stepped out from behind the granite plinth, only to hear something whistling through the air before his vision exploded...

*

Joe recovered his senses slowly to find that he was stretched out on the cobbled ground in front of the same restaurant, his head throbbing mercilessly. The other thing he realised instantly was that a man was leaning over him and going through his pockets...

Joe found he still had the Webley in his hand, and in a flash had it cocked against the man's temple.

'Be very careful!' Joe ordered gruffly. 'I've had a hell of a day so I am in a mind to use this.' It was only as he spoke that he realised that this man was certainly no shaven-headed monk but a young European with a rich head of wavy red hair above a weak-chinned insipid face. Although that still didn't mean he couldn't be the man who had just scythed him down from behind with what felt like a baseball bat...

Even with his head throbbing and his vision fuzzy, Joe realised that he'd seen this man somewhere before too...

This man had also been in the lobby of the Imperial Hotel on the Monday night, the evening of the attempted bombing. It seemed as if half the people who had congregated in the lobby of the Imperial that night were meeting again in the Pleasure Quarter tonight. This particular guy was the Englishman mentioned by Toby with the ridiculous name. What was it again? Peregrine something or other. That was it...the Honourable Peregrine Cavendish.

The man had a ridiculous accent to match his silly looks. 'I thay! I'm awfully thorry,' he stammered.

'You were going through my pockets,' Joe said balefully, jamming the barrel even harder against his head.

'I thaw thomeone hit you. He was going to thlit your throat but he ran orf when he thaw me coming. I was just trying to help. I was looking for your wallet, to find out your name, old chap.'

Joe didn't believe a word of that story. 'Who was it who hit me, then? What did he look like?'

Cavendish blinked in fear. 'It looked like one of those monk chappies. Shaved head, don't you know.'

'Was he blind?' Joe demanded.

'Thertainly didn't look it.' Cavendish suddenly peered at Joe's face. 'I thay, you're the chappie who ran out of the Impewial on Monday night with the bomb in his hands aren't you? The American chappie with the funny name? Apple thomething or other?'

'I've got a funny name!' Joe would have laughed out loud but for the excruciating pain in his head. Reluctantly he lowered his Webley and put the safety catch on again.

Cavendish helped Joe to his feet. 'You're hurt, old chap,' he said solicitously.

Joe felt his head gingerly, which was bleeding profusely from a cut somewhere on his scalp.

'I'll take you thomewhere thafe,' the man offered hopefully.

'I don't think so!' Joe said sharply, feeling his hackles rising again.

'Perhaps you should tell me where *you* want to go then, and I'll twy and help you get there,' Cavendish said reasonably.

'Do you know a bathhouse called the House of the Red-Crowned Crane?' Joe could think of nowhere else to go.

'My thecond home, old boy,' the Englishman announced breezily.

*

Aiko-san was proving unexpectedly proficient at dressing head wounds.

She had shaved away a little of his hair on the right temple and cleaned the cut with alcohol. Then she applied some gooey Japanese medication that seemed surprisingly effective in stopping the bleeding.

She showed him her handiwork in a hand mirror. 'I think all right now,' she said, pronouncing herself satisfied.

'Better than all right.' He smiled at her but she didn't reciprocate, still the same implacable white mask. 'As good as new.' Apart from the steam hammer reverberating inside his head, of course.

Aiko tilted her head. 'Who do this?'

A good question, thought Joe. Well, he certainly had succeeded in provoking a response by blundering back into the *Yoshiwara* tonight so perhaps he shouldn't complain too much. 'I don't know,' he responded with a wry shrug.

Aiko frowned slightly under the heavy make-up. 'You go to police?'

'Oh, I tried that already. It would be no use going there again for help,' Joe said resignedly. If this was Plesch who was orchestrating these attacks against him, then Joe knew that it was quite pointless hoping the local police would protect him.

Joe thought back to the two men he'd seen tonight: Maienfeld and the supposedly blind monk. Joe was almost sure that Maienfeld could not be Plesch – he was simply the wrong height and body shape to be Plesch. But that didn't mean he couldn't be an accomplice of Plesch, of course. And then there was the gun-toting "blind" monk – could that have been Plesch himself, back from the grave? That seemed even more unlikely, but Plesch had been a past master of disguise, and had proved himself before to be a difficult man to kill...

'Is other man a friend?' Aiko asked expressionlessly, indicating the doorway leading to the rear of the establishment. Cavendish had left Joe to have his head wound tended to by Aiko in a tatami mat room next to the restaurant, while he had gone off to the bathhouse at the rear with the other girl, Sumiko.

'No, I only just met him,' Joe said, 'and I think he's a total dumbbell, to be honest.'

She was seated on the floor in characteristic Japanese keeling fashion while he was perched uncomfortably on a raised cushion that she had provided for him at a low, black-lacquered table. She tilted her head again in characteristic Japanese fashion. 'What is "dumbbell"?'

Joe grunted cynically. 'A fool.'

She nodded knowingly. '*Ah so desu.*'

'If he's not a fool, then he's the best actor I've ever met, anyway,' Joe ventured further.

'I hear gun shooting before,' she said carefully, after a long pause. 'Was it to do with you?'

'Yes. Somebody doesn't like me apparently.' He stopped to look at her delicately shaped face and features. In this brighter light of the tatami room her eyes had looked almost blue, just for a moment. Surely that was impossible, though: no Japanese had blue eyes, did they? And yet there was something strangely familiar about her face that he hadn't noticed the first time he met her – something in the shape of the nose and her slender jaw line that triggered a memory in his sub-conscious...

She sensed his close examination and turned her head away slightly. 'I hear shot *last* night too.'

Joe smiled ruefully. 'Guilty again, I'm afraid. Although I didn't fire that one either, and, unlike tonight, it wasn't even aimed at me.'

Aiko looked puzzled. 'Oh...'

Joe raised a difficult subject. 'Did you hear the sad news that the man who was here last night with me – Pryor-san - is dead?'

Aiko nodded. 'I hear. Yes, so sad.'

Joe wondered who had told her, but he supposed this place did have a powerful bush telegraph as he'd suspected.

'Yes, three men tried to rob us,' Joe went on, 'and they killed Pryor-san. But I was fortunate enough to be saved by a young Russian – a man who called himself Raskolnikov. Tall and young, with dark curly hair. Have you ever seen a man like that here?'

Aiko blinked slowly. 'Russians come here sometime to bathhouse. But, regretfully, all fat and old.'

Joe smiled at the way she said that, already becoming thoroughly enchanted with this woman again, despite the fragile way he was feeling.

'How about a Swiss man called Maienfeld? Does he ever come here?'

'So sorry. No Swiss men come here,' she declared flatly, then relaxed a little. '*Biru o motte kimashoo-ka?* Shall I bring you glass Fuji beer, App-re-doon-san? Or *Scotchu whiskii*? Make feel better.'

He wasn't quite done with his questions yet, though. 'Do you happen to know a monk who stays in this area? With a shaven head, wearing grey?'

'All monk like that,' she said complacently.

'This one is blind – or pretends to be, anyway. He was the man who tried to shoot me tonight.'

'Then not very good Buddhist, this monk,' Aiko decided with a slight giggle.

'I suppose not.' He looked at her closely again. 'And I think I will have that beer...'

*

'Tell me about your life, App-re-doon-san. *Doko de umaremashita-ka?*' She excused herself. 'Oh, *gomen nasai*, where born?'

'Me? In Philadelphia. That's a city in the United States, in the state of Pennsylvania.'

Aiko smiled faintly. 'I know. And parents?'

'Both dead, I'm afraid.'

She inclined her head gracefully. 'So sorry.'

'My mother died when I was small. But my father died only four years ago. Heart attack.' Joe remembered with some bitterness how his father had been driven into an early grave by the pressures of endless work and his long court battles with his unscrupulous competitors in the electrical engineering business.

'And your work? What you do to make money?'

'I own a company making electrical generating equipment. I'm here to try and sell my equipment to a Japanese company.'

She seemed to weigh him up with a long glance. 'So young. And yet you own company?'

'It was my father's company I inherited. Appeldoorn Industries.'

Aiko hesitated. 'Married, App-re-doon-san?'

Joe nodded. 'Yes, over a year now.'

'Tell me about wife.'

It was an odd sensation for Joe to be prompted into thinking of Eleanor right now, and by this painted, sultry-looking siren of a woman. He was still missing Eleanor hugely, particularly after the drama of the last three days, yet on the whole he was glad Eleanor wasn't here with him in Japan. It would have been one more major worry for him if he had to concern himself with her safety too. At least he only had his own welfare to worry about at the moment.

Joe described Eleanor for her as best he could, in much the same words as he'd used with Motoko. It seemed Japanese woman were very interested in the looks of Western women, perhaps because they were so different from them. And yet Joe couldn't help noticing that Aiko-san was very tall and well-built for a Japanese, although much of her height perhaps was down to her elaborate coiffure. She didn't wear a wig as *geisha* did, though; this was her real hair, Joe could see, gleaming, raven-black and embellished with golden ribbons. Her silk kimono was beautiful too: salmon-pink and decorated with falling drifts of white plum blossom.

'And her character...?' Aiko wanted to know even more about Eleanor.

Joe laughed. 'That's easy. She is very possessive and has a fearsome temper to match her beautiful red hair, so if Eleanor ever found out about me taking to a woman like you in a Japanese bathhouse, I would get my head in my hands...'

Aiko seemed confused so Joe wasn't sure how much of that speech she had understood. 'How meet Ereanor-san?'

Joe shrugged. 'It's a long story. Far too long to tell now...'

'Any other woman ever in your life? Must be many, I think,' Aiko declared knowingly.

Joe smiled. 'That would be telling. But of course there have been some.'

'And some special one before Ereanor-san?'

Joe reflected for a moment. 'Yes, one special one.'

'Who was she?'

Joe had no idea why he was opening up like this to the blandishments of this Svengali-like woman with her mysterious white-painted face. 'She was an Englishwoman I met in Europe when I was working as a detective there.'

Aiko-san was about to say something more when Cavendish and Sumiko finally returned from the bathhouse. 'I thay, may we join you? This looks jolly comfortable, what...!'

*

Cavendish's return quickly destroyed the intimate mood of the evening.

Aiko soon withdrew from the room with Sumiko and only reappeared occasionally again after that to bring fresh drinks and snacks.

123

'You were a long time,' Joe told Cavendish suspiciously, still by no means sure that this young Englishman could really be as much of an upper class moron as he appeared to be. 'That must have been the longest bath in *Yoshiwara* history.'

'Oh, I wasn't in the bath for long, old chap. I went down to the river afterwards and tried my luck on one of the boats. Borrowed a hundred yen from a chap I know.'

Joe knew by now that there was organised gambling events held on many of the larger boats moored along the Sumida, run apparently by the local criminal gangs, men with fearsome reputations and reputedly an outrageous taste for elaborate body tattoos. Joe wondered how such men got along with an even stranger visitor from another world, like this man Cavendish.

'How did you do?' Joe asked him coolly.

'Oh, cleaned out, as usual,' Cavendish admitted frankly. 'I'm into one of the gangs here for five thousand yen now...'

'*Five thousand!*' That was a fortune to most people.

'Oh, I'll be all right. Pater will always give me the money, if I'm despewate enough, although he'll be bloody angry about it...'

'How old are you, Cavendish?' Joe asked him curiously. The man acted about twelve years old.

'Twenty-eight, old chap...' A thought seemed to occur to him. 'Now that you mention it, I do need a little cash to help me over the next few weeks. You don't have any money to thpare, do you?'

'Who, me? Why would you think that I would lend you money?'

'I did thave your life, old chap,' Cavendish pointed out in an aggrieved voice.

Joe grunted disbelievingly. 'You were going through my pockets; that's all I saw.'

'That monk who hit you would have thlit your throat but for me coming along and scaring him off. Tho, be a good chappie and lend me a hundred yen,' Cavendish remonstrated.

For whatever reason, Joe did pay up, although knowing fine well he would never see the money again. He wondered, though, why the "monk" hadn't just shot him after felling him with that blow, but perhaps he had been out of ammunition after his earlier reckless shooting spree.

Cavendish was counting his money with satisfaction. 'Are you ready to go back to town now, old chap? It's nearly midnight - the witching hour. I've got a boat waiting at the jetty.'

Despite the attractions of Aiko, Joe had certainly had more than enough of the *Yoshiwara* for one night and wanted to get back to the safety of town before it was too late. Perhaps it was time to be circumspect now and avoid danger if he could for the next few days. And the best way of doing that was to get out of the city completely, where Plesch, or whoever it was that was dogging his footsteps, couldn't follow easily. So Joe nodded at Cavendish. 'Yes, I'm ready to leave.' But he still didn't trust this man, so he felt again for the reassuring bulk of the Webley in his pocket. '*After* you,' he said menacingly, allowing Cavendish to rise from his seat first, before bowing a smiling farewell to a silent Aiko-san.

*

In the early hours, the *Yoshiwara* was quiet again after all the earlier commotion.

Amelia, gazing at herself in her mirror, was wiping away Aiko-san's face piece by piece. Tonight had been the hardest deception of all. At times this evening, she had felt an almost irresistible urge to reveal her identity to Joseph - particularly the moment when he had declared his special feeling for an Englishwoman...

How strange it had been to hear a man opening up his heart in that way. She had just enjoyed possibly a unique experience – hearing a man speak his true feelings about her to her face, and with absolute honesty. And he had been talking about *her*, she didn't doubt it, a fact that had given her a warm glow of contentment.

Yet she had enjoyed the deceit too, and the sexual excitement of getting this close to Joseph again in this different guise, without him realising it.

Then that man Cavendish had reappeared and she'd been very glad that she hadn't revealed her true identity to Joseph prematurely.

She thought again about what she'd seen of Cavendish tonight, and it was gradually bringing her round to agree with Randall's viewpoint - although it pained her greatly to admit it, even to herself. It did seem as if Cavendish couldn't possibly be the informer after all. He was indeed far too stupid - "dumbbell" was exactly the right word for him. The classic despised younger son of the English aristocracy – the runt of his particular litter: in-bred, weak-chinned and irredeemably hopeless.

Or else, was he instead a superb actor...? That didn't seem likely, though, given his true blue background.

Yet he was the only man in the Embassy who had access to all the secrets that had apparently been leaked to the Russians – Amelia had spent a lot of time over the last weeks narrowing down her investigation of everyone in the Embassy, one by one - and Cavendish's gambling addiction and near penniless state had seemed to confirm that he must be the one.

Although not *quite* the only possibility, Amelia reminded herself uneasily. There was still the Ambassador himself, Baronet Sir Stephen Hawtry-Gough. He had access to all the same secrets as Cavendish too, of course. But that idea was unthinkable, wasn't it? The Ambassador himself? A career diplomat for thirty years? - selling, or giving, secrets to the Russians? That possibility seemed even unlikelier than Cavendish being a traitor...

She glanced outside her window and saw the half moon was just setting over the rooftops of the *Yoshiwara* behind a bank of silvered cloud. A dog howled in the distance; in the street below she heard a woman giggle seductively in the shadows.

Turning back to her mirror, her attention shifted again to worrying thoughts of Johan Plesch. She had no remaining doubts that he was here operating in Tokyo, and inevitably in a disguise – or in a series of disguises - as impenetrable as her own.

She asked herself the same question yet again. Did Plesch really send those three men last night to kill Pryor and Joseph? It seemed more and more likely now, as she learned more of the facts of the case. It really wasn't his style to hire others to do his dirty work – he liked to work alone as much as possible - but if he was desperate to shake off Western agents on his tail, then he might have been forced to make emergency recourse to such a measure.

She wondered about the strange vagaries of life. It seemed that Joseph had been saved last night by Shelepin of all people – she couldn't imagine who else would match that description and who would mockingly call himself "Raskolnikov".

But what was Joseph's puzzling interest in "Herr Maienfeld"? She knew fine well that this "Herr Maienfeld" was Obodovsky's pathetic attempt at a secret identity in Tokyo – as if anyone could really mistake that Russian oaf for a Swiss businessman, Amelia thought wryly. But why was Joseph so interested in the Russian?

Was Joseph perhaps an official agent of the Americans after all? Did that explain his interest in "Herr Maienfeld"?

She thought again about tonight's equally perplexing events, and one question dominated all others. Who was this blind monk who had tried to complete the job on Joseph tonight?

The inevitable suspicion arose in her mind. When she'd last seen Johan Plesch up close in London two years ago, on the roof of that house of pleasure in Mayfair, he had been sporting a bald head as a disguise. *So could that shaven-headed monk have been Plesch himself...?*

CHAPTER 11

Thursday January 28th 1904

Amelia saw a line of morning shadow momentarily darken the window of the cabin as the houseboat glided under Shinobashi Bridge, and knew from this that they would soon be back at their regular berth in Nihombashi.

Sumiko stood behind her at the mirror, adjusting the grey wig and helping her complete her transformation from Aiko-san into the plain and plump Mrs Evadne Smythe.

'Do you really like changing yourself into such an ugly *gaijin*, when you can be the beautiful Aiko-san instead, *Ameria-san*?' Sumiko was puzzled by Amelia's willingness to make herself look so old and unattractive, even in the interests of surviving as a spy in this dangerous city. It was touching to Amelia in a way that Sumiko accepted her so much as an honorary Japanese now that she was prepared to insult Westerners freely in her presence, almost forgetting that Miss Peachy was one herself.

Amelia looked at herself in the mirror, and admired the artful way in which she had cleverly aged her face with shadows and lines. Her skill with paint and powder was so accomplished now that the changes were hard to detect as artificial. And yes - in answer to Sumiko's question - the truth was that she did enjoy stepping outside herself and into the guise of these different characters, even unattractive ones. In fact she probably preferred the challenge of playing an older woman. She particularly enjoyed the challenge to her as an actress of bringing the plain middle-aged Mrs Evadne Smythe to life – of convincing other people of her reality – as much as she did with Aiko-san.

Sumiko frowned at her in the mirror and at Mrs Smythe's unprepossessing outfit of heavy cotton bloomers, layers of petticoats, whalebone corset and dowdy velveteen dress and bodice. 'Do Western women really wear all this stuff? No wonder they sweat so much, and look so red-faced and cross all the time. I would be angry and red-faced too. And why so fat?' She poked the padding of Amelia's dress. 'Are all *gaijin* women really as fat as this?'

'They call it "well-endowed", little dumpling.' Amelia loved calling her that – no one, she imagined, could be shaped less like a Chinese dumpling or a rice ball than the slender and willowy Sumiko so the incongruity of the name still amused her.

'This is not "well-endowed",' Sumiko complained, cupping one of Amelia's padded breasts. 'This is just "fat". So I shall call you "fat dumpling" from now on.'

Amelia smiled at her. 'You can call me anything you want, little dumpling.'

Sumiko grew pensive. 'Are you coming back in a few days?' she asked uncertainly.

Amelia wasn't absolutely sure if she would ever be going back to the *Yoshiwara* after this, and becoming Aiko-san again. But she hadn't said anything to Sumiko about her plans, and hadn't behaved any differently to all the other trips she'd made downriver, *so how on earth did this girl know...?*

'You've taken all your small private things this time – old photographs, bits of jewellery,' Sumiko explained when Amelia raised her eyebrows questioningly. 'You never did that before.'

'You're much too clever for your own good, little one,' Amelia said sadly. 'But I think I will be back – it just may not be for a week or so until everything is resolved finally here. I will send a message to you when I need you to return with the boat.'

Sumiko seemed doubtful and still a little rebellious in her mood. 'You are doing something dangerous in the next few days?'

'Perhaps,' Amelia admitted. 'I don't know for sure.'

'Then I shall stay here in Nihombashi with the boat...just in case you need to escape quickly.' Sumiko's jaw had hardened determinedly and she clearly wasn't going to take no for an answer.

Amelia nodded and bowed gratefully, deciding not to argue for once, touched by Sumiko's real concern for her safety. '*Soo sh'tai desu ga...Sumiko-san, o-tetsudai wa domo arigato gozaimashita.* I'm grateful for your help...'

*

Amelia thought Lady Rosemary was looking happier today than she'd ever seen her, a new pink satin glow to her cheeks that she hadn't noticed before. If Amelia hadn't known better, she might have suspected that Lady Rosemary had taken a lover. But that could not be the reason surely - not the wife of the British Ambassador? Yet Lady Rosemary did have that particular unmistakeable look of a middle-aged woman re-invigorated by a love affair...

'You're looking well, Rosemary,' Amelia complimented the older woman, above the chink of Royal Worcester teacups.

'And you too, Evadne,' Lady Rosemary returned the compliment with less honesty but with similar warmth. Amelia had met Lady Rosemary in the lobby of the Imperial soon after arriving in her rickshaw from the quayside and had accepted an invitation to take luncheon with her in the grand dining room of the Imperial, with its palms and sweeping al fresco painted ceiling.

'Is your husband still away in Kyushu, Evadne?' Lady Rosemary asked politely.

'Yes, he is, I'm afraid. And he will be away for another three months at least.' Amelia had wisely used the name of a real individual, a railway engineer called Mr George Fairburn Smythe, as her putative husband. The bachelor Mr Smythe would no doubt have been astonished to learn of an unknown wife claiming his name and spending much of her time in Tokyo while he prowled the mountains and forests of Kyushu surveying a new railway line. But fortunately Mr Smythe never came to Tokyo at present so that the embarrassing possibility of meeting his mysterious wife didn't have to be faced. So, all in all, it was the perfect arrangement for Amelia, since it gave her full rein to mix with the British expatriate community without the need to constantly explain to them what a middle-aged Englishwoman was doing on her own in Japan. She could also plausibly explain her frequent absences from the Imperial as a return to a fictitious bungalow on the Tokkaido Road near the Izu Peninsula, fifty miles from Tokyo, where she claimed to be patiently keeping house for the return of her hardworking husband.

They had ordered tomato soup and a plate of cold cuts for their luncheon. This frequent change of identities was no problem for Amelia's acting abilities, but it was causing her digestive system some stress at least, as she had to constantly change between the austere Japanese cuisine of the *Yoshiwara*, and the much richer Western diet she encountered when staying in town. The latter now tasted very odd to her, if not distasteful, when she was now so accustomed to the subtler tastes of *miso soup, natto, umeboshi* pickled plums, *soba* and *udon* noodles.

'You're not eating, Evadne.' Lady Rosemary was having no such problem herself in tucking enthusiastically into the tasty selection of cold beef and pork.

'No, my appetite is poor today. I'm not doing proper justice to the chef at all, am I?' Amelia happened to glance up at that moment to see a very handsome young Japanese woman at a neighbouring table giving her a long and penetrating examination. Amelia was disconcerted by the look and worried that her grey wig might have slipped unknowingly, or that she might have betrayed herself by some inappropriate action. But it seemed to be no more than normal curiosity, and the Japanese woman soon apparently lost interest in her, and went back to her own soup and her quiet conversation with her woman companions.

'Who is that Japanese lady in western dress over there, Rosemary?' Amelia asked surreptitiously, after a minute or so. 'Do you happen to know her?'

Lady Rosemary shifted her eyes to the table indicated, then whispered in response. 'Yes, I know her. She was introduced to me at the party at the American Embassy on Tuesday night. Her name is Fumiyo Isogai – she is the daughter of the politician Shintaro Isogai, who leads one of these odd political parties here, and is very active politically in her own right. She's *very* left-wing, so Stephen says, always criticising the actions of Western governments in Asia.' She coughed. 'As if *we* are to blame for the state of the entire world.'

'We have laid claim to most of it,' Amelia pointed out. 'So perhaps we must take some responsibility for current troubles.'

Lady Rosemary looked at her oddly for a moment, and Amelia realised uncomfortably she had just uttered a very unusual sentiment to come from the mouth of a no doubt reactionary woman like Mrs Smythe.

Amelia decided to change the subject rapidly. 'I haven't seen you since that appalling incident on Monday night here. Do the authorities know yet who tried to blow the hotel up?'

'Stephen seems convinced it wasn't an attack on Westerners as such. He thinks it was one of these Japanese nationalist groups – you know, fanatics with swords and cropped hair – who want to turn the clock back on fifty years of progress.'

'They do seem to hate the West, those people,' Amelia agreed.

'They certainly do, that's true. But they hate left-wing Japanese politicians like Miss Isogai's father even more, apparently. She and her father were in the lobby on Monday night when the bomb was thrown, and Stephen thinks they could have been the real targets.'

'Brave of her to take lunch here again, then,' Amelia observed with another glance in the woman's direction.

'I suppose so,' Lady Rosemary conceded. Although the security here is very tight now – you saw the way armed soldiers at the entrance search everyone coming in and out now.' She thought for a second. 'Still we must be grateful. Although these Japanese fanatics might have been trying to kill Miss Isogai and her father, they certainly wouldn't have been squeamish about the possibility of killing a few dozen Westerners at the same time too. You weren't downstairs at the time of the attempted bombing, were you?'

Amelia glanced across at Fumiyo Isogai and shook her head. 'No, I didn't witness it; luckily I'd gone upstairs to my room by that time. I heard a young American man saved the day.'

Lady Rosemary smiled complacently. 'He certainly did. And not only brave, but he is a very sweet boy too. I met him on Tuesday night at the American Embassy party too.' Lady Rosemary smiled secretively. 'And I was *very* impressed with him, if you know what I mean. Such a handsome, well-spoken young man…' As Lady Rosemary said this, Amelia noticed that her skin seemed to glow even pinker for a moment.

Amelia was slightly disconcerted by this intimate confession from Lady Rosemary. Could Joseph be the reason for Lady Rosemary's apparent happiness? Could she have started an affair with Joseph since Tuesday? There hardly seemed to have been enough time for that, though, unless Joseph and Lady Rosemary were both very fast workers. But Amelia nevertheless found herself a little put out even by the possibility…

*

At 2 p.m. Amelia retired to her suite on the third floor. She went straight to the window and was just in time to see Lady Rosemary leaving the main entrance below, her elegant hat tied down with ribbons against the strong gusting wind.

Lady Rosemary had clearly had an urgent appointment this afternoon because she had been most anxious not to let her luncheon overrun by even a few minutes. Amelia had been able to sense the clear anticipation building in her companion throughout lunch, and had not the slightest doubt by now that Lady Rosemary had an illicit liaison with a man planned for this afternoon, somewhere in the vicinity of the Imperial Hotel.

Amelia had been tempted to follow her and discover who she was meeting, but hadn't in the end because it seemed a prurient and unnecessary intrusion into the life of a woman she liked well enough. Yet now that she was back in her room overlooking the entrance to the hotel, Amelia was still curious enough to rush to the window and see if Lady Rosemary might actually be meeting someone on the forecourt of the hotel.

Her lover couldn't really be Joseph, though, surely…? Amelia had already decided that was highly unlikely, but even the slight possibility of such a thing was enough to make her go to the window quickly and look.

Amelia saw Lady Rosemary decline the offer of a horse-cab or rickshaw in the forecourt, and walked instead along the outer moat of the palace, still showing signs of bomb damage from Monday night's incident, towards a distant grove of maples. The white walls and green tiled roof of the palace were perfectly reflected in the dark green water of the moat, with the low winter sun already casting long fingers of shadow across the thin skin of ice on the surface. Amelia watched Lady Rosemary progress slowly approach the maple grove and there meet someone under the stirring trees by the moat. It was certainly a man with dark hair, and probably a tall young Western man at that, she decided. But was it Joseph…?

Annoyingly, the bare frosted branches of the maples were just thick enough to make identification of Lady Rosemary's mysterious companion

131

impossible from her third floor window, and Amelia wished now that she had taken the opportunity after all to follow her when she'd had the chance. It was too late now, though, because Lady Rosemary and her companion were already walking away under the maple trees towards Hibiya Park, with an afternoon of intense and secret passion ahead of them, no doubt...

*

It would perhaps have eased Amelia Peachy's mind to know it, but Joe Appeldoorn was in fact sixty miles away from the city of Tokyo at this precise moment, and definitely feeling more relaxed, now that he was removed from the imminent threat of anarchist bombs, knife-wielding assassins and murderous monks. Out here at Hakone, he felt in a different country from the city of Tokyo, and even the vengeful threat of a re-born Johan Plesch seemed a distant and remote possibility that could be safely ignored for the present.

Joe had been thoroughly enjoying his day so far with Mr Maeda's American technical representative. Larry Longrigg had met him personally first thing this morning as arranged at Atami Station. Joe had ridden a pretty little steam train pulled by a miniature puffing locomotive as far as the coastal town of Atami, where Larry had been waiting on the platform at 7 a.m. to greet him. Larry had then taken him on a guided morning tour by carriage of the Hakone region, a mountainous area inland from Atami. Hakone was a revelation to Joe: an entirely different and more beautiful Japan from the vast sprawling city of Tokyo with all its endless crowds and noise. By contrast, Hakone was a scenic mountainous area of shaded forest walks and bubbling hot springs, falling steeply towards the blue Pacific just to the east of the Izu Peninsula.

'This whole area of hot springs is the collapsed remains of a huge volcanic cone that some people think was active only a few thousand years ago,' Larry told Joe at one point. 'They think the cone could have been twenty miles across! Can you imagine a mountain that size spouting lava, Joseph...?' Larry engaged his toothy smile again, which Joe was getting used to by now, and which he found strangely endearing. Despite the man's natural ugliness - the heavy freckles, the wild sprouting red hair and the thin awkward body - Larry Longrigg also had a natural self-effacing charm that somehow overcame all his physical disadvantages and made Joe warm to him more and more as the day went on. Even after only a few hours together, Joe was already well on the way to thinking of this man as a good friend.

Larry had taken him first by carriage up twisting switchback roads to Hakone-Yumoto, a pretty hot-springs resort village in the mountains. From there they had trekked on foot, penetrating even higher into the forests of the Hakone region, and exploring the fascinating *Owaku-dani* – the "Valley of Great Boiling" - where the trail was criss-crossed with steaming vents of sulphurous gas and steam. Then they had crossed the final crest of the hills and down towards Lake Ashi – *Ashinoko* - a stretch of clear blue water nestling between feathery green hills and with a perfect view of the snow-capped cone of Mount Fuji in the azure distance.

At 12 noon they met up with Larry's driver and the carriage again, and got a ride from the village of Hakone-machi on the lakeshore up to Larry's house at Moto-Hakone, located among pine groves on a steep green north-facing hillside above the lake. Beyond the crest of the hill above the house, the southern side of the forested hills fell away on the far side in a vertiginous drop of fifteen hundred metres to the black volcanic sand shoreline of the Pacific Ocean. 'I'll take you up there later and show you the view if you like,' Larry had offered, indicating the crest. 'That's where I fly my gliders from. Wonderful up draughts.'

Larry Longrigg's house was an atmospheric place, a traditional three-storey *gassho-zukuri* house of timber beams and columns moulded together with exquisite craftsmanship, and with a steep roof thatched with Miscanthus grass.

Joe enjoyed lunch with his host in a bare tatami room looking out through sliding rice paper screens at the moss-green garden, the only sounds the soughing of the wind, the distant trickle of water, and the rhythmic clatter of the bamboo deer-scarer as it filled with water from the stream and fell at intervals to discharge its load. Joe noticed that the rice paper of the shoji screens had often been pierced by the beaks of inquisitive birds - Japanese bush warblers and white eyes – and been mended characteristically with small squares of paper cut by meticulous fingers.

Joe had no doubt whom those loving fingers belonged to – they had to belong to Larry's Japanese wife Haruko, who had cooked a Western lunch especially for their guest. Haruko wasn't beautiful, or even pretty, with a broad flat Oriental face and sallow skin, yet Joe could see how completely intoxicated Larry was by her. And her quiet graceful presence was what made this house special for Larry; in her butterfly kimono, she was to him that classic *musumé*, that exotic creature from a Far Eastern land that so many Western men dreamed of.

*

After lunch, Larry took Joe up to his workshop, a barn-like wooden structure set on its own clearing nearby on the hillside.

Larry was effusive in his praise for the products of Appeldoorn Industries. 'I went to the warehouse in Yokohama yesterday and inspected your equipment in detail. Your technical specifications are very clear and well thought out, Joseph. And the steam turbines appear to be the best quality I've seen...'

'We've run them continuously for a month during tests and had not the slightest problem with them,' Joe boasted. 'It's because of the quality of the alloy we use for the turbine blades – an alloy my father developed himself.'

Larry nodded approvingly. 'He must have been a special guy, your father.'

Joe appreciated the praise for his father's work. 'He certainly was.'

Larry smiled that jaw-wrenching smile again. 'But you're being coy, Joseph. Not all of this is down to your father, is it? There's clearly a lot of recent design work from yourself, too.'

Joe smiled modestly. 'Some, maybe. I have worked hard over the last year to try and improve my father's basic generating system. We can produce high voltage alternating current transmission at one-twenty or thirty-three kilovolts and with a choice of transformer types. You do realise the system is based on hundred volt output at fifty cycles, but can also create a hundred volt DC supply if required?'

Larry was deep in thought. 'Of course. I was particularly impressed with your brush commutators, which are vastly superior to anything I've seen out here before.'

Larry had a few more technical questions about the manufacturing details, which Joe answered easily. Joe was trying not to show his satisfaction prematurely because it seemed clear by now that Larry Longrigg was going to recommend the system wholeheartedly to Maeda.

But he was still hugely relieved when Larry finally offered him his hand and said, 'Congratulations, Joseph. I'm pleased to tell you that I am going to recommend to Mr Maeda that he signs a contract with you to use your generating system in his new power stations.' His blue eyes twinkled but his voice still had a note of caution. 'The one thing I can't advise Maeda on is price, though. He'll make his own judgement about that whatever I say, and beat you down to the bone. And I'm afraid he won't be swayed by sentiment – not even by the fact that you saved his daughter's life on Monday night...'

*

Larry showed Joe around his workshop and demonstrated some of his own interesting inventions. This was certainly an idyllic place for a small private workshop. Through the open *shoji* screens, Joe could see white moths fluttering in the feathery foliage outside, and hear mice scurrying along the beams above. Warblers sang sweetly from distant bamboo thickets even though spring was still a few weeks off.

Larry explained the workings of a wireless transmitter he was developing that he claimed was better than Marconi's. Then he pointed to a metal box with a glass panel. 'And this is a device, I've invented to measure the intensity of Becquerel waves...'

Joe found his attention grabbed instead, though, by a set of large photographs displayed on a wall at one end of the barn. These photographs were striking in two ways, apart from their size: one was that they were in glorious natural *colour* – a quality of colour Joe had never seen before in hand-tinted pictures; and two was the fact that they were mostly intimate pictures of Larry's wife, Haruko, in a very revealing state...

Joe wasn't sure whether he should be looking at these clearly private pictures. These were as erotic as any seventeenth century Japanese prints Joe had seen – with Haruko apparently in a state of ecstasy, shamelessly lifting the folds of her silk flowered kimono to reveal both her breasts and the secret space between her legs.

Larry didn't seem at all embarrassed, though. 'Like my pictures, Joseph? Look at how beautiful the colours of the kimono come through.'

Joe coughed uneasily; his attention had been focused elsewhere than the colours of the kimono. 'Are they hand-painted?' he asked.

'No, Joseph, I told you. This is *true* colour photography using blue, green and red filters, a practical development of Maxwell's method. I plan to sell this system in time to one of the big US companies and make a fortune.'

Joe smiled at his enthusiasm. 'Then what? Return to America?'

Larry deliberated. 'Maybe. I don't know yet. It would be a difficult decision to leave this place, but I do miss my own home.'

'If you do return, what about Haruko?' Joe asked. 'You think she'll fit in Lansing, Michigan society?'

Larry looked uneasy. 'What are you suggesting, Joseph? Leave her behind?' Larry examined one of the more conventional pictures of Haruko and smiled tenderly. 'Of course I'll take her with me. Could *you* abandon such a woman?'

*

At two o'clock in the afternoon Joe stood nervously on the crest of the hill, the wind clutching at the winged contraption to which he was attached with harnesses. Below, the hillside fell away in a series of near vertical cliffs to the shore of the Pacific and the town of Atami. From here Joe could see the emerald green hills of the Izu Peninsula beyond Atami, projecting far out into the rippled blue ocean and its swirls of whitecaps.

Joe remembered the only other time his feet had left the ground – a mad nerve-racking flight suspended under the gondola of a Zeppelin – which was enough to put anyone off the idea of humans flying for the rest of their life.

'I think I've changed my mind about trying this,' Joe said weakly.

'It's perfectly safe, Joseph, if you follow my instructions. This is my development of the German aviator Otto Lilienthal's Glider. It's very easy to fly. Just do what I told you. You don't have to go right off the end of the cliff. Just try a short hop of a flight. You'll see how easy it is.'

How easy to get yourself killed, more likely, Joe thought angrily. He had been expecting some sort of toy flying machine, not this huge contraption of wooden frame and canvas wings.

'Didn't Lilienthal kill himself a few years back, jumping off a hillside wearing just such a dangerous contraption?' Joe asked dryly.

Larry demurred. 'He was unlucky, that's all. The spars on Lilienthal's broke under the strain. But I've *designed* my frame scientifically for stability and strength. I've flown from here dozens of times without mishap.'

'Perhaps you'd better demonstrate then,' Joe suggested quickly.

Larry shrugged as if he was dealing with an irrational child, and helped Joe out of the harness with Haruko's help.

Then Haruko helped Larry into the harness in turn. She smiled at Joe, but he had a little trouble meeting her eye, wondering if she knew that Larry had shown him those revealing colour pictures of her.

Larry checked the buckles one more time then, with another jaw-splitting smile directed at his wife, he ran down the grassy slope towards the cliff edge and simply launched himself off into the void. Joe braced himself for disaster, his muscles tense, but was relieved and astonished when Larry powered effortlessly into the air above the cliff.

Then Larry put on a quite extraordinary show of skill, floating, diving and soaring on the air currents above the green hills like an unlikely eagle, his thin red hair blowing wildly, his goofy smile visible even from here.

Haruko came across and joined Joe to watch, and seemed to notice his slight embarrassment. 'Did you see my pictures, Mr Appeldoorn?'

'Err...yes, I did. Err...very beautiful.'

'Yes, I think so. I am not pretty woman, Mr Appeldoorn, but Larry-san makes me beautiful in picture. I very proud.'

Joe looked at her more easily. 'Yes, they are beautiful.'

Haruko looked up at her husband in blissful admiration as he defied the elements and indulged in fantastic feats of aerial acrobatics above their heads. 'Look at him soar, Mr Appeldoorn. He is like a God, isn't he...?'.

CHAPTER 12

Later that same afternoon, Joe watched the sun settling low over western mountains, the green tranquillity of the pretty seaside town of Kamakura laid out on the slopes below for him to admire.

Joe had taken the same puffing little steam train back from Atami, along the line of the old Tokkaido Road, first to Yokohama, then on a branch line to the old town of Kamakura, where he had been collected at the railway station by a driver and four-wheel carriage sent by Motoko.

Joe hadn't been too comfortable with the idea of accepting Motoko's invitation to come here, still not knowing quite what she had in mind for the evening, and knowing full well that her father was still away in Kyoto. But, on reflection, the risk of some minor social embarrassment still seemed infinitely preferable to remaining in Tokyo as a sitting duck at the Imperial Hotel, if, as seemed more and more probable, Johan Plesch was really alive and in Japan, and wanting to exact revenge on him. Joe had decided by now that he had to accept that this unpalatable fact might be true, and that his best tactic was therefore to keep on the move, until he could sign his business deal and then get the Hell out of this country while he still could.

Before going on to the house, the carriage driver had taken him on a short tour of this scenic former capital of Japan, with its atmospheric temples and ancient shrines nestling against the wooded green hills ringing the town. They drove down Wakamiya-oji, Kamakura's tree-shaded main street and the driver, who had a few words of English, pointed out the statue of the Great Buddha in imposing jade-coloured stone on its green hillside and the azalea-lined steps to the thatched hall at Sugimoto-dera Temple.

Joe had still been wary as the carriage finally pulled up to the entrance gate to the house, still unsure what to expect of the coming evening. Dinner with Motoko wasn't a chore of course – but was that all she had planned? Or could it be she had something more intimate in mind? She had been insistent that he stay the night too, but then there simply wasn't enough time to return to Tokyo tonight even if he wanted to. He tried to remember exactly what she had said yesterday morning when she had invited him here, and he did worry that Motoko might be about to offer herself as a special reward for saving her life on Monday. Perhaps this was a weird Japanese tradition he'd never heard of, although he doubted that. If made, though, such an invitation would be a difficult one to turn down, and even if he managed to resist the temptation, he was going to end up upsetting someone in this powerful family, that much was certain...

But on remembering the words she'd used, Joe was now partly reassured that Motoko was not intending to offer herself to him as a prize this evening because she had also mentioned she was inviting another special guest to dinner tonight that she wanted him to meet. Surely that meant this was just going to a conventional dinner...

*

The house was extraordinary.

Joe had been impressed enough with the perfection of Larry Longrigg's house on its hillside above Lake Ashi, but this house owned by the Maeda family was a palace by comparison. Actually it was not a single house, but a whole complex of linked wooden buildings arranged in a U-shape around the garden, almost like a temple.

Motoko was clearly taking great pride in showing him the family treasure. She walked him through the main part of the house, explaining the various features and their purpose. 'This is built in the style of a *minka* house, but much larger than normal because it was built for an important person. It built in Momoyama period, year sixteen hundred in Western calendar, and was given by Shogun Ieyasu Tokugawa to favourite courtesan. Her name Murasaki-sama; she great beauty.'

In her delightful silk kimono, the beautiful Motoko was giving the memory of Lady Murasaki a run for its money, Joe thought, his mind forgetting his earlier doubts and beginning to dwell on thoughts of possible sensuous pleasures to come.

'*Engawa* is space outside, like Western veranda,' Motoko was explaining, in guide mode. 'And *doma* is this area of earth just behind entrance. *Shoji* is outside sliding door; *fusuma* is inside sliding door of wood or heavy paper to divide room. This is *tatami* mat. *Tokonoma* is larger straw-and-rush mat...'

He and Motoko went outside and walked in the tea garden, despite the evening chill. They traced a route along paths of white stones between the gravel, past bamboo screens and miniature pines. The stones of the path had been freshly sprinkled with water - 'to welcome a special guest,' Motoko explained. 'This is *rojo;* it mean "dewy path".' She seemed to notice the patch of shaven hair on his right temple for the first time. 'Have you had accident since yesterday?' she asked curiously.

'Just a minor one,' Joe responded lightly, reluctant to go into details. Considering he'd been whacked over the head yesterday, he felt surprisingly well, although the cut was still a little tender to the touch. 'Is your father still in Kyoto?' he asked, changing the subject adroitly.

Motoko nodded enigmatically. 'For a few more days. He telephone me from there to ask favour of you. He want you come to Kyoto as guest this weekend; stay at famous Japanese inn – *ryokan* - by Kamo River. He would like introduce you to business associate, and to famous General Yoshida.'

Joe certainly wasn't displeased to hear of the invitation; it meant he could stay away from Tokyo and the Imperial Hotel for a little while longer. 'Yes, of course,' he agreed. 'That's very kind of him.'

'I come Kyoto too,' Motoko said with a smile, before turning solemn again. 'Sorry to mention painful topic, but have you any news of sad death of Pryor-san? Have police caught someone?'

Joe shook his head. 'Not that I know.' He felt like adding, *I don't think they're even trying to...*

'You not in danger here, Joe-san. No more bomb. No more men with knife.' Motoko's eyes twinkled. 'But in future stay away from bad woman in *Yoshiwara*. Understand?'

Joe didn't need any further persuasion to stay away from the fleshpots of the *Yoshiwara*, although the fact that he might not see the seductive Aiko-san again was a little disappointing.

'We have dinner now,' Motoko announced charmingly, pointing back towards the house, freshly lit by lanterns.

Joe had seen servants moving about silently and almost unnoticed in the house and outbuildings, like spirits. But one of them finally approached Joe and Motoko, and Motoko introduced him. 'This is Okuma-san. Head servant here. He look after me since I little girl.'

Okuma-san bowed low and said something rapidly. The Maeda family's head servant was a sturdy brown man with close-cropped hair and limbs like oak; he could have been any age from forty to sixty, Joe thought.

Motoko translated for him. 'He thank you from bottom of heart for saving Motoko-chan.' She smiled deliciously. 'I agree with sentiment.' She watched Okuma-san depart with a glow of quiet affection in her almond eyes. 'He seventy-seven year old, you know, but won't take life easy.'

Joe was amazed at that, and shook his head in disbelief. 'Is anyone else coming this evening?' he asked casually as they stepped onto the *engawa* and exchanged their outside shoes for indoor slippers. 'You did say you were inviting someone else.'

'Yes, I do. But it surprise.' Motoko smiled mysteriously. 'You see inside.'

They went inside the house to a tatami mat room overlooking the garden. Outside, Joe could hear the doleful clanging of a temple bell, the trickle of water over mossy rocks, the rustle and swaying of bamboo, the tinkle of a wind chime.

Then a *fusuma* screen was slid open to reveal a larger room where a low lacquered table lay ready with fresh *tatami* mats laid all around.

Standing there to greet Joe was a vision of old Japan – a beautiful young woman in a green silk flowered kimono that made even Motoko's look a little dowdy.

Motoko smiled triumphantly. 'This is surprise for you, Joe-san. This is Umegiku-san. Most accomplished *geisha* in Japan.' She saw the questioning look on Joe's face. 'Face not painted white tonight because this evening not formal occasion. She travelled from Gion-kobu district of Kyoto today to entertain you at dinner. I invite.'

*

Umegiku did indeed entrance Joe, who was soon drawn into a different world by her playing of the *shamisen,* her classical dance with the fan, her demonstration of the tea ceremony - *cha no yu* - and her undoubted grace.

Motoko smiled her delight throughout dinner at the effect the sensuous Umegiku-san was having on her guest. '"Geisha" mean "talented performer", Joe-san,' she explained. It seemed to Joe that Motoko was just as diverted by the seductive skills of the *geisha* as he was. 'However Umegiku-san prefer term "Geiko" – means "child of the arts".' Motoko looked at Joe. 'You not disappointed she not paint face and lips for you? I can ask her if wish. Her attendant is here too.'

Joe shook his head in alarm that he might have been looking dissatisfied in any way with the evening's entertainment. 'No, of course not.'

Motoko was clearly enjoying being the intermediary between Umegiku-san and Joe, although Joe could sense from his limited knowledge of Japanese that Motoko was embellishing what he said considerably and making it perhaps more provocative and sexually charged, judging from the occasional gasp of surprise, perhaps even pleasure, from the *geisha*'s lips when she heard what he'd ostensibly said.

Joe had done his best to study some Japanese on the long voyage across the Pacific and he finally decided to try a little directly on the *geisha*. '*Umegiku-san, anata no ocha no o-temae wa doo ni itte imashita yo.*'

Motoko almost dropped her cup in her surprise, then clapped her hands delightedly. 'Ah, *sugoi*, Joe-san,' she said.

Umegiku-san too looked almost shocked and glanced slightly accusingly at Motoko. '*Ah, gaijin wa Nihongo hanasu koto ga dekiru.*' Joe caught the meaning and the clear surprise in her voice - the foreigner can speak Japanese…

'*Hai, sukoshi dekimasu.*' Joe also turned to Motoko. 'I hope I just said that she was a real expert at serving tea,' Joe added.

'Yes, you did. Moment,' Motoko interrupted, and went into a huddle with Umegiku-san, after which she glanced knowingly in Joe's direction.

*

An hour later, after much saké and songs and giggling from the girls, a very inebriated Motoko said, 'It's time for me to leave you now, Joe-san. I sleep in another room. Umegiku-san will look after you by herself now.'

'What?' Joe was hoping he'd misheard.

Motoko explained patiently, as if to a child. 'Umegiku-san will sleep here too, in this room. On quilt – *futon* - on floor.' Her voice dropped to a conspiratorial whisper. 'She will pillow with you, if you wish, Joe-san. I think she like you very much. You lucky. The house at your disposal, Joe-san. I see you tomorrow.'

Joe nearly panicked. 'I can't. What can I say to her?'

'Enough. You already say enough. You man, she woman. What else to say?'

'Better she sleeps somewhere else, I think,' Joe said desperately.

'No, Joe-san. That would be very rude of you to reject her.'

'What about my wife?' Joe pleaded.

'She not here, Joe-san, and she not know. So not mind,' Motoko said primly, then glanced across at Umegiku's curious expression at this whispered interchange. 'This would cause great offence to Umegiku-san. This your fault. If you not want her, then why you charm her that way at dinner?'

This was good coming from *her*, Joe decided irately, when Motoko herself, on her own initiative, had done most of the seducing on his behalf.

Motoko's eyes widened solemnly. 'She might even kill herself over disgrace, if you refuse her generous offer,' she warned.

She had to be joking, Joe thought uncertainly. But it was tricky being sure with a girl like Motoko, who Joe suspected now was no shrinking violet but a rather skilled practitioner of the womanly arts herself...

*

In the morning Joe saw Umegiku-san and her attendant to the entrance of the house and to her waiting horse-drawn carriage, which was there to take her back to the railway station for her return to Kyoto. Joe knew enough not to touch her in public – that would be a disgraceful breach of good manners - but only to bow formally in return to her much lower bow. Then he walked back through the sunlit morning garden, whistling to himself.

A kimono-clad Motoko suddenly appeared through the trees with a knowing smile on her pretty face. 'Happy, Joe-san?' Clearly she had been watching Umegiku's departure with avid interest.

'Yes, happy. Thank you. *Kono aida-wa domo arigato gozaimashita.*'

'*Doo itashimashite.* Was last night enjoyable?' Motoko was obviously very keen to hear all the interesting details of Joe's hopefully torrid night of

141

passion with Umegiku-san but Joe wasn't prepared to oblige her.

'Very much.' Joe kept a poker face just to spite her.

'Did she do anything *special* to enhance your enjoyment, Joe-san?' Motoko was not prepared to give up without a fight in order to satisfy her prurient curiosity as to what a *geisha* might do for their specially regarded clients.

'Oh yes, that she certainly did,' Joe said, bringing the discussion to a firm close.

*

In mid-morning, Joe and Motoko took a walk through sun-dappled winter woods at the back of the house, which led them eventually out onto a cliff-top path above the wind-tossed ocean, with a steep wooded slope rising behind. Below were small rocky islets set in the frothing blue sea, with the odd grove of pines clinging to their pinnacles, while all around the hidden submerged rocks, the Pacific surf crashed and raged.

Motoko wasn't talking as much this morning as usual; she still seemed a little miffed by Joe's reluctance to tell her any details about last night's liaison with Umegiku-san. They had reached a slight promontory on the coastal path when a young man suddenly appeared from the woods ahead of them and stood waiting, in slightly threatening attitude. He was clad in a black kimono, but looked young and tough, despite a handsome face, and Joe was beginning to regret leaving his Webley revolver in his bag back at the house.

But it seemed this wasn't to be a repeat of the robbery in the *Yoshiwara*. Motoko had gasped a little in surprise when she first saw him, but she obviously knew the man well because she ran ahead and spoke to him, exchanging rapid staccato sentences in Japanese. The interchange was far too quick for Joe to pick up even a word, but he could sense some anger and suppressed emotion in both of them just from their attitudes.

Joe felt highly uncomfortable being witness to this intimate encounter that he didn't understand, but he held back out of politeness.

Motoko turned her head to him and seemed to sense his discomfit. 'Will you please excuse for moment, Joe-san. I all right. Please walk on ahead and I follow in minute.'

Slightly reluctantly, he did as he was told. A hundred yards along the path he glanced back uneasily to check what was going on and saw the man clearly about to raise his fists in anger and strike Motoko. Joe yelled at him and ran back, an action that stopped the man in his tracks, his hand still raised.

Joe was still a few yards away from them when there was a massive rumble beneath his feet, and the whole ground started to vibrate violently. Joe had never been in an earthquake before, but he realised instantly what this must be. He was flung to the ground by the violence of the shaking, as

142

rocks and debris began to rattle down the hillside towards him. The shaking didn't last long, though – perhaps ten seconds – and Joe breathed a sigh of relief, believing the worst was over.

But then he saw, with a feeling of disbelief, that the entire hillside above him - trees and all - was now starting to slide: an uncanny and terrifying sight.

Joe turned to look at Motoko and the young man again, who had both realised the danger too, and were running for the protection of an outcrop of solid rock three or four metres high. The young man made the shelter of the rock face just as the earth on each side of the rock began to slide too. Motoko was slower to reach the protective outcrop in time but the young man, with lightning fast reflexes, reached out a sinewy arm and grabbed her wrist, pulling her to safety just before she would have been swept away by the mudslide.

Joe wasn't so fortunate, though. He was too far away to reach the shelter of the stable rock face in time, and he felt his feet sliding away from under him as the whole mass of soil on which he stood, turned to near liquid by the intense shaking, began to accelerate under the pull of gravity.

As Joe slid down with the moving mudslide and reached the cliff edge, he made a despairing effort to reach the branch of a tree bedded in solid rock and prevent himself from being carried over with the tidal wave of mud and gravel.

His fingers did somehow find the branch of the tree, and he hung on desperately to it for a moment. But then the force of the mudflow uprooted the tree too and Joe found himself on the move again and thrown violently over the edge of the cliff, down towards the crashing surf and jagged rocks a hundred feet below...

CHAPTER 13

Friday January 29th 1904

Joe hit the surface of the water just as a huge Pacific wave rolled in, its crest on the point of breaking as it ran into the shallows. So, instead of ploughing directly into solid rock with a few inches of water sloughing over it, Joe gratefully found fifteen feet of dense green salt water that absorbed his fall without complaint, then spat him back onto the cliff face, where he found himself gasping and half-drowned on a narrow rocky shelf.

His problems weren't over yet, though, because he could see a whole series of other massive waves approaching the cliff, and these would not help him, he knew, but would quickly batter him into submission if he couldn't get higher up the cliff.

He tried to scramble a couple of metres up the soft rock face, but he wasn't anything like high enough before the next wave struck, and it hit him cruelly with massive breath-sucking force. Joe didn't know how he managed to cling on to the rocks with several tons of glassy green water washing over him and trying to sweep him back into the ocean again. Joe could taste blood and salt in his mouth, and his ribs were stiff and sore from the pummelling he'd just received.

He knew he couldn't survive another such impact and, once the wave had retreated for a few seconds, he tried frantically to inch his way further up the sheer rock face to safety, using his old climbing skills to aid him. But the rock, now freshly stripped of all topsoil, was as greasy as the floor of an abattoir and Joe felt his fingers losing their grip just as another mighty Pacific wave loomed up behind him. He was bracing himself for the sea's final coup de grace when a rope appeared magically from above – as mysteriously as the Indian Rope Trick - and he just had time, with fumbling fingers, to wrap it around his torso twice before the tons of foaming water hit him again.

The rope nearly cut him in two when the impact came, and left him dangling over the water, but did at least prevent him being sucked back into the sea and smashed against the rocks. As the sea subsided briefly yet again, Joe used the rope and his feet to claw his way rapidly up the cliff face to safety, employing all the remaining strength in his arms and legs. Once he was above the crest of the waves, he could relax a little and rest, watching as another huge moving mass of grey-green water, as big as a freight train, rushed in and foamed just below his feet.

Then he continued upwards, foot by foot, until he was back near the level of the cliff top path, although he saw that a two hundred-yard length of it had been swept away completely in the landslide.

A strong brown hand reached down and pulled him up the last few feet, and Joe recognised the goblin face of Okuma-san.

Motoko appeared beside him, almost weeping with relief. '*Aaah, yokatta, yokatta*...You safe!'

It took several minutes for Joe to get his heaving lungs back to some sort of normality again, as he lay gasping on this stable plateau of rock above the vertical cliff face and the churning ocean far below.

Joe looked at the palms of his hands, which were blistered and bleeding where he'd burned them on the rope. His right arm felt as if it had nearly been dragged out of its socket. But he was in one piece thanks to someone's quick thinking.

Motoko came over and explained. 'You owe life to Okuma-san. He follow us on walk – to look after me – and see what happen.'

Joe tried to stand up finally. 'Lucky he had a rope with him.'

'Yes, he always take rope to collect sea bird egg on cliff. Very lucky.'

There was no sign of the young man who had saved Motoko's life earlier, and Joe, even though recovering, tactfully thought it better not to question Motoko about him.

But, as soon as he had his breath fully back, he did go over to Okuma-san, who was sitting with philosophical calm on a nearby rock, looping the recovered rope back around his neck. The old man spoke gruffly but had tears in his eyes as Joe thanked him with a deep bow – Joe could see Okuma-san was inordinately happy to have repaid an important debt of honour so soon.

Joe understood by now what an emotional race the Japanese were, and certainly far removed from the conventional view of the inscrutable Oriental. In many ways they seemed to him quite as passionate and easily prone to tears as Latins.

Joe went back to Motoko. 'That was a big earthquake. Do you think there will be a lot of damage in the town?' he asked worriedly.

Motoko looked puzzled, then dismissive. 'Not big earthquake, Joe-san. That small earthquake. Quite common here...'

*

Still in her guise of Mrs Evadne Smythe, Amelia sipped her morning tea and looked with an intrigued eye at the bustle and babble of the Imperial Hotel lobby swirling around her.

A passenger steamship had arrived this morning in Yokohama from Hong Kong and Shanghai, and the lobby was filled with porters and a flustered set of newly-arrived travellers, milling around amongst their stacks of heavily laden trunks and baggage: there were loud-mouthed top-hatted American businessmen and their heavily corseted wives in hats and feather boas, an English bishop in gaiters and his remarkably plain grown-up daughter, a Scottish judge and his querulous family from China, a retired monocled colonel with a grumbling overweight wife, and a bevy of young American missionaries too, all with shining parted hair and a fresh proselytising gleam in their eye at the chance to save the souls of the poor benighted Oriental.

Amelia was in an ill temper for several reasons, one certainly being that she felt acutely uncomfortable in the corset and petticoats and heavy drawers of an English lady again after getting so used in recent months to the delicious comfort of a silk kimono.

But her present ill temper stemmed from other much more serious considerations too. She had now almost abandoned her theory that Peregrine Cavendish could be the nigger in the British Embassy woodpile. But the alternatives were surprisingly narrow – in fact only the ambassador himself seemed to have had the necessary access to all the secrets that were known to have been passed to the Russians. But she was at a loss to know how to prove such a devastating possibility, even if she herself took it seriously. She would need incontrovertible proof to make such an improbable accusation stick, of course, so would have to set a subtle trap for the ambassador to fall into – should he be the guilty party, that is. But she would have to obtain Randall's cooperation to set such a trap, and she could imagine what the tiresome Randall would say if she dared to tell him where her suspicions now resided.

So she was wavering between difficult choices as she reasoned what to do next. But whatever action she finally decided to take, she knew it would have to be soon. The diplomatic rhetoric between this newly resurgent and confident Japan, and Tsarist Russia, had reached fresh heights of poisonous invective in the last twenty-four hours, and everyone sensed that both countries were moving relentlessly towards war. It now seemed to Amelia only a question of "when" these two countries would go to war, not "if".

Amelia had to make sure that no more embarrassing British Embassy secrets reached the ears of the Russians in the meantime - via Shelepin or anyone else. If the Japanese were even to suspect that their British allies had somehow allowed secrets about Japanese military preparations to be leaked to the Russians, then several major treaties and potential arms deals between Britain and Japan might be duly torn up and thrown away.

As if on cue, Amelia saw Major Kiyoshi Sawada and some of his staff enter the Imperial Hotel and stride through the lobby on their way upstairs to one of the rooms they used for vetting suspicious new arrivals to Japan. She knew that, despite his relatively junior rank, this man was a close confidante of General Yanagi Yoshida, the leader of the *Genro* and the de facto ruler of this country, the eminence grise behind Prime Minister Katsura.

Sawada was the chief spy catcher in Japanese counter-intelligence, and reported directly to Yoshida, a reflection of his unique authority. Although the British were allies of the Japanese, she knew she would get short shrift from Sawada if she was recognised and caught by the Japanese authorities. In that respect she had to be as wary of Japanese counter-intelligence as Shelepin, although her ability with the art of disguise gave her much more freedom of movement to move about in Japanese society than he probably had.

Yet at least Amelia had no fear for her life, if she were unmasked by Sawada and his Japanese spy hunters – it would be highly embarrassing, of course, but she would probably only be deported after a bit of diplomatic wrangling between allies. Whereas Shelepin must know that if Sawada caught him, he would be interrogated painfully and could meet a very unpleasant end indeed...

A further reason for Amelia's ill-tempered mood this morning was that she had also come to the Imperial hoping to keep a protective eye on Joseph for the next few days, in the event that Johan Plesch really was here and bent on his murder. This did seem entirely plausible now given the events of the last few days, and the several attempts on Joseph's life. Joseph had received much publicity in this country as a result of the attempted bombing of the hotel last Monday, and perhaps this incident had alerted Plesch to his presence here, and offered him the chance to take his revenge. Therefore, like it or not, Joseph could be the key to smoking Plesch out of hiding, much as Pryor seemed to have intended. Pryor and the Americans could no longer benefit directly from this situation, but perhaps she could. It would be a substantial coup for her if she could make up for past failures and identify Plesch here in Tokyo, then arrange for him to be finally dealt with. But Joseph's life undoubtedly meant more to her than it had to Pryor so she couldn't possibly use him as an innocent and unknowing pawn in quite the same way. Instead she needed to proceed with a more cautionary plan than Pryor, which would hopefully not expose Joseph to too much unnecessary risk.

But her plan had been still born so far: she'd made a few enquiries with the hotel staff and discovered that she couldn't watch Joseph's back as she'd hoped, for the very simple reason that he had, according to the hotel staff, left Tokyo for a few days - to go either to Hakone or Kamakura, depending on which member of the hotel staff you believed. But at least it probably meant that Joseph was safely out of harm's way for these next few days...

Amelia became suddenly flustered as she saw Clive Randall enter the lobby too. For a moment his eyes raked over the scene and lingered suspiciously on her. She held her breath expectantly, then sipped her tea, trying to look as much like a bored middle-aged English lady as possible.

But fortunately it seemed Randall hadn't recognised her after all, because he proceeded to walk straight past her and mount the main staircase two steps at a time as if late for an urgent appointment. Amelia wondered if he was meeting Sawada – she knew that they did exchange sensitive information on occasions, which was one further reason why Amelia didn't want even Randall to know that Mrs Evadne Smythe and Amelia Peachy were one and the same person. He might betray that secret too, as he had with her secret guise as Aiko-san, and she needed to use the identity of Mrs Smythe in order to track down the traitor in the British embassy. Her private mission to catch a British traitor was one secret that had to be kept from the Japanese at all costs.

Amelia watched Randall disappear up the stairs, then suddenly became aware of another pair of eyes trained on her, those of Jacques, the handsome young French desk clerk.

'Is everyzing all right, Madame Smythe?' he asked crisply, his brilliantined hair shining like polished metal in the sunlight falling through the coloured skylights in the entrance portico.

Amelia sighed inwardly. This man was the bane of her life when she was here, always angling for tips for one thing or another, and believing his attentions must be so welcome to an apparently middle-aged and lonely woman. 'Yes, everything is splendid, Jacques, thank you.' Amelia tried to send Jacques on his way with a firm dismissal but the Frenchman seemed reluctant to get back immediately to the desk. Amelia had wondered several times if Jacques might be a government agent of some sort too – certainly in the position he was in, he must get to hear all sorts of sensitive information.

'Is your 'usband still away, Madame?'

Amelia nodded. 'Yes, he is - still in Kyushu for another three months at least, I'm afraid.'

'Oh, zat is so sad for a lovely lady like you, Madame. You must be very lonely wizout 'im.'

Amelia blinked in surprise. *Was it her imagination or was she being propositioned?*

Jacques stopped in mid-flow however, suddenly conscious that another woman was standing by, listening closely to this conversation. Amelia was surprised to recognise the Japanese woman, Fumiyo Isogai, whom Lady Rosemary had pointed out to her yesterday. Miss Isogai stared coldly at Jacques for a moment before saying surprisingly, 'May I join you for tea…?'

*

'It was very good of you to rescue me from that man, Miss Isogai,' Amelia said circumspectly after she had introduced herself as Mrs Smythe.

'Oh, you know who I am, do you?' Now that she had sat down and joined "Mrs Smythe" in a cup of English tea, Fumiyo Isogai seemed less than interested in her new companion, Amelia thought, her attention clearly elsewhere as if she was waiting for someone else.

Amelia sipped her tea. 'I do – a friend of mine, Lady Rosemary Hawtry-Gough, pointed you out to me yesterday.'

Fumiyo glanced up from her tea in surprise. 'Really? I doubt that the wife of the British ambassador approves of me, though.'

Amelia smiled. "Perhaps not. I believe you are seen as a woman full of dangerous notions and radical ideas.'

Fumiyo almost smiled back. 'I certainly hope so…' – she glanced over at the hotel desk – '…that desk clerk gigolo is a disgrace. He's propositioned every wealthy woman in the hotel, including myself. But he gets away with it constantly.'

Amelia turned to look at Jacques, who was now back at the desk and smiling broadly at the English bishop's plain twenty-year-old daughter. The girl responded with a shy smile that revealed a set of braces like a barbed wire fence on her front teeth. Amelia studied the girl for a moment and wondered if she could ever use that particular plain look as a disguise – it certainly was a promising possibility as it would deter the attention of almost every man alive. 'I imagine he must have made a few conquests in his time here,' she said, indicating Jacques and the bishop's daughter.

Fumiyo frowned. 'I hope I didn't act presumptuously in breaking up your conversation with the man. I supposed his attentions were unwelcome to you, but perhaps…'

'Yes, of course they were unwelcome,' Amelia said hurriedly.

Fumiyo asked a few questions about Amelia's putative railway engineer husband, which Amelia answered politely and evasively as the lobby gradually quietened after the sudden influx of new arrivals checking in.

'And what do you do for a living, Miss Isogai?' Amelia asked, studying with approval her elegant kimono and beautifully styled hair. 'Are you involved in politics like your father?'

Fumiyo still seemed very distracted. 'Oh, me?…No, not really. Presently I teach mathematics to Japanese girl students at a local high school. These girls are mostly from poor backgrounds but some are very intelligent. For the life of me, I really can't see why the careers of scientist and engineer and doctor are open only to men, and not to women. With our present system, we are ignoring the talents of half of humanity, and we can't afford to do that any longer. That's what I want to try and achieve here in Japan – a chance for women to make good careers for themselves, not always to be shackled to the kitchen and the marital bed, if they don't want that for their life's work.'

'Bravo.' Amelia wondered if Miss Isogai was being deliberately provocative in stating such opinions to the staid-looking English lady she appeared to be.

Fumiyo did seem a little surprised that "Mrs Smythe" was apparently so willing to agree with her viewpoint, and she became even more forthright. 'And I have been trying to start a clinic in the district of Asakusa for advising young women about birth control. For married women as well as prostitutes, I mean. I hope that doesn't shock you.' Fumiyo's eyes gleamed with challenge, as if looking deliberately for an argument.

Amelia herself had come across a young Scottish woman called Marie Stopes in London two years ago, who was studying botany at University College and who had been passing out leaflets around the slum areas of the East End with a similar revolutionary idea in mind. But she was still surprised to hear a Japanese woman openly mentioning such radical things in public. 'No, not at all,' she responded. 'But I think you will have a long struggle ahead of you.'

'True.' Fumiyo became more cautious in her mood. 'But I do help with my father's political work too, of course, and that will further women's rights here in the long run.'

'Will Japan go to war soon with the Russians, do you think, Miss Isogai?' Amelia asked, curious to know what the Japanese themselves thought of the likely coming conflict.

'I sincerely hope not.' Fumiyo was adamant. 'It would be a disaster for this country.'

'Because you think you will lose?' Amelia suggested warily.

Fumiyo snorted angrily. 'No, on the contrary, because I think we might well win.'

This woman was full of surprising opinions, Amelia thought. 'Why would that be a problem for Japan, then?'

Fumiyo sighed. 'It's a problem for us because Japan is a country presently trying to evolve a sensible political structure for itself. We are presently torn between the rule of a few rich powerful men supported by the military, and the new political parties who want to give ordinary people some say in their lives. A victory over the Russians would give the military even more power and make any progress to universal franchise slower and more difficult. If we start to embark on foreign wars of conquest, Japan could easily become a military dictatorship with even less freedom for its people than now, if we are not careful.' Fumiyo frowned as if suddenly regretting such frank talk with a stranger. 'Forgive me, Mrs Smythe. I can see I'm boring you with this political talk...' She stopped in mid-sentence as Major Sawada appeared on the stairs again and came back down to the lobby.

Amelia could see that Fumiyo was watching Sawada with close attention, as if weighing him up. When Sawada left the hotel, Fumiyo got straight to her feet. 'I've really enjoyed our little talk, Mrs Smythe, but would you please excuse me? I have an urgent appointment to attend,' she added, before hastening after Sawada.

*

Within a minute, a curious Amelia had followed Fumiyo Isogai out into the mid-winter morning sunlight, keeping a discreet distance behind her.

Amelia saw her quarry heading in the direction of Hibiya Park, although the man who seemed to have prompted her rapid decision to leave the hotel, Major Sawada, had completely disappeared from Amelia's sight by now.

Amelia had been sure that Fumiyo had decided to follow Major Sawada for some reason, but that didn't seem to be the case after all. Once she got to Hibiya Park, Fumiyo no longer appeared to be in any hurry at all. Having entered the park, she wandered at a leisurely pace down an avenue between rows of bare gingko trees, lined with noodle vendors and stalls on each side selling magic fans, creamy-puff rice waffles and bloated cardboard masks.

Fumiyo stopped and bought some noodles from one of the stalls and ate them standing up. Amelia watched her consuming her noodles from the cover of a gingko tree but only gradually became aware that, as she was eating, Fumiyo remained standing next to the same individual the whole time, a man with whom she seemed to be exchanging the odd whispered word.

Yet the man didn't look the sort of person who would have much in common with a woman like Fumiyo Isogai – this was a shaven-headed blind monk...

Shaven-headed Buddhist monks were common in this city, of course, but blind ones much less so. Amelia thought it was an interesting coincidence that the man who taken several shots at Joseph Appeldoorn on Wednesday night had apparently been someone pretending to be a blind monk...

She considered again the possibility that this someone could have been Johan Plesch himself...

Suddenly Amelia's attention was diverted from Fumiyo and the shaven-headed monk, though, as she felt the earth begin to rumble beneath her feet, and then to shake violently. People were flung to the ground by the rapid back-and-forward movement of the earth as Amelia distinctly saw trees and lampposts sway rapidly like slender reeds of tall grass.

Amelia managed to keep her feet but all around her women and children screamed and staggered for shelter. She watched in breathless trepidation, waiting for the shaking to become more intense, and for the buildings around the park to start toppling and collapsing like dominoes.

But the quake passed in a few seconds and Amelia was reassured that this was only a minor event, and not one of the major earthquakes that frequently occurred in this mountainous volcanic country.

As the vibrations stopped, she returned her attention to the noodle stall where Fumiyo had been eating. But she saw with dismay that Fumiyo was gone.

And so unfortunately was the monk...

CHAPTER 14

Saturday January 30th 1904

Despite it being a Saturday, Shimbashi Station still reverberated with all its usual early morning bustle as Joe met Motoko on the main concourse. On Platform 1, their express train to Kyoto was being prepared for its departure in half- an-hour, while on Platform 2 another earlier express bound for Osaka was just about to leave, with much frenetic activity, loading of luggage, rushing of last minute arrivals, banging of carriage doors, all of this human activity played out against a harsher background chorus of mechanical noises: the grind of iron wheels on rails, the screech of a whistle, the hiss of expectant steam from the hulking black locomotives waiting at the platforms.

Although this place had the general architectural look of a European railway station, Joe saw that it also had a unique cultural identity of its own that set it apart from anywhere in Europe, certainly with regard to the interesting examples of humanity who thronged its busy platforms. Groups of noisy schoolboys, still mostly wearing traditional Japanese costume rather than Western-style school uniforms, giggled and horse-played with each other as they ran down the length of the platforms; shop girls in their pretty peach and sky-blue kimonos scurried across the concourse in droves, heading to work no doubt in the department stores of Nihombashi. Emaciated delivery boys swayed along with huge panniers of noodles and rice balanced improbably on their heads, while the few Westerners waiting on the concourse for the express to Kyoto looked down their long European noses at all this clamorous Oriental activity around them.

Joe could not help but notice a haughty-looking English lady, wearing a coat of fox fur, who inspected all this Eastern activity around her with exaggerated perplexity through her gold pince-nez. Joe was struck as much by the woman's disturbing ugliness as by her patronising manner; he decided uncharitably that she had the perfect face to match the dead animal that had provided her luxuriant fur. An exuberant elderly Italian in a frock coat and gaiters remonstrated with his porters, his rich and mellifluous tones echoing around the curved hammer beam roof of the station. The man's penetrating tones could even be heard above the slow hiss of steam and all this Oriental babble which was an impressive feat of sorts.

Despite all this extraneous activity going on around him, Joe's attention was concentrated more particularly, though, on his beautiful companion than on anything else. As he waited in line with her to go through the gate to Platform 1, Joe saw with amusement that Motoko seemed as excited to be making this trip as a young girl boarding a train for the first time. But perhaps this was just her natural exuberance, Joe thought, or else a result of her general happiness after their narrow escape from that earthquake and landslide yesterday in Kamakura.

Motoko had not been absolutely correct, though, in saying that yesterday's earthquake had been an ordinary one. The newspaper report in the Japan Mail today had suggested that it had actually been a significant quake that had been felt right across the Kanto Plain, including the cities of Tokyo and Yokohama. Yet Motoko had been right at least in thinking that the effects of it would not be serious. Joe had seen some minor structural damage in Kamakura and Yokohama on his way back to Tokyo yesterday afternoon, but remarkably little considering the violence of the ground movement during the quake. Everything in the city of Tokyo seemed to be working normally today, and all the fallen building debris from the quake had already been cleared from the streets; this was clearly a nation that seemed capable of shrugging off the challenges of nature with an almost casual resilience.

Finally they were allowed to go through the gate and onto Platform 1, along with their porter and their luggage. As he walked down the platform on this fine winter morning, past the gleaming painted carriages of the waiting train, Joe was still undeniably nervous because of recent events, and couldn't help keeping his eyes peeled for any shaven-headed monks who might be in the vicinity, or even for that supposed Swiss businessman, Herr Maienfeld. That man seemed to have a worrying habit of turning up where he wasn't expected...

'Perhaps I should buy a newspaper before we claim our compartment,' Joe suggested, as Motoko ordered the porter in rapid Japanese to take their luggage ahead and put it on board. Joe went over to a nearby newspaper stall looking for anything to read in English. But he saw only further copies of the Japan Mail that he had already read in his hotel earlier, so he quickly gave up on that idea and returned to the train, which was now ready for imminent departure. The carriages were designed in the manner of European trains, Joe saw, with a through corridor on one side, giving access to well-appointed private compartments, with seats in each for up to six passengers. But Motoko had booked a whole compartment for just the two of them, and soon Joe was settled comfortably opposite her in a luxuriously upholstered seat, and with plenty of room to stretch his long legs...

Still conscious of this plausible threat from the assassin Plesch, Joe had returned to the Imperial Hotel yesterday afternoon in a wary mood (particularly after his narrow escape in the morning from the landslide) gone straight up to his room, and, behind double locked doors, had gone to bed early for once in preparation for the trip to Kyoto. At first light this morning he had appeared discreetly in the near deserted lobby to make a hopefully unobserved exit from the hotel, then taken a carriage from the Imperial to Shimbashi Station to meet up with Motoko again as planned. Motoko had already assured him that she had made all the other arrangements for the rail journey herself, including booking a private compartment to ensure that they would be able to travel in both comfort and security...

Now, in the light of a fresh day, and with the train ready to depart for Kyoto, Joe had almost managed to put all his worries aside for the moment, even the most unsettling one - the thought that Johan Plesch might still be alive and in Japan, and bent on vengeance.

As the train finally began to chug away from the platform in a great cloud of steam, Joe tried to weigh up afresh the actual evidence of this being true, and it did seem to him that perhaps he had just been a victim of ill circumstance and bad luck, rather than because of a deliberate campaign of revenge. Oddly, the fact that he'd nearly lost his life in that earthquake and landslide at Kamakura yesterday had rather reinforced that view, if anything. After all, even Johan Plesch couldn't organise an earthquake to order, could he?

And Major Sawada - and everyone else he'd spoken to, for that matter - seemed convinced that the attempted bombing in the Imperial Hotel on Monday night had to be the work of a Japanese ultra-Nationalist or anarchist group, not the work of a foreign assassin.

So what did that leave? Only the murder of Toby Pryor, and his last enigmatic words. And the armed monk in the Yoshiwara, of course.

Those events were frankly more difficult to explain, except as personal attacks on him. But perhaps he'd just been attacked in the Yoshiwara on those two separate occasions because he was a Westerner, and this had nothing to do with Johan Plesch at all? Perhaps the simple truth was that this was just a more dangerous town for foreign visitors than he'd been led to believe...

Yet a significant doubt remained in Joe's mind that meant he couldn't ignore this potential risk from Plesch altogether. But thankfully Joe had seen nothing out of the ordinary as he'd boarded the train, and now for the first time in many hours, he felt completely safe again, and even content, with the pretty face of Motoko opposite, beaming at him in anticipation of the pleasant eight-hour rail journey to Kyoto.

*

Motoko became pensive soon after, though, and said little for the first hour of the journey, seemingly happy to watch the exquisite scenery unfold in silence, as the train, after crossing the Kanto Plain and passing Odawara and Mishima, left the rocky Izu Penisula behind and reached the Pacific coast again.

With the rippled blue ocean on one side, and an endless vista of fallow rice paddies on the other, and with Mount Fuji looming emblematically in the hazy distance, this view through the carriage window seemed to Joe the quintessence of Japan. This mystical mountain had a particularly strange and ghostly look today. The snowy cap, with a thin layer of pearl-white cloud arrayed below it, appeared by a trick of the light to be detached from the rest of the mountain, almost floating ethereally above it as if literally a home for the Gods.

'Beautiful, *né?*' Motoko breathed, as if in a state of religious ecstasy at this strange sight.

Joe nodded in agreement. 'I hope Umegiku-san didn't suffer any distress from the earthquake yesterday,' he went on.

'We Japanese used to moving earth,' Motoko said philosophically. 'I sure you cause Umegiku-san much more disturbance than earthquake. Maybe you want see her again when you reach Kyoto?' she added with a sly smile. 'Earthquake cause no real damage in Tokyo or Kamakura yesterday.' She shivered slightly. 'But one day, of course, earthquake will destroy city. "*Inevitable*" – is that right word?'

It was the right word, perhaps, but Joe was still taken aback by the bleakness of her forecast. 'You really believe that Tokyo will be destroyed by an earthquake one day?'

Motoko wrinkled her pretty nose. 'Oh yes, Joe-san. But that won't be end of Tokyo. When it happen, we build again...and again...'

She was a remarkable girl, Joe thought, and a good example of her remarkable people.

*

At 1 p.m., having passed Hamamatsu, they took lunch together in the restaurant car, which was clearly modelled on that of a European express train. With its thick maroon carpet, obsequious soft-voiced waiters, windows partly curtained with draped swirls of velvet, neat tables on each side with rose-coloured lamps, and silver cutlery shining on crisp white linen, it did resemble the restaurant cars of the Compagnie Internationale des Wagons-Lits, the service originated by the famous Belgian, M. Georges Nagelmackers.

The restaurant car was warm and inviting, and the tables mostly occupied by European travellers. Motoko did seem a little nervous at eating in such a place, although Joe thought that she'd handled the dining room of the Imperial Hotel the other night without any noticeable problems that he could remember. She had dressed in Western costume for the rail journey – a tight-fitting outfit of green satin and white lace that showed off her slender figure to perfect advantage, and with a pert little feathered bonnet to complement her sweet face.

As Joe was sitting down at an unoccupied table, he glanced along the carriage and vaguely recognised the face of a plump middle-aged Englishwoman eating at a table alone at the end of the car. Joe's natural suspicions were working overtime at the moment so he racked his brains as to where he'd seen her before. Then it came to him – this was the same woman he'd seen sitting in the alcove of the Imperial lobby on the night of the bombing five days ago. What was her name again? He'd heard Jacques, the desk clerk, use it. Mrs Smythe, that was it...

This seemed quite an unsettling coincidence to Joe that she should turn up here on the train to Kyoto, although it could just be perfectly innocent of course. There were relatively few Westerners in Japan, he reminded himself, and they would tend to congregate in the same places and at the same social gatherings with each other, places like the Imperial Hotel, and this train for that matter. So perhaps the coincidence wasn't that unusual at all. Nevertheless he still kept his eyes trained on her uneasily for a few minutes while he and Motoko ordered lunch.

Joe opted for Wiener Schnitzel and Vichyssoise, and Cataratto white Italian wine, while Motoko went for Bisque and lobster. During lunch, Joe kept a wary eye on the disparate faces of all his fellow diners, not only Mrs Smythe, trying to discern any sign of a possible threat from any of them.

The haughty looking Englishwoman in the fox fur was there, as expected, now in company with an equally repellent-looking middle-aged Englishman in a tweed suit. A much prettier and younger Englishwoman was travelling alone with a child of ten or so. She had a truly spectacular bosom and the tiniest waist Joe had ever seen, and she smiled wistfully in Joe's direction whenever he caught her eye, which was quite often.

An elderly French couple complained noisily about the quality of the food throughout their meal but seemed resolved to eat every last morsel anyway. At the next table in front of them, a youngish German by his dress and looks, examined his fellow passengers with sour displeasure. There was no sign of Herr Maienfeld, or any travelling monks, Joe was glad to see.

On the opposite side of the carriage, at the table immediately adjacent to their own, was the elderly Italian with the stentorian voice whom Joe had seen on the Shimbashi Station concourse. This man seemed determined to engage Joe in conversation, particularly as Motoko seemed out of sorts and very quiet.

'My name is Valdini, Giuseppe Valdini.' He leaned across after the wine waiter had passed and stretched out his hand. Valdini had a striking baldhead, quite as bare and dome-like as that of Hageyama, and tufted grey eyebrows over a craggy drawn face. 'I am *Professore* of medicine, from Milano.' He indicated the bottle on Joe's table. 'I think you should not have ordered the Cataratto. Much better the Moscato or the Saint Nicola.'

'Oh, I am happy enough with this,' Joe assured him.

The Italian's voice boomed through the dining car, despite the rattle of the train and the deadening effect on sound of the thick carpet and velvet curtains.

'So how long have you been in Japan, Mr Appeldoorn?' Signor Valdini asked, after Joe had introduced himself in return.

'Only a week or so.' It did seem surprising that it was so short a time, given what had happened to him.

'And how are you enjoying Japan? This to me is a unique land, unlike anything I ever encountered.'

Joe nodded ruefully. 'I certainly agree with that. What are you doing here, Signor?'

'I am here to do some – how you say? – research in diseases, particularly smallpox. I try to identify cause of disease. I extend the work of Professor Martinus Beijerinck of the University of Delft, who has identified the causative agent of tobacco mosaic disease as a filterable virus, not a toxin. I believe many diseases, like smallpox, are also caused by filterable viruses, which are much smaller than bacteria, and therefore impossible to see with microscope. Perhaps smaller than a thousandth of a millimetre.'

'Interesting,' Joe said without enthusiasm.

The Italian doctor lapsed into silence as Motoko groaned. 'So sorry. No good feel, Joe-san. Have to go back to compartment.'

'Perhaps the lobster didn't agree with her? Shall I help you and take a look at your lady companion, Mr Appeldoorn?' Valdini offered with a concerned look.

*

It was after three o'clock in the afternoon by now and the train had passed Nagoya and left the coast, heading into the forested mountain interior of Western Honshu on its way to Kobe.

The carriages swayed and lurched from side-to-side as Joe half-carried Motoko back to their compartment near the rear of the train. He was getting worried because she was clearly in some distress, her legs leaden and her eyelids drooping.

The locomotive began to ascend a long curved incline up through dense pine and cedar forest; because of the curve, Joe could see the engine breathing fire up ahead, a long plume of steam and smoke rising from the stack.

Valdini was following behind and tut-tutting his concern as he went. They finally reached the compartment and Motoko was almost unconscious now so Joe lifted up all the arm rests and laid her out gently on the padded velvet seats on one side of the compartment.

'Shall I take a look at her?' Valdini suggested diffidently, closing the compartment door to the corridor behind him and pulling the window blinds down for privacy. Joe stood aside to let him examine her.

'What's wrong with her?' Joe asked. 'Any ideas? Could it really be food poisoning?'

Joe watched the Italian as he loosened a few buttons on Motoko's bodice and took her pulse. Joe absently put a hand in the pocket of his English worsted jacket and was puzzled to find a piece of paper that he didn't remember putting there.

'I don't think this is food poisoning, Mr Appeldoorn,' Valdini was saying. 'It looks almost as if she's been drugged. I wonder who could have done such a thing.'

Joe had pulled out the slip of paper by now, and his blood froze as he read the message scribbled rapidly by hand in English on the note...

"Beware of the Italian. He is v. dangerous..."

As Joe fumbled to put the note back in his pocket, Valdini suddenly lashed out with the back of his hand and sent Joe sprawling...

*

Joe woke up to find it was already nearly dark outside, and that he was in his own seat in the compartment. He must have been out for hours, yet that was puzzling because Valdini certainly hadn't hit him that hard.

Then he remembered feeling the prick of a needle as he'd fallen, and realised in panic that the Italian had injected him with something...

Joe's eyes brought the features of the compartment slowly into focus again: Motoko was apparently sleeping now, stretched out on the other compartment seat where he'd laid her earlier. The blinds to the corridor windows were still pulled down for obvious reasons: at the opposite end of his own seat, next to the corridor, sat Valdini, with a Mauser pistol in his hand.

But no longer the genial elderly Italian – instead, someone else entirely. The man hadn't changed his appearance at all from earlier today, yet somehow he looked twenty years younger and infinitely more threatening...

'Herr Plesch,' Joe said through dried, cracked lips, wondering how he was managing to stay so calm when his nervous system should instead be erupting with fear.

Perhaps the calmness was a chemical calm only, induced by whatever concoction Plesch had injected into him. Yet it was more than just an unnatural calm that seemed to possess him: his mind did truly seem to be working in an enhanced way, his perceptions heightened somehow, sensations of colour and sound and texture intensified. This extended to his view of Plesch/Valdini who seemed magnified in every detail. The eyes still had the same disturbing yellow caste that he remembered from two years ago, yet everything else looked different: the shiny skin of the skull with almost no hint of stubble, the drawn sallow cheeks, the pores of his aquiline nose visible, the wiry tendons and strong musculature of his neck.

'Joseph. So nice to see you again,' Plesch said in perfect English. 'You don't mind me calling you "Joseph", do you? I feel I've earned the right to such familiarity.'

Joe's voice was hoarse and strained, and he tried to clear the discomfort in his throat with a cough. 'Why did you drug me, Herr Plesch? Why not just kill me outright?'

Plesch sighed. 'Too many people about in the restaurant car, that's all. Now that we have left Kobe, and we're on the final leg to Kyoto, the train is two-thirds empty so it's much easier to dispose of unwanted baggage without being seen. Much better, too, to dispose of a body under the cover of darkness in this wild stretch of mountainous country coming up. And, anyway, I've missed your company, Joseph, so I thought I would like to catch up on old times. Call me a sentimentalist, but there you are.'

'Your doctor act was very convincing,' Joe said begrudgingly.

'That's because it's not an act, Joseph. I did indeed train as a physician, until I realised that my own species is hopelessly corrupt and degenerate, and therefore not worth the trouble of trying to save. With a few honourable exceptions anyway.'

Joe thought back to the last time he'd seen Plesch in Switzerland. 'How did you survive that fall from the cliff into the Rhine? Why did you survive? God must have a strange sense of humour.'

'Strange indeed...' Plesch stroked the barrel of the Mauser with his left forefinger, removing an invisible film of dust. 'That's a very difficult question, Joseph. Who can say how or why? It wasn't my time to die, that's all.'

Joe nodded at the man's shining skull. 'What happened to your hair?'

Plesch grimaced. 'A temporary sacrifice only, I assure, but I do rather like the effect. I deliberately lost twenty kilos too for this part, and I also imbibed a chemical concoction that includes gunpowder as one of its constituents. Its long term harmful effects are negligible; however for a few days it does give the skin this marvellously authentic sick grey pallor and age it a good twenty years or so.'

Joe grunted cynically. 'And there was me hoping you might really be at death's door.'

Plesch looked hurt. 'Now, now. That's ungracious of you, Joseph.'

'That face you are wearing is also very useful for playing a blind shaven-headed monk too, I suppose,' Joe suggested tartly.

Plesch frowned. 'Ah, you spotted that as me. I must say I'm disappointed, then. I thought that I was rather convincing in that role, and so unlike my normal self.'

Joe was curious to know the truth. 'Did you throw that bomb into the lobby of the Imperial Hotel on Monday night?' he asked. 'You were there that night...'

'I was there, but surprisingly the bombing was nothing to do with me. I was as disconcerted as everyone else when that man threw his device into the lobby. I was there outside the hotel for a liaison with someone else entirely – my own client. You shocked me, charging through the door at me like that, and for a second I thought you'd recognised me by some unfortunate miracle. Until that moment I had no idea you were even in Japan but, alas for you, your heroic escapades brought you rapidly to my attention after that.'

Joe nodded knowingly. 'So you did send those three assassins to follow me and Pryor to the *Yoshiwara*?'

'Not me personally, but my Japanese client did arrange it on my behalf. You and Mr Pryor gave me no choice but to deal with you quickly before you became a nuisance again. When American agents begin to dog my footsteps like this, I have no choice but to retaliate.'

Joe was genuinely puzzled and irritated by this. 'You still suspect I'm an agent of the American government? I am no agent, Herr Plesch, and I did not come to Japan to pursue you.'

Plesch laughed sarcastically. 'No? Really? I find that very hard to believe. But you want to know something, Joseph. I could have killed you very easily on Wednesday night in the *Yoshiwara* after I hit you with that old chair leg, I had all the time in the world to slit your throat or put a bullet through your head, even with that silly Englishman approaching. Yet for some reason I couldn't do it, not with you lying there, helpless. It's a strange weakness that I've developed of late, is it not?'

'So why do it now?' Joe asked disbelievingly.

Plesch sighed. 'Ah, because my client has finally insisted on closing any loose ends. And you are certainly one of those. My client believes you are far too dangerous a fellow to be left alive, in view of what we are planning to do. I heard by chance that you came very close to meeting a natural end in Kamakura yesterday, which would have been very convenient all round. But, like me, you have an unfortunate habit of cheating death, Joseph. So I'm afraid I'm under strict orders to ensure you give us no more trouble.'

The last rays of sunlight were just staining the western sky. The train was rattling and wheezing as it twisted up a tortuous length of mountain line with steep precipices and ravines falling away on both sides.

'I think it's time, Joseph.' Plesch lifted the blinds to the compartment and looked out into the corridor. Satisfied that it seemed to be empty, he stepped outside and motioned Joe with the Mauser to follow.

'Come on!' he ordered. 'I don't want to kill that pretty creature too – that's why I put a sleeping draught into her Bisque. You see, I really am a sentimentalist at heart, whatever you may think. I dislike killing women except when it's absolutely necessary, as it was with the late and unlamented Miss Peachy. But if you give me any trouble about this, I guarantee I'll kill the girl too. So be warned, and move yourself quickly before I lose patience.'

Joe stood up reluctantly and followed Plesch out into the corridor. The windows looked almost black now with the near darkness outside, and the view dominated by the darkening mass of the encroaching hills and their dense stands of fir and cedar trees.

Plesch led Joe at gunpoint to the main carriage door. 'Lower the window!' he ordered.

Joe did as he was told, allowing the wind to roar through the carriage.

The train was travelling at breakneck speed along the upper edge of a steep-sided river valley, a sheer drop and a foaming boulder-strewn torrent of water rushing below them, with another precipitous slope of tall fir trees rising on the other side of the valley.

Joe wondered if he could possibly jump the man, but he knew from experience that, despite all appearances to the contrary, the man was physically unsurpassed as an athlete. For all his nondescript looks, something other than normal red blood coursed through that evil man's veins, and his body seemed composed of a different form of matter to conventional muscle and sinew.

Joe felt the barrel of the Mauser jammed into the back of his skull and prepared for his end with a silent prayer and a wildly thudding heart.

But saviours come in unlikely forms, and Joe was suddenly aware that the plump Englishwoman Mrs Smythe had appeared from nowhere in the corridor, apparently in a volatile and unpredictable mood. Actually she seemed drunk and almost out of her mind, muttering strangely to herself like a mad woman.

Joe heard Plesch curse softly to himself, and he pulled his gun back out of sight to let this strange deranged woman pass.

Joe didn't want to get Mrs Smythe killed too, no matter how bizarre a person she was, so said nothing but made only a slight bow of acknowledgement to her as she passed.

But suddenly the woman screamed at him unnervingly. 'You animal! You unspeakable bastard!' She looked at Plesch and sobbed. 'This man forced his way into my compartment earlier and made disgraceful advances to me! Sir, I need your help to bring him to account. Please call the guard at once!' And she swung her heavy handbag at Joe, using it like a slingshot, but, instead of hitting him, somehow managed to strike Plesch in the jaw with a force that sent him reeling against the nearby bulkhead.

The woman then pushed Joe away and reached with feverish speed inside her bag.

But Plesch had recovered enough from his own surprise by now to kick out viciously in return with a foot directed into the pit of Mrs Smythe's stomach, which blow sent her flying along the floor of the corridor, where she hit her head with savage force against a metal stanchion.

Plesch had lost his pistol somewhere in the melee but wasn't to be denied and, grabbing Joe's neck in a vice-like grip, tried to force him bodily through the open window and out into the yawning chasm on that side of the train.

But, despite having his neck throttled, Joe had enough strength left to hit his attacker in return, directing a blow to his solar plexus with the back of his right elbow; Plesch was thrown back by the fierce blow against the steel wall of the nearest compartment. Joe could see that Plesch was badly winded by the impact but still dangerous, so he kicked the villain's feet away from under him, sending him tumbling to the floor. Sprawled on his back, Plesch glanced along the wildly lurching carriage and must have realised instantly that he was in significant trouble now, because railway attendants and guards were arriving from both ends of the train.

Knowing how dangerous the man was, and seeing him still trying to get to his feet again, Joe wisely decided to forget any old-fashioned notions of fair play, and kicked the man full in the face to finish this contest for good.

Joe nursed his aching neck muscles as he went over to see to the unfortunate Mrs Smythe. As he bent down to try and assess her injuries, though, he had an undoubted moment of exultation as he realised that Plesch was trapped now – the man was unconscious and would soon be taken into custody by the arriving guards...

But that unspoken optimistic thought was soon replaced by disbelief as Joe realised from a blur of movement at his side that Plesch was not unconscious at all, but had been feigning. Joe was sure that he had kicked that man in the face hard enough to have put even Jack Johnson into a permanent coma, yet the man remained as slippery and unbeaten as ever. Before Joe had even realised his intention, Plesch had got to his feet, climbed out through the open window in one fluid motion, and launched himself straight up in the air with considerable gymnastic skill onto the roof of the carriage.

Joe, incensed to see the man escaping yet again, rushed back to the open window and stuck his head out after him, only to have it nearly taken off by Plesch's boot as the man swung his leg at him from a horizontal position on the edge of the carriage roof. But the foot just missed him and Joe had the sense to duck back inside again.

The puzzled guards and attendants had arrived by now, while Mrs Smythe was just getting groggily to her feet. Her grey hair was all awry as if it was a wig that had come loose, but Joe had no time to reflect on that strange sight. He could hear footsteps pounding on the carriage roof over his head, and realised that Plesch had given up in his intention to murder him, and was now just trying to make good his escape along the roof of the train.

If Plesch managed to get back into the forward part of the train and into a carriage, he might even be able to pull the emergency cord and stop the train. He might even get away completely, Joe realised with dismay, as he looked at the unimpressive collection of train guards who had come to his assistance. These small and elderly railway employees did not seem equipped in any way to deal with a criminal as ruthless as Johan Plesch, that much was certain. Joe wanted the guards to stop the train immediately but in all this babble of confusion he couldn't seem to make them understand this simple request. There was no emergency cord nearby that Joe could see to pull himself, though, so before he really knew what he was doing , Joe had climbed through the window after Plesch. Using the projection of a ventilation chimney on the roof, he hauled himself up on top too, where he lay flat on his chest, gasping with the effort, his heart thudding to match the wild shaking of the carriage beneath him.

With disbelief he glanced up from his prone position and saw Plesch running - *running for God's sake!* - along the length of the train towards the front coach and the locomotive. Reluctantly Joe got to his feet, trying his best to keep his balance on the juddering roof, and then followed Plesch at a much slower pace, scared of losing his footing.

God, this was terrifying! It was almost impossible to keep his feet, what with the slippery curved roof, the shrieking of the wind, the near darkness, the sparks of fire and the billowing steam of the locomotive ahead like a vision of Hell. Joe heard the scream of wheel flanges on rails as the train followed a sharp curve, and felt a shiver of primal fear as he saw a vast chasm yawning on one side, and a raging torrent of a river far below.

The only things in Joe's favour were the ventilation louvers on the roof, which gave him something to hold on to - at intervals at least - as he inched his way methodically up the length of the train after Plesch.

Plesch had reached the front of the train by now, with only the coal tender and the locomotive ahead, belching smoke and soot into their faces. He turned to face his pursuer as Joe finally caught up with him. For a man who had been through the wars, including being kicked in the face, Joe saw that the man seemed remarkably untouched by his ordeal, without so much as a bruise to show for all that physical damage. The man truly seemed to possess an almost supernatural physical resilience, as if he was in league with the Devil himself...

Plesch grunted. 'It was unwise of you to follow me, Joseph. You're no physical match for me, as we have proved in the past several times. But you never seem to know when it's time to desist, do you?'

Before he could defend himself, Joe found himself being throttled by hands like hydraulic steel vices rather than things of flesh and blood. Joe's vision began to fade, his head swimming and bursting with pain, as if it was going to explode under the pressure of those relentless steel fingers.

Then, through a red mist turning black, Joe saw the yawning mouth of a tunnel ahead, growing with extraordinary speed, like being sucked into the jaws of some immense leviathan.

Plesch heard the sound of the locomotive change as it approached the tunnel and looked around at the very last second. Joe found his neck suddenly released from the vice and had just a second to fling himself flat before the train roared into the tunnel.

Joe was conscious of deafening noise and a dense cloud of smoke and steam. When the noise level suddenly dropped again and the train reappeared again into the cold blast of the starry night air, Johan Plesch was nowhere to be seen...

CHAPTER 15

Sunday January 31ˢᵗ 1904

The last day of January had dawned cool and dry in the ancient city of Kyoto. Joe was still recovering from the exertions and trials of the last few days, but had nevertheless got up at first light and gone for a walk in the tranquil mossy garden of the Japanese *ryokan* where he was staying. Joe had seen enough of the city late the night before to understand the basic layout of this vast place. Kyoto was a huge rectangular grid of quiet tree-lined streets, of temples, shrines and seductive alleyways, encroached on three sides by green mountains. Here was certainly an older, more timeless Japan than the parvenu Tokyo: on the rickshaw ride from the station to his inn, Joe had seen shuffling *geisha* returning from late night festivities, little stone statues everywhere, and shrines lovingly cherished on every street corner.

At ten o'clock in the morning, Maeda and his daughter Motoko called at the *ryokan* to take him to General Yoshida's house for the planned audience with this important man.

The general's house – a surprisingly modest one considering his much-vaunted status - was located in the foothills of the Eastern Mountains – the *Higashiyama* – facing onto the famous Philosopher's Walk, a path that meandered along the banks of a cherry-lined canal at the base of these scenic forested hills. The house, for all its modest size, also had a fine view of the nearby beautiful Silver Pavilion – the *Gikaku-ji* - except, as Motoko explained to Joe with quintessential Japanese logic, the Silver Pavilion had *never* been silver. Expensive wars of the time had soon put paid to the idea of coating it in silver, and now it had only the patina of five centuries and an illogical name to give it all the charm it needed.

Joe was understandably nervous at meeting this well-known leader, who was the nearest thing Japan had to a Bismarck, or even perhaps a Napoleon. He was supposedly retired but Joe understood enough of the way Japanese

166

politics worked by now to realise that these members of the *"Genro"* never really retired until they were dead and buried, and still ran things closely from behind the scenes.

In deference to a Westerner, the meeting took place in Yoshida's study which was furnished with Western furniture and chairs. But Motoko had been deliberately excluded from this discussion, Joe saw to his slight annoyance. Seated at his writing desk, General Yoshida was a small, wiry, grey-haired man, yet he carried that indefinable stamp of ruthlessness that all great leaders, good or bad, seem to carry. Yoshida was not in uniform but wore instead the *montsuki*, the formal black silk kimono, and the striped *hakama* ankle-length loose trousers, with *setta* sandals on his feet.

Yoshida was patently curious at first about yesterday's reported events on the train from Tokyo, and put his own questions directly to Joe with Maeda standing nervously by, listening to every word with strained attention. Yoshida's English was good if heavily accented.

Joe gave them a bare and entirely fictitious outline of the story. 'Yes, this Italian passenger, Signor Valdini, apparently went insane and decided to kill himself,' Joe said in response to Yoshida's probing. 'No one seems to know why he did it. A very sad business.'

Yoshida chose to demur. 'Suicide is not sad if done for a good reason, Mr App-re-doon. In fact it can be an uplifting and deeply spiritual experience when done properly. But to hurl oneself off a train lacks a certain style, and that is sad. You have only one life to give, after all, so it should not be thrown away without due preparation and planning. The art of suicide is something very close to the Japanese heart, after all.'

Joe nodded warily. 'So I believe. But it's a hard thing for Westerners to comprehend, when we value life so much.'

Yoshida frowned. 'Oh, we Japanese value life deeply too. It's just that we know when the right time to depart has come. It's a question of timing and finesse, that's all...'

*

The train had finally been brought to a screeching halt just after the locomotive made it through the tunnel, and Joe had nearly been sent sliding off the front carriage roof by the violent deceleration, to join Plesch in Kingdom-come.

The train had stopped there for more than an hour while the train crew and coach attendants searched with flaming torches through the tunnel and along the railway line on the approaches, looking for the mortal remains of "Signor Valdini". But none had been found so Joe suspected he must have fallen into the ravine on the right hand of the line just before the tunnel, where the raging torrent of the river would have carried his body miles away in double-quick time.

Joe had decided not to reveal the truth of the incident to the Japanese train crew or to the police – the story was just too wild and improbable for a sensible explanation and he preferred instead to hold fire until he could return to Tokyo and speak to Ambassador Reinhold. And perhaps, on further reflection, he would just forget about the incident entirely and not even broach it with his own Embassy – it was definitely time to start thinking of his own interests and not to go getting involved any more in things that were no longer his concern. He certainly didn't want to have that sinister man Sawada hounding him again, which would undoubtedly happen if Sawada glimpsed any of the truth of what had really happened on this train journey to Kyoto...

Fortunately the Japanese guards and coach attendants on the train had seen no sign of firearms being used, or of the violent struggle that had preceded their arrival, and Joe had managed to persuade them that the Italian doctor had simply gone insane and climbed up on the roof of the train to kill himself (although he had seemed sane enough to the train attendants when having lunch in the restaurant car earlier in the day – a difficult anomaly to rationalise.) It was even harder for Joe to make the train crew believe that he had followed Valdini up onto the roof of the train simply to try and save the man from jumping – even the biggest dullard of a coach attendant would doubt such a wild story.

Motoko had woken up by the time the train finally made it to Kyoto after its long stop in the mountains, and in a slurred and weary voice she had helped Joe convince the uniformed policemen in Kyoto Station who came to question him about the incident that it was really nothing to do with him. The Kyoto City police inspector, Ishii - a man with pebble glasses an inch thick but whose brain was obviously much better than his myopic vision – had clearly been highly doubtful of Joe's version of events, but, without a shred of evidence to the contrary, had been forced to accept it and finally allow Joe go to his *ryokan* late that Saturday night.

Motoko of course knew nothing about the truth of the incident anyway, and Joe had decided to leave her in blissful ignorance. There was no need to burden her with more grief after all the other traumas of the last few days – the bombing at the Imperial Hotel, and then the earthquake - and he was convinced by now that Plesch must be well and truly dead this time, and that his own troubles in Japan were therefore behind him.

So Joe was undoubtedly feeling more relaxed this morning, particularly after he realised that he had achieved justice of a kind for Toby Pryor too, even if the man who had actually run Toby through with his blade might still be alive and free.

The only really perplexing question that remained over the incident on the Kyoto express concerned the unknown fate of Mrs Smythe: somehow the woman had managed to disappear completely from the train after the incident. Joe had looked for her afterwards on the train, and at Kyoto

Station, but she was nowhere to be found. In the excitement, the coach attendants hadn't apparently noticed her disappearance and Joe had thought it better not to bring it to their attention, perhaps because he now had his own theory concerning the identity of the mysterious and apparently deranged Mrs Smythe...

The woman had been wearing a wig, he remembered later, and, while there might be an innocent explanation for that, another thought had occurred to him. Clearly the woman had been trying to protect him when she had come to his rescue with that absurd fabricated tale of being assaulted by him earlier. Perhaps she was also the one who had scribbled that warning note about Valdini, and slipped it into his pocket – although unfortunately he'd not read it until too late. He was convinced now that the woman also had to be an American agent in disguise, therefore probably an associate of the late Toby Pryor, and someone who had been helping him in his task of hunting Plesch to earth. Joe recalled now that Pryor had been quite insulting and derogatory about the woman when Joe had happened to mention her existence to him in the lobby of the Imperial on Monday night. But that could have been Pryor playing games as usual, using sexual insults about the woman to mask her real identity and purpose. This "Mrs Smythe", whoever she really was, had obviously been assigned to follow him to Kyoto and protect him, should Plesch make a move. If that was true, then she had done her job brilliantly well...

Joe was sure by now that her disappearance afterwards was also no accident, which was why he had made no issue of it with the guards. He might never discover the real identity of the woman now who had saved him, but at least he could play his own small part in protecting her secret. In her own way, this woman seemed as remarkable a person to Joseph Apeldoorn as the late Amelia Peachy...

*

Joe's thoughts came back to the present and his reason for coming to Kyoto, as he realised Yoshida had just said something that he'd completely missed.

Maeda quickly intervened to help him. 'General Yoshida was just asking if you were enjoying seeing the sights of Kyoto, Mr Appeldoorn...'

'Kyoto means "Capital City", Mr App-re-doon,' the general repeated patiently. 'This was the home of the Japanese Emperor for centuries - until quite recently in fact. Emperor Kammu laid out this capital a thousand years ago in the Chinese manner, which is why everything is square and perfectly arranged. This city is repository of all ancient Japanese traditions and patriotism, the golden heritage of Japanese people. You have nothing like this in America, I believe.'

Joe shook his head. 'We have a few important sites and artefacts: Plymouth Rock, the Liberty Bell, Monticello - but grand symbols are not really the American way. Our real heritage is our constitution, and the shared values of our people.'

Joe was beginning to understand by now that this wasn't just a courtesy meeting - he was here primarily to be vetted for some reason. It seemed Maeda could not apparently sign this contract with Appeldoorn Industries until General Yoshida had personally given him a stamp of approval. This man really was the power behind the throne in Japan, even apparently to the extent of deciding the winning of important commercial contracts. Forget Prime Minister Katsura, Joe thought; *this* was the real man that mattered.

Yoshida appeared to be in his seventies, but not showing any signs of mental or physical decline yet that Joe could see. He was the archetypal elderly Japanese in some ways, short and squat with tiny slits for eyes, yet his skin was as smooth and unlined as a child's. His manner was undoubtedly autocratic and, although not actually hostile, Joe found the way the man spoke to him – perhaps because of his youth - a little patronising. To his slight discredit, Maeda behaved around the old General in an overtly subservient way that rather demeaned him in Joe's eyes. Yet he supposed that this was the way things were done in Japan – the strict proprieties of rank and status had to be maintained at all time.

At the conclusion of the meeting, Yoshida generously offered to show Joe his private garden, which was a typically restrained Japanese design, with rocks and gravel, and mounds of bright green moss, interspersed with small pines and maples.

Motoko had joined the group again but was walking deliberately behind the men as custom demanded. Yet her mood was less subservient towards Yoshida than her father's, and Joe noticed that she was throwing the odd direct comment into the conversation, which made her father glance at her uncertainly from time to time. She was also giving Joe long and thoughtful looks this morning too, as if seeing him in an entirely fresh light from before.

Yoshida finally complimented Joe on his heroism in the Imperial Hotel on Monday night. 'I heard you saved the life of Motoko-chan and many others, Mr App-re-doon, by your quick thinking. Well done!; the Gods will recognise you for your bravery one day. You may even be reborn as a Japanese one day...'

Joe acknowledged the praise and smiled faintly at Motoko behind. 'Motoko-san already more than repaid the favour to me on Friday.'

Yoshida was curious. 'Oh, how so?'

Joe told the story of the earthquake at Kamakura, and of how he'd been rescued from the sea almost by a miracle.

'Okuma-san was fortunate to be able to repay a debt so quickly,' Yoshida observed primly.

Joe smiled. 'Not as fortunate as I was to receive it.'

Yoshida pondered that. 'You have certainly had an eventful time in our country in the few days you have been here, Mr App-re-doon. An American friend of yours died too, I believe. So sad.'

'Unfortunately we live in violent times. But Mr Pryor was an acquaintance only, not really a friend.' Joe thought again uneasily about Plesch and what he'd been doing here in Japan. He'd obviously been planning some major mischief or other – Joe now remembered his references to his mysterious "client". But hopefully that plan, whatever it was, would be still born now that Plesch was finally dead, so perhaps he could safely go back to being just a businessman again, and one perhaps who was about to finally sign a lucrative contract to supply his company's electrical generating equipment...

*

Afterwards Motoko took Joe to see some of the sights of Kyoto and they returned by the Philosopher's Walk, following the banks of the Shishigatani Canal, under the sun-dappled shade of the bare cherries.

Earlier she had taken him to view one of Kyoto's mightiest treasures, the thousand images of the Goddess Kanno in the Temple of Sanjusangen-do. Standing in front of this bewildering phalanx of glistening golden figures - silent, many-eyed, accusatory, attended by Gods of Thunder and Wind - Joe had been struck again by the inexhaustible mystery of Japanese life...

'I take it that General Yoshida has to approve of me before your father can sign the contract?' Joe commented. 'That's why I was brought here, isn't it?'

Motoko bowed in apology as she walked under the bare branches of the cherry trees at the entrance to the temple. 'So sorry. I should explain before. But don't worry. General very impressed by you. He owns half Imperial Hotel, you know, so you save his property too on Monday. More important than Motoko's life.'

Joe smiled at her. 'Not to me it isn't.'

Motoko bowed gratefully again in gratitude. Joe was tempted to take advantage of this intimate moment to ask her about the young man who had accosted her on the cliff top outside Kamakura, and then subsequently saved her life. But it still seemed presumptuous of him to ask such questions when he still knew so little of Motoko's past life.

They walked on to their next temple. Motoko was a little pale today and still seemed under the weather after her escapades yesterday. Joe suspected that the drug that Plesch had slipped into her Bisque soup on the train yesterday had to have been quite a powerful barbiturate for her still to be suffering after effects in this way. 'Are you feeling all right now?' he asked her worriedly. '*Ima atama ga ii desu-ka?*'

'I all right.' Motoko gave him another glowing smile. 'I enjoy hear you speak Japanese, Joe-san. Per'aps you stay here longer in Japan and learn more.'

'Maybe. We'll have to see.'

'What really happen yesterday on train?' Motoko asked suddenly as they continued on their way. 'There are things I not understand.'

'Me too,' was all Joe would say to that. 'But I hope it's all over now.'

They had reached the Nanzen-ji Temple by now with its rows of pines out front and a truly colossal San-mon, a two storey wooden gate, fit for giants to enter. 'This temple built to console souls of those killed in famous Summer Siege of Osaka Castle in Tokugawa time,' Motoko explained. 'This later became hideout of famous Japanese outlaw, Goemon Ishikawa, who was caught and boiled alive in iron pot.'

After the last few days, Joe thought dryly that he knew what that experience of being boiled alive might feel like.

Motoko stopped in her tracks and looked apologetic again. 'I have one more favour to ask, Joe-san. Mr Kiratani – you remember him from American Embassy on Tuesday - has asked to see you again. Can you go to his house this afternoon?'

*

Yukio Kiratani's house was grander than General Yoshida's, a substantial Kyoto villa set on the hillside above Maruyama Park, with the green mountains of the Higashi-yama rising steeply behind.

Joe had not been keen about coming here, except as a favour to Motoko, so was even more perplexed and put out when he found he had to go in to see Kiratani alone, especially knowing Kiratani could not speak English. For some reason, Motoko herself would not go in, but preferred to wait in Maruyama Park for Joe to return. She assured Joe that there would be no problem of communication because Kiratani's daughter would act as his translator throughout. Motoko seemed deeply troubled about something, but wouldn't say what when Joe pressed her. But of course, she had been engaged to Kiratani's son, Joe remembered now, so perhaps it was simply embarrassing for her to call at the house in person.

Joe was met at the gate by Kiratani himself, and his eldest daughter, Keiko. Kiratani made a great show of welcoming his barbarian visitor, while the rather plain and understated Keiko hovered discreetly in the background, translating her father's words as they went. Her English seemed impeccable.

They sat on the *engawa* of the house, with the skyline of Kyoto's temples and shrines visible through the encircling trees. Green tea was served in broad bowls without handles. Keiko complimented Joe on his seating stance on the hard wooden deck. 'You sit well for a foreigner, Appeldoorn-san.'

From the front veranda of the house, a mossy garden fell away in a series of steps, interlaced with deep fish-pools in which giant carp lazily stirred.

A man dressed in black was exercising in the garden with a samurai sword, performing all the classic movements with the curved blade as he danced around the straw figure of an opponent – unsheathing the sword, then in an elegant ballet, striking out at his straw enemy with a series of impeccable thrusts, parries and a final merciless coup de grace.

'My son, Joji,' Kiratani said. Joe didn't need Keiko's translation this time.

Joe had recognised him at once – this was the young man who had argued with Motoko on the cliff top outside Kamakura. He made no sign of recognition in return but Joe didn't doubt who he was, and now fully understood why Motoko preferred to wait below in Maruyama Park.

But what was less clear was why Kiratani has asked him to come here in the first place, because the man didn't seem to have a great deal to say. There were long uncomfortable silences between them while Joe struggled to think of some suitable topic of conversation. He answered Kiratani's polite questions about his proposed business deal with Maeda, but fortunately did not have to face any further questions about yesterday's incident on the train, or about the death of Toby Pryor, both of which Kiratani apparently seemed unaware of.

Joe couldn't help his attention wandering frequently to the rather sinister figure in the garden. Joji Kiratani looked even more dangerous and threatening with a curved sword in his hand than he had on that cliff top at Kamakura. It was perhaps just as well that his engagement to Motoko had fallen through because he did seem an odd choice of prospective husband for a sweet girl like her – this young man had a fanatical gleam in his eye, and a fixed manic look of concentration on his face, as if nothing else mattered to him in the world but the perfection of his strokes with the sword, and the elegance of his body movement.

Kiratani finally got around to what seemed like the actual point of this meeting. 'I believe you have been talking to a Major Sawada about the bombing incident at the Imperial Hotel on Monday night?' Keiko translated the question in a sing-song voice without any emotion. 'Have you managed to identify the perpetrators of Monday's outrage yet? There has been some suggestion that foreign anarchists could be implicated.'

Joe remembered what Plesch had said to him on the train and for some reason believed him. 'I don't think that's true. Major Sawada seems convinced that it was the work of a local Japanese group.'

Kiratani frowned. 'Could you recognise the man who threw the bomb?'

Joe shook his head. 'No, I never saw the person myself. Other witnesses outside reported a Japanese man in a homburg hat running away, but I think no one could identify him from that.'

Joe was puzzled by Kiratani's reaction to this answer as Keiko translated for him – *was that relief in his face?*

Kiratani seemed happy to change the subject now and talk about more general things through his daughter. 'These are difficult times we live in, Appeldoorn-san – it is hard to keep the spirit of Japan alive under the pressures of the modern world. We cannot freeze time or preserve our society in aspic, I know. But many suspect that we are moving too fast, replacing our own civilisation with alien and decadent values that we will not be able to control.' Kiratani looked at Joe. 'I hope this doesn't offend you, but most of these new values stem from your own country. America grows ever more powerful, and seems unstoppable in its ambition.'

'No offence taken,' Joe said hurriedly. 'I can certainly see why Japan might feel threatened by the rise of America.'

Kiratani seemed appreciative of that diplomatic answer. 'It is difficult bringing up children. Have you any children of your own, Appeldoorn-san?'

Joe smiled. 'No, not yet. I've only been married one year.'

Kiratani looked solemn. 'It is the hardest thing in life to be a good parent and to instil sound values in the young, especially when our culture is changing at such bewildering speed.' At this point he glanced uneasily at his son in the distance.

Joe too was suddenly startled by the son's actions. With a terrifying scream Joji finally sliced through the solid straw figure, removing its head and half its torso in one lightning move. Joe couldn't imagine how sharp that blade must be to be able to cut through such a thickness of tough dried straw with one stroke.

Kiratani seemed caught between admiration for his son's skill and some deeper underlying disquiet as he said, 'Yes, very difficult to raise children...'

*

After saying goodbye for the day to a subdued Motoko, Joe returned to his quiet *ryokan* on the east bank of the Kamo River, directly opposite the red Torii gate of the famous Shimogamo shrine.

He took off his shoes and put on slippers before entering the building and passing down the series of corridors to reach his own wing of the building. As he entered his own rooms, the sunlight was fast fading in the garden outside, green shadows spreading across the moss and stones, the sound of birds settling down noisily in the groves of maples and elms for the coming night.

The *fusuma,* the inside sliding door of wood or heavy paper that divided his allocated room, was suddenly slid open from the other side to enlarge the room. A woman in a lilac-coloured *yukata* appeared from behind the screen. Joe naturally thought she was a member of the *ryokan* staff and waited for her to say something.

But she just stood there, waiting in the shadows, out of reach of the last rays of the sun.

Finally she came forward tentatively into his own part of the room, and Joe realised with perplexity who it was...

'Aiko-san!' He was struggling to understand how and why this woman should materialise here and now of all places, so far from her own home in the *Yoshiwara*.

Yet her face was no longer painted white with cupid red lips but only made up more naturally, and like that she seemed different – more human – more familiar...

Then with a shock he realised the unbelievable truth and, for a moment, anger at being deceived by her again outweighed the euphoria of knowing she was still alive.

His anger didn't last long, though, and was soon replaced by bewilderment. His voice was hoarse as he asked, 'Amelia! Is it really you? Or are you a ghost come back to haunt me?'

'No, I'm entirely flesh and blood,' she said simply. With that she slipped the *yukata* off her shoulders and let it fall to the tatami mat floor. 'As you can see.'

Then she came forward slowly and laid her head softly against his chest. '*Gomen nasai,*' she said, apologizing, then took his right hand and moved it down the flanks of her own abdomen until his fingers touched the line of scar tissue.

'Remember this scar?' she asked in a breathless whisper.

'I remember,' he answered as she parted her lips and kissed him.

CHAPTER 16

Monday morning came to this Kyoto *ryokan* with the stealing of rosy dawn light across the moss and gravel of the garden, and the noisy chattering of bulbuls and mynahs in the surrounding *keyaki* trees.

Joe Appeldoorn stirred under the *futon,* then was suddenly awake again. For a moment he had no idea where he was or who he was with, but then, with a slight feeling of disbelief still, he saw the sleeping face of Amelia Peachy beside him.

He was even now having trouble getting used to the idea that Amelia was alive and well. There was still a small amount of residual anger stirring within him, but this resentment was now a minor thing when compared to his undoubted happiness at seeing her alive and well again. He reminded himself, though, that this woman had manipulated him mercilessly in Switzerland two years ago to her own ends, inveigled herself into his affections, and had then abandoned him. And later she had ruthlessly misled him, quite content to let him suffer and go on believing she was dead, when it suited her own interests. And now she had returned to his life and seduced him yet again – was she simply up to her old tricks, he wondered uneasily.

Yet he couldn't deny that she had certainly saved his life on the train from Tokyo two days ago by her brave and reckless action, so that implied some real remaining affection for him on her part. Joe had not spoken to her yet about the incident on the train, but he had no doubt now who had been playing the part of "Mrs Smythe"– Amelia did have an extraordinary chameleon-like ability to change not only her physical appearance, but her whole personality and even character...

He lifted the futon slightly to glimpse her naked body lying beside his, and it was a seductive and entrancing sight. Even in this light he could make out the slight ridging of the scar on her creamy white abdomen - the result of a bullet wound that he had personally stitched in a Zurich hotel room two years before...

'Are you enjoying your peep show, Mr Appeldoorn?' she asked lazily, suddenly smiling at him through sleepy eyes.

Joe almost blushed but didn't replace the futon. 'Very much, Miss Peachy, I have to admit.'

Amelia opened her eyes properly. 'Good. I hate men who are so hypocritical that they can't admit to enjoying the sight of a female body.' She leaned across, her body tight against his, and kissed him tenderly on the lips.

He took her face in his hands and kissed her in return. 'So what right do you have to come into my life again like this, like you own me?' he asked breathlessly, unable to keep a slight note of complaint from his voice.

'I didn't exactly plan it this way, you know.' She frowned at his tone. 'And I can leave now if you really want.'

He ran his hands up her slender flanks. 'No, don't do that,' he apologized. 'We have little enough time together as it is. I have to get up in a few minutes.'

Amelia ran her fingers against the rough stubble of his jaw. 'No, you don't. You see I've booked the entire *ryokan* for the next two days. There are only us and the staff here now. And they are very discrete, as all Japanese women are.'

Joe was impressed as ever by her forethought and planning. 'How did you know where I would be staying?'

'I am a spy, Mr Appeldoorn, and a good one,' she said primly. 'If I can't find out where one particular foreigner is planning to stay in Kyoto, I wouldn't deserve to be a successful secret agent, would I?'

Joe laughed. 'Well, that's as may be. But I'm afraid we still have to get up. My client, Mr Maeda, and his daughter, Motoko, are coming to take me on a further tour of the city at ten. Although, to be honest, I have had more than enough of Japanese temples by now...'

Amelia lifted her neck a little so that she could focus her dark blue eyes on his face. 'She was the Japanese girl on the train? The one making cow eyes at you the whole journey?'

Joe coughed dryly. 'She was my travelling companion, if that's what you mean. I certainly didn't notice her making eyes at me.'

Amelia gave him a knowing look. 'Take it from me – she was. It seems that you have made yet another female conquest, Joseph. We women are like putty in your hands with that handsome face of yours... '

Joe smiled ruefully. 'I can't imagine *you* ever being putty in anyone's hands, and especially in mine. And I am sure that Motoko is entirely resistant to my plain face and coarse Western manners. But nevertheless, I still have to get up to keep my appointment with her and her father.'

Amelia relaxed her body again, and gently took the lobe of his right ear between her teeth. 'Put her off, Joseph,' she breathed in his ear. 'Say you're feeling sick, or you're simply tired. That may even be true after last night,' she added dryly. 'Spend the whole day with me, Joseph, please. For old time's sake. It may be the only time we'll ever have...'

*

Amelia, now dressed again in her lilac-coloured *yukata,* sat cross-legged on the tatami mat opposite him while they shared their unappetising-looking Japanese breakfast of salty fish, rice, pickles, *miso* and strips of seaweed.

Amelia's acceptance of everything Japanese had obviously gone a longer way than his, Joe thought, as he watched her eating what was on offer with apparent relish, even to the extent of apparently enjoying the infamous *natto.*

Joe was still curious as to how she could have survived that incredible fall from a precipitous cliff face into the Rhine two years ago, and then being carried over the greatest waterfall in Europe. 'Even Plesch thinks you died in Switzerland, you know. He told me so on the train, and I believe he was sincere for once.'

She put down her chopsticks with a sigh of satisfaction. '*Go-chisosama deshita.* No, not in Switzerland, Joseph. He soon knew I'd survived that exhilarating ride over the *Rheinfall,* just as he did himself. No, on the contrary, he thought I died rather later, in a frozen lake in Russia.'

'In Russia? What were you doing there?' Joe was still resentful at her callous disregard in not telling him the truth about her survival in Switzerland. 'Why did you not tell me that you were still alive? Did you not know the grief I was going through?'

'You weren't grieving immediately, Joseph,' Amelia pointed out soberly. 'That was not possible in your condition. You were lying in a near coma in a hospital in Schaffhausen, as I recall, so there was no way I could tell you immediately of my survival. I don't know how I survived the fall, to be honest, but somehow I missed all the jagged rocks and managed not to drown in the maelstrom afterwards. And, having survived, it was better for me, in my line of business, to keep it a secret. I had come through that fall without any significant injury so of course I suspected Plesch might have too. Therefore I needed to keep my survival secret until I was sure Plesch was no longer a threat.'

'You could still have told me later, when I had recovered sufficiently from my wounds,' Joe interjected harshly.

'How do you know I didn't try to?' Amelia rejoined quietly. 'But at the time, I still had the life of the King to protect, and in April I was ordered back to London. I went back to my life as a pretend courtesan, this time in a London bawdy house frequented by the King...'

178

'You mean like Catherine in *Le Royale*?' Joe remembered the sweet little English prostitute he'd met in a Zurich bordello and fallen for, only to discover later that she was actually this English government agent in yet another disguise.

'Well, I chose a rather more vulgar character than Catherine this later time, to better suit the style of the place, which was several steps down from *Le Royale*, I'm sorry to say. And that was a huge mistake with Bertie at hand – he has rather a penchant for vulgar-looking women. The King was told this time of my identity, but it didn't make any difference - he still behaved disgracefully and chose to treat me as if I was really one of his harlots. I had to fight to keep him and his octopus hands off me all the time. It did make me wonder at times what I was doing protecting such a man.'

'And? What happened?' Joe was curious despite himself.

Amelia looked embarrassed. 'What happened? Thanks to my ineptitude, the King was stabbed one night in this bordello and nearly died...'

'Plesch again?' Joe interrupted.

Amelia grimaced. 'Indeed so. I had missed spotting him that time, but then his disguise was truly brilliant and difficult to see through. An elderly bald Italian!' Amelia paused expectantly, waiting for Joe's reaction.

'Ah, Signor Valdini!' Joe said, understanding. 'That's how you recognized him at once on the train!'

Amelia nodded. 'Yes. It's comforting to know that he's human after all, and beginning to repeat himself in his disguises.'

'So what happened after this incident? How did you get to Russia?'

'Plesch escaped me again in London,' Amelia admitted, slightly shame-faced. 'He made an incredible leap from a rooftop in Mayfair in order to escape; I had misjudged him and his inhuman physical skills yet again. But I didn't give up there, and I pursued his trail across Europe, first to Berlin, and then eastwards to Russia. I finally tracked him down to a village near the town of Kuibyshev, a thousand miles east of Moscow. It was there, on a frozen lake, that he threw a stick of dynamite at the sled I was travelling on and saw me fall through a hole in the ice. That's why he was so sure I was finally dead. No one should have lived through that immersion in a frozen Russian lake – it made the fall over the *Rheinfall* seem trivial by comparison.'

'More fool him, then. You obviously have as many lives as a cat, Miss Peachy,' Joe said in admiration.

'Perhaps.' She gave him a slightly melancholy smile. 'But I must be rapidly running out of them.'

*

Later they walked in the garden where the spring-like warmth and the shelter of the surrounding hills were bringing it back to life. In the dappled sunshine, early dragonflies hovered above the lotus leaves in the pools and giant koi twisted their orange bodies in the shallows. A tiny tree-shaded shrine in the stone courtyard of the *ryokan* was decorated with statues that were rough with cream and purple lichens. Amelia ran her hands along the rough stone, feeling the lines of complex *Kanji* characters with pleasure as if reading Braille.

'Did you not recognize me as Mrs Smythe at all, when you saw me first in the lobby of the Imperial?' she asked coyly. 'Or even on the train?'

'No, not at the time.' he hesitated. 'Well afterwards, I had a strange inkling after the events on the train that Mrs Smythe must have been an American agent sent to protect me, but I still couldn't quite believe it. I certainly didn't think it was you, but then why would I? You have been dead and buried these two years...'

Amelia seemed in a coy mood. 'Nor even Aiko-san? Did you never suspect Aiko-san and Amelia Peachy could be one and the same person?'

Joe shook his head vigorously. 'Certainly not. Your masquerade as a Japanese was quite your most extraordinary transformation yet, although the dark blue of your eyes should perhaps have made me suspect something. How on earth did you learn the language so quickly?'

Even without makeup, Amelia was still managing to look remarkably Oriental today, Joe decided, as she shuffled sensuously through the garden in her lilac *yukata* and sandals, and with her dark hair tied up prettily with ribbons. 'I've always had a talent for mimicry, Joseph, as you know. And I had a superb teacher in my friend Sumiko-san. And, remember, I've been here for nearly nine months, which gave me considerable time to study and learn.'

Joe still couldn't quite believe that he been duped by the same woman's deceit so easily again, just as in Switzerland, and perhaps even more completely this time, if anything. 'You did it to me again, didn't you? Do you enjoy making a fool of a dumb American? Is that it?'

Amelia put his arm through hers. 'Don't be like that, Joseph. But yes, I do admit that I did enjoy talking to you as Aiko-san; I saw quite a different side to your character then.'

Joe relented in his tone. 'And how about Miss Cordingly? Is she here in Japan with you too?'

'Ah, you would like to meet Charlotte again, I can tell,' she said playfully. 'Would you like me to dress up as Miss Cordingly? Is that it?'

She was mocking him but Joe undoubtedly felt a stirring of excitement at the thought.

'I'm afraid the props and outfits of Miss Cordingly are back in Tokyo, so you will have to make do with the real me for now.' She smiled secretively. 'Although perhaps I can think of something else to divert you later...'

*

They went for a walk by the Kamo River, along a woodland path where querulous macaques rustled the trees and came begging for food.

'What are you doing here in Japan, Amelia?' Joe asked. 'Were you still chasing Plesch? Is that what brought you here?'

Amelia stopped to admire a white Camelia flower. 'These are such perfect blooms, aren't they, and remarkable flowers to see in the depth of winter. But it's sad that they have no perfume to match their visual beauty.' She turned her head to look searchingly at Joe. 'No, I didn't suspect Plesch was here until I heard a report of the possibility a few weeks ago.'

'Then what are you doing here?' he asked again, puzzled.

Amelia sighed. 'I shouldn't be telling you this, but I don't suppose you will let the issue go until you do know. I'm trying to catch a British traitor. Someone in our Tokyo embassy is selling or giving our trade and military secrets to the Russians.'

Joe was relieved it was nothing to do with him. 'And when you've caught this person, what then?'

Amelia touched the sepals of the Camellia bloom again with a slightly wistful expression. 'Then I suppose I shall go home again.'

*

They sat on a fence post by the boulder-strewn gushing river and he took her left hand and examined the lines on the palm. She seemed almost embarrassed by this public display of affection and sentimentality, but she let him keep hold of her hand anyway. 'I suppose I was very unlucky to come to Japan when I did and encounter Plesch again,' he remarked.

Amelia played with the fingers of his hands in return, examining them and stroking the tops. 'I doubt it was purely bad luck, Joseph. I think you told your State Department about your encounter with Plesch in Switzerland, didn't you?'

Joe thought back to what had happened. 'Some officials came to see me on my return to the States eighteen months ago. Eleanor has relatives who are high up in the government in Washington and she had mentioned the story in passing to one of them. So they sent their agents to question me. I had no reason not to tell them the whole story. I thought Plesch was dead at the time, and I believed you were dead too so I saw no point in secrecy.'

Amelia turned to him. 'Pryor was a top American agent, Joseph. Did you not realise that? It was he who probably arranged to get you here, with Ambassador Reinhold's connivance. They needed you to help track down Plesch – perhaps even as bait for their trap.'

Joe nodded. 'I had guessed as much by now. Although he was clever in diverting suspicion from himself: he even accused *me* of being a spy which certainly diverted my suspicion of him.'

Amelia took his hand again and gripped it tightly. 'He was very proficient agent.'

'And yet he is still dead,' Joe pointed out worriedly.

Amelia still held his hand in hers. 'That's true, which shows the measure of the people we are up against. Don't think too badly of Pryor, though: he needed your help to get Plesch but wasn't sure if you would volunteer if you knew the hidden agenda behind this business trip.'

Joe was still angry, though, at what his own government had done to him. 'Of course I would have refused to get involved, if I'd known what was going on. I'm not absolutely crazy.'

'So it was very wise of Pryor to use a little subterfuge, then,' Amelia pointed out.

'You would no doubt have done the same thing, wouldn't you, if you were in the same situation?' he said to her accusingly.

'Perhaps,' she admitted brazenly, 'if I had to. It's a hard and deceitful world we live in, and we all have to make sacrifices in order to defeat evil people like Johan Plesch..'

Joe reflected a little more. 'Were the Maedas in on this deception too, do you think?'

Amelia shook her head. 'I doubt it; I suspect the Americans would have been using them as mere pawns too.'

A dismal thought occurred to Joe. 'So it's not the quality of my company's products that got me this invitation to Japan at all, is it, but a bit of political chicanery?'

Amelia finally released his hand and stood up. 'Don't look a gift horse in the mouth. Perhaps the reasons for you and Maeda finding each other were less than straight, but that still doesn't mean that your business deal doesn't make perfect sense for the two of you. Take my advice and take full advantage of the situation. Make your lucrative deal, Joseph, and then go home. You've earned it.'

Joe shrugged uneasily. 'That's one way to look at it, I suppose.'

'Again, please don't blame Pryor too much, Joseph; he was trying to catch the murderer of his President and he ended up paying with his own life, after all, while you're still here, alive and well. *And* getting the reward of sleeping with a notorious and seductive British agent, I might remind you,' she added facetiously.

Joe grunted sourly. 'Perhaps it's a little unwise of you to remind me what an unfaithful louse I am. I was doing my best to forget it...'

*

They began to retrace their steps to the *ryokan* again.

'Tell me about Saturday,' Joe said. 'How did you know Plesch would try and murder me on that train?'

'I didn't know for sure. But after it became clear to me that Plesch was here in Japan, and apparently stalking you, I resolved to follow you and try to protect you. After all that we meant to each other in Switzerland, I couldn't just stand by and see you murdered...'

Joe looked at her in surprise – perhaps she really did have some deep feelings for him after all, despite her sometime ambiguous actions.

'...you'd gone to Hakone or Kamakura, or somewhere, for a few days, so I was unable to keep track of you, but then you returned to the Imperial Hotel on Friday afternoon and I heard of your return from the hotel staff. The hotel porter let me know you were going to Kyoto by train early on Saturday morning so I had time to make my own preparations to follow you.'

'And?'

'On the train I spotted "Signor Valdini" quite quickly. It was I, of course, who slipped that warning message into your pocket but unfortunately you didn't read it until too late.'

Joe was curious. 'He didn't recognise you in the guise of Mrs Smythe either?'

Amelia was emphatic. 'I'm sure he didn't. He really was still convinced that I died in Russia, I think – after all, even most of my fellow British agents still believe it. And that's why I have been living secretly in Tokyo as Aiko-san and Mrs Smythe – there is no official record of Amelia Peachy being here at all. Only one man at the British Embassy knows I'm working undercover here, a man called Randall.'

'I can see why you would want to keep your being here a secret,' Joe admitted begrudgingly.

'In the dining car on the train, I spotted that Plesch had slipped your cute Japanese companion something - perhaps to make her sleep. I hoped it was nothing worse, but there was nothing I could do about it anyway without breaking cover.'

'So you were waiting for something else to happen?' Joe said.

'Yes, and I was very uneasy when I saw "Valdini" accompany you to your compartment.'

'You didn't intervene immediately, though. How did you know he wouldn't kill me straightaway?'

Amelia shrugged. 'Because it's not what I would have done. It was more logical for him to keep you alive until it was easier to dispose of your body later. It's not easy, after all, to carry a dead body over your shoulder and throw it out of a crowded moving train without being spotted.'

Joe had a thought. 'I wonder why he didn't just shoot me and just leave my body in the compartment on the train.'

'That's an easy one. Because that would have started a manhunt – finding the body of a murdered *Westerner* on a Japanese train. Every passenger on the train would have been questioned, and Valdini had been seen with you earlier. So far better to have a missing passenger than a clearly murdered one.'

'So you watched and waited for Plesch to make his move.' Joe laughed. 'I must say, you play the deranged woman rather well, Amelia.'

Amelia enjoyed the compliment, he could see. 'My career as an actress still stands me in good stead, Joseph. I have played some strange characters in the works of Shaw and Ibsen in my time, so Mrs Smythe was no great stretch for me. Yet Plesch still got the better of me, though; I had planned to knock him unconscious with one good blow of my bag – it is weighted with lead shot. But the man is so fast and has such inhuman reflexes and abilities.'

Joe looked at her shrewdly. 'It sounds sometimes as if you really did admire him.'

'"Admire" is not the right word, Joseph. But there was a certain artistry about this man's dedication to killing, as deadly as any big cat or predatory shark.' Amelia smiled ruefully. 'I was still shocked when I recovered my senses, though, and saw that you'd followed Plesch up onto the roof of that train. Even *I* wouldn't have done anything so foolish, Joseph. What on earth possessed you?'

Joe couldn't explain it himself. 'Rage, I suppose. The man had even tried to pretend some sympathy with me, even as he put a gun to my head to blow my brains out. The hypocrisy of that devil just drove me mad for a second, I guess...'

As Amelia bent to admire another wayside flower – a patch of winter aconite flowering bright yellow at the edge of the woods - Joe forgot completely what he was saying as he saw the fabric of her lilac *yukata* tighten against the lines of her slender figure. It was still almost impossible for him to believe that this truly was the same woman who had been on the Kyoto train. 'What happened to "Mrs Smythe" after the train stopped, anyway?'

She straightened her back. 'I slipped back to my compartment afterwards and quickly changed my clothes. I had the costume of a Japanese boy coolie ready in my bags and, with my face blackened with dirt and it being nightfall, I soon managed to disappear among the searchers looking for signs of Plesch's body.'

'And then?'

'Like all the other searchers, I didn't find any sign of Plesch. Afterwards I had a long walk through the night along the line to the next station where I caught a local train to Kyoto. Then I was able to collect Mrs Smythe's luggage and belongings at the station by pretending to be a boy sent to pick it up. After a bath and a change of clothes, I could then become a lady again.'

Joe tried to be positive, yet there was a niggling doubt in his mind because no one had found Plesch's body . 'Plesch must be dead, this time, surely?'

Amelia was more philosophical and wary. 'He could be, that's all I'm prepared to say. But I won't believe it for certain until I see the body. That man doesn't have nine lives; he has *ninety*...'

*

They made love again in the *ryokan* that afternoon, to the sound of birdsong and trickling water from the garden.

Joe had switched off his mind to everything else by now but her presence – for the moment he gave no thought to the traumas of the last week, to his business dealings, or even to thoughts of Eleanor. Only this woman and this tranquil inn and garden, and this moment of supreme sexual enchantment, existed for him.

Afterwards he held her in his arms, his mind returning to the first time they had ever made love, in a hotel overlooking the blue water of Lake Constance in Bavaria. This was a different setting from that one but just as perfect in its way. 'What happens to us now?' he wanted to know.

She frowned as if surprised at his lack of clarity over such a simple issue. 'What do you mean – "what happens now"? You will go back to your wife, I assume. And I will go back to my life of pretend and subterfuge.' Her voice had layers of meanings he couldn't fathom or even separate properly in his mind – a degree of irony certainly, but also a sense of melancholy realism, and a deep underlying unhappiness...

'That's it? Nothing more than this one day? Is this all we'll ever have?'

She held his face between her hands and looked at him frankly. 'You will never leave a wife to whom you made an oath for life. You're not the type...'

'Yet I'm clearly not the faithful type either, though, am I?' he said bitterly. 'Better not remind me of Eleanor. It's confusing, I know, but I love her deeply too. I really do.'

Amelia kissed him thoughtfully, keeping her lips in contact for a long time as if unwilling to let go of the sensation of his lips against hers. 'I'm sure you do, Joseph. But who can say what love is really? In my own way, perhaps I love you too. Eleanor really shouldn't complain. *She* took you away from *me* after all, not the other way round, and she has you for the rest of her life. I will only be with you this one time. It's I who should complain of life's unfairness.'

Joe was struck by her practical and accepting attitude – she made their liaison today seem like perfectly reasonable behaviour. 'What is the matter with me? I can't resist you, can I? Am I bewitched?'

'For our last evening together, you will be, I promise.' She gave him another mysterious smile. 'I have a special surprise planned for you...'

*

'Could Plesch really be alive?' he asked her again a few minutes later, unable to put the thought of that devil entirely to one side, even though it

185

threatened the intimacy of this moment with her. 'No man could survive a fall from a moving train into a ravine and a torrent, could they?'

Amelia too seemed reluctant to answer, but did finally. 'But nobody saw him fall, did they?'

'True,' Joe admitted.

Amelia clearly didn't really want to talk any more of Plesch but she too couldn't quite help herself, it seemed. 'During your private tête-à-tête with the man, did Plesch give you any idea what he was planning in Japan?'

Joe tried to recall. 'He did say that he had a client. And that his *client* wanted me killed, more than him.'

Amelia sat up suddenly. 'Then that means the client must know you personally,' she said in surprise.

That thought hadn't occurred to Joe before, but he saw that it had to be true. So the mysterious client who had commissioned Plesch to kill someone had to be one of the people he'd come across in Japan in the last week or so... 'If Plesch is dead, then the planned mission, or assassination, will now be off, though, won't it?'

Amelia looked concerned. 'Perhaps so. If he is really dead, anyway. But do you remember anything else that Plesch said about this client that might identify him?'

Something suddenly jarred in Joe's memory. 'Yes, I do. Plesch denied vehemently that he'd had anything to do with the bombing at the Imperial on Monday night. You were there that night, of course, in your guise of Mrs Smythe,' he suddenly remembered ruefully. 'But Plesch mentioned he had been there too to meet his client. S*o* that means his client must also have been someone who was there in the hotel that night...'

Joe saw a sudden gleam in Amelia's eye and wondered if she had come to some secret conclusion of her own about the possible identity of this person. But if she had, she clearly wasn't going to enlighten him. When he asked her if she had any ideas of her own, she responded with a firm and unequivocal negative. 'It's time for both of us to forget Plesch,' she said. 'Tomorrow I go back to Tokyo where I have to resume my search for a traitor.'

Joe shook his head in disbelief. 'And just when I thought I was beginning to see a softer side,' he commented wryly.

'Perhaps you will see a different side to me later,' she said enigmatically. 'I need you to leave me for an hour or two now, Joseph. Go for another walk and don't come back to the *ryokan* until seven. I have to prepare something special for dinner tonight.'

Joe was suspicious. 'What have you got planned, Amelia?'

She smiled. 'Be patient, Joseph. You'll see...'

*

Darkness had fallen and the garden was lit by oil lamps when Joe returned at seven, stepping across the raised stones of the garden path. He opened the *shoji* screen carefully, unlaced his shoes, and entered the tatami mat room in slippers.

The room was in near darkness and he felt a sudden prickling of fear on the back of his neck, wondering if Plesch could have risen from the grave yet again and found this hiding place. But then he became aware of a shimmer of silk in the gloom, and he knew there was no need to worry.

Amelia sat there calmly at a low table, dressed in full *geisha* outfit and makeup. He was stunned into silence for a moment by the sight.

'Why are you dressed like that?' he finally asked in a whisper.

'Doesn't it please you? I thought it would please you,' she said in Aiko's sing-song voice.

'Yes,' he said honestly. 'It pleases me greatly.' He realised how well this woman understood him - how much she comprehended his deepest desires and unspoken thoughts. This was a moment, and an image of her, that he knew he would never be able to forget as long as he lived.

He couldn't take his eyes off her face, painted pearl-white, but with her eyebrows and the outer corners of the eyes extended with red and black lines into the shape of a falling tear that seemed to say so much of her mood. Her formal *geisha* wig was decorated with ornamental pins and ribbons, her kimono green silk with the red of the underkimono showing through at sleeve and hem. Where had she obtained all these things in such a short time, he wondered in bewilderment. She turned her head slightly, and his eyes, now adjusting to the light, saw that the sensuous nape of her neck had been left bare of paint in the erotic shape of a "W". Her red lips were delicately shaped into a bow.

His heart was soaring and racing wildly. This was no longer the English Miss Amelia Peachy but the exotic Aiko-san, a creature from a different world. Every gesture, every note of her voice were inviting pieces of acting, a mannequin combination of the innocent and the sensuous.

'*Ereanor-san sonna koto o shimasu-ka?* Would Eleanor do this for you?' she asked in breathless *geisha* Japanese, as she arranged his seat and served him tea...

*

In the morning, she was the resourceful Amelia Peachy again, and Joe had to pinch himself to remember the passionate and uncontrolled way she had made love to him in the dark of night.

They walked together in the garden one last time. A little dawn mist clung to the surface of the wet gravel and damp moss, and a beam of sunlight was just filtering through the bare branches of the maples and the green needles of the dwarf pines. Somewhere, far off, a temple bell was beating its doleful message of enlightenment. Joe was feeling desolated at the thought of losing her again, but he did his best to hide his distress.

'You're travelling as yourself today, Amelia,' he pointed out unnecessarily. 'Is that safe? Perhaps you really do think Plesch is dead after all.'

'Perhaps I do, Joseph. But regardless, my own identity is as safe for travelling here now as any. I don't believe I'm known by anyone here. But I will have to return to being Mrs Smythe when I get back to Tokyo.'

'In order to spy on your own compatriots?' Joe was surprised at the harshness in his own voice, when all really wanted to do was put his arms around this woman and never let her go.

Amelia seemed to be trying to contain her emotions too, but making a better job of it than him. 'One of them is betraying us, Joseph. It could cost many Japanese, or British, lives if any more military secrets were to be revealed.'

Joe nodded resignedly and took her hand. 'I suppose so. Thank you again for last night. It was everything you promised...*and more...*' His voice tailed away sadly.

Amelia gripped his hand for a second in return. 'It was wonderful for me too, Joseph, not just for you.' She paused. 'My advice remains not to tell your embassy of anything that happened on the train coming here, or anything about Plesch. You remember how talking to your government got you into this trouble in the first place.'

'I'll bear it in mind. So what do we do now, Miss Peachy?' Joe asked with a slight feeling of desperation.

Amelia was expressionless and in control of her emotions again. 'We resume our separate lives, Joseph. Perhaps it's better for us that we only have this limited time together. There will be no time for our friendship to become stale and turn to indifference. When people have so much time together, they squander it recklessly. We did not; we made the most of the time we had. So although I am a little sad today to be leaving you again, I am also happy that we found each other again. Please remember me, won't you?'

Joe swallowed hard. 'How could I ever forget you after last night?'

Amelia turned to go. 'For what it's worth, Joseph, I want you to know that I did come back to try and see you after Switzerland. In fact I did see you again, although you did not see me...'

Joe looked up sharply. 'When was that?'

'It was on the quayside at Cherbourg, after you'd recovered, and you were about to board your ship back to New York.'

Joe was even more confused. 'Yet you didn't come and speak to me, did you?'

Amelia smiled sadly. 'No, Eleanor was there with you. So I didn't know what I could say to you by then, except goodbye...'

CHAPTER 17

Tuesday February 2nd 1904

By late afternoon, the train had passed Shizuoka on the final leg of the return journey from Kyoto and, from the carriage window, Joe could see Mount Fuji rising like a vision above a layer of attendant mist. The pale winter sky above the mountain had a hard metallic look, like a dome of pewter, polished and beaten to a dull shine.

Joe smiled at Motoko in the opposite seat, as the carriage was jolted back and forward on an uneven length of line, and she was nearly lifted of her cushion into the air. Motoko was not her usual sunny self today, though, and didn't respond to Joe's smile at once. Joe, despite his own preoccupations, could see she seemed deeply troubled by something, as she had for the whole journey.

Yet she finally raised a smile of sorts. 'How you feel today, Joe-san? No more headache?' she asked solicitously. She was wearing a ridiculous little feathered hat for the journey that made her look as sweet as a sixteen-year-old, and a high velvet burgundy collar with silver buttons encircled her slender white throat.

'Pardon me?' For a moment Joe had forgotten the excuse he'd made yesterday to the driver sent to the *ryokan* by Motoko's father, to justify missing the promised further tour of the sights of Kyoto. 'Oh, yes, I'm fully recovered now,' he said, remembering that he was supposed to have had a fever and headache. 'Did you enjoy your day anyway, with your father? I don't suppose you often have the chance just to spend a relaxing day together when your father is such a busy man.'

Motoko didn't answer but looked downcast; Joe realised that he had just said something wrong but couldn't imagine what.

'Did you speak to him yet about the possibility of you studying Western fashion in New York?' Joe inquired curiously.

'No, not good time for such request,' she declared bleakly.

Joe decided to change what appeared to be a painful subject. 'Shall we have something to eat in the restaurant car?' he suggested brightly. 'We still have time before we get back to Tokyo.'

She finally smiled more warmly in response. 'After last time? I don't think good idea. I avoid lobster, and Italian doctor, from now on. Why that man kill self, I wonder? So strange! He seem happy man, if loud.' She turned her pretty face to look at her own muted reflection in the glass. 'I not hungry anyway, Joe-san.'

In all honesty Joe didn't have much appetite either; he had his own reasons today for feeling dejected and confused after Amelia's brief return to his life. Her short lived return had left him only with a profound feeling of emptiness, despite the enchantment of those thirty-six hours they had spent together in Kyoto. Now, his mind was awash with conflicting emotions: bewilderment, sorrow, and perhaps even some subdued anger at the way she had been able to simply walk away from him again as if nothing had happened between them.

Amelia had taken a carriage at first light this morning from the *ryokan* to Kyoto Station, and he had watched her go with a numb feeling of resignation and sorrow. Soon after her departure, though, anger and resentment had stirred up in his mind too – *why had she bothered to come back only to abandon him again so soon?* It would have been better for her to have let him go on thinking that she had died in Switzerland rather than to know the truth: that this woman whom he treasured so much was alive and well, and breathing air, and talking to people, and laughing and smiling - and perhaps being melancholy and sad on occasion too – and doing all the myriad other interesting things that made up her life.

But he would never be allowed to share any of it with her again. In some ways, knowing she was alive and well made the thought of never seeing her again much harder to face than when he'd thought she was dead.

He tried to think of Eleanor too – in his selfishness, he didn't want to lose her and her sweet nature and loving personality either. *Who said that a man can only really love one woman at a time?* Joe was sure that he loved both these women, if in rather different ways. It was a ridiculous restriction of man's nature to say such a thing, he thought. Tell that fable to a Mohammedan...

But neither Eleanor nor Amelia struck him as women who would be prepared to share a man with each other, although Miss Peachy was definitely much less conventional in her attitude to male-female relationships than Eleanor, he guessed, and did not apparently feel bound by the normal constraints of middle-class morality to the same extent.

Certainly Eleanor was the type of woman who expected a hundred percent devotion from her man, and who gave her love completely in return. So she would be deeply hurt by the betrayal of an unfaithful husband and might not be able to forgive him for it, if she ever discovered the truth. Joe had been entirely faithful to her until his visit to Japan – but then in America he hadn't seen a woman to touch her for beauty or personality or general appeal. Despite Motoko's belief to the contrary, Joe had not made love to the beautiful geisha Umegiku-san last week, although the night they had spent together in that house in Kamakura had certainly been both memorable and erotic enough, and would no doubt have got him into hot water with Eleanor if she ever heard about it...

But his unfaithfulness with Amelia ran so much more deeply than that gentle flirtation with a *geisha*. Amelia Peachy was not a real *geisha* but it seemed she knew more about a man's passions than even those accomplished Japanese ladies. Miss Peachy knew how to penetrate his very soul and leave him tormented with an impossible longing...

But Joe knew that he would have to suppress that impossible longing somehow, and put it behind him, otherwise it would destroy his marriage, and possibly his life. So, although it would be hard, Joe knew he would have to try and forget Amelia Peachy a second time – she had walked out of his life yet again and that was it: it was over. And he told himself that he should simply be grateful for that memorable day she'd given him, a day of loving and special memories that would have to last him a lifetime now...

The train was now traversing the coastal plain near Mishima where coolies in conical straw hats were working in fallow rice fields, industriously preparing the ground for the spring sowing. The white steam of the powerful black locomotive billowed out in clumps behind the train carriages and cast racing shadows across the stubbly yellow fields and the rows of tireless workers, bent to their task. Joe was struck by the juxtaposition of the old and new faces of Japan – the timeless cycle of rice cultivation, presided over by the snorting steam power of twentieth century technology. This was a society and country still in a huge state of flux – who could tell what miracles might be achieved here in the next fifty or a hundred years...?

Joe, seeing the sad look still on Motoko's face, finally asked her what was wrong. 'Is it to do with Joji Kiratani and the argument you had with him at Kamakura? Is that what's troubling you, Motoko-san?'

Motoko seemed reluctant to answer at first, but then relented. 'Ah, you see him in Kyoto and recognise from Kamakura.' Her sweet face took on a tormented and haunted look for a second. 'I shamed to admit, but love him still, Joe-san.'

Joe was surprised. 'I thought you had broken off your engagement with him.'

Motoko nodded solemnly. 'I do.'

'Why did you break it off, if you still love him?' Joe was trying to understand this little mystery.

Motoko averted her eyes in embarrassment. 'He change. Not same man as before. I see change happen and I try stop. But can't. He angry at modern Japan. Angry with me. He want keep old ways: wear kimono, not kowtow to West. He want all foreigner to leave Japan.'

Joe was gentle with her, speaking softly. 'Right or wrong, it's too late to stop change in Japan now, Motoko-san. The genie will never be pushed back into the bottle.'

She looked confused by that reference to the Arabian Nights so he tried another more conventional explanation. 'Japan is becoming a powerful country, and will be rich and prosperous one day. Japan will have to try and find a way to reconcile its past with its future – decide what cultural things must be kept, and what can be allowed to lapse. The essential Japanese character and culture should be preserved, of course, but I'm afraid the Japanese will have to adapt to the modern world like everyone else.'

Her almond eyes flashed for a second. 'I know that. It Joji-san who not know that.'

'So what was the argument on the cliffs about?'

'He want me to change mind. Marry him. Give up fashion and business career.' She sighed resignedly. 'I can't, not even for him, even though still love him.'

Joe nodded thoughtfully. 'He saved your life during the landslide, didn't he?'

'Yes, he did. You saw it. He risk own life to save me. Still at heart good boy.'

'But?'

A shadow fell across Motoko's innocent face. 'Joji now also violent and unpredict'ble. Can't say what he might do. Per'aps something terrible...'

'What do you mean?' Joe could hear the tension in her voice.

'His father tell me, few weeks ago, he think Joji join anarchist people.'

Joe felt a sudden deep sense of foreboding. 'You mean one of these ultra-Nationalist groups, like the one who tried to bomb the Imperial Hotel?'

Motoko bowed her head solemnly. 'Exactly. I think Joji know about bomb last week. He not do it himself, but he know of plan, I think.' She bit her lower lip. 'You remember telephone call I get that night in Imperial Hotel. I think it my father, but was him - Joji. Something went wrong and we disconnect. But he sound strange so I wait – expect another call. I not tell you the truth about that – Joji call back and tell me, "Get out of hotel at once!" His voice scared.'

'How did he even know you were there?' Joe asked.

'He must be outside, per'aps. He must see me in Imperial Hotel dining room with you, so try to find another telephone and warn me get me out of lobby before bomb thrown.'

Joe thought this all sounded depressingly plausible. 'You know this for sure?'

'No, not for sure. When he met me in Kamakura, I accuse him.'

'Did he admit his involvement?' Joe demanded.

'No, he deny, but I not believe. He one of *Kokuryukai* - "Black Dragon Society". I think they do it.'

'Was that all he said on the cliff? He looked as if he was about to strike you just before that earthquake happened.'

'He angry seeing me walk with *gaijin*.' She blushed furiously. 'He say I dishonour Japan. I say I never want see again!'

'That was just before he saved you?'

Motoko nodded reluctantly. 'Yes, he save me. But I can't change mind. It never work between us now. It all over! But I still can't tell police truth...'

Joe didn't know what to say to her...

'Be careful, Joe-san,' Motoko went on. 'Do not go anywhere alone. Joji jealous. He kill you per'aps if he find you alone. I scared for you.'

Joe felt the blood draining from his face at the thought of this man harbouring a grudge against him: he remembered the way that the man had casually dismembered that straw mannequin with one vicious cut of his fearsome curved Samurai sword. 'Then you have to report him to the authorities, Motoko-san, if he really is that dangerous and unbalanced.'

Motoko looked desperate. 'No. Can't! Please don't tell Major Sawada any of this. I think of Joji's father. This would destroy him if son branded criminal...'

*

As evening fell over the city of Tokyo, Randall realised with a slight feeling of shame that he had lost his fight completely. The fight, that is, to resist the allure of Miss Amelia Peachy...

Since their last meeting in the room above the bathhouse in the *Yoshiwara,* he had thought of nothing else but this woman. The memory of her in those tight pyjamas, with a pearly sheen on her brow, had filled his waking moments since then - and many of his un-waking moments too. Clive Randall was a man who had always looked down with contempt on those simpering long-haired poets and pathetic individuals who fawned around sexually attractive women. Yet now, for the first time in his life, he had found himself firmly hoisted by his own petard, and tormented by unhealthy thoughts for just such a woman.

It did not make him feel any better that she had clearly done this to him deliberately – seduced him quite blatantly. But at least that must mean that she desired his physical attentions equally in return, and must welcome his proposal with gratitude if he should decide to offer her that honour.

He had run into her quite by accident in the lobby of the Imperial

193

Hotel, and despite the risk of being observed by passers-by, had insisted on her coming up to the first floor and giving him an immediate report of her activities. In this meeting room on the first floor that had been rented this week for a British embassy trade function, she looked quite different from the sultry creature dressed in pyjamas that he'd met last Wednesday, but no less alluring. In fact she was restored this evening to the looks and dress of a young English lady of impeccable dress sense and manners - in a stylish afternoon dress of emerald green velvet, her raven hair tied with ribbons, a glimpse of decorous white petticoats beneath her skirt, and perfect ankles laced in gleaming black shoes. And Miss Peachy seemed in an equally modest mood to match her dress, almost refined and slightly melancholy if anything, Randall noted with approval. Dressed like this, she would even be welcomed at his mother's ivy-covered country manor house in Malvern, and among the best society of Worcestershire. His mother might not even be too dismayed if Miss Peachy was then presented to her as his intended bride, provided she looked and behaved like this. (Although he would of course have to conceal the truth from his mother of Miss Peachy's extraordinary past – actress, circus performer and government spy; that kind of risqué background would be difficult to explain to their staid neighbours in the heart of the Worcestershire countryside.)

But at night Randall decided that he could be magnanimous and safely allow his bride full rein for her passions. Once safely married and in the privacy of their bedroom, he would even allow her the freedom to satisfy her full exotic taste for dressing up as much as she desired. Randall could imagine her now, displaying those long legs and that perfect body in a variety of enticing costumes, all for his own private delectation...

'Is something wrong, Mr Randall? You seem distracted.' Her voice was icy and peremptory.

Randall was startled out of his daydream. 'Where have you been for the last six days, Miss Peachy? I have been trying to contact you urgently, but none of the girls at that bathhouse would tell me where you'd gone.'

'I told them expressly not to,' Miss Peachy declared with satisfaction. 'So I'm glad they obeyed me.'

'No doubt you are. But that still doesn't enlighten me as to where you have been.'

Miss Peachy seemed reluctant to tell him, but finally relented and said, 'I went to Kyoto, Mr Randall.'

'For a bit of spiritual enlightenment perhaps?' Randall still couldn't stop himself mocking her, despite his newfound attachment for her, perhaps because she always seemed a little rebellious in mood. Once they were married, though, he would have to put a stop to all this rebellious nonsense, of course, and show her firmly who was boss.

'No, I went there because I thought I might have a clue to the whereabouts of Herr Plesch.'

Randall was suddenly alert again. 'You did? And did it come to anything?'

Miss Peachy looked suitably chastened. 'Unfortunately not.'

Randall was suddenly suspicious. 'I did read a report that a European man killed himself in a bizarre way on a rail journey to Kyoto at the weekend. That was nothing to do with you, Miss Peachy, I take it.'

She smiled faintly. 'Of course not. Who was this European man?'

Randall wasn't quite deceived by her innocent expression; he remembered that this woman was a highly accomplished actress, of course, therefore often had a suspicion that she was dissembling with him deliberately. 'He was a prestigious Italian doctor, I believe, although, strangely, his embassy is denying they know anything about the man.'

'*Sic transit Gloria.*' Miss Peachy seemed wary for a moment under his close inspection, her eyes narrowing.

'Quite.' Randall thought for a second. 'So no trace of Plesch in Kyoto, then?'

'No. Perhaps he's not here in Japan after all,' Miss Peachy suggested. 'Maybe the Americans, and Mr Pryor, got it wrong.'

'Then that should be one less problem for us to worry about,' Randall said coolly. 'But your major concern should still be catching this traitor of ours, Miss Peachy, and so far I haven't been greatly impressed with what you've achieved in that regard.'

'You may be right about Cavendish, after all,' Miss Peachy admitted begrudgingly. 'The man is far too stupid to be a traitor.'

Randall tried not to look too satisfied with himself at this admission from Miss Peachy, even though he disliked her insulting manner towards his well-connected colleague at the embassy. 'Then who is it? I know for a fact that the Japs will attack Port Arthur soon without a declaration of war, Miss Peachy. They have confided this information to us, including details of the precise time and troop deployments, in return for our help in supplying details of Russian naval movements. So far the secret has been kept in the British Embassy here and has not even been disseminated back to London for fear that our unknown traitor will get to hear of it. This is one secret that the Russian spies in Tokyo must never get...but we can hardly guarantee that when we have no clue yet as to the identity of this person...'

Randall could see this information had intrigued Miss Peachy, and in her preoccupied mood she began to pace in front of the window, her figure outlined against the lights of the Imperial Palace.

He could feel himself being aroused again by her sensual movement, by the swirl of her skirts, and the rustle of her petticoat along the wooden floor.

She stopped suddenly and regarded him with feigned disapproval again, which did not fool him for one moment. 'Yes, Mr Randall, what is it that you're looking at, may I ask?'

'Nothing at all, Miss Peachy,' he assured her. 'I just want you to understand the urgency of this matter. We need to unearth our Embassy traitor before it's too late. If the secrets of the Japs' military plans fall into Russian hands, and it is shown that the leak originated from our embassy here, the repercussions would be disastrous for our future relations. Do you understand?'

'I understand perfectly.' She hesitated, still apparently uncomfortable under his frank inspection. 'May I go now, Mr Randall?'

'Yes, you may. But send me a daily report on your progress from now on, otherwise I shall camp outside that bathhouse of yours. Is that quite clear?' With equanimity Randal watched her walk slowly to the door and close it gently behind her.

He had been tempted to tell her today about his feelings for her, but perhaps now was not the best time to turn the girl's head with thoughts of marriage, and the generosity of his offer. He still needed her to unearth this traitor, after all, and there was more than enough time for declaring himself to her later, once she'd completed her mission...

*

Amelia quickly ascended two floors and entered the main corridor on that level, anxious to return unseen to her own room where she could turn herself back into the plump and middle-aged Mrs Smythe again. Luckily she had a whole wardrobe of oversized and unfashionable clothes available in her room for the character of Mrs Smythe, to replace those she'd had to abandon on the way to Kyoto when she had made her escape from the train.

She had only just arrived back from Kyoto this evening when Randall had walked into her by accident in the lobby of the Imperial, and insisted on getting an immediate report. And the truth was she didn't feel entirely safe walking around Tokyo dressed as herself: she attracted far more unwanted attention here as Miss Amelia Peachy than she ever did as the familiar Mrs Smythe, who was so well-known to the hotel staff and other long term guests here as to be almost invisible.

Soon after she'd entered the spying game, Amelia had realised one incontrovertible truth: how much more easily it was for a plain or older women to merge into the background than a young and attractive one. Plain women, or any woman over forty, tended to become quite invisible after a while, just so much background wallpaper, ignored by the attentions of men, and even ignored by their own sex except as sources of gossip and rumour.

Amelia was reflecting on this sad truth for women in general when the bedroom door she was passing was suddenly flung open and a strong hand yanked her inside the room. Then another hand was placed firmly over her mouth, before she could protest.

Her heart was thumping wildly against her ribs, and she was just about to retaliate violently in kind when she recognised the handsome eyes and dark curls of the man who'd once pulled her with equally strong hands from a frozen Russian lake...

Shelepin released his hand from over her mouth; he was alone in the room, Amelia was relieved to see.

He smiled at her. 'I see, *dushinka*, that Japan agrees with you. You look remarkably well, considering your hectic life here. I hope that this return to your normal character doesn't signify that you will no longer be masquerading as the delectable Aiko-san? That would be a great pity...'

Amelia sighed mentally in disappointment. If both the Russians and the Americans now knew of her secret identity in the *Yoshiwara* then that truly was the end of Aiko-san as a viable role...

Shelepin was still talking. '...I spotted you in the lobby with your boss, Mr Randall, and I was waiting in this empty room for you to return to your own suite - thirty-six.'

Damnation! - she swore to herself. Then that meant Shelepin also knew of her identity as Mrs Smythe, which meant in turn that role might also have to be retired soon as well...

Despite a feeling of being thoroughly outclassed by this man, Amelia tried to recover her poise. 'And you too look very well, Gregor Nikolaivich. But I warn you that you're taking a huge risk in coming here to the Imperial Hotel openly like this. Major Sawada frequents this place often and he is determined to find you and arrest you, I fear.'

'I leave playacting and disguises to wonderful actresses like yourself, *dushinka*,' Shelepin murmured. 'I cannot be anything but myself.'

'My playacting - as you call it - has kept me alive these last few years, Gregor Nikolaivich. I'm sure Sawada knows exactly what you look like, and is just waiting for you to take a foolish risk like this, coming here.'

Shelepin didn't look concerned at all. 'And would you give me away to him, *dushinka*?'

Amelia bit her lip. 'Only if you gave me no choice, Gregor Nikolaivich.'

Shelepin smiled grimly. 'There's always a choice in life, isn't there? Anyway I am only in the Imperial briefly for a meeting of my own; I don't intend to make a habit of this. So I trust you will allow me to walk free this one time. I hesitate to mention it - I normally detest people who want favours returned – but you do owe me your life, *dushinka*.'

Amelia kept her face expressionless. 'True. So I would certainly regret it deeply if I had to hand you over to Japanese counter intelligence.'

Shelepin grimaced. 'Not as much as I would.'

Amelia sighed. 'There is nothing for you here in Tokyo, Gregor

Nikolaivich. You'll never be allowed to get away with whatever British secrets you're hoping to purloin. We know you have been dealing with a traitor in our embassy, and we now know who...' Amelia had been about to say "who *he* is" but had a sudden flash of insight at the last second and changed it instead to, '...who *she* is...'

Amelia could see immediately from the look in Shelepin's eyes that her sudden intuition had been a correct one. How could she have been so blind? she wondered. Who else would Shelepin have been able to seduce so easily into betraying secrets...?

But how much did Shelepin's lover really know of what was going on? Was she a willing traitor to her own country, or simply another dupe of a handsome face and manly physique?

Amelia couldn't be too critical of the woman, though, when she remembered that she herself had yielded just as easily to this man's physical attractions too.

Amelia took his hand and squeezed it. 'Take my advice, Gregor Nikolaivich, and leave Japan at once. Otherwise I won't be responsible for what happens to you.'

Shelepin leaned forward until his lips were only an inch or two from her face, and she felt her heart racing again. He shook his head in mock disappointment. 'You've changed, Amelia. You weren't always as hard and practical as this, *dushinka,* I fear...'

CHAPTER 18

Wednesday February 3rd 1904

Seated at an alcove table under a Phoenix palm in the busy lobby of the Imperial Hotel, Joe sipped his morning coffee and studied the aimless activity around him.

Major Sawada, seated next to him, was partaking of *gyokuro* green tea, which should perhaps have relaxed his temper Yet the tea did not seem to be working because was in a particularly sinister and baleful mood as he made Joe uncomfortable with his unsettling and probing questions. 'Where have you been for the last few days, Mr Appeldoorn? I haven't seen you here for a week. Did I not ask you to keep me informed of your whereabouts at all times?'

Joe suspected that Sawada knew exactly where he'd been during the last few days, although hopefully he didn't know all the details of what he'd been up to. '*At all times*? Did you really say that? I don't recall you being quite so definite as that,' he said innocently. 'Well, I can tell you now what I've been doing. I visited the house of Maeda-sama in Kamakura, then spent a few days with the Maedas in Kyoto. We visited a General Yoshida -' Joe had thought that name might impress Sawada, but it seemed clear that Sawada already knew all about that meeting from his complete lack of reaction – 'and I also called at the house of a man called Yukio Kiratani.'

'A great Japanese patriot,' Sawada commented with approval.

'So I believe.' Joe decided not to mention the name of Kiratani's son, Joji, though, remembering his solemn promise to Motoko on the train yesterday.

Sawada frowned. 'I did hear reports that an elderly Italian doctor committed suicide on Saturday by throwing himself off an express train on to Kyoto – coincidentally the same train on which you were travelling. And that you of all people then tried heroically to save him?'

Joe inclined his head modestly. 'Tragically I couldn't prevent him jumping to his death.'

Sawada pursed his lips. 'I was very surprised to hear that you were involved yet again in another violent incident during your brief stay in Japan. Violence and death seem to be following you around, Mr Appeldoorn. The bombing here in the hotel, Mr Pryor's death in the *Yoshiwara*, now this Italian meeting a strange fate? I begin to suspect that no one can be as naturally unlucky as you. Do you really still claim not to be an agent of the American government?'

There was sudden cough, and Sawada looked up to see the vast bulk of American Ambassador Reinhold looming up beside him. 'I couldn't help overhearing your conversation, Major,' Hageyama said with an ill-concealed temper. 'Are you really accusing Mr Appeldoorn of being an American spy?' He simmered for a moment, eyes glittering. 'Well, I can assure you that it's simply not true. Mr Appeldoorn is an entirely innocent American businessman, here to make a commercial deal between your country and mine. I would also remind you that he saved the lives of at least thirty innocent people in this hotel last week by his heroic action, and you should therefore be a damned sight more grateful to him than you are, instead of treating him as some sort of spy! Do I make myself perfectly clear?'

Even Sawada seemed slightly embarrassed to be upbraided in public like this, and shifted uneasily in his seat. 'Then please accept my apologies, Mr Appeldoorn, if my questions appear presumptuous. If you'll excuse me now...'

*

'That man is a complete asshole!' the ambassador muttered - loudly enough, though, for a passing Western guest or two to hear and raise their eyebrows in astonishment at such language from an eminent man.

Joe wondered if the ambassador's spirited defence of him had anything to do with a guilty conscience. He didn't doubt now that what Amelia had told him had to be true – that the American embassy here must have certainly connived in the plan to bring him to Japan, as a sort of tethered goat to smoke out the assassin Johan Plesch. For a moment Joe was sorely tempted to accuse Reinhold of this duplicitous behaviour but in the end decided he had enough enemies in Japan already without making more.

'Thank you for that support, Ambassador. That man seems convinced I'm an embassy spy – I wonder where he could have got hold of such a notion?' Joe declared innocently.

The ambassador had the grace to look even more discomfited before deciding rapidly to change the subject. 'Did you experience the earthquake on Friday, Joseph? I believe it was worse in Kamakura and the Izu Peninsula than here.'

'I did feel it. But I personally suffered nothing untoward from it, fortunately.' Joe didn't feel like elaborating further.

The ambassador took Sawada's recently vacated seat, and lowered his voice to a whisper. 'So, enlighten me, Joseph. Who was this mysterious Italian who killed himself on your train to Kyoto? I've had a request from the police in Kyoto – an inspector called Ishii - to help identify the man, although, since no body was found, that might be difficult. I was surprised to learn of *your* involvement in this incident; this Inspector Ishii mentioned your name in particular as one of the witnesses to what happened. The Italian embassy is denying that such a man as this Signor Valdini even existed, which is why the Kyoto police are trying other foreign embassies in the hope of discovering his true identity.'

'I have no idea who the man was. I simply tried to help, after the man went crazy and climbed up onto the roof of the train,' Joe said with finality, hoping the ambassador would leave it at that, and not pursue the matter further.

The ambassador frowned – perhaps he suspected the real truth about this "Signor Valdini's" identity, Joe thought. But he took the hint anyway from the tone of Joe's voice, and changed the subject yet again, if reluctantly. 'Actually I was hoping to find you here this morning, Joseph. I have another invitation for you. It would give me great personal pleasure if you could join us at the party that the American embassy is hosting at the Japanese pavilion in the grounds of the *Rokumeikan* tomorrow night.'

'Any special reason for the party?' Joe asked curiously.

The ambassador looked surprised. 'Of course there is. The party is being held to celebrate fifty years since Commodore Perry first opened up Japan to the West back in 'fifty four. Fifty years of close ties between America and Japan...'

'Are the Japanese celebrating that too?' Joe asked ironically.

'Maeda and Motoko will be there,' the ambassador said, apparently not picking up on the sarcastic note in Joe's voice, 'as well as a host of other Japanese luminaries, including General Yoshida and Prime Minister Katsura.' He paused. 'We are making a gesture of sorts in holding it in the Japanese pavilion, rather than in the original building, which was seen as an unfortunate symbol of Western cultural dominance during the early Meiji years. We're trying to change the image we have of being overbearing dictatorial foreigners, and we now want to be seen by the Japanese as their true equals, not their superiors.'

He sounded genuine and contrite to Joe, in more ways than one, so Joe finally smiled in agreement. 'Then I'll be glad to come,' he said.

*

Joe lingered over his coffee after the ambassador had gone on to a meeting of local business people in the grand ballroom. Joe had been invited to the meeting too, but had had more than enough of business meetings for the time being.

A voice startled him out of his deeply introspective mood. 'Mr Appeldoorn, you look a little lonely sitting there. May I join you for tea too?' Joe glanced up in surprise to see Fumiyo Isogai regarding him quizzically.

Joe stood up with alacrity and offered her the seat recently vacated by Ambassador Reinhold. 'I'm drinking coffee, but please do join me, Miss Isogai.'

Fumiyo ordered tea for herself from the passing lobby waiter, before appraising him with a faint smile. 'You've been in the wars recently, Mr Appeldoorn, I hear, by all accounts.'

Joe wondered idly who she had heard these accounts from. 'True,' he acknowledged.

'An anarchist bombing, a friend murdered; an earthquake; a suicide on a train? It's quite a catalogue of ill fortune, isn't it?'

'It is indeed. It seems you're very well informed about my personal circumstances, Miss Isogai. You more or less accused me of being a foreign spy the last time we met, as I recall, although my knowledge of Professor Hilbert's list of unsolved theoretical problems in mathematics seemed to lessen your suspicion of me a little. Perhaps it's time for me to reciprocate. I wonder how it is that *you* know so much about my affairs.'

She smiled deprecatingly. 'You think *I* am a spy of some sort? That's an interesting notion...But I would hardly need to be a professional spy in order to have heard your name this week, would I? Believe me, Mr Appeldoorn, your name is being widely discussed in all sorts of important places after the events of the last week or so. I hold no monopoly on such knowledge; your name seems to crop up naturally at every social affair I have been too recently.'

Joe raised an ironic eyebrow. 'Really? I had no idea I had become so famous in Tokyo. Or is it *infamous?*'

A waiter returned to serve Fumiyo her tea, and she took the opportunity to change the mood of their discussion. 'Shall we talk of pleasanter things, Mr Appeldoorn?' she said brightly. 'How is your business deal with Mr Maeda progressing?'

'Satisfactorily, I think. I had to go to Kyoto at the weekend, though, in order to be vetted by Mr Maeda's patron...'

Fumiyo nodded in understanding. 'Ah, you mean General Yoshida...'

'Indeed,' Joe confirmed.

'And how did the meeting go?'

Joe gave a non-committal shrug. 'I'm waiting to hear. But hopefully I passed the audition and we can now move on to detailed contract negotiation.'

Fumiyo smiled. 'You're clearly learning the Japanese way of doing business, Mr Appeldoorn. The key is patience, because Japanese negotiation requires painfully slow deliberation and much manoeuvring. And of course, all the social proprieties to be rigorously observed.'

Joe smiled at her in return. 'Yes, I am beginning to appreciate that.'

Fumiyo studied him again with a long cool look of appraisal. 'So what do you truly think of my country, Mr Appeldoorn? Does it please you? Interest you? *Infuriate* you?'

Joe phrased his answer as diplomatically as he could. 'All of those things, I suppose. Your nation is certainly unique, Miss Isogai, and will one day become a major world power. Perhaps that day will come sooner than even I suspect. When the Japanese put their mind to something, they seem capable of achieving anything.'

Her eyes moistened unexpectedly at this encomium from a foreigner, and Joe was reminded what an emotional people the Japanese were, despite their reputation to the contrary. 'True,' she said, 'but as a nation we are also capable of being led into dark and destructive pathways by unscrupulous and corrupt men.'

Joe wondered at that sudden note of bitterness and derision in her voice.

'War with Russia is coming,' she said worriedly. 'I fear for us as a nation if we should be seduced into going down that militaristic road. It will lead us only to disaster.'

Joe had read the papers today where the main story concerned the growing tension between Japan and Russia, which was now at fever pitch. 'From what I've read, it's probably too late to stop that war with Russia now, Miss Isogai,' Joe declared bleakly.

Fumiyo seemed almost dazed for a moment. 'Yes, you're probably right. But perhaps we sane Japanese must still try to avert this disaster, nevertheless.'

An uncomfortable silence developed, while the bustle and commotion in the Imperial lobby continued around them.

'Are you going to the party in the *Rokumeikan* pavilion tomorrow night, Mr Appeldoorn?' Fumiyo finally asked.

'I am.'

'Then perhaps I might see you there.'

'Is that really your sort of occasion?' Joe was surprised: the arrival of the Americans fifty years ago in Japan hardly seemed a cause for celebration for someone of Fumiyo Isogai's political persuasion.

She looked a little embarrassed. 'Perhaps not. But I like dressing up for parties as much as any young woman, I assure you. Perhaps we'll have another chance to talk again tomorrow night...?'

*

Amelia listened to the reassuring lap of water against the hull of the houseboat as it ploughed a steady course at three knots back up the river, under the full power of its little steam engine. She had decided to return to the *Yoshiwara* for one final day with Sumiko, even though she knew she was no longer safe there when so many of her enemies had now penetrated her secret identity.

Amelia had boarded the houseboat in Nihombashi dressed as Mrs Smythe, and was still in that costume, though longing now to take off all these petticoats and this heavy skirt in favour of a kimono again. But for the moment she was content to relax in a chair with Sumiko's nimble fingers easing the tension in her neck muscles.

'Thank you, little dumpling,' she said, when Sumiko had finished and was about to go off and fill the vertical Japanese bath in the cabin.

Sumiko hadn't forgotten her promise of a week ago to be rude to her in return. 'Not at all, "Fat Dumpling".'

Amelia patted her cheek affectionately; Sumiko had been overjoyed when she'd reappeared at the quayside half-an-hour ago and asked to be taken back to the *Yoshiwara*.

'Are you coming back for good?' Sumiko asked hopefully.

'No, I don't think so, little one. I need to return to town by tomorrow night. There is a big party at the *Rokumeikan* being given by the Americans.'

'Yes, I know all about it,' Sumiko said eagerly. 'All of Tokyo society will be there, so they say. Two friends of mine are serving there as waitresses for the evening. They know the lady who caters these events for the American Embassy.'

Amelia was immediately interested. 'Do they? Do you think this lady would be able to make room for two extra serving girls at tomorrow's party, Sumiko-san?'

Sumiko looked suspicious. 'Which extra serving girls?'

'Why, you and I, of course, little dumpling,' Amelia said with satisfaction.

*

After Amelia had bathed and washed her hair, she then changed into the kimono of Aiko-san and re-did her face in oriental style.

Then she sat uneasily, contemplating her dramatic change of image in the mirror.

For one of the few times in her life, Amelia was torn between conflicting loyalties, between the professional and the personal.

Lady Rosemary was the first of her moral dilemmas; Amelia had no doubt now where the leaks in the British Embassy must have originated...

Lady Rosemary had access through her marital bed to all the secrets that her husband possessed, and it was clear now that Shelepin was the person who must have seduced her into revealing those secrets. Talking to him yesterday in the Imperial, Amelia had suddenly realised that *he* had been the man whom Lady Rosemary had met last Thursday outside the hotel, and the consequences of that had come to her in a flash. His hair was shorter now than she remembered, which was one reason why she had not recognized him at once from that distant glimpse last Thursday.

But did Lady Rosemary really know what she was doing? – that was the question. Did she really know that she was giving British state secrets to a Russian spy? Amelia suspected not - Gregor Nikolaivich was a distracting lover and a past master at drawing information from an unsuspecting woman.

And that was Amelia's problem. She liked Rosemary and wanted to protect her from her own indiscretions if she could. But how could she prevent Shelepin gaining access to the date and details of the planned Japanese assault on Port Arthur without destroying the life and reputation of Lady Rosemary at the same time?

An uneasy thought struck her. Perhaps she was already too late? Perhaps Lady Rosemary had already passed on this dangerous information to her lover during one of their regular liaisons? If so, then Shelepin could already know the date of the planned Japanese invasion of Port Arthur.

Yet Amelia decided that this wasn't likely. For one thing, the embassy was being particularly cautious about disseminating this vital information so perhaps Lady Rosemary would not have heard this secret yet from her husband. Also, the fact was that Shelepin was still here in Tokyo, and Amelia suspected that if he had stumbled on the details of Japan's invasion plans, he would already have left for Vladivostok to warn the Russian Pacific fleet directly of what was about to happen. So Amelia thought it likely that everything was still to play for. Somehow she had to prevent Lady Rosemary from giving her Russian lover any more information. She could of course tell Randall and have Lady Rosemary watched or even arrested. But that would mean disgrace for the woman, and perhaps even the death penalty if she was tried and convicted for treason, therefore Amelia was reluctant to take such a drastic step immediately. If Shelepin did obtain this information from Lady Rosemary despite her best efforts to the contrary, then Amelia knew that she couldn't also simply let him leave Japan with that secret. Yet she didn't want him caught by Sawada and his Japanese counter intelligence thugs either.

So what to do...? She was certainly caught on the horns of a difficult dilemma.

She'd advised Gregor Nikolaivich as firmly as she could to leave Japan, of course, but she knew him too well to believe that he would simply go as easily as that. Shelepin had to suspect that the British were privy to Japan's military plans, and that Lady Rosemary was his best chance of learning those secrets...

Amelia decided that she would have to warn Lady Rosemary of what was at stake here, and not to make any more liaisons with a dangerous man like Shelepin. But what if she was wrong, and Lady Rosemary was actually a *willing* traitor to her husband and her country? Perhaps she was helping this woman too much, a woman who simply didn't deserve such consideration...

*

The boat was now nearing the crumbling jetty landing nearest to the *Yoshiwara,* and Amelia prepared to disembark with Sumiko.

She watched the low marshy ground sliding past her view, and wondered why she loved this ugly place so much. Yet she did love the *Yoshiwara.* It was a place that had affected her deeply and worked its way into her soul. Today the distant view of the main gate of the *Yoshiwara*, this high arched entrance to the old Pleasure Quarter of ancient Edo, seemed particularly poignant, perhaps because she knew that this might be the last time she ever returned here.

For the first time in her life, Amelia felt unnerved about the future. She no longer had any clear idea for her own future plans, and her life was now clouded in doubt and uncertainty. The meeting with Shelepin yesterday had been a further distraction to her troubled mind, yet her inner emotions were concentrated more on Joseph than anything else, and particularly the time they had spent together in Kyoto.

It had been the hardest thing she'd ever done to leave him in Kyoto. After the incident on the train, she'd resolved that she would see him this one last time, explain herself properly to him and clear the air between them, then walk out of his life forever.

But the reality of doing that had been infinitely harder than she'd imagined. The moment she revealed herself to him had told her the truth: that she wanted this man more than anyone she'd ever known - more than Shelepin, more than John Ballantyne, more even than dear tragic Luigi...

Amelia Peachy recognised that her personal view of life could never be naïve or girlishly romantic any more; she'd seen too much of the weaknesses and foibles of humans for that, and particularly of men. Yet this man, Joseph Appeldoorn, had stirred unfamiliar feelings of passion in her that probably came as close as her hardened heart could ever get to falling in love...

Damn him! Why couldn't he have waited for her in Switzerland? The way that he had given in so rapidly to that Eleanor woman's blandishments was quite disgraceful. That girl had shamelessly worked her way into his affections, of course, but that still didn't excuse him. It was true that he had thought she was dead at the time, but nevertheless, how could he have given into that transparent woman so easily...?

The irony was that she'd revealed herself to him in Kyoto in order to excise him from her own mind. But, in doing so, she had inadvertently done exactly the opposite. On the morning she had left him at the *ryokan* in

Kyoto, all Amelia had wanted to hear was the sound of his footsteps running after her carriage, and his voice begging her not to go...

Dressing up in *geisha* costume for their last dinner together had not been her original intention, but by that time she'd been desperate to make him commit to her again, to break the strong bonds he had with his American wife by a brazen act of seduction of her own. Yet there had been an element of humility in that act too – for a self-reliant person like her to adopt the subservient and doll-like manners of a *geisha* in order to win a man's devotion was entirely out-of-character, and deliberately humbling. And she'd seen, just from the look on his face when he saw her dressed that way, that she had shaken that man to his core.

She thought about his hands on her now, and the idea that she would never see him again filled her almost with despair. Yet, if she was being honest, she still had hopes that it was not yet over between them. With that act of seduction in Kyoto, she knew that she had planted a seed of sorts, a seed that might grow into something mighty again, if he wanted it.

But she had resolved now not to make any more moves herself in this game. It was now up to Joseph to make the next move. If he really wanted her, then he would have to make the important decision that mattered, and come after her...

CHAPTER 19

Thursday February 4th 1904

The Japanese pavilion in the grounds of the *Rokumeikan* was an elegant building – certainly a lot more elegant, Joe thought, than the original *Rokumeikan* building itself, which was looking abandoned and unloved these days, a little like a rich Englishman's garden folly left to rot and decay after the money ran out.

The pavilion, on the other hand, had a cypress-bark roof with curved eaves, and the usual cool calm Japanese interiors of tatami mats and gossamer screens, with one main room as big as a banqueting hall and many passageways leading off it to smaller more intimate rooms.

Because of the dry and relatively balmy night, the party had spilled out from the pavilion onto the terrace and into the surrounding garden. Joe had escaped briefly outside with some fellow guests and was admiring the ceremonial brass gongs and the display of fine Satsuma porcelain arrayed in front of the pavilion. A glitter of reflected light in the garden indicated the outline of the nearby ornamental lake over which globular red lanterns cast an orange radiance. From inside the pavilion came the murmur of conversation and the clink of saké cups.

Joe was suddenly aware that the intimidating figure of General Yoshida was bearing down on him in bull-headed style, with another kimono-clad gentleman in tow.

He bowed. 'Ah, we meet again, Mr App-re-doon. This is a great pleasure; I did not expect to see you again so soon. May I present Katsura-sama?'

Joe bowed to Yoshida's companion formally and said, '*Katsura-sama, hajimemashite,*' before he'd fully registered that this was the Prime Minister of Japan he was being introduced to. Katsura too was an army general, but a less striking figure than Yoshida. He looked every inch what he no doubt

208

was: a compliant front man and puppet, there to do his real master's bidding.

'Did you enjoy the performances tonight, Mr App-re-doon?' Yoshida asked.

'I did indeed.' The American embassy had made a major effort tonight, Joe could see, in providing a mix of Western and Japanese entertainment for the edification of their distinguished guests. So there had been virtuoso displays of the *koto* and *shamisen* to match the playing by a Western string quartet of a Bach Brandenburg Concerto; while a dance display by a team of visiting American ballet performers had been balanced with a *geisha* performing several elaborate fan dances. Joe hadn't been able to take his eyes of this latter entertainer in all her impeccable silk brocade and painted glory, but mainly because of the reminders she brought him of both Umegiku-san and of his weekend in Kyoto with Amelia. It struck him how eerily accurate Amelia's mimicry of a *geisha* had been; to his inexpert eyes, at least, she had been able to summon up all the strange charm and erotic enticement of these doll-like and exotic creatures.

He felt another twinge of melancholy, though, at that reminder of Amelia, as he wondered where she might be tonight, and who she might be with...

'I am looking forward to the fireworks,' Yoshida said, with all the enthusiasm of a small boy anticipating a great treat.

'Yes, me too.' Joe felt compelled for some reason to agree, even though he had been unaware up to that moment that there were to be any fireworks tonight...

*

Major Sawada sidled up to Joe as soon as Yoshida and Katsura had moved on to more important guests.

'I sense the General approves of you, Mr Appeldoorn,' Sawada stated with no great conviction. 'This stamp of approval from such a great man should be of great assistance to you in closing your business deal here satisfactorily.'

Joe assumed he must be talking about Yoshida, since Katsura had hardly said a word, but was puzzled nonetheless. 'On what basis do you make such a judgement, Major?'

Sawada shrugged. 'Oh, General Yoshida respects bravery, and you showed plenty of that when you foiled that bomb plot last week in the Imperial Hotel. You have also displayed some suspicious and dubious behaviour during your time in Japan, of course, but it seems the General does not hold such meddling behaviour against you.'

'So the General is appreciative that I saved his hotel – I believe he is one of the owners of the Imperial?'

Sawada smiled enigmatically. 'He is indeed. But I am sure the General's approval of you is only partly gratitude for your help in foiling that bomb plot. He also has a great respect for experts on Western technology like yourself. He wants Japan to learn from the West and from people like you...'

'And then what? To compete with us? To defeat us?'

'"Defeat" is an emotive word, Mr Appeldoorn. But to compete with the West on equal terms, certainly.'

Joe lifted his eyebrows questioningly but did not respond further.

'Are you enjoying the party?' Sawada asked politely.

Joe could see that Sawada clearly had something else he wanted to say to him but, with the usual obliqueness of Japanese manners, had to get there by an elliptical and devious route.

'I am,' Joe confirmed

Sawada finally looked embarrassed. 'Then I hesitate to spoil this evening for you. But I have troubling news which I feel you need to be made aware of.'

'What news?' Joe felt a prickling of tension.

'It does concern the bombing at the Imperial Hotel last Monday, where you performed so heroically... ' Sawada somehow made the word "heroically" still sound like an insult, Joe thought. 'We are sure now that the bombing was indeed the work of the *Kokuryukai* - the "Black Dragon Society"...'

Joe's pulse quickened. 'Have you made any arrests?'

Sawada nodded thoughtfully. 'Indeed we have. Many of the conspirators are in custody. Regrettably however, not all, including some of the major ringleaders of the plot. In particular I have just issued a warrant for the arrest of an individual called Joji Kiratani who has been heavily implicated in the plot...ah, I can see you are familiar with that name...'

Joe kept his face as blank as he could. 'I believe I told you yesterday. I was at Yukio Kiratani's house in Kyoto at the weekend. Joji, I believe, is his son. He was there at the house too, although I never spoke to him. This is bad news for the father to see his son accused of such a heinous crime.'

'It's also unfortunately bad news for you, Mr Appeldoorn,' Sawada said tartly. 'I wish to warn you of this for your safety. For some reason Joji Kiratani appears to believe that you and Maeda-san's daughter betrayed him to the authorities...'

Joe was getting worried. 'Me betray him? Where could he get an idea like that from? How could I betray him? I barely knew of his existence.'

'You did foil his original plan at least, so that wouldn't have made you popular with his movement anyway. And, from talking frankly to his associates, it seems Kiratani has formed the opinion that you and Miss Maeda have been – shall we say – overly intimate, and that you therefore felt the need to betray him to the authorities in order to have the field to yourself...'

Joe could imagine cynically that this discussion with Kiratani's associates might have involved some unpleasant interrogation techniques in order to produce this supposed level of frankness. But at the moment, he was more concerned about his own welfare in the face of this startling new threat. 'That is nonsense, Major...'

Sawada smiled, but the result wasn't reassuring to Joe – it was like watching a snake bearing its fangs. 'Of course it's nonsense. I don't give it any credence to these accusations at all. But I can only tell you from the evidence of Kiratani's associates in terror that he does seem to believe this. Kiratani is a young hothead, Mr Appeldoorn, and capable of anything, so I advise you strongly to watch your step until we can catch him...'

*

Ambassador Reinhold bustled up to Joe as soon as Sawada had left him. 'That asshole Sawada wasn't bothering you again, Joseph, was he?'

Joe shrugged ruefully. 'No, not this time. I think he was actually trying to help me this time, although he still couldn't help playing the heavy a bit. He was just telling me the latest news concerning his investigation of the Imperial Hotel bombing.'

'And? What is the latest news?'

'He has arrested quite a few people, it seems. And one or two of them may even be guilty of something,' Joe added sarcastically. 'I think Sawada uses the scattergun style of policing: if in doubt, lock 'em up. Better that a thousand innocent people get accidentally punished than a single real criminal should go unpunished.'

Hageyama nodded thoughtfully, but seemed prepared to defend Sawada for once. 'Well, he does have a tough job, what with all the crazy people in this country plotting to blow things up.' The ambassador relaxed. 'Let's talk of pleasanter things, Joseph. Have you heard that we've organised a big fireworks display on the quayside of *Tsukiji* later in the evening?'

'I have,'

'Well, try and find yourself a good spot to see it – it will be something special to mark this momentous event. Some of the VIPs - Yoshida, Katsura, our embassy people, and some of the British, including Sir Stephen and his lovely wife - are going to board a steam yacht called the *Yoshino Cherry* to get a better view of the fireworks from the river.'

'Can I go along?' Joe didn't know why he asked that, since he had little real interest in the display.

The ambassador looked embarrassed. 'Unfortunately not. There's only room for thirty or so guests and staff on the yacht. But you will be able to see most of the fireworks from the garden here anyway. It will be quite a sight' He clapped Joe on the shoulder. 'Enjoy the rest of the party, Joseph. Why don't you go and talk to some of the pretty American girls who are here tonight? There's a ballerina girl from Philadelphia who's a knockout in her white silk tights – and she looks very lonely backstage there after her performance so I'm sure she would appreciate a kind word from a fellow Philadelphian.'

'Yes, I'll have to do just that,' Joe said with pretended enthusiasm.

As the ambassador moved on to speak to more of his guests Joe walked back into the pavilion, but with no real intention of searching out any ballerina in white tights, despite the attractiveness of that picture in his mind. Instead, within a minute, he ran into Sir Stephen and Lady Rosemary Hawtry-Gough and the British spy Randall whom Toby Pryor had pointed out to him in the lobby of the Imperial. Joe remembered that this man was the only person among the British who knew that Amelia was working undercover in Japan, therefore effectively her boss...

Lady Rosemary seemed delighted at the accidental meeting. 'Mr Appeldoorn, how nice to see you again! Isn't it, Stephen?'

Sir Stephen looked less thrilled than his wife at the chance encounter, but inclined his balding head slightly to acknowledge Joe's existence. 'Mr Appeldoorn, do you know Clive Randall, the head of our Japanese language section at the embassy?' Sir Stephen was an inch or two shorter than Joe, yet still somehow seemed to be gazing down at him from a great height.

'We haven't been formally introduced,' Joe said in response, before turning directly to Randall. 'But I believe you were in the lobby of the Imperial during the unpleasantness last Monday week, Mr Randall.'

Randall gave him a cool and patronising smile in return. 'Ah, I see you are an observant fellow, Mr Appeldoorn.' Randall was undoubtedly a good-looking man, Joe could see, with a head of thick blond hair and the physique and presence of a natural athlete; yet there was something unsettling about him too, a glimpse of an unpleasant and devious nature lurking beneath that personable exterior. 'I never complimented you on your quick thinking that night, Mr Appeldoorn...'

'*And* on his courage, Clive,' Lady Rosemary added, with a dazzling smile. 'Don't forget that.'

Randall twisted his handsome face into a semblance of a smile too. 'Of course. No one could doubt Mr Appeldoorn's...err...*courage.*'

Joe was rather enjoying seeing the man being discomfited in this way. 'I met a Major Sawada tonight,' he confided, 'who is in charge of the investigation of the bombing, and he seems confident that he has caught most of the plotters already.'

'That's splendid news, Mr Appeldoorn,' Lady Rosemary enthused, rewarding Joe with yet another warm smile. She did look very fetching tonight, Joe thought, in a flame-coloured silk gown that showed off her wonderful bosom to perfect effect, and made her appear at least ten years younger than the slightly sad-faced woman he remembered from their first encounter a week ago.

'I wonder if you would excuse Mr Randall and myself for a few minutes, my dear,' Sir Stephen apologised half-heartedly to his wife. 'Embassy business,' he explained. 'I'm sure Mr Appeldoorn will be more than happy to keep you company until I return, won't you, sir...?'

'Gladly,' Joe interjected.

'...But remember that we are going to leave to go on board that yacht to watch the fireworks at ten,' Sir Stephen cautioned his wife.

*

'You *are* a very good-looking young man, Mr Appeldoorn; I'm sure many people must tell you that – especially elderly biddies like myself,' Lady Rosemary remarked, almost as soon as they were alone.

'You're hardly elderly, Lady Rosemary,' Joe claimed gallantly.

Lady Rosemary smiled. 'Next to you, I feel truly ancient. But no matter - shall we take a turn through the garden? - it's wonderfully atmospheric here at night. And there is something I need to say to you...'

Joe was a little uncomfortable but went with her anyway, following her down a twisting gravel path lit by hanging lanterns.

'Please don't be too embarrassed at my forwardness, Mr Appeldoorn, but I need to apologise for my behaviour last week at the embassy dinner. And do not worry yourself that I am about to repeat any of those intimate advances. I don't know what came over me that night – a little too much champagne perhaps - but I freely concede that I enjoyed the experience nevertheless,' Lady Rosemary admitted. 'I still get pleasure from the company of handsome young men even though those young men may no longer get quite the same degree of pleasure in return.'

Lady Rosemary stumbled slightly on the uneven gravel path and Joe linked his arm naturally with hers, wondering if she was drunk. 'Perhaps you should hold on to me, Lady Rosemary. It's a little dark here, and the path is rather uneven.'

'Gladly. Tell me, Mr Appeldoorn, what is your first name?'

'Joseph.'

Lady Rosemary smiled. 'That's a nice name. It suits you well. May I call you "Joseph"?'

'Of course. But only if I can call you "Rosemary".'

'Agreed, Joseph.' She smiled again, looking quite radiant and girlish in the soft-hued light of the garden lanterns.

'How old are you, Joseph, may I ask?' she asked.

'Twenty-five.'

She sighed. 'Ah, to be twenty-five again! I must truly seem like an ancient relic to you. Time is a strange thing, Joseph.' She paused to summon up some remembered lines. '"*And time that gave doth now his gift confound, time doth transfix the flourish set on youth, and delves the parallels in beauty's brow*." Shakespeare did put the dilemmas of life extremely well, did he not?'

'He certainly did,' Joe agreed. He wondered what Lady Rosemary had been like in her youth – she had probably been a radiant English beauty in her time. Getting older was a trial for everybody, but it was particularly difficult for a beautiful woman, he decided regretfully...

She immediately confirmed that by what she said next. 'One minute, life seems an endless vista of parties and invitations and boundless delights spread out before you, a life where it's always spring or summer. Then one day you look in the mirror and see the little laughter lines spreading and the gloss in your hair fading, and realise that the possibilities are no longer endless. The parties and the invitations gradually diminish. Other concerns and worries seem to take over your life. And before you know it, you realise that you are now in the autumn of your life. And you spend your time now longing to break free and re-discover that feeling of youthful joy again somehow, even if only for a few hours. No wonder that so many women of my age, with no children to worry about, either take younger lovers, or else take to drink...'

Joe didn't know what to say.

'Tell me, Joseph. Do you think a handsome young man could ever really love a woman of my age without having an ulterior motive? Or are young men just deceivers who always want something mercenary in return? Could a young man like you genuinely love an older woman just for herself, do you think?'

Joe was acutely uncomfortable with the direction of this conversation but realized this woman was deeply disturbed about something. 'I'm sure I could have loved an older woman if the circumstances were right. It would depend on the woman, of course. Why are you asking me these things, though, may I ask? Are you trying to discover whether young men are truly to be trusted?'

She looked confused for a moment. 'No, I'm talking hypothetically, that's all, Joseph. Please excuse the tired ramblings of a sad middle-aged woman. Forgive me, I really shouldn't be saying such intimate things to you. I'm embarrassing you.'

'You're not,' Joe insisted gamely.

'I believe I am. But you are a very sweet young man to lie so charmingly. Shall we go back to the party? You must have had quite enough of an old biddy like me by now...'

*

An unsettled Joe returned to the pavilion to find Motoko standing near the main door, apparently waiting for him, and in sombre mood. Joe guessed what might be the cause of her dark mood...

Joe smiled at her, trying to lift her spirits, which seemed to have been depressed ever since her return from Kyoto.

Motoko didn't smile back in response, even though she looked as beautiful as Joe had ever seen her, in a kimono of red watered silk, and with her hair decorated in formal Japanese style, held up with gold combs.

'What's wrong?' he asked, seeing her face still clouded with worry. He assumed that her mood had to do with the news that Joji Kiratani was being hunted for the Imperial Hotel bombing after all, despite her own resolve not to give him away to the authorities.

But it seemed it was not Kiratani's fate that was worrying her after all. 'My father not let me go to New York,' she announced in a tiny voice. 'He name a husband for me instead. He want me marry soon. He angry with me.'

'Why?' Joe was mystified.

'He say "wife and mother" is best career for woman; he think fashion design not suitable job for daughter of powerful man.'

Joe wondered what had prompted Kenzoburo Maeda to suddenly turn into such a strict and reactionary Japanese parent when he had until recently seemed quite amenable to the idea of Motoko having a career in business. Joe decided that he must tell Motoko the news about Kiratani. He didn't want to add to her worries but she had a right to know the worst. 'Have you heard that a warrant has been issued for the arrest of Joji Kiratani?' Joe asked Motoko.

'No!' Motoko was shocked, her face instantly losing colour. 'You promised you say nothing to the police or Major Sawada!'

'I didn't say anything to them,' Joe explained patiently. 'I kept my word. But Major Sawada already seems well enough aware of the facts, I'm afraid; he probably had some of the *Kokuryukai* members he's taken into custody interrogated and tortured. Unfortunately Joji apparently believes as you do: that *I'm* somehow responsible for his troubles. And Sawada certainly hasn't done much to discourage such a belief.' In fact it might well suit Sawada very well, Joe realised with deep disquiet, if an extremist like Kiratani disposed of a man he suspected to be an American agent interfering in Japanese domestic matters, before being caught and dealt with himself...

Motoko was abject with distress. 'Then I have drawn you into terrible danger...'

*

A few minutes later Joe was watching Motoko in deep conversation with her father in a distant corner of the room when someone appeared at his elbow.

'Enjoying the party, Mr Appeldoorn?' Fumiyo Isogai asked, glancing around at the groups of disparate guests holding difficult and strained-looking conversations. 'It always leaves me a little uneasy, seeing the uncomfortable attempts of East and West to try and understand each other, don't you think?'

'You think that's impossible? For East and West to understand each other?'

Fumiyo seemed in as dark a mood as Motoko. 'Probably it is impossible. The West, after all, hasn't got a very good record when it comes to dealing with the conquered peoples under their control.'

'Are you a conquered people? You seem more like conquerors yourselves these days,' Joe suggested, 'since your international adventures in China and Manchuria.'

'Not if I have anything to do with it,' Fumiyo denied. 'I would much prefer that we Japanese leave our Korean and Chinese neighbours firmly in peace.'

'And Russia? Will you leave them in peace too?' Joe asked cynically.

'That will be more difficult to achieve, but perhaps, given time, the Russians will have internal problems of their own to divert their attentions away from us.' She smiled suddenly with a visible effort, transforming her stern face instantly into one more pleasant and amenable. 'But this is a party, Mr Appeldoorn, so shall we talk of lighter things than politics?'

Out of the corner of his eye, Joe happened to catch sight of two of the Japanese serving girls in plain quilted kimonos, who were serving guests saké and snacks to the guests. Fumiyo noticed his sudden odd distraction with these girls with slight puzzlement and quickly excused herself. 'I see a friend over there who wishes to speak to me, Mr Appeldoorn. So please enjoy the rest of the evening.'

'Are you staying here for the fireworks display, like me, or have you been invited on board the *Yoshino Cherry* to watch from the river?' Joe asked as she turned to leave.

'I am going on board the steam yacht,' Fumiyo said.

'Then you're obviously a lot more important than I realised, Miss Isogai, so perhaps I should have been more polite to you.'

She smiled graciously again. 'No, I am not important at all; I had to pull a few strings to join the boat party. But don't worry, Mr Appeldoorn. You are better off staying here to watch the fireworks. We will be so close to them on the river, we might even have to suffer some sparks and singeing of our clothing...'

*

Joe made his way across the room towards the two serving girls. He had recognised one of them as Sumiko-san from the House of the Red-Crowned Crane, so by process of elimination suspected the other might be Amelia up to her old tricks again...

Yet it was frankly hard to believe, though. This other girl bore no physical resemblance either to Amelia herself, or even to Aiko-san. This Japanese girl looked sallow-faced and frankly plain, and her eyes seemed authentically Oriental.

Joe watched from a distance from a while, unwilling to commit himself and speak to her, and perhaps make a huge fool of himself in the process.

But then the girl herself solved the problem by noticing his attention, and eventually coming over to his quiet corner of the room to offer him some sweet *Wagashi* delicacies: dry persimmons coated with red bean jelly, and *chofu* - sweet rice cakes.

As she bowed to him and offered the dish - '*Okyaku-sama, nani o meshiagarimasu-ka?*' - Joe mentally gave up the ridiculous notion that this could be Amelia. Until, that is, she hissed at him under her breath in a thoroughly annoyed voice, 'What are *you* doing here, Joseph?'

Joe was too astonished to react for a moment as she went on, whispering angrily, 'I told you to stay away from your embassy people. They have been using you shamelessly, and yet you walk straight into the lions' den again.'

Joe was fascinated by the transformation in her face, her eyes in particular – how had she managed to achieve such a genuine oriental shape? And even her other features looked different, shorter and rounder chin, a flatter, broader Oriental nose and plump cheeks. With her actress's black arts of make-up and subterfuge, she seemed capable of turning herself into virtually anyone – it was unnerving to say the least. 'And what are *you* doing here, masquerading as a serving girl?' he demanded in reply.

'It's nothing to do with you, Joseph. But if you must know, it concerns that Russian man who saved you last week – the one who called himself "Raskolnikov". His real name is Shelepin and he is an agent of the Tsar's government; I know him well too...'

'*How* well?' Joe asked suspiciously.

'This is not the time for jealousy, Joseph. Shelepin is a ruthless man and has formed a liaison with an important woman in the British community here – I fear she is the source of the leaks of British diplomatic secrets that I told you about. And I'm afraid he may be in the process of trying to obtain some particularly sensitive information from her tonight that we simply can't afford to lose. I'm trying to stop Shelepin from getting this information...and this lady from destroying herself.'

He still couldn't take his eyes off her, but he had a sudden feeling that he knew who Amelia was talking about. 'You mean Lady Rosemary, don't you?'

Amelia was suspicious in return. 'Perhaps I do. How do you know Lady Rosemary?'

'What information is Shelepin hoping to obtain from Lady Rosemary?' Joe asked.

Joe noted a long hesitation before Amelia answered reluctantly, 'The timing and details of an imminent Japanese assault on Russian forces in Port Arthur.'

'And you British know that for certain, do you?'

'We do,' Amelia whispered, while she served Joe a *Yakiimo* – a sweet-potato cinnamon-flavoured cake – that she pretended he'd asked her for.

'Well, I can see why that would be embarrassing for the British if such a secret were to be let prematurely out of the bag. But would Lady Rosemary really willingly give Shelepin such information, even if he is her secret lover?'

'Perhaps not willingly. Perhaps she doesn't understand what's going on. Maybe she just thinks she's exchanging a lover's normal confidences with him.'

Joe thought back to his enigmatic conversation with Lady Rosemary in the garden, and realised she had been trying to broach a difficult subject with him. 'I think she probably does suspect the truth about her lover now – that Shelepin is using her.'

'I can't rely on her coming to her senses by herself,' Amelia snapped. 'I will have to stop her – for her own good.'

Joe was uneasy. 'Are you going to turn her in to your boss, Randall, then?'

Amelia sniffed coldly. 'Not if I can avoid it...nobody deserves that fate...'

*

At 9:15 Joe saw the party of generals and VIPs getting ready to leave the *Rokumeikan* to go to *Tsukiji* and board the steam yacht *Yoshino Cherry*, in preparation for viewing the upcoming fireworks display from the Sumida River. He noticed Fumiyo Isogai among the party, looking a little uneasy and sheepish among all these military men and career diplomats with whom she seemed to have so little in common.

Hageyama was walking around in a fluster, looking for Sir Stephen and Lady Rosemary Hawtry-Gough. 'They should be in the party to go down to the river but they've damn well disappeared somewhere at the last minute.' The ambassador cursed softly in Japanese. '*Shimatta!* Well, we'll just have to go without them; I can't keep Yoshida and the rest waiting. If you see them, Joseph, can you tell them to make their own way to the quayside, and we'll arrange to ferry them out to the steam yacht from there.'

'Yes, I'll certainly do that.'

Joe watched the ambassador stride over the dry winter grass to the driveway where the carriages were drawn up waiting to leave. The ambassador took the last vacant seat - next to Major Sawada as it happened - and Joe wondered sourly what those two would find to talk about for the next few minutes. Joe spotted Amelia and Sumiko sitting with the gaggle of servants in the humbler carriage bringing up the rear of the entourage heading to the quayside and realised she was going to be on the *Yoshino Cherry* too. Presumably Amelia was hoping to keep an eye on Lady

Rosemary tonight to make sure she had no opportunity of passing any secret information to this Russian Shelepin. But Joe now wondered if Amelia knew that Lady Rosemary had just disappeared somewhere with her husband, so might not get on board the boat tonight after all...

*

The mood of the party guests remaining in the pavilion was subdued, as if they had all suddenly realised that they were lesser lights in the Tokyo diplomatic firmament.

Joe was too busy deciding what to do next to worry about such social sleights. He saw that Randall too had remained behind, which surprised him. Randall clearly didn't know that Amelia had managed what he hadn't - to get on board that boat in the harbour full of VIPs. It occurred to Joe that the quality of Miss Peachy's disguise tonight might have been as much to fool her own boss as all these other people around her. It seemed that Amelia genuinely didn't want to throw Lady Rosemary to the wolves if she could stop Shelepin some other way.

Motoko and Maeda were leaving the party altogether, and Maeda came across and bade Joe good night in a friendly enough manner. Joe had no reason to believe that the falling out tonight between father and daughter need impinge on his business deal at all – assuming, that was, he could manage to avoid sword-wielding fanatics and bomb-throwing anarchists for the remainder of his stay in Japan. He longed now just to get the contract signed with Maeda, leave this country for good, and get back to Eleanor's warm embrace. But for the loss of Amelia, and some genuine remaining warm feelings for Motoko, he would have no regrets about going home as soon as possible.

Then Maeda said the words Joe had been hoping to hear. 'Can we meet at Mr Longrigg's house at Hakone tomorrow at two and hammer out the final details of the contract? Hopefully we can sign the initial agreement then if all goes well.'

Motoko seemed to be bearing up too and gave Joe a touchingly sweet and wistful bow before she climbed into her own carriage with her silent father. Joe watched politely as the carriage headed down the drive for the main gate.

After they had gone, though, Joe set off instantly for the garden where he had walked earlier with Lady Rosemary, thinking she might have returned there. And it was near the spot where they had talked that Joe soon spotted a man skulking suspiciously in the shadows of the maples. Joe worked his way closer and tried to get a better view of the man. Finally he realised who it was: the man he had last seen in the *Yoshiwara* on the night he was attacked by Plesch - the supposed Swiss businessman he knew only as Herr Maienfeld.

Joe ducked behind a tree out of sight and continued to watch the man.

Then he was forced to follow Maienfeld as the man made his way along a mossy track at the back of the garden towards the darkened bulk of the main building, the *Rokumeikan*.

Joe saw Maienfeld reach the rear of the *Rokumeikan* building and a line of steps leading down into a basement.

Another man was coming up the steps, breathing heavily. He and Maienfeld exchanged a few rapid words in Russian, and Joe, spying on them from behind a pine tree, was convinced the newcomer was his old friend Shelepin, alias "Raskolnikov". The two men were almost in a frenzy of excitement so something unexpected had clearly happened to rouse them into this frantic mood. Joe was still wondering what to do next when the two Russians disappeared at a run into the shrubbery.

Joe was about to try and follow them, but some sixth sense made him turn back and investigate the basement instead. He went down the worn stone steps, hearing the rustle of dead leaves beneath his feet. A door at the bottom of the steps leading into the basement was slightly ajar and he pushed it open. Inside, he saw by the dim light from outside that the basement appeared to be empty, redolent with the dank smell of decay and long disuse.

Joe moved uneasily across the damp wooden floor, then cursed when he tripped over something.

He reached out for the obstacle and his blood froze when he realized that the object felt soft and warm to the touch...

Joe already knew what it must be, but reached in his pocket and with trembling fingers lit a safety match to confirm his grim discovery. The flickering light was just enough to show him the dreadful truth - not just one body sprawled untidily on the floor, but *two*...

Sir Stephen Hawtry-Gough and his wife, Lady Rosemary, both with their throats cut from ear to ear...

CHAPTER 20

Joe had run the two miles to the quayside in just over ten minutes, and his lungs were still heaving with the exertion. Now he stood panting on the quayside, forcing air back into his weary body, as he reasoned frantically what to do next.

The *Yoshino Cherry* was easy to see, moored prominently out in the middle of the river - more a small steamship of several hundred tons than a "yacht", Joe realised - with a gleaming white superstructure, as brilliant as the flowers of the mountain cherry blossom after which it was named, and a double funnel painted with thin red and blue bands.

It was now ten past ten, and Joe knew the fireworks were due to begin at eleven o'clock and go on for a half hour or so, so presumably the *Yoshino Cherry* wouldn't be returning the guests to the quayside until midnight at the earliest - and possibly much later than that. Therefore Joe understood that if he wanted to tell Amelia what had gone on at the *Rokumeikan*, he would have to get on board the yacht somehow.

He wondered again why he had come here directly and not just reported his discovery of the bodies to the security staff at the Rokumeikan as any sane person would have...

That would have been the obvious thing to do, and certainly the easiest, but it seemed the easy way was never Joe Appeldoorn's way, he thought ruefully. Perhaps he was doing this because he felt some personal responsibility for what had happened tonight; it was clear to him now that Lady Rosemary had been trying to ask him in the garden earlier for his help and advice in dealing with her Russian lover Shelepin, and he had been too stupid to realise it because of his own preoccupations. If he had listened to her properly, he might even have been able to save her. But the least he could do now was to try and catch her killer before he got away: the truth was that his heart felt sick for the fate of that nice woman, and he was determined to make her killer pay for his sins, even if it was the very same man who had saved his own life only last week...

Joe had little doubt of the truth. The Russian had callously slit Lady Rosemary's throat, presumably in order to silence her after he'd finally obtained from her the secret information he craved - the plans for the Japanese assault on the Russian citadel at Port Arthur.

And Amelia Peachy was probably the only person who might be able to track down the Russian before he could flee the country, so somehow he had to get to that yacht and tell her what had happened.

Joe remembered that he had talked briefly to that man Shelepin during their boat ride together down the Sumida a week ago, and although the man had seemed a formidable enough individual, he hadn't given Joe the impression of being someone quite as ruthless and violent as this. In trying to assess the likelihood of the man's guilt and what his fate should be, Joe couldn't consider the positive aspects of the man – the fact that he saved his own life, for example – as some mitigation against the negative, the taking of two innocent lives. That helpful and courageous act in saving him from the three assassins in the *Yoshiwara* didn't make up in Joe's mind for the brutal slaying of an innocent woman and her husband.

Still there were major things at stake - the outcome of a possible Far East war and the loss of many Russian and Japanese lives, as well as the question of national prestige - and perhaps Shelepin had thought he was justified in his terrible act if it meant he could warn his fellow countrymen of what was coming their way. Amelia had told him that Shelepin was a ruthless character, after all, and now he had gone and proven it.

Joe didn't know why Shelepin had seen the need to kill Lady Rosemary's husband too but perhaps the British ambassador had followed her to her final assignation with the Russian and interrupted them, so had to pay with his life too.

As for the so-called Swiss businessman "Maienfeld", he was obviously a Russian too, Joe now understood, and a confederate of Shelepin's

Joe still wasn't quite sure that he was doing the right thing in seeking Amelia's help first, though. In the end he had decided on the course of action simply because he didn't know who else to trust. The US ambassador and Sawada were the only other possible people he could talk to, and both were already on the *Yoshino Cherry* as well, he reminded himself. He did fully intend to tell Ambassador Reinhold what had happened eventually – but not until he had alerted Amelia to the situation first...

As for Major Sawada, Joe was a little more reluctant to go talking to that man, when Sawada already suspected him of all sorts of dubious and devious goings-on in Japan. But Sawada certainly had a close vested interest in catching Shelepin too so Joe decided he would have to be the third person to inform of the deaths of the Hawtry-Goughs, provided Amelia didn't object anyway...

So now Joe stood on the quayside at *Tsukiji*, massaging the cramp in his leg muscles after his energetic run, and straining his eyes to make out details of what might be happening out on the steam yacht moored in the river. Even though ablaze with lights from bow to stern, it was still too far away to make out much detail apart from a few lounging figures at the rail. Most of the guests and crew seemed to be inside, which was understandable: there was a stiff cold breeze blowing across the darkened water that probably explained why those on the boat preferred the comforts of a heated cabin for the present.

Joe didn't have to stand long at the quay wall before a candy boat nudged up to the jetty and a man shouted from the stern, '*Okyaku-sama, booto iru?*'

'*Hai. Asoko ni ikitai desu.*' Joe pointed to the *Yoshino Cherry*. '*Ikura desu-ka?*'

The man held up the fingers of both hands. Ten yen was a bit steep but Joe wasn't in a mood for haggling and nodded rapidly as he descended the seaweed-covered concrete steps three at a time and jumped across the gap of dark frothing water onto the bobbing boat.

*

Joe mimed to the candy man that he didn't want to be seen boarding the steam yacht, and the man enthusiastically entered into the spirit of the thing, circling discreetly around the *Yoshino Cherry* and then moving in and landing Joe on the steps and small landing stage on the far side of the ship, the port side, when no one was about on deck.

Joe made it up the steps and over the rail in a few seconds; then, smoothing his hair, waved to the candy boat and its small crew as it departed up river.

Now that he was on board, Joe was relatively safe from discovery, being dressed in eveningwear and looking like all the other invited guests. Only Sawada and Ambassador Reinhold – Hageyama - were likely to question his presence if they spotted him, so it was only a matter of avoiding them until he could first speak to Amelia.

Joe moved forward along the deck gallery on the port side of the yacht. He was unarmed, of course; he hadn't dreamed of taking his Webley revolver to the *Rokumeikan* pavilion party tonight, and – rightly or wrongly - had decided not to waste time going back to his room at the Imperial Hotel to collect it. Shelepin couldn't possibly be on board so Joe certainly hadn't come here expecting to encounter any direct danger – only to warn Amelia that Shelepin was getting away under all their noses while she was serving drinks on a river excursion.

Joe had reached the outside wall of the main lounge, located aft of the funnels, and he glanced through a window. He could see a gaggle of guests inside and hear a suppressed murmur of conversation, but couldn't see any sign of Amelia. The ambassador's booming voice was in evidence, though, as was his vast bulk, holding forth to a group of pretty Japanese diplomatic wives in formal kimonos, who giggled and covered their mouths at the ambassador's racy banter.

Then a nearby door suddenly opened and a beam of light fell across the timber flooring of the deck ahead as someone left the main party for a break on deck. Joe found himself unexpectedly facing General Yoshida yet again this evening. The general saw nothing amiss however, obviously not realizing that Joe hadn't been one of the party invited on the yacht in the first place, and he did nothing but bow slightly and say, 'Not long to the fireworks now, Mr App-re-doon.'

Joe hardly trusted himself to speak. 'Absolutely. I seem to have lost my bearings, though. I was looking for the two girls serving drinks and snacks. Have you seen them? I'm feeling hungry again.'

'I believe they are in the smaller lounge up front. I noticed the prettier one too...' - the general's eyes twinkled roguishly - 'her name is Sumiko-san, in case you're wondering.'

The last thing Joe wanted was the general joining him in his search for Amelia and Sumiko, but he smiled back. 'Well perhaps I'll just take a turn or two around the deck before I go looking for them.'

The general fortunately didn't seem to want any exercise, only a quiet smoke of a cigarette, while leaning against the rail and looking up at the stars.

As he lit his cigarette and tossed his match into the water, he glanced suddenly at Joe. 'Have you had an accident, Mr App-re-doon?'

Joe looked down and suddenly realized that he had a large patch of blood on his shirtfront – it had to be Lady Rosemary's blood, of course, picked up when he'd examined her to make sure that there was no chance of her still being alive.

Joe didn't know how he managed to keep his voice as casual as he did. 'Yes, I cut my hand on a sharp piece of metal as we boarded the yacht and I must have got some on my shirt...'

'Let me see. It must be a bad cut to have bled so much.'

Joe kept his right hand firmly clenched, annoyed at his stupidity in inventing a story so patently easy to disprove. He fought to control his rising panic. 'No, really, it's fine now.'

'Let me look,' the general insisted. 'As a soldier, I do have some experience of wounds, you know.'

'No, it's fine. Please don't trouble yourself,' Joe insisted

'Well, I'm afraid you can't go back to the party with your shirtfront like that,' the general suggested practically. 'You will need to get a fresh one at the very least. I shall speak to the boat crew and perhaps they will have a suggestion.'

'I've tried them already. There are no clean shirts available that would fit me, so I will have to make do as I am.' Joe had a sudden inspiration. 'That's why I'm waiting outside on deck for the fireworks to begin; I didn't want to upset the ladies with the sight of my bloodied shirt.'

Yoshida regarded him with a trace of suspicion now. 'Very thoughtful of you, Mr App-re-doon...'

*

After that encounter, Joe found a darkened corner of the deck in the shelter of a lifeboat and tried to get his pulse rate under control again. If he wasn't careful, he was going to find *himself* accused of the murder of the British ambassador and his wife – he had her blood all over his shirt, and people must have seen her walking off with him in the garden of the *Rokumeikan* earlier in the evening. Someone might even have noticed his bit of under-the-table thigh-stroking intimacy with Lady Rosemary at the American Embassy party last week, which would probably seal his fate now if it ever came out...

Joe suddenly froze in the shadows as he spotted Major Sawada prowling the deck, like a big cat looking for prey. Joe stood stock-still until Sawada, after studying the patchwork of city lights from the starboard rail, made his way aft again.

Joe was just thinking he was in the clear when a woman's voice startled him from the shadows.

'What are you doing here, Mr Appeldoorn? I thought you said you weren't included among the guests invited on the yacht to watch the fireworks.'

Joe turned his head but remained in the shadows so as to hide the bloodstains on his shirtfront. 'Ah, is that you, Miss Isogai?'

'It is.' Fumiyo stepped forward into the light from a distant lamp. For some reason she looked as nervous as Joe, as if worried he might be unhinged and about to attack her. 'You didn't answer my question.'

'Ah, you've caught me out! I'm afraid I sneaked on board without permission.'

Fumiyo frowned. 'Why? Is seeing the fireworks from the river really that important to you?'

Joe shrugged flippantly. 'Apparently.'

'How did you get on board?' she asked, still apparently nervous of him.

'Oh, a candy boat brought me over from the quayside.'

'Perhaps you would have been better advised to stay where you were.' She sounded angry to Joe for some reason, which seemed like an overreaction in the circumstances.

'Why do you say that?' he asked.

'As I told you, we may be a little closer to the fireworks here than is comfortable...'

*

After Fumiyo had left him, apparently to return to the main lounge, Joe started moving stealthily forward again, past the bridge and the steps down to the engine room and crew quarters, trying to locate Amelia.

Eventually he found the front cabin, which was not that much smaller than the main lounge, and which contained a similar high-spirited gathering. With relief he finally saw the slender and recognizable figure of Amelia, even if her face, made-up to be so plain and sallow, still looked disturbingly unfamiliar. She was moving around the cabin serving *saké* and whisky to the guests, while Sumiko did the same with the food – more *Wagashi* and *Kaiseki* dishes.

Unfortunately Sawada was also in the cabin so Joe couldn't simply walk in to attract her attention. Instead he was forced to continue skulking at a window and wait for her to come within his line of sight where she might happen to see his gesticulating hand.

It seemed to take forever for such an opportunity to arise but eventually Amelia was more or less facing his window as she served some *saké* to an elderly Japanese politician. Joe waved frantically through the window but from her lack of reaction she obviously hadn't seen him. Then she disappeared from sight again and Joe let out a quiet howl of frustration.

But then a voice behind him made him jump. 'What are you doing here now, Joseph? Are you mad? How did you get on the boat?'

Joe turned rapidly to find Amelia hiding in the shadows with him. 'I thought you hadn't seen me.'

'I could hardly miss you!' she observed dryly. 'But why are you here?'

There wasn't an easy way to say this. 'I came to tell you something.'

'What is it? Can it really be that important that you barge in here and threaten my cover?'

'Yeah, I think it is...I just found Sir Stephen and Lady Rosemary Hawtry-Gough, in the basement of the *Rokumeikan*, both with their throats cut.'

Amelia's face was a blank cipher in the dim starlight, but there was a catch in her voice. 'That's impossible!' she declared flatly. 'What game are you playing, Joseph?'

'It's the truth.' He showed her the blood on his shirtfront. 'This is Rosemary's blood. That Russian spy, Shelepin, did it.'

'Now I know you're insane. Shelepin is ruthless, God knows, but he wouldn't do such a thing to a woman.'

'I tell you; I saw Shelepin running away from the scene, with another accomplice, the man masquerading as a Swiss called Maienfeld.'

Amelia nodded. 'His real name is Obodovsky and he is a natural killer, I

226

agree - but not Shelepin. He would never kill a woman for no reason.'

'Perhaps he had a good enough reason? He's definitely the one I saw coming out of the basement where I found the bodies.'

Amelia shook her head again vehemently. 'It still can't be him. Are you sure the other body was actually her husband, Joseph?'

Joe grunted in frustration. 'Yes, I'm sure. I talked to the man tonight at the party, only an hour before I found him dead.'

Amelia was thoughtful. 'Then that's strange. You see, I talked to the man tonight too. In fact I served him a whisky and soda.' She paused dramatically. 'What's odd is that it was only *fifteen minutes ago or so...*'

'What! You've seen Sir Stephen here on the boat?'

Amelia was clearly alarmed. 'Yes. He turned up late, came on a separate boat. Said his wife was feeling ill and had to go home, but she didn't want him to miss the fireworks... and he was looking remarkably healthy for a man with his throat cut...'

*

Amelia had gone pale even all her sallow make-up. 'It has to be Plesch...!'

'*What?* He can't possibly still be alive,' Joe protested. 'I saw him fall off the top of a moving train near Kyoto only five days ago, and you're telling me that he's here on this boat disguised as Sir Stephen in order to murder someone.'

Amelia was in grim mood. 'It can't be anyone else. It's certainly not Shelepin who has taken Sir Stephen's place, that's for sure. He must have killed Sir Stephen and Lady Rosemary in order to assume the British ambassador's identity and get on this yacht tonight. The most powerful men in Japanese politics are all on board tonight; any one of them could be the target. Or even *all* of them...'

'It's impossible. Not even Plesch could manage that.'

Amelia thought rapidly. 'With help he could. Remember - he has a client who's helping him. A client who knows *you* personally.'

Joe tried to think who it could be, but nobody came to mind. 'You must have seen this "Sir Stephen" arriving late on the yacht. Was he carrying anything when he came on board?'

Amelia wrinkled her smooth brow as she racked her brains. 'Let me think. Yes, he did have a suitcase with him! Souvenir presents for everyone, that he would give out later, that's what he said...'

Joe felt his blood run cold. 'Souvenir presents, eh? We have to find that suitcase, Amelia,' he suggested calmly. '*And quickly...*'

CHAPTER 21

Thursday February 4th 1904

Joe and Amelia had first investigated all the lounges and cabins on the main deck to locate the bogus "Sir Stephen" – and had even looked on the bridge where Amelia had been forced to offer the suspicious watch crew some *sashimi* as her excuse for going there. Amelia had also enlisted Sumiko's assistance to look for the thin balding *gaijin* too, but the three of them had found no sign of him, and it seemed - ominously – as if the man had mysteriously vanished into the ether.

Joe looked worriedly at his watch, which now read ten minutes to eleven. 'Then he's either below decks, or else he's already done his dirty work and left. What time did this "Sir Stephen" turn up on the boat?'

Amelia frowned as she tried to recall. 'About ten, as I remember – about fifteen minutes later than the rest of us. And I think it was about twenty minutes after that I served him a drink.'

'Do you think it really could have been Plesch?'

Amelia was baffled for once. 'If it was him, then it was a truly brilliant disguise, because even I didn't recognise him.'

Joe gave her a wry look. 'Look who's talking! I bet he didn't recognise you either, dressed like that. But if this imposter was Plesch, did you see him after you served him that drink?'

'No, I don't believe so. I'm sure I haven't seen him in the last half-hour.'

'Then he's done his dirty work and left, that's what I think,' Joe stated bleakly. 'He had more than enough time between arriving and being served a drink by you to leave a bomb somewhere.'

Amelia was slipping out of character under the pressure of looming disaster and, despite the plain and unattractive way she looked, was behaving like the formidable Miss Peachy of old. 'But where would he leave it, Joseph? You're an engineer. Where is the place it would do most damage?'

Joe racked his brain. 'Below deck somewhere, I suppose – in the engine room or crew's quarters or utility spaces.'

Amelia shook her head groggily in despair. 'Then we'll never find it in time.'

Joe tended to agree with her, but he knew there was no alternative but to try. 'We'll never persuade everyone to evacuate the ship in the time we've got. It'll be much quicker if we can find the device and disarm it. And we might do it in time if we split up. I think the engine room is the most likely place for Plesch to have chosen to conceal a bomb since there's probably no one down there at the moment, what with the main engines having no steam up. The ship is only working off a small steam-powered generator at the moment...' - Joe listened intently – 'I can tell from the sound and the vibration of the deck that it isn't the main engines working.'

Amelia glanced around nervously. 'But just in case Plesch didn't do the obvious, where else might he have put a bomb? The crew's quarters, you said?'

'The crew's quarters would probably be too risky, with people coming and going all the time. Also it would be too easy to spot an unfamiliar object lying about. This thing has to be the size of a suitcase, remember.'

'How about the forward hold?' Amelia suggested with a frown. 'I know for a fact there is a sizeable hold in the bows for storing baggage and so on. I had to go down there a few minutes ago to bring up some more bottles of saké.'

'Could be,' Joe conceded. 'So you go and look there, then, while I search the engine room. Sumiko...' Joe nodded at Amelia's silent worried-looking companion, 'had better go back to serving drinks in the lounge otherwise someone might notice your absence and come searching for you.'

Amelia didn't argue but had a rapid whispered exchange with Sumiko in Japanese, and then nodded her head in agreement. 'I don't want anything to happen to that girl, Joseph,' she added worriedly after Sumiko had scurried back forward.

'We'll meet again on deck in fifteen minutes,' Joe proposed. 'If we've found nothing by then, then we'll raise the alarm and then we and Sumiko will go over the side, and Yoshida and his cronies will have to take their chances.'

Amelia had a thought. 'But that would make it already five past eleven.'

'Is that a problem?'

'Not necessarily, but it strikes me that if the bomb has a clock, then a convenient time to set it off would be at about eleven, the start of the fireworks.'

Joe's heart sank as he recognised the likely truth in what Amelia had suggested; if it were true, they probably had less than *ten minutes* to find the device if it existed, and disable it.

'Then we'd better really hurry,' he said tersely.

Amelia was about to set off when Joe grabbed her arm and pulled her briefly back to him. 'Can I kiss you for good luck?' he whispered.

'You'd better not,' she smiled primly, showing discoloured teeth. 'You might spoil my make-up or even loosen my nose; it's a false one.'

'I don't believe I've ever heard that particular excuse from a girl before when I attempted to get a kiss,' he said as he clung to her for a second.

'Just find that suitcase, *Mr* Appeldoorn,' she warned with a dangerous glint in her eyes. 'Then you can have all the kisses you want.' With that she was gone, with only one backward glance in his direction.

Despite the danger of the task ahead, Joe was doing his best to stay positive as he set off in the other direction for the main staircase leading down to the lower decks. Two flights down brought him to the lowest level of the ship, just above the hull, and a quick reconnoitre along the main corridor at this level soon located the engine room.

Joe found he had been right about there being no crew about; most of the engine crew probably had shore leave with the ship moored in the river. From the manufacturer's brass plate fixed to the main boiler, Joe saw that the *Yoshino Cherry*, for all its quintessentially Oriental name, had been built by John Brown's shipyard on the Clyde in Scotland, and that the gleaming engine, cylinders and pistons, silent and immobile at present, were a modern reciprocating steam engine manufactured by Boulton Watt of Birmingham.

There were a myriad places among the gleaming valves, stopcocks and pipe fittings where a suitcase-sized bomb could be hidden, though, and Joe set rapidly to work, trying not to listen to the mental wheels of panic turning in his head as he imagined the clock on this thing ticking rapidly down.

Then he found it almost by accident...

It was hidden behind a large pipe and flange plate, still contained in the leather suitcase that "Sir Stephen" had presumably brought on board. The size of the suitcase shocked Joe for a second; this didn't look anything like the small black object thrown into the Imperial Hotel lobby last week, yet even that much smaller device had been powerful enough to cause massive death and destruction. This one had to contain ten times as much explosive power so Joe didn't like to dwell on the thought of how much damage this one might do if it went off.

On gingerly opening up the suitcase (fortunately the saboteur hadn't bothered locking it), Joe found that this was a more homemade-looking device than the one used in the Imperial Hotel. But that was little consolation to him, seeing that the case was packed with stack upon stack of circular cakes of Atlas Dynamite — at least forty of them! - and surmounted by a mass of detonators. On top of the detonators was the triggering device - a simple revolving winder triggered by an alarum to fire a small starting pistol at the detonators.

The clock mechanism was ticking loudly; in this coffin-like room with its reflective steel walls and bulkheads, the noise of it seemed deafening. Joe recalled that dynamite was nothing more than nitro-glycerine absorbed into a diatomaceous earth called *Kieselguhr* to make it stable. Which it normally was, until set off by a detonator, in which case it erupted just as powerfully as any nitro. Joe had seen the effects of a close nitro-glycerine explosion on human flesh and bone; a friend of his father's – a mining engineer working in the wilds of South America - had suffered such an accident, and the explosion had left him alive but looking barely human, without arms and half his face.

This quantity of dynamite was evidently large enough to rip this whole ship apart and send it quickly to the bottom of the river, together with the remnants of its human cargo...

Joe saw that the alarum on the clock was set to five minutes *after* eleven so whoever had set the timer – Plesch, if Amelia was right about him – had allowed a few minutes for the fireworks to start. That was the only slight bit of good news – that he had five more minutes grace to disarm this bomb than he'd had any right to expect.

But it was already nearly eleven so he only had those bare five minutes to save the ship. Joe quickly assessed his options. Could he just move the timer on the alarum back and delay the explosion long enough for everyone to abandon the ship? Or perhaps disconnect the winder from the trigger of the firing pistol? Yet that would be extremely risky...

Joe decided that disconnecting the clock mechanism from the winder would be the least dangerous option to follow in this case, but he was still worried that he might accidentally set off the winder anyway by trying such a thing, or worse, that the trigger on the starter pistol might be so sensitive – a hair trigger action – that just the slightest movement in the vicinity might detonate the whole thing immediately.

Joe was about to try this risky operation nevertheless when a voice behind him hissed in a baleful whisper, 'And just what do you think you're doing, Mr Appeldoorn?'

Joe jumped so suddenly that his hand nearly hit the alarum and set off the firing pistol at once.

Major Sawada stepped forward into the light, pointing a pistol directly at Joe's head. 'Stand back from there, Mr Appeldoorn, or I shall shoot you immediately. Do you understand?'

'I didn't plant this thing here, Major,' Joe responded testily. 'I'm trying to disarm the damn thing; there's only five minutes left – less now! – before it takes us all to Kingdom come. So I suggest you let me get on with it.'

Sawada was clearly caught in two minds by this unexpected response, still not trusting Joe at all, but also now with a bead of sweat on his upper lip and a hint of fear in his eyes as he took in the mass of explosive concealed in the open suitcase.

Sawada's voice was hoarse. 'If you didn't put this device here, who did?'

'Probably a man called Plesch, Johan Plesch.' Joe could see that name meant something to Sawada.

'Why would he do that?'

Joe laughed humourlessly. 'Because someone paid him to, I suppose. One of these lunatic ultra-right Nationalist groups perhaps, who see Yoshida and the rest of the gentlemen upstairs as traitors to the Japanese Yamato spirit.'

'Almost right, Mr Appeldoorn,' a woman's voice said softly. Joe looked up to see Fumiyo Isogai standing behind Sawada with a gun of her own placed against his temple. 'Would you drop your gun, Major? Then we can wait together for Armageddon...'

*

Fumiyo still held her gun on Joe and Sawada, after Sawada had reluctantly placed his own weapon on the steel chequer plate floor.

Joe could do nothing else for the moment but hope that Amelia would come looking for him, when he didn't meet her on deck at eleven as planned.

'Is all this true, Isogai-san? What this foreigner says.' Sawada asked her in Japanese.

'*Hontoo ni soo desu, Sawada-san,*' Fumiyo said. 'But shall we speak English for Mr Appeldoorn's benefit? It seems the least we can do when we three must die alongside us each other for the sake of the Japanese nation.'

'*You* hired Plesch to do this!' Sawada was almost catatonic with rage. 'And you really intend to kill everyone on board here?'

'I do - because it's the lesser of two evils by far. But since Herr Plesch has left the ship already and is far away by now, I will have to deal with you myself. I was going to leave the ship too, but now, because of this unfortunate intervention by you two gentlemen, I will have to stay to ensure the bomb goes off.'

Joe was frankly puzzled too at such bizarre behaviour. 'You would sacrifice your own life? While Plesch simply goes free?'

Fumiyo seemed as calm as if she was taking tea in the lobby of the Imperial Hotel. 'This is not his fight, Mr Appeldoorn. Like all Westerners, Plesch is a simple mercenary and he has completed the task that I paid him to do – to get this bomb on board this vessel tonight.' She frowned. 'I can't expect a foreigner like you to understand what is at stake here. But I will gladly give my life, together with yours, in the cause of Japan. A war with Russia, stirred up by those warmongers on the deck above us, will lead us only to disaster, Mr Appeldoorn.'

Sawada snarled, 'But we can win, you stupid woman! This is a chance for Japan to stamp its authority on this part of the world. Don't you understand that? We stand on the threshold of greatness as a nation. This could be the start of an empire that will rival - perhaps even outdo - that of the British.'

'Exactly.' Fumiyo was icy in her contempt. 'This war with Russia would no doubt be a triumph for the military, and that would be disastrous for the future of this country. The military already dominate our government, and a success against Russia will lessen even further the calls for democracy and the rule of the people. We will end up with a complete military dictatorship, with no chance of ever breaking free. That's why Yoshida and the rest of the *Genro* — these reactionary elderly statesmen upstairs - must all die tonight...'

Fumiyo looked at the alarm clock almost with triumph as Joe saw that the hands on the dial were now nearly on four minutes past eleven. Only sixty more seconds to live...

*

Sawada's self-control finally snapped and he dived for his own gun on the steel plate floor; but Fumiyo calmly shot him twice through the heart before he got anywhere near it. Sawada was thrown back against a bulkhead by the force of the shots, leaving a vertical slime of red gore on the riveted steel wall as he slid untidily to the floor.

'I hate violence, don't you, Mr Appeldoorn?' Fumiyo sighed theatrically, but then gasped with pain herself as she found her head wrenched unexpectedly from behind. Joe saw that Amelia had finally arrived belatedly on the scene, and that she and Fumiyo were now wrestling fiercely for control of the pistol. The two of them reeled across the deck in a savage parody of a dance, both gouging and kicking each other like a couple of Klondike bar girls.

Before he could make a move to intervene, Joe heard the gun bark once again, a terrifying sound in the echoing vault of the engine room. Joe couldn't be sure for a moment if either of them had been hit by that shot, since both women seemed equally transfixed with expressions of pain and shock. But then Joe felt an immense wave of relief flood through him as he saw Fumiyo slowly collapse onto her face on the deck. Yet he had no time to pause and congratulate Amelia on her survival, which might be a temporary reprieve at best given the precariousness of their situation...

Joe immediately crouched down again to concentrate his attention on the time bomb, while a white-faced Amelia, limping painfully, came over to join him.

'I should have guessed it had to be *her* who hired Plesch,' she observed coolly. 'I believe I saw them together once.'

Joe was barely listening to her as he contemplated the baleful ticking mechanism in front of him. 'You did? *Now* you tell me...'

Amelia was perspiring heavily after her fight but still gasped with fright when she saw the fateful position of the hands on the clock. 'For God's sake, disconnect that winder from the clock, Joseph...*now!*'

Joe could hardly hear the ticking of the clock over the intense thudding of his own heart. He could feel his gorge rising like volcanic magma as his hands hovered near the connection between the clock mechanism and the winder. 'Are you sure I should do this?' Joe was nearly palpitating with terror as he saw the second hand of the clock ticking down the final few seconds. But finally he summoned up the resolve from deep within him to move his shaking fingers, and disconnected the end of the winder from its attachment to the clock mechanism as carefully as he could. Then he held his breath for a moment as he shared a look of mutual agony with Amelia.

As he realised that he had succeeded in stopping the detonation, Joe finally let out a long sigh of relief. Somehow he had made the mechanism safe...*but with probably no more than two seconds to spare...*

Then he nearly jumped through the roof at the sound of a deafening explosion from outside.

Amelia smiled with relief too and ruffled his hair. 'Only the fireworks, Joseph...' She helped him slowly to his feet; in her arms, he felt as limp and incapable of proper movement as a rag doll. 'I think, after that, you do deserve your kiss now...or possibly even two. But can you bear it from an ugly little Japanese woman like me...?'

CHAPTER 22

Friday February 5th 1904

Joe Appeldoorn gazed out at the rippled azure water of the Pacific and enjoyed the sensation of the cool sunshine and salt breeze of the ocean on his face. He felt relaxed and at relative peace with the world again, with one tantalising exception. What was he to do with this impossible and unfathomable woman walking at his side? She was certainly an impossible woman to deal with, yet also distracting, overwhelming, enigmatic. And, he had to admit to himself, just being near her made him feel extraordinarily alive.

Joe was caught now in an impossible conundrum, torn between this extraordinary Englishwoman and his beautiful wife. He knew of course that his first loyalty must be to his sweet Eleanor. Yet leaving Amelia again seemed simply unthinkable too...

Amelia Peachy walked modestly beside him, dressed as herself for once – a formidable English lady spy in stays and tight lace bodice, green buttoned zouave jacket in velvet and full-length worsted skirt. Yet she was looking decidedly uncomfortable in those restricting Western clothes, Joe thought with amusement, as if she was longing to return to wearing the kimonos of Aiko-san.

'It's very pleasant here, isn't it, Joseph?' she said as they followed a meandering path next to a beach of grey-black volcanic sand.

'It certainly is.' Joe nodded his approval and glanced around this pretty fishing village located in a secluded cove on the east coast of the Izu Peninsula, only a few kilometres along the coast road from Atami. Izu was barely sixty miles from Tokyo but a different world, the echo of an older feudal Japan still lingering here in the way the peaceful houses were arranged in quiet tiers on the slopes above the cove, the smell of wood smoke from fires, the industriousness of the people – mending nets, smoking fish, cutting wood, cleaning door fronts – and the raucous cries of their children playing *Chanbara* with wooden swords.

'Those children are acting out the story of the *Forty-Seven Ronin*,' Amelia said, pointing at them. 'Do you know the story at all?'

Joe shook his head with a smile, still quietly enjoying looking at her rather than at the children playing. 'No, I've never heard of it.'

'It's a famous true story from that older blood-stained Japan of yesteryear that seems to satisfy all the secret recesses of the Japanese soul. The good Lord Asano was taunted by the evil Lord Kira into showing the blade of his sword in the Shogun's - the military ruler's – presence. As a result Asano was beheaded, his estates confiscated, and his Samurai retainers, led by their leader, Oishi, forced to wander the land as *ronin* – renegades. After two years of waiting, though, on a frozen winter's night, Oishi and his forty-six other *ronin* scaled the walls of Kira's castle and hacked off Kira's head, which they carried to the grave of their lord, Asano. There they all killed themselves to atone for their failure to protect their Lord properly. So, you see, the story contains every element of life the Japanese revere: violence, courage, loyalty, self-sacrifice, retribution...'

'And suicide,' Joe added tartly. 'What is it about the Japanese and suicide anyway? Why was that woman, Fumiyo Isogai, so determined to die for her cause, for example? She seemed remarkably westernised on the outside, but there was obviously something tormenting her inside, some fanatical belief in Japan's destiny. '

'If you have to ask that question about suicide, then you don't really understand these people, Joseph,' Amelia observed. 'I suppose I had to do what I did, yet I was sorry to be the one to end her life. So much of what she said actually made perfect sense. Yoshida and people like him *will* take this country into a dangerous militaristic future.'

'And we've helped them do it,' Joe said ruefully.

Amelia sighed in silent agreement with that uncomfortable fact, but then raised a smile at one of the boy "*ronin*" who seemed fascinated by her and was following her about like a dog. This particular boy was a fat and ugly little ragamuffin who no doubt was usually forced to play the evil "Lord Kira" in order to participate with the other prettier village boys in the game of *Chanbara*...

It was the day after all the excitement on board the *Yoshino Cherry*. It had taken Joe the best part of the night to explain his side of the story to the late Major Sawada's counter intelligence colleagues, who had soon descended on the boat in numbers after he had been discovered alone in the engine room of the steam yacht with two dead bodies, one of which was their own former chief. Also there had been the matter of explaining a suitcase full of dynamite...

*

Ambassador Reinhold had been Joe's major ally in dealing with these highly suspicious and officious army intelligence officers, and he had managed to whisk Joe quickly away from the boat to the sanctuary of the American Embassy before the security officers had fully cottoned on what was happening. Then the ambassador had forced the interrogating intelligence officers to come to the American Embassy where Joe had explained the night's events as he understood them. Joe guessed that the interrogation would have been a lot longer and more unpleasant if it had taken place at army headquarters, but there in the American embassy he had felt reasonably protected and able to give a good account of himself. Even in simplified form, though, it took some explaining: four people murdered - including the British Ambassador and his wife, and the daughter of an eminent politician, Fumiyo Isogai – *and* a suitcase full of dynamite cakes sufficient to have killed a lot more important people. Fumiyo's part in the plot had been the hardest thing for Sawada's men to accept about Joe's story: although certainly a troublesome political radical in their view, they had difficulty believing that Miss Fumiyo Isogai could really have organised such an outrage. Yet the death of Major Sawada, shot by a gun with Fumiyo's fingerprints on the handle and trigger, was difficult to explain otherwise. (Joe was grateful at this point that the new-fangled science of fingerprinting had already made it to Japan, and had been enthusiastically adopted by the eager forensic bloodhounds of the Japanese Counter Intelligence services.)

Joe had changed the facts of last night's events only in one important respect: he had omitted Amelia and Sumiko's part in the night's proceedings completely from his account. (At Joe's insistence Amelia had returned to the lounge at once to continue serving drinks, before anyone else arrived in the engine room to investigate the three shots that had been heard all over the ship - even if those shots had been thought by most people on board to be just a noisy part of the fireworks display.) Joe had declared himself responsible for killing Fumiyo in a struggle with her, after she had callously shot Sawada twice in cold blood. Joe claimed that, after finding the bodies at the *Rokumeikan,* he had gone to the yacht to warn Sawada that some anarchist outrage might be attempted during the river excursion. And that he and Sawada had discovered the bomb together in the engine room and were dealing with it, until Fumiyo arrived and tried to stop them.

Well, it was *almost* the truth...

Joe suspected that if he hadn't been an American protected by his embassy, the Japanese authorities would have simply locked him up at this point and thrown away the key. The officer in charge of the interrogation – a grey-haired army major called Kimura - seemed convinced that Joe must actually be an agent of the American government, so Joe had resigned himself to that situation by now. Everyone had to believe that now after last night's events…

There were certain elements of the story that clearly didn't make sense to Kimura – particularly how Joe had managed to divine, just from finding the bodies at the *Rokumeikan,* that this heinous murder of the British ambassador and his wife somehow presaged an attack on the steam yacht moored in the Sumida. Kimura and his interrogation team picked up on this point immediately, as well as on many other weaknesses and inconsistencies in the story, particularly Joe's assertion that the murder of the ambassador and his wife had almost certainly been carried out by a professional assassin called Johan Plesch. But Joe's nationality seemed to give him protection from the worst excesses of these dour counter-intelligence men, and in the end Kimura had begrudgingly left him at the embassy without demanding his arrest, although still clearly sceptical of large parts of his evidence…

*

This morning, after only a couple of hours of sleep at the embassy, Joe had been confident enough that he wouldn't be arrested by Kimura and his men, to leave the protection of the embassy and return briefly to the Imperial Hotel. There, he found a note from Amelia pushed under his bedroom door, asking him to meet her here in this village at twelve noon, if he could. Joe already had his other meeting arranged with Maeda at Larry Longrigg's house in Hakone at 2 p.m., so it had proved possible, by taking an earlier train to Atami and then hiring a carriage there, to come here first.

He had certainly been anxious to see her again. Yet he was beginning to wonder why she had asked to meet him here, when she seemed reluctant to say much. In fact the whole conversation between them, as they had walked through this picturesque village, had been stilted and awkward.

Finally, though, she said with more warmth, 'I wanted to make sure that you didn't leave Japan abruptly without seeing me again, Joseph. And I know you have a meeting at Hakone today with your client, Maeda, so I thought this would give us a small chance to talk again.'

He shook his head in bewilderment. 'Do you know *everything?*'

He saw the faintest of smiles. '*Almost* everything.'

'Why meet here of all places, though? Why not at Hakone, for example?'

Amelia looked embarrassed. 'Because I had to be here today on British government business. I have information that Shelepin will leave by boat from this very village, probably this evening.'

Joe had been hoping that she would be finished with her spying activities in Japan by now, and that she might even have some free time to spend with him so that they could try and resolve their future. But, as usual, it seemed sadly that work took priority with Amelia Peachy. 'Are you still interested in him?' he demanded peevishly. 'He didn't kill anyone, did he?'

Amelia was uncomfortable. 'No, but I still can't afford to just let him leave Japan unchallenged. Lady Rosemary may still have let slip some important secrets to him before Plesch murdered her. And this village is a well-known point of departure for people fleeing the country. According to my source, there are fishermen here who make a good living ferrying spies and criminals out of the country to Korea or China.'

Joe was slightly annoyed. 'If you're going to pursue anyone, it should be Plesch, shouldn't it? You should have seen what that devil did to Lady Rosemary...'

Amelia was solemn for a moment. 'Yes, I liked her too, Joseph, so I would dearly love to deal with Plesch once and for all. But according to one of Randall's best sources, Plesch has already left the country late last night, in a ship from Tokyo Bay bound for Fukien in China. He must have gone directly on board that vessel after he was finished with his evil work on the *Yoshino Cherry*. So we've lost him – yet again...'

Are you absolutely sure about that?' Joe asked, disappointed at the news that Plesch had escaped justice once more.

Amelia shrugged regretfully. 'As sure as we can be. Randall's informants are usually reliable.'

'Why must you pursue Shelepin though? Is he really so important to you?' Joe continued to argue. 'I talked to Lady Rosemary last night and it seems clear to me now from what she said that she'd become suspicious of Shelepin's motives in seducing her. So the chances are that she wouldn't have told him any fresh secrets he didn't know before last night anyway. And did Lady Rosemary even know about the plans for the Japanese attack on Port Arthur? I doubt it – there probably wasn't time for her to hear such rumours. So why can't you just let him go?' He touched the back of her hand encouragingly. 'He did save my life in the *Yoshiwara*, remember.'

'I do remember...and I might even thank him for it in different circumstances,' Amelia said succinctly. 'But I still can't let him leave Japan – not without being sure that he isn't on his way to warn the Russian Pacific Fleet of Japanese military plans anyway.' She seemed embarrassed at her own obstinacy. 'But I don't need your help, Joseph. I can deal with Shelepin by myself. That's not why I asked you to come here. I can't say for certain how long my business with Shelepin will take, though. But promise me you won't leave Tokyo in the next day or so until we've had a chance to talk properly. I'll find you at the Imperial when this business is over, so that we can...' Amelia lapsed into an uncomfortable silence, not sure of the right words.

Joe could sense that despite her mask of calm she was as confused about the future direction of her life as he was. 'Didn't you say that our time together in Kyoto would be all there'd be?'

'I did say that,' she said hesitantly.

Joe could almost swear that he saw a trace of a tear in Amelia's eyes for a moment. 'Has something changed?'

She nodded. 'Yes, Joseph, something profound has changed. *I've* changed...'

*

Joe stood on the high ridge overlooking Larry Longrigg's house and watched in amazement as Larry put on a virtuoso performance of gliding above his head, riding the wind and the up draughts like a soaring eagle or kite. Behind Joe, the wooded slopes spilled down through pine and cypress groves towards the town of *Hakone-machi* and the blue waters of Lake Ashi, with Mount Fuji asserting its commanding presence on the distant northern skyline as ever. To the south, in front of him, the hillside fell away even more steeply, in a series of wooded slopes and cliffs, to the shores of the Pacific and the town of Atami. From here Joe could clearly see the line of the Izu Peninsula projecting far out into the ocean, and, but for a green hill or two in the way, could perhaps have even espied the quiet cove and the fishing village where he had left Amelia an hour or so before.

Maeda and Motoko, and some of Maeda's company accountants and clerks, stood beside Joe, straining their necks to watch this exhilarating show of skill above their heads with equal amazement, as Larry demonstrated the impressive capabilities of his improved Lilienthal Glider.

Larry was putting on a quite extraordinary display of flying prowess today, even more dramatic than the one he'd given privately for Joe last week: circling, swooping and ascending on the air currents above the verdant hills of Hakone, an ungainly human transformed improbably into a magnificent bird of prey. Perhaps the enhanced performance owed something to the more favourable thermal currents today – it was warmer than last week and Joe himself could feel the gusting rising power of the air. But perhaps there was also an element of increased bravado in Larry's performance as he did his best to impress his mentor Mr Maeda in particular.

Larry's wife, Haruko, being used to the sight, was the only one among the spectators who was making no audible gasps of astonishment, as Larry continued to defy the elements and weave his magic spell across the sky with graceful loops and turns.

Maeda smiled at Joe, his smooth dark hair still refusing resolutely to be ruffled, even by the billowing wind on this high ridge. 'I think I see a glimpse of the future here today, Mr Appeldoorn,' he commented. 'Imagine if such machines could be powered in some way...'

Joe felt obliged to say something, surprised that reports of the Wright Brothers' flight hadn't already reached Japan. 'Have not you heard, Mr Maeda? Someone in North Carolina in America already did just that, only last month. It was little more than a kite with an engine, though, from what

I heard.'

'Everything has to start somewhere.' Maeda wasn't to be denied his dream, it seemed. 'Imagine if you could scale these flying machines up, though, so as to carry passengers and cargo. Ships and trains might become a thing of the past.'

Joe smiled at the man's absurd optimism. 'Even the Wright Brothers don't think that's possible, Mr Maeda. They see airplanes only as a form of recreation.'

Maeda looked thoughtful. 'Well, we shall see. But inventors don't always see the full potentials of their own discoveries, do they? It often takes businessmen like me to see that...'

'True,' Joe agreed as Larry finally brought his glider back into land with consummate skill, touching down as delicately as a crane on a flower meadow. It did look a flimsy and unwieldy contraption on the ground, though – a framework of large wings and wooden spars held together with wires and glue. It seemed frankly unbelievable that such a thing could allow a man to soar and fly free like an albatross.

Haruko helped her husband out of his harness, and Larry tried to smooth down his wild red hair, which was an interesting contrast in styles to Maeda's perfectly controlled coiffure.

Larry smiled one of his jaw-wrenching smiles. 'So, what did you think of that, Maeda-san? That's the first time you've seen me demonstrate my machine. Do you think it has a future?'

Maeda smiled. 'For certain, Mr Longrigg. We must talk about it later. But today we are to here to sign the contract between *Nippon Electriku Kaisha* and Appeldoorn Industries. So shall we go down to the house and carry out the formalities in your beautiful garden?'

Haruko bowed almost to the ground at this compliment to her home, and to her husband.

On the way down the track through the woods, Joe fell in beside Motoko, who seemed to be seeking him out particularly for some reason. 'I hear you involve in more shocking event yesterday, Joe-san. The British ambassador and his wife dead at the *Rokumeikan*, and some say another bomb found on pleasure ship in river. Somebody try to kill Yoshida and Katsura and other *Genro*.'

Joe was uneasy. 'Where did you hear these things?' he asked her.

Motoko was coy in return. 'I have some important friend, you know. Is it true?'

'Yes, it's true,' Joe finally admitted. 'But hopefully all this trouble should be over now.'

Motoko studied him curiously. '*Oto-san* – my father – says you American secret agent. Spy! That exciting if true. Is that true?' she asked hopefully.

Joe adopted a wry expression. '*Et tu*, Motoko?'

'*Nani?*' she asked, puzzled. She fluttered her eyelashes enticingly at him, just as he remembered her doing the first time he met her, on that boat ride up the Sumida. That already seemed a long time ago now, but it was only twelve days, Joe realised with some surprise. 'Everyone say you agent,' she told him primly. 'You not normal businessman anyway. Otherwise why all this trouble for you in Japan?'

That was an extremely good question, Joe thought, which he did not have a very cogent answer for. 'I assure that I am not working for the American government, Motoko-san. Everything that happened to me here was mostly just bad luck. But there was an evil man here who wanted me dead...a German called Plesch. He and I are old enemies.'

Motoko tilted her head in her distinctive Japanese way. 'This was man who kill Mr Pryor?'

'Yes. At least he arranged it. '

'And this evil man is dead too?' Motoko asked worriedly.

Joe shrugged. 'Unfortunately not; I think he got away last night. But I believe he's no longer in Japan so he's not a danger to me anymore.'

'I make even more danger for you in Japan,' she apologised with almost a blush.

Joe wondered what she was talking about with that cryptic remark. Did she mean Joji Kiratani, or perhaps Umegiku-san, he asked himself? Both were dangerous distractions in their way, Joe thought wryly, although certainly not in the same fashion. Of the two, he would take the distracting attentions of Umegiku-san any day of the week. But it seemed the threat from Kiratani at least was not as serious as Joe had been fearing – the man was being hunted by the police after all, so had probably far more pressing things on his mind than getting even with a foreigner for some imagined sleight...

Motoko went back to her father's side, while Joe, deep in thought, fell a little way behind the rest of the party as they filed down through the final grove of trees immediately above the house. By the time Joe emerged from the wood, the others in the party had already turned the corner of the house and had followed a gravel path around it to the front *engawa* where the contract was going to be signed by Joe and Maeda, and by the NEK Company secretary, a dapper little man in pebble glasses and frock coat.

Out of the sight of the others now, Joe was crossing the small mossy garden at the back of the house when, out of the corner of his eye, he saw a blur of movement at his side. Before he could even react further, Joe felt the barrel of a Mauser pistol jammed hard against the side of his head.

Plesch....

*

His looks were almost restored to those of two years ago in Switzerland. This was recognizably the same man now, only thinner and with his hair still just black stubble, of course. He certainly looked nothing like either the blind monk or the elderly Italian doctor whose identities he'd been using up to last week.

'You came back for me, Herr Plesch. I'm flattered,' Joe said, trying not to let his internal panic show.

Plesch smiled grimly. 'What else could I do in the circumstances, Joseph? Our lives do seem fated to be curiously intertwined, do they not? So it's only fitting that I should be here for the end of yours.' He moved behind Joe, but still kept the Mauser trained on the back of his skull. He prodded Joe into movement and forced him to follow the rest of the party around to the front of the house.

Joe saw everyone's smiles freeze on their faces as he came into sight, held at gunpoint by this homicidal maniac. Only Larry Longrigg seemed unafraid, standing up to his full height and inspecting Plesch with open curiosity as if he was some sort of unpleasant rodent who had dared to invade the sanctity of his home.

Motoko whispered something in her father's ear so she at least probably understood exactly who this individual was: the murderer of Toby Pryor, and of Lady Rosemary and her husband. And the man who had very nearly wiped out the entire Japanese government yesterday evening. Perhaps she had even recognised him as Signor Valdini from the train to Kyoto, although Joe doubted whether even Motoko could be quite as perspicacious as that.

Plesch bowed in mock acknowledgement to the assembled party: Motoko, Maeda, Larry, Haruko and the rest. 'I am not a monster, Joseph,' he whispered in Joe's ear. 'I don't want to have to kill these people too. But if they try to follow us, I promise I will kill them all. Every last one, even the girl. Is that clear? Shall we go, Joseph? There's a nice clearing in the woods below the house – a pleasant place for a final confession and absolution.'

Joe didn't want to get Motoko and the rest killed, and hung his head deliberately in apparent submission. He called out to them, pleading. 'Please don't interfere, Maeda-san! This man will kill you all if you try and interfere. Leave this to me and him to resolve. It's a personal matter between us.'

'Well put, Joseph.' Plesch indicated the way and Joe, stumbling a little on the rocky path, set off down the track through the cypress woods, while Motoko and the rest of the party could only stare after them in uneasy silence.

Joe hardly knew what he was saying, as he looked around desperately for some possible means of escape. 'You surpassed yourself last night, Herr Plesch. In the guise of Sir Stephen, I mean.'

'Did I?' Plesch tut-tutted. 'I think not. Englishmen are so easy to mimic, after all. As a race they are completely lacking in any imagination, and so abominably stupid on the whole. It really pains me that such people rule a quarter of the world.'

Joe was simply trying to keep the man talking for a little while longer, clinging to his own life as long as he could. 'So how did you find me here?'

'You came here to sign a contract with Mr Maeda; the meeting was even reported in the *Japan Mail* this morning. I simply followed him and his beautiful daughter in their fine automobile, and they led me straight to you. It was that simple.'

'You have a car of your own here? It must be a good one to keep up with a Lanchester.' Maeda and Motoko had come from Tokyo this morning in their chauffeur-driven English Lanchester, Joe knew, so it would certainly take a fast and powerful car to keep up with that.

'Yes, I have. So don't worry about me getting away afterwards, Joseph. My car is ready nearby to whisk me off to my final rendezvous in Japan.'

'In Izu?' Joe guessed that Plesch must have deliberately covered his tracks last night by pretending to leave on that tramp steamer to China, and that he'd always been intending to leave from somewhere rather more private than the main roadsteads of Tokyo Bay. It occurred to him that Plesch might even be leaving instead from the very same fishing village where Amelia was waiting. It had to be somewhere relatively close that he intended to use, so how many nearby villages could there be that were prepared to risk the wrath of the law and smuggle criminals out of Japanese waters? That almost gave Joe some cause for satisfaction – the thought of Plesch walking directly into her and seeing a ghost. A ghost who would finally take proper retribution from him hopefully...

He could feel Plesch's Mauser trained on his back and knew that trying to jump him in this situation would be suicide. His mind was racing, wondering if this could be the same weapon that Plesch had used in the train to Kyoto, or even perhaps the same one he'd used to shoot him two years ago in Switzerland – there would be a certain irony in that, if he had come all the way to the other side of the world, only to end up being shot again by the same weapon. Though probably it was a different gun from the one in Switzerland because that one, he remembered, had gone over the cliff into the Rhine with Plesch shortly afterwards.

'Why is my death so important to you now?' Joe asked, without turning his head.

Behind him, Plesch seemed in philosophical mood. 'Because until I met you, Joseph, I had never failed at anything I did. Yet you have changed all that, thwarting so many of my plans. Now I don't seem able to succeed in anything. I failed again last night, for reasons that I simply cannot comprehend. I did get paid a great deal of money beforehand by Miss Isogai, yet I don't feel that I truly deserve that money in the circumstances. You seemed truly blessed with a God-like luck that defies rational belief. So you know the real reason why I must kill you? It has nothing to do with hatred or revenge, Joseph, despite what you must think; in fact I like you and respect you, as I told you before. Even when I had the chance to kill you last week, I didn't take it although I must say I regretted my decision afterwards. The fact is you have to die because you seem to be the one person in the world who makes me doubt myself - and self-doubt is a luxury that someone in my profession simply can't afford to have. Even now I don't want you to suffer, though; I hope this will be quick and painless for you.'

'Like Lady Rosemary last night?' Joe said dismissively.

'She had to die, Joseph; I trust you can see why. I was going on board the yacht dressed as her husband, and I was sure my impersonation could survive the attention and curiosity of most of the people there quite easily. But she of course was the one person my disguise could not fool, so I had simply no choice in the matter. Cutting throats is not pleasant, but it is quiet and it is quick. I don't believe she suffered unduly...'

This man was so deluded that he didn't even believe himself to be an evil man, Joe could tell. He saw himself merely as a craftsman of sorts, a man providing a necessary service. Joe felt the blood rise in his face with anger and disgust at this man's wickedness, but also because he saw that he had arrived at his final destination: a small sunlit clearing surrounded by tall cypresses and filled with the sound of birds. 'Here will do nicely, Joseph,' Plesch said softly behind him.

Joe felt the Mauser placed against the back of his skull and held his breath, waiting for eternity, as Plesch said, 'Farewell, Joseph.' But the expected brief explosion and the descent into infinity never came, as Joe found himself instead knocked to the ground by someone, where he ended up on his chest, badly winded and struggling for breath.

Joe was sure that Plesch must have simply decided to knock him to the ground first, before he delivered the coup de grace, but when he looked up, squinting into the afternoon sun, he saw that Plesch was on the ground too, and that the ungainly figure of Larry Longrigg was standing grinning over him, holding Plesch's own Mauser in his bony freckly hands.

And Motoko was there too, God bless her...

They'd clearly ignored Plesch's dire warning, Joe realised, and must have taken a short cut through the woods and effectively ambushed Plesch from the trees somehow. Joe had no idea how Larry had managed to sneak up and disarm someone as dangerous as Plesch, but Larry was proving a surprising character in all sorts of ways.

But Joe could see that Plesch was not yet beaten, only temporarily subdued at most, as his powerful sense of self-preservation and his uncanny powers of recuperation brought him back to full dangerous consciousness. Joe wished he had the guts to take the Mauser off Larry now and pump several shots into Plesch's brain while he had the chance, but he seemed as incapable as ever of doing such a callous and inhuman thing, despite the palpable evil of this man.

Then Joe saw Larry just relax his guard slightly and turn the barrel of the Mauser momentarily away from Plesch's head – and that was all it took for Plesch to explode into action again. Joe tried to shout a warning to Larry but it was already too late; Plesch was on his feet again somehow and had his hands gripped around Larry's scrawny windpipe, as they tussled for control of the gun. Joe heard a bone snap like a rotten twig and saw Larry scream and fall to the ground. Joe attempted to get his winded body to work but it seemed as if Plesch had cast some black spell on him, weighing his body down with lead and destroying his normal reflexes.

Plesch had the Mauser in his hand again and Joe thought he was done for yet again as the man turned it in his direction. But he was saved one more time by Motoko who kicked Plesch in a very un-lady-like way in the side of the knee.

Plesch howled in pain and dropped the gun, which rolled down the hillside into a fast flowing stream. A disarmed Plesch now looked up the hillside to see the rest of the gathering – even Haruko – charging and howling down towards him. At which point even a man like Johan Plesch decided that it was a suitable time to withdraw and concede defeat. After one final baleful look at Joe, he turned and hobbled off – in real pain, it seemed – down through the forest to the nearby road.

Still badly winded, Joe was after him in a second, but warily, not sure how badly hurt the man really was. Even unarmed he was lethal enough anyway, as Joe knew only too well. Joe could hear Plesch ahead of him from time to time, splashing through streams or slipping on rocks, as he made his own way down the steep slope, sometimes slipping and stumbling himself, and once nearly falling headlong.

Eventually he saw the line of the surfaced road leading into *Hakone-machi,* but got there in time only to see a silver-painted Daimler tourer disappearing at high speed into the distance. This was no Mercedes as Plesch had once used in Switzerland but still a more than fast enough car for Plesch to escape in. If he were headed for Izu it would be impossible to catch him now by any form of horse-drawn transport. And there wouldn't be anything else but horse-drawn transport in a sleepy little town like Hakone, Joe guessed. Larry's own automobile was currently in bits while he was working on it, so there was no hope of using that to pursue Plesch. The one hope of following the silver Daimler had to be to use Maeda's Lanchester, so Joe ran along the road the two hundred yards to the driveway up to the house where Maeda had left his own car and chauffeur.

The car was still there all right, all gleaming chrome and shining green paintwork and polished walnut and leather interior. But the brown-liveried chauffeur was out to the world, lying stretched out by the car with blood oozing from a nasty wound in his head. The bonnet of the car was open too, and Joe saw at once that the spark plugs on the cylinders had all been smashed to pieces with a hammer. Plesch must have done this beforehand: he was taking no chances of being followed...

*

'Are you sure about this, Joe-san?' Motoko was looking fearful as she stood on the high ride above the house, with the wind billowing her hair. 'I scared for you.'

'It's the only chance of getting down the mountain before him,' Joe shouted above the gusting wind. 'I think Plesch is probably making for a village down on the Izu Peninsula near Atami.' Although that was only a complete guess, he remembered dismally.

Even Larry was looking worried. 'Maybe this is not such a good idea. Why not just let the police catch this guy?'

Joe regarded him quizzically as he checked the straps holding him to the flimsy-looking mechanism, Larry's Lilienthal Glider. 'He'll be gone from Japan in a few hours at most and the chance will be gone. And I can't let Plesch go; I'll be looking over my shoulder for the rest of my life if I do.' Joe tried to hide his own disquiet. '*You* said flying this thing was easy.'

'It is easy,' Larry remonstrated, 'but only after a bit of training. And the wind is getting up and might make it difficult for a beginner. Why not let me go instead?'

Joe could see Larry was in agony with his broken forearm, even though Haruko had set it for him as best she could with makeshift splints and linen bandages. 'What? With a broken arm? Don't be ridiculous.'

It was already forty-five minutes since Plesch had escaped and Joe knew it was now or never if he wanted to have any hope of getting to Izu ahead of him.

From this vantage point, the mountainside below seemed to fall away near vertically a thousand metres or more to the Pacific, a terrifying sight for someone who didn't like heights. Joe could see the wooded hills of the Izu Peninsula, hazily blue in the afternoon sunshine, which now seemed hopelessly distant and beyond reach from here. This now seemed as crazy a venture to him as trying to fly to the moon, and he knew that if he waited any longer he would allow himself to be talked out of this madness.

So with a yell he suddenly began to run down the short grassy slope to the cliff edge and launched himself off into the void...

CHAPTER 23

Friday February 5th 1904

The sensation of flying was extraordinary. Even more extraordinary than the unique experience of dangling accidentally from the mooring cable of a Zeppelin, as he'd done two years before.

This experience was much closer to the true flight of birds, he thought – at least those giant birds that soared on wind currents like the albatross rather than those tiny birds that madly flapped against the air, like songbirds. And Joe, after an initial rush of blood to the brain at the dizzying space beneath his dangling feet, had soon got used to the unaccustomed sensation and the feel of these large wood and fabric wings into which his body was strapped.

Larry had taught him the basics of the controls – how to turn, to dive and pick up speed, and most importantly to detect when he was about to stall and fall precipitously out of the air. The most surprising thing was that it was even possible to *climb* - by finding suitable columns of warm air rising at the edges of the mountains. Joe had expected that flying one of these gliders would be nothing but a mad plummet to the ground, hardly distinguishable from an uncontrolled fall to earth. Yet he now had the feeling he could stay up here all day if he wanted.

He spent the first five minutes not worrying too much about his direction, only about trying to perfect his control. Just once he glanced back at the crest of the hill and saw that he was at least a hundred metres higher than his launch point, and that Motoko, Maeda and Larry were waving at him enthusiastically from the highest point of the ridge.

Yet there were still some heart-stopping moments too when a particularly heavy gust of wind would catch the fragile craft unexpectedly and nearly flip it over and send it hurtling to earth. And the slender wings did flex and strain most alarmingly in flight, particularly when being buffeted by strong vortices and air currents, so Joe finally decided to try and head towards the ocean and the Izu Peninsula while the craft was still in one piece.

When he pushed the nose of the glider down, the speed built up so alarmingly that Joe thought the wings might fall off, and he was forced instead to descend in a series of shallow turns left and right that brought him gradually lower.

Below his feet he could see mountain streams falling off the edges of cliffs, dense woods, outcrops of shale and scree where the steep slopes had collapsed, tracks rutted by wooden cartwheels. As he left the mountains behind, he began to fly over rice paddies and irrigation canals where coolies in their conical straw hats strained their eyes at this strange apparition in the sky.

The surface of the Pacific displayed more texture as he got lower, the smoothness revealed to be moving wave crests and occasional white caps. The land came into sharper relief too: the feathery outlines of cypress and pine, and the bare branches of cherries and maples. The stepped rooftops of Atami drew closer, matching the fall of the hillside down to the ocean.

Joe was just watching the activities of people in the streets of Atami far below when he became conscious of a vehicle moving fast along the coast road approaching the town from the west.

The vehicle was silver and had to be an automobile from the speed. But by diving more, Joe found that he could easily keep up with it, and even pass the car at will, if he desired.

But where was Plesch going? If it was back towards Tokyo, then Joe had no chance of catching him once he disappeared into that rabbit warren of streets. If, on the other hand, Plesch was really heading for a rendezvous at that village on the Izu peninsula with some fisherman who would smuggle him abroad, then there was a chance. Joe could see that he would be able to outpace the car and get to the village before Plesch, if that was truly where he was going.

But it still wasn't clear yet where he was going. The silver Daimler was still on the old Tokkaido road heading back in the general direction of Yokohama and Tokyo. If he was intending to go to Izu, he would soon have to turn off right.

Joe held his breath as he hung in the air above the town of Atami, waiting to see if Plesch would turn off the Tokkaido road...

He did turn...he *was* going to Izu...

And Joe, with a whoop of satisfaction, turned his glider in that direction too.

*

The only problem was that Larry had omitted to tell him one important thing about flying this glider: *how to land the damned thing...*

Yet how difficult could it be? All you had to do, surely, was to get near to the ground and then try and reduce your speed by turning into the wind.

Joe reasoned that the most sensible place to try and effect a landing was the sandy beach in front of the fishing village where he had left Amelia a few hours before. Although what the villagers and the children playing the "*forty-seven ronin*" would make of the sudden appearance of a flying machine, he couldn't anticipate.

He was low enough to be skimming over the treetops now and for the first time could appreciate just how fast he was going – at least forty miles an hour – as fast as a train. He tried to slow down by his usual tactic of turning in S curves, but he was now too low for this to be effective - his feet were already brushing the tops of the branches.

Suddenly he shot out from beyond the protective line of coastal trees and saw that he was directly above the cove and the grey sand beach where he'd walked earlier today. But he was still far too high to land, and also moving much too fast and spinning dangerously out of control. Suddenly he saw the mast of a beached fishing boat directly ahead and had to turn desperately to avoid it. But this change of direction now brought him in direct line with a small hut ahead. He saw that he could not turn again in time so did his best to get over it by lifting his feet as high as he could. He skimmed across the roof tiles with his feet but the whole glider suddenly lost momentum as it cleared the roof and flipped completely over onto its back, thumping finally into the sand with a force that rattled every bone in Joe's body.

Joe found himself hanging upside down in the shattered wreckage of Larry's glider, but still mercifully in one piece, if dazed and bruised by the experience.

He became aware of a figure running towards him and tried to lift his head to see who it was.

The figure slowed to a walk and a voice said breathlessly, 'Sometimes you do surprise even me, Mr Appeldoorn.'

*

Amelia helped him out of the harness and checked him for injuries. But Joe knew that he'd done no serious damage to himself, only a few bruises and some scraped skin on his knees and elbows.

But the glider was a write-off and Joe wondered how he was going to break that news to Larry.

'Plesch is on his way here,' he told her breathlessly. 'He didn't leave last night on that steamer to Fukien; he's still here and on his way to this very village, most likely.'

While he told her the full story of what had happened up at Hakone and how he came to be flying a glider, Amelia helped him carry the wreckage of the craft up the slope and into the shelter of the rocky pinewoods behind the beach where it would attract less attention. Fortunately Joe had landed at the end of the cove remote from the village so his badly choreographed crash landing hadn't been witnessed by more than a handful of perplexed children and old people. And no one was likely to believe them anyway, Joe thought wryly.

'Are you *sure* he's on his way here?' Amelia sat on a rock beside a track through the pinewoods and offered Joe some rice balls soaked in soya with a black seaweed paper coating – *o-nigiri* – that she'd got from one of the villagers.

Joe was hungry enough to accept them. 'He's certainly on the only road that comes here, so it's either this village or one further up the east coast of the peninsula that he's heading for.'

Amelia was definite in her opinions. 'It must be this village, then! There isn't another place within twenty miles of here where an ocean-going vessel could land. Although this is only a small fishing village, the jetty here extends a long way out into deep water so quite big ships can berth here if they want. That's why it's a popular place for spies and criminals to arrive and depart from Japan.'

Joe cocked an eye at her suspiciously. 'How do you know about this place when the Japanese authorities apparently don't?'

Amelia hungrily selected another rice ball. 'Because this is where I landed for the first time in Honshu when I arrived here last year. A boat brought me here from the port of Nagasaki in Kyushu; I had reasons for not landing normally at Yokohama.'

'What reasons?'

'Several, but mainly because I was disguised as a young Frenchman and didn't particularly want to be questioned too closely by Japanese port officials.'

Joe smiled. 'A French *man*? You might be able to pass for almost any woman, Amelia, but I refuse to believe that you could ever make a convincing man.'

Amelia smiled to herself. 'Then I think you'd be surprised, *Mr* Appeldoorn. In fact I made a very handsome moustachioed Frenchman.'

Joe thought the conversation was taking a surreal tone and reminded himself of the seriousness of what might be coming. 'Have you seen any sign of Shelepin yet?'

'No, but I don't expect him to show himself much before dark.'

'It's going to be fun if he and Plesch have happened to choose the same boat to take them out of the country, isn't it?' Joe observed tartly.

'I doubt the coincidence will extend as far as that.' She leaned over and wiped a dribble of soya sauce from Joe's chin. 'You're such a messy boy, Joseph...' she chided him affectionately. Then her eyes widened suddenly and she uttered a scream of warning as Joe heard a scything noise behind him, and only just ducked in time to see a curved sword blade flash by his head with only a whisker to spare.

Joe rolled over and got back onto his feet in an instant, to find himself confronted by Joji Kiratani, dressed in a black kimono, sword in hand, a look of demented bloodlust in his eyes.

Joe was almost mesmerised with fear for a moment, but Amelia came to his rescue yet again, as a Browning automatic pistol appeared magically in her hand.

She muttered a threat to him in guttural Japanese, pointing the gun at his head. Kiratani showed no fear at all – were none of these damned Japanese scared of dying? Joe wondered irately. Instead Kiratani seemed to be simply weighing up the options of continuing his attack, or withdrawing.

In the end he chose the latter, and vanished abruptly into the woods behind like a wraith – so quickly it seemed hard to believe he had really been there. Amelia had seemed quite content to let him go.

'Who on earth was that?' she asked calmly.

Joe was still trying to get his wildly beating heart under control. 'His name is Joji Kiratani. He thinks I've stolen his girl…' - Amelia rolled her eyes in derision at this – 'and, more seriously perhaps, he also thinks I betrayed him to the authorities. He belongs to the "Black Dragon Society", the organization that attempted to bomb the Imperial Hotel last week.'

Amelia stared at him disbelievingly, then said dryly, 'Joseph, is there *anyone* in this country that you haven't annoyed in the two weeks you've been here…?'

*

'How did he find you so easily, do you think?' Amelia asked.

Joe and Amelia had found a safer place from which to keep watch on the distant jetty: lying down in the long grass on top of a high rocky cliff backed by dense thorn bushes. From here it would be much harder for Kiratani to sneak up on them again, if he felt so inclined.

'I don't know. But Plesch found me here easily enough, so perhaps Kiratani followed the Maedas too.'

Amelia made a wry face. 'And with you flying through the air over Hakone and Atami like an ungainly bird, I suppose it's not too surprising that he spotted you, now I think of it.'

Joe was slightly insulted. 'What do you mean – *ungainly*?'

'You did fly straight into a hut, Joseph,' she reminded him tartly, 'which hardly suggests any great measure of control or elegance in your aeronautical endeavour.'

'I don't think I did badly for a first attempt,' Joe protested. He thought again about the demented Kiratani. 'I think my friend Joji must imagine himself as someone like those famous *"forty-seven ronin"* in the story you mentioned earlier – a gallant samurai keeping alive the traditions of Japan in a decadent age. Traditions like suicide, and hacking your enemies to death, anyway,' he added sarcastically...

They relapsed into inconsequential small talk after this as the afternoon wore on. It was late in the day when Amelia suddenly woke from her lethargy and pulled out a pair of powerful field glasses.

'What can you see?' Joe asked her impatiently.

She seemed almost disappointed. 'It's Shelepin on the jetty, talking to a Japanese fisherman. They must be making their deal.'

'So what will you do?'

Amelia sighed. 'Go down there and talk to him, I suppose.'

'And what if he knows what he's not supposed to know? The details of Japanese military plans against his country?'

Amelia avoided his eye. 'Then I suppose I shall have to stop him leaving...'

Suddenly they both heard a twig break behind them, and Joe turned in disbelief to see that Johan Plesch had outflanked him and outthought him yet again...

*

Plesch had a shotgun in his hands and he was pointing both barrels at Joe, yet seemed fascinated more by Joe's companion.

'Ah, Miss Peachy! Still alive. This explains so much, doesn't it? Here we all are together again, like old friends.'

Joe could see that even Amelia was too shocked at this unexpected development to respond. Her Browning pistol was in her jacket pocket on a nearby rock, and impossible to reach anyway with the open barrels of a shotgun pointed at her face from a distance of only six feet.

'Even this doesn't explain how *you* managed to get here from Hakone in such a short time, Joseph. I drove flat out yet you managed to beat me here.' For once, Plesch couldn't understand how Joe had out-manoeuvred him, and seem disturbed by his own failure to understand this unusual turn of events. 'It was unlucky for you that I happened to leave my car on the road above the village, and decided to use this cliff top path to get down to the beach. But very fortunate for me...'

His finger squeezed on the trigger and Joe jumped back in horror...

Horror, because Plesch no longer had a head or even a right arm – he was just a monstrous headless one-armed torso spurting fountains of blood in all directions.

Joe and Amelia both jumped to their feet, watching the body collapse into a heap, next to the head. Plesch's lips were still moving on the detached head as if in bewilderment, and the fingers of his dismembered arm twitched and danced in mad rhythm.

Joji Kiratani stepped forward into view, the blood still dripping from the curved blade in a scarlet stream. He wiped it absently with a cloth as Amelia bravely stood before him.

Joe could sense impending disaster as this madman squared up to her in return. 'No!' he screamed, trying to pull her away, but she pushed him savagely away and faced him with a frown of deep concentration on her face. She was hardly dressed for fighting and Joe braced himself for Joji to take off her head with one brutal lightning cut of his blade.

She seemed to Joe to be almost in a trance, standing right on the cliff edge, her eyes a strange colour, her body held like a coiled spring.

As if in slow motion Joe saw Joji raise the blade again to slice it downwards through Amelia's slender unprotected neck, and yet she still seemed to be doing nothing at all to defend herself.

Joe could hardly believe what happened next: the blade fell with the speed of light – yet amazingly Amelia was no longer standing where she'd been, but crouched in a different position entirely, and moving so fast that she seemed almost a blur. Joji's blow had overbalanced him, the power of the missed through stroke with the sword tilting him forward off balance. But with nothing but air to restrain him, he began to topple outwards over the cliff. He looked in wonderment at Amelia as he went, as if she was some sort of devil spirit come to send him to his doom, and he fell silently, without a scream, hitting the rocks far below with a sound of breaking flesh.

Amelia looked down at his broken form on the jagged scree below. 'I think even Luigi would have been proud of me today,' she murmured.

*

The purple hush of evening was stealing across the glassy surface of the ocean. To the north the mountains of the Japanese mainland were outlined black against an apricot sky and the last vestiges of sunlight.

The fishing boat was preparing to leave as Amelia walked quietly along the long jetty, her buttoned boots clicking on the timber decking. She could smell the competing aromas of the sea, the tang of salt and kelp, of shellfish and spray. She felt strangely at peace considering what had just occurred on top of the cliffs at the back of the cove. She had used all her accumulated skill acquired over years of practice in acrobatics to defeat that man, and the glow of satisfaction at her own achievement had left her with an extraordinary sense of elation. Best of all, though, had been the clear wonder in Joseph's eyes at her almost superhuman skill in avoiding that sword blade...

Shelepin saw her coming alone and stepped off the boat to greet her warily. Behind him the last rays of sunset still painted the sky above the mountains of Hakone with russet streaks.

As she approached him, she pulled out her Browning pistol.

'So, *dushinka,* it has come to this,' Shelepin said calmly.

'It has, Gregor Nikolaivich.'

'You must know by now that Lady Rosemary is dead, *dushinka*?'

Amelia nodded. 'I do, Gregor Nikolaivich. Everyone knows; her murder is the talk of Tokyo.'

Shelepin looked sombre as he pointed at the pistol in her hand. 'You cannot believe that I had anything to do with it, surely?'

'Of course not. It was our murderous friend Plesch.'

Shelepin nodded knowingly. 'Ah, I'd heard he was here, but I didn't know what he was up to.'

Amelia remained expressionless. 'It's of no consequence now. He's finally been dealt with, you'll be pleased to hear. Lady Rosemary has been avenged.'

Shelepin closed his eyes and whispered something under his breath that sounded like gratitude. 'Are you sure he's dead this time?'

'Yes, I'm *absolutely* sure this time,' she said dryly.

Shelepin was conciliatory. 'Will you let me leave, then?'

Amelia hesitated. 'I'm not sure I can, Gregor Nikolaivich. You're still a threat to my country, and to our allies.'

Shelepin realised the truth quickly. 'Ah, you're worried that I might have learned some sensitive information from Rosemary about Japanese military intentions, aren't you?'

'In a word, yes.'

'Then don't worry. Lady Rosemary may have heard something of such things from her husband, but if so, she refused to tell me anything more. She accused me of being a spy and seducing her in return for secrets...'

'Hardly unfair of her, Gregor,' Amelia pointed out acidly. 'You *are* a spy.'

Shelepin was contrite. 'Yes. But the irony was that I had fallen entirely in love with Lady Rosemary and genuinely wanted her to leave her husband for me. And I think she might even have done it – chosen to leave her husband and her English life behind, and to embark with me on a new life in Russia.'

Amelia was surprised, yet there was a ring of truth in Shelepin's words. 'Really? Is that true?'

'It is true. Rosemary was a wonderful woman. Very like you in some ways, I think, a free spirit. But unlike you, she had been caged like a bird ever since childhood and the spark was almost gone. I like to think that in her last few months on earth I made that spark burn bright again.'

'She never told you anything about Japanese military plans?'

'Nothing that I didn't know already. In fact she was very cautious in recent weeks about what she said to me. She didn't trust me any more - that was clear. Which was sad for me when, for possibly the first time in my life, I was finally being genuine with someone.'

Amelia studied his face with shrewd eyes. 'Tell me frankly, Gregor Nikolaivich. What do you know of upcoming Japanese military plans?'

'I already know from other sources than Lady Rosemary that the Japanese will probably attack Port Arthur and Korea very soon. That much is obvious to everyone except my own incompetent government. I don't know any exact information: neither the planned deployments of troops or vessels to be used, nor the precise date and time of the assault. I'm not sure it would do me any good even if I did possess such information, *dushinka*. You see, my superiors simply cannot countenance the possibility that the Japanese will attack them, and even less the possibility that the Japanese might succeed in their plans. I have already tried to convince them of the danger, but no one will listen. Even if I brought them irrefutable evidence now, they wouldn't believe it. To them the Japanese are a backward nation of rice farmers, quite incapable of waging a modern war.'

Amelia thought he might be telling the truth for once. 'Then they might be in for a rude awakening.'

Shelepin laughed in frustration. 'But *I* can't awaken them. I've tried already. So you may as well let me go; it will make no difference.'

Amelia nodded reluctantly, then instantly made up her mind and lowered her pistol. 'All right. Go then, Gregor Nikolaivich. With my blessing.'

He came closer. 'I loved you too, *dushinka*, in my way. I want you to know that, and to know what an exceptional woman I think you are. But you will never submit to a man, will you? Promise me you never will. You should always be a free spirit; I never want to imagine you caged and tamed like Lady Rosemary, reduced to being the bored wife of some rich boring Englishman. It would destroy you. Promise me you'll never do it.'

Amelia glanced back along the jetty to the village and the line of cliffs beyond, a thin line of gold against the dying colours of the sky. 'I think I can certainly promise that, Gregor Nikolaivich...'

*

Joe walked along the jetty to meet her, as she stood watching the fishing boat raising sail and pulling away from shore.

'I suppose we will have to report what happened to someone,' Joe said diplomatically as he arrived beside her. 'We can't just leave two bodies there like that for the villagers to have to deal with.'

Amelia shook her head vehemently. 'No, Joseph. I've spoken to the headman of the village already. I know him quite well. He saw what happened and he will deal with the bodies. He will bury them privately with due reverence.'

'That's more than Plesch deserves.'

'Certainly,' Amelia agreed. 'But the last thing these villagers want is police and army security descending on them *en masse*. So they prefer it this way.'

There was a long pause. 'You just let Shelepin go in the end,' Joe observed, nodding at the distant boat where a figure stood in the stern with his right arm raised in farewell. 'Why did you do that?'

Amelia continued to gaze out to sea. 'He says he doesn't know the Japanese invasion plans.'

Joe frowned. 'And you believed him?'

'I'm not sure if I do or not. But frankly I almost don't care any more, Joseph. I'm tired of all this.' With that she reached out her hand and gripped Joe's fingers as they watched the sails of the fishing boat fill with wind and head out into the Pacific...
    '

CHAPTER 24

Reuters Agency, Tokyo. *February 10th 1904.*

It is reported that a surprise night raid by Japanese torpedo boats of Admiral Togo's fleet on the night of 8th February has crippled the Russian Far East Fleet – the Tsar's First Pacific Squadron - at Port Arthur on the Liaotung Peninsula of Manchuria. Two battleships – the Retivizian *and the* Tsarevich *- together with the cruiser* Pallad, *have reportedly been badly damaged and sunk in the channel, trapping other Russian warships in the harbour. Two more cruisers, the* Variag *and the* Koreitz *are also reported to have been disabled by Japanese warships off the west coast of Korea...*

...The Japanese government say that they have a legitimate claim to Port Arthur. In 1898, in a move that angered the Japanese government, Russia had forced the Empress of China to grant them a lease on the Liaotung Peninsula, in order to have access to an ice-free port in the Far East. Port Arthur, although a windswept and desolate location, does not generally freeze up in the winter as does the port of Vladivostok, and is also surrounded by high ridges suitable to be equipped with defensive forts.

In Tokyo thousands of flag-waving students have demonstrated their approval of their government's pre-emptive strike on the Russians. Only today, though, has the Emperor of Japan, seated on the Throne occupied by the same dynasty from time immemorial, officially declared war on Russia by making a grave Proclamation to his loyal subjects.

The Emperor blames Russian imperial ambitions in Korea and Manchuria for causing the conflict.

So complete has been Russian surprise at the attack that the first news of the Port Arthur disaster is believed to have been reported to the Tsar by his foreign minister while he was attending a performance at the opera in St Petersburg.

Today the Japanese have been quick to exploit their advantage in the conflict and 8000 Japanese infantry have disembarked on the Korean Peninsula to begin their march on Seoul, the capital...

Friday February 19th 1904

Randall smiled complacently at Miss Peachy. 'It seems that you were right and that Shelepin knew nothing at all about the Japanese plans, then.'

Miss Peachy however didn't seem in a mood to be congratulated. 'Actually I believe he had a very good idea of what was about to happen, but knew he could never convince his superiors in time.'

Randall frowned. 'Then it was rather cavalier of you to allow him to leave unhindered, wasn't it?'

'Perhaps. But as I say, I saw little risk of the Russian authorities believing the rumours of a Japanese attack.'

Randall decided to ignore that remark and be magnanimous; today was not a day for recriminations after all.

They were meeting in the same rendezvous as last time: the meeting room on the first floor of the Imperial Hotel. Miss Peachy was dressed in an afternoon gown of emerald green velvet again, her glossy hair worn up and dressed with ribbons, just the way he liked her – every inch the English lady on the surface, yet something sultrier and more sensual stirring just beneath the surface.

'This attack has been a triumph for General Yoshida, and for Admiral Togo,' Randall commented. 'Who would have ever thought that our little yellow friends could be quite so efficient and competent? They've clearly learned a lot from us in the last few years.' He relaxed in his chair and inspected her figure yet again as she paced in front of the window. There *was* something cat-like and provocative about Miss Peachy, even when dressed as decorously as this, a hint of the wild in the way she was never still, never fully relaxed.

'So you are to be congratulated on achieving your original mission and unearthing the source of our diplomatic leaks. I do feel some genuine pity for Lady Rosemary but she was a foolish woman to get involved with that Russian. Yet the secret of her foolish infatuation must die with her and her husband. Don't you agree - to protect both their reputations?'

Miss Peachy nodded. 'I do agree.'

God! She was driving him wild again! So docile today in a way, but how well that green velvet skirt suited her delicious figure. What he would give to have his way with her here and now... But he told himself to be patient.

'And this even greater triumph - in foiling the attempt of this strange anarchist woman, Fumiyo Isogai, to blow up the entire Japanese cabinet on board that ship – is an even more telling achievement, Miss Peachy. Quite extraordinary! And, even more, you have also finally administered fitting justice to Herr Plesch for his wicked deeds. I have written a secret memorandum to Sir Charles and detailed your part in these proceedings so you will get the full credit you deserve.' This wasn't quite true, of course; in fact Randall had subtly credited his own leadership as the major reasons for these successes, and Amelia Peachy's part had been relegated to a few short paragraphs at the end.

She regarded him with her usual enigmatic expression. 'Thank you, Mr Randall. Can I go now?'

'There's no pressing hurry, is there?' he remonstrated.

Miss Peachy picked up her bag. 'I have plans for the rest of the day, and the weekend.'

Randall was puzzled why she should be in such a hurry now. 'May I ask something, Miss Peachy? What are your long term plans? Sir Charles will no doubt want you back in London sometime soon.'

Miss Peachy seemed disinterested at best. 'I believe I want to stay in the Far East for the present and travel a little.'

Randall was surprised. 'Well, you've certainly earned a holiday.'

'Actually it's something rather longer than that I have in mind. I am actually intending to leave the government's service permanently, Mr Randall.'

Randall was taken aback even more. 'Retiring, you mean?'

'I wouldn't call it that exactly. I need a change in my life, that's all.'

'Are you considering marriage at all in the future, Miss Peachy? Is that your reason for wishing to leave government service?' he asked hopefully.

She looked annoyed. 'I am not.'

Clive thought this was an opportune time, though, to press his own case. 'I'm surprised to hear that you're not considering marriage. You must be considering it at some stage soon, surely. You *are* a very attractive woman, Miss Peachy.'

She looked astounded for a moment by his compliment, then wary. 'I am?'

'Certainly. Surely you have some inkling of the way I feel about you, Miss Peachy. Our relationship has been more than purely a business one, I trust. I feel we have become rather close of late.'

'You do?' Miss Peachy seemed almost at a loss for words.

'I too will be returning to England in a few months and perhaps retiring from the diplomatic service in due course. And then I plan to take up a career in business and politics.' He cleared his throat, which had suddenly become unexpectedly dry. 'In short, I would like to offer you *my* hand in marriage, Miss Peachy. I assure you I could make you *very* happy indeed. There would be no more tramping the world for you. No more danger. Just the sedate and affluent life of an English lady, and the delights of the Worcestershire countryside. Doesn't that appeal to you?'

But she was already on her way to the door. 'To be honest, sir, it doesn't. So I thank you very kindly for your offer but –' she opened the door and smiled sweetly at him – 'frankly, Mr Randall, I would rather be boiled in oil...'

*

Joe stood with Larry and Haruko on the hilltop above their house.

'Thank you for your help that day,' he said yet again. 'How is the arm anyway?'

Larry held up his plastered forearm. 'Another month before I can use it again.'

'You won't be able to fly even when you can use your arm properly. Not after what I did to your glider,' Joe apologised.

'Oh, it doesn't matter,' Larry said gallantly. 'I'm planning to build another one in time – much bigger, and with a motor to power it. I might not have beaten the Wright Brothers but I want to be the first at least to make a powered flight in a heavier-than-air machine on Japanese soil.' Larry changed the subject with apparent reluctance, glancing uneasily at Haruko. 'Have you seen the demonstrations in Tokyo supporting the war? I've heard they're getting pretty vicious and unpleasant.'

Joe nodded. 'I have, and it leaves me a bit uneasy too. I guess they're being heavily orchestrated from behind the scenes by the military. I just hope the Japanese are not going to get a permanent taste for war and conquest; they might live to regret it.'

Haruko chirped up. 'We are not so foolish, Joseph-san.'

Her husband disagreed. 'Everyone is that foolish, I'm afraid.'

Certainly there was an air of jingoism in the air in Japan that hadn't been there recently, Joe thought. The reputation of Shintaro Isogai's liberal political party was now in tatters, discredited by his daughter's anarchist activities. Although there'd been no direct press reports of the events on board the *Yoshino Cherry,* everyone in the political world seemed to know perfectly well what she had tried to do there.

On the other hand, Yukio Kiratani seemed to have suffered no similar loss of reputation to Isogai, even though his son Joji had been implicated in an anarchist bomb plot of his own. Perhaps because the target of his bomb had not been the ruling oligarchy, and perhaps also because Joji had conveniently disappeared without trace; rumours were being bandied about that he had killed himself by committing *seppuku* – that agonising ritual form of suicide in which a man slit open his own belly with a horizontal cut of a short sword, and then watched his own intestines spill out of his guts without screaming. And the Japanese still had a secret reverence for the sort of courage and self-sacrifice that would enable a man to do something like that to himself...

*

Joe walked down the hillside to Larry and Haruko's garden where he had earlier that day finally signed the contract between *Nippon Electriku Kaisha* and Appeldoorn Industries.

Maeda had already returned to Tokyo after the little ceremony today but Motoko had stayed on at the house, to Joe's distinct pleasure.

'You're looking happy,' he noted with a smile. Although "radiant" would have been a far better description, as she bubbled with good humour and high spirits.

'I not happy, Joe-san. I miserable, but hiding it well,' Motoko said.

His face fell. 'Really? Why?'

She gave a delicious giggle of happiness. 'I joking. I very happy today. *Oto-san* say Motoko can go to New York. Not marry this year. Maybe another year all right. So we shall meet again in America, I hope. I want to meet wife, Ereanor-san. We become friends perhaps.'

Joe was a little uneasy. 'I'm very happy that you're coming to America, Motoko-san. But if you do, it's probably better if you never mention *Umegiku-san* to her. Eleanor might not understand.'

Motoko gave a conspiratorial smile. 'I not stupid, Joe-san. Of course not tell. *Umegiku-san* was my present to you – grateful thanks for my life.'

'Well, you've thanked me enough now. And saved me at least once yourself. So we're all square.'

'*Nani?*' She looked puzzled by the expression.

Joe shook his head with a laugh. 'Never mind...'

*

A few hours later, as dusk was falling, Joe walked through Hibiya Park with Amelia.

They'd seen comparatively little of each other in the two weeks since the events on the Sumida aboard the *Yoshino Cherry,* and out at Izu. There seemed to be no deliberate reason for this mutual reticence to meet, but Joe sensed that both Amelia and himself had been consciously distancing themselves from each other for a while, almost as a test of their feelings and their commitment.

'I like walking here in the early evening, especially now I can be myself again,' she commented.

'No more dangerous assassins to catch?' Joe teased her. 'No more anarchist plots to foil?'

Amelia smiled. 'Apparently not. The world appears to be safe and stable for the moment.'

She sounded almost disappointed, Joe thought.

She was dressed in green velvet and looked more like the Amelia Peachy he remembered from Switzerland two years ago, as if she was deliberately shedding this Oriental patina she'd acquired over the last year. Yet her mood was hard for him to gauge; she seemed both melancholy and happy at the same time, flitting from one mood to the other. Just being beside her caused a stirring of emotions in the recesses of Joe's soul, though: passion, wonder, delight...

If this wasn't love, then he didn't know what it was. It was something entirely different from what he felt for Eleanor, yet he could have sworn *that* was love too, so he was in a badly confused mood.

Hibiya Park, with its atmospheric maples and gingko trees, was a popular trysting place for young Japanese, especially at sunset on a Friday, so Joe and Amelia seemed to belong there by natural right. The young Japanese girls, walking shyly alongside their beaus, did have an unnatural amount of charm, Joe thought, as they flirted and smiled and dodged between the noodle vendors, the toy pedlars and the "cookshop men" with their burning charcoal braziers.

Amelia stopped and admired a Japanese baby girl in a Western baby carriage; with her fat red cheeks and tufts of black hair, the baby looked out of place in this alien vehicle, but gave Amelia a gurgling smile anyway. 'Do you like babies, Joseph?' she asked innocuously.

'Well enough,' he answered diplomatically, wondering at the reason for the question.

Mendicant musicians competed for their attention, playing flutes and drums, while vociferous pestering salesmen tried to sell them tickets for the latest music hall show.

The moon rose above the horizon as they walked, a great round honey-coloured moon that seemed huge and swollen as it floated up above the surrounding rooftops. 'So where do we go from here?' Joe asked her finally, a deliberately ambiguous question.

Amelia seemed reluctant to speak but finally blurted out, 'Come with me, Joseph. Let's go back to Kyoto and spend some time there together.'

Ah, there's the rub, Joe thought. If I do that, then I'm lost to this woman forever. I'll never be able to free myself of her again.

But did he really want to free himself of her forever...?

Then on the far side of the path he happened to catch sight of a *geisha*, tottering in high clogs on her way to an evening assignation, her glossy hair jet black, her face vivid with colour, her kimono gaudy with silks and sashes, and his heart gave a lurch as he remembered Amelia dressed that provocative way....

Amelia saw the direction of his eyes and smiled, seeming to know exactly what he was thinking. 'I promise to bring my own kimonos, if you wish, Joseph...'

.

EPILOGUE

Saturday 12th March 1904

An early Saturday morning in the middle of March and Amelia sat in front of the mirror in the room above the bathhouse - *the Red-Crowned Crane* - in the *Yoshiwara*. She knew this would be the last time she would ever sit here talking to Sumiko, and her heart felt leaden at the thought she would never see her friend again.

Sumiko stood behind her, apparently unconcerned about Amelia's imminent departure from Japan, but Amelia suspected the insouciance was a clever act.

'Will you stay with the American?' Sumiko asked, brushing out Amelia's long hair.

'I don't know yet,' she answered honestly.

'You spent a whole two weeks with him in Kyoto. Is he a good lover? He must be!'

Amelia tut-tutted. 'Mind your own business, little dumpling.'

But Sumiko persisted, anxious to be initiated into the strange rituals of Western men and women. 'Does he kiss on the lips? Western men like to kiss on the lips, *neh*? A little peculiar, isn't it?'

'Do you want to come to Yokohama and see me off, little dumpling?'

Sumiko seemed to consider the suggestion before declining politely, but Amelia saw just a trace of a tear in her eyes as she did so. She pretended not to see in return, though; that would be a huge loss of face for Sumiko-san if she made an issue of it.

'Who will be the new owner of the House of the Red-Crowned Crane?' Sumiko asked with a slight sniffle.

'Look in the mirror over there and you will see the new owner.'

Sumiko had half-ducked to look before she realised who Amelia meant. '*Me?*' she asked in a tiny and disbelieving voice.

'I have signed the ownership of the bathhouse over to you completely, little one,' she announced. 'You own everything as of today. You can throw me out of here right now, if you wish.'

Sumiko was humbled by such an unlikely offer and she seemed to shrink in size until she appeared to Amelia like a little girl. 'I don't deserve this great honour,' she said in an even tinier voice.

Amelia patted her arm. 'You *do* deserve it, Sumiko-san. But please don't stay here too long, little one. Sell up within a year or three - that's my advice - and then go home to Akita and marry a handsome rice farmer and have lots of beautiful white-skinned babies...'

*

Joe was sitting in his room at the Imperial when he heard her knock at his door.

She looked as wonderful as usual, as she came diffidently into the room, dressed for travel in a silk gown and white-trimmed jacket.

Joe couldn't dispel all the myriad images of Amelia in his mind after those two extraordinary weeks of love in Kyoto. If that time together was all they would ever have in their lifetime, then perhaps it was enough. Joe had felt a sustained level of happiness in her company that had surpassed even his joy in being married to Eleanor; yet his relationship with Amelia always had an edge of melancholy and regret to it too, perhaps the painful realization of knowing that this intensity of happiness could never possibly last.

She simply wasn't the sort of woman to settle down with one man and raise children, supervise dinners, and undertake all the other trivial domestic things that Eleanor seemed perfectly happy to do. That sort of life would only make Amelia Peachy miserable and resentful in the end, he felt, and Joe never wanted their relationship reduced to the prosaic and the drab.

She accepted his offer to share his morning coffee, and Joe poured a cup for her from the still hot coffee pot. As she sipped it, she said, 'I'm leaving on the steamship SS *Pearl River* from Yokohama at seven this evening, Joseph.'

His eyes fell. 'Bound for where?'

She caught her breath nervously. 'Hong Kong first. I...'

In their awkwardness Joe had spoken at the same time so excused himself. 'Sorry. You were saying...?'

'I was about to say that I would appreciate it greatly if you would come with me, Joseph. I never thought I would hear myself say this to anyone, but our two weeks together in Kyoto have convinced me that I do genuinely care for you. I can't promise you anything if you do decide to come with me – God knows I am an impossible person to be with all the time – and even I don't know if our relationship could possibly work. But for the present, I want to be with you as much as possible – it's that's simple.' With that she rose to her feet and retraced her steps to the door. As she was closing the door behind her, she added, 'If you don't come, I'll understand, though...'

*

Joe went for a long walk on his own in Hibiya Park trying to decide between these two wonderful, and yet entirely different, women in his life. Faced with such an impossible dilemma, how could he decide between them?

In his preoccupied state, he returned to the hotel with his mind still completely undecided, vacillating from one extreme to the other. He opened his room door with the key to find his room in near darkness with the drapes tightly closed. He was feeling his way to the window to open them when he was suddenly smothered with an avalanche of warm kisses and the sensation of wonderful soft breasts pressed against his body.

'Eleanor!' he gasped in surprise.

She smiled triumphantly. 'Are you pleased to see me, Mr Appeldoorn?'

'Of course! But how did you get here?'

She pressed her rose-petal lips against his and pulled his head down to her white bosom. 'Oh, I've missed you so much, you beast! I couldn't bear it after you left. I was so thoroughly miserable that my grandfather said I should come after you. So I did. Crossed the Wild West and the Pacific, and with only my maid Ruthie for companionship.'

She smiled triumphantly and pulled him towards the window where she opened the curtains to let in the sunshine. Joe saw that she was only wearing her corset, drawers and silk stockings. 'You came back too soon from your walk; I was putting on something special to greet you.' She looked down at her tiny waist and splendid bosom. 'But I suppose this outfit will do well enough, will it not?'

Joe was still dumbstruck. 'This is marvelous you coming here, sweetheart. But I am nearly done here, you know, Eleanor. I was planning to go home in a week or so anyway.'

Eleanor shook her head with a laugh. 'No, Joseph, you're not. My grandfather said we never had a proper honeymoon so he's bought us tickets to go around the world together from Yokohama. We shall return to New York *the long way round!* Isn't that a wonderful surprise?' she said, hugging him again.

Out of the corner of his eye, Joe happened to glance down into the forecourt in front of the hotel, and saw Amelia standing with her trunks beside a four-wheeler carriage as she made ready to leave for Shimbashi Station.

Joe saw her glance up briefly at his window and stepped back out of sight involuntarily.

'Where is the ship going first?' Joe asked distractedly.

Eleanor puckered her brow. 'Hong Kong, I believe. I've always wanted to visit Hong Kong, haven't you, Joseph...?'

266

THE END

ABOUT THE AUTHOR

Gordon Thomson is a civil engineer by profession, a Geordie by birth, and Sunderland supporter (and therefore masochist) by inclination. His professional engineering career took him all over the world - Africa, the Far East, South America, as well as Holland and the UK - and this experience of exotic places and different cultures is what gave him the urge to try writing.

He has a Japanese wife and two grown up sons, one of whom was born in Holland, so he does claim to be a citizen of the world, if a very English one.

This story is one of a series of adventure stories featuring the Edwardian secret agent Miss Peachy, which are intended to be, as one reviewer kindly put it ,"…Boys' Own or Girls' Own stories for adults…"

He has previously published the Victorian thriller *Leviathan,* and the Restoration mystery thrillers *Winter of the Comet* and *Summer of the Plague.*

Printed in Great Britain
by Amazon

34311249R00156